48 Hour Pass – Hong Kong

Lieut-Colonel Walter Rowley OBE was born in Preston, Lancs in 1913. Following the family tradition of the British Army, he was commissioned in September 1941 at Sandhurst and spent the Second World War in France, India and Burma. From 1945 to 1961 his service took him to Germany, Hong Kong (the background of this book), Singapore and Malaya, and included a 6-month attachment to the American Army based in Chicago, USA.

He was appointed an Officer of the Military Division of the Order of the British Empire in Her Majesty's Honours List of June 1960.

In August of the following year he retired from the Army, and took a post which was to continue his life of travel although in a very different sphere. Walter Rowley was fortunate to be interviewed by Fred Pontin (now Sir Fred Pontin) – they struck up an immediate relationship that was to change the course of Walter's life. He joined Pontins Holidays and gained Managerial experience with them in the U.K., Majorca, Spain, Morocco, Greece and Yugoslavia.

Walter became totally involved, to the point where, indeed, Pontins became as much a part of his life as had the Army previously.

From 1974 onwards Walter held two appointments with Pontins – Public Relations Executive, and Special Event Holidays Executive, and he is still retained by Holiday Club Pontins as a Consultant.

A man who thrives on activity, he is a Founder-Member of the Under-privileged Childrens' Charity Club formed in 1975 in Bristol, and is Secretary of the Parochial Church Council of St Bridget's Church, Brean, Somerset, in addition to being Chairman or Member of many other local Committees.

Jean and Eric

48 Hour Pass – Hong Kong

Best Wishes

Walter Rowley

Walter Rowley OBE

A Square One Publication

First published in 1995 by
Square One Publications,
The Tudor House
Upton upon Severn, Worcs WR8 0HT

British Library Cataloguing in Publication Data

Rowley, Walter
48 Hour Pass – Hong Kong
I. Title
823.914 [F]

ISBN 1-872017-90-8

Typeset in 10.5pt Times on 12pt by Avon Dataset Ltd, The Studio, Waterloo Road, Bidford-on-Avon, B50 4JH
Printed by Biddles Ltd., Guildford, England.

To my daughter Louise,
with happy memories of our life in Hong Kong.

Contents

1

THE MAN FROM SINGAPORE

It was exactly a quarter to ten when the room amah knocked at the door, and he wished her a very pleasant "good morning" in English as she came in to collect his laundry.

Gordon Hamilton always spoke in English, he didn't think anyone knew that his Cantonese was almost perfect, not even old Taipan Chin, as he called the head of espionage in Hong Kong, whilst Chin could have no idea that all his asides to his servants, or to anyone, were fully understood by Hamilton. This was why he was so confident in the old man, who gathered so much information from everywhere, from Taiwan, Red China, Hong Kong, everywhere, so that, if anyone knew what was going on, it was Chin, as Hamilton hoped to find out that afternoon.

He had been in Hong Kong for four days, during which time he had done his best to give the impression of being on a business cum pleasure stay in the Colony, and perhaps one which was rather more pleasure than business.

It had been necessary to spend the best part of two mornings with Edgar Willis, his counterpart at Headquarters here, and in that time he had really settled all the official business. Apart from that he had done everything and gone everywhere he could in the time available, which was necessary even if some of it was very boring, especially as he had done everything and gone everywhere many times before, but when dealing with the Chinese, it was essential to have their sort of patience and thoroughness, which were but two of his many attributes and a good reason he had been so successful in the job he held.

There was so much to see in Hong Kong, and as always, so many memories came flooding back to him whenever he was here. Back he had gone, on the Peak tram, to Victoria Peak, with its glorious view – as good as anywhere in the world he reckoned – with the ever growing Victoria city and the space of new luxury hotels, reaching for the sky just beneath him, the crowded strip of water between Hong Kong island itself and Kowloon alive with shipping from every country in the world, and the picturesque Chinese junks – diesel oil powered now and not relying on sails as he once knew them – as busy if not busier than ever. Across the water and spreading out in front was Kowloon, with Kai Tak Airport to his right, and beyond the airport Kowloon Peak.

Spreading further back, disappearing into the heat haze, the New Territories – triangular in shape, with Kowloon the entry and the apex, where farming life went on still as he had known it as a boy, and for years and centuries before that.

But what a difference now to those good peaceful days of his youth, before the Second World War. He could remember his father and mother bringing him up to the Peak on a tram. He had loved those carefree days and was sure the memory of them would stay with him for ever.

As always in Hong Kong, he had been shopping, though apart from a couple of shirts he hadn't really bought anything. Still it was fun to look around the shops and to be offered a cold glass of coca-cola by a friendly Indian shop owner, his attitude still friendly when he bowed and blessed you on leaving the shop, even if you had not bought anything.

Edgar Willis and he had played golf one afternoon at the Fanling Golf Club. This was something he never missed when in Hong Kong, and the drive through the New Territories had been as enjoyable as ever.

Yesterday he had lunched at the Hong Kong Club with Sam Reynolds of the Hong Kong Police, then there had been a session at the Press Club, with a typical Chinese meal in the evening in one of the many happy restaurants of this wondrous city which came alive at night, and then a Hong Kong pub crawl in some of the places Sam Reynolds knew so well.

On the morning after his arrival, before going to see Willis, he had gone into his favourite tobacco shop to mooch around, as he generally did –

"I just want to buy a few cigars," he told the smiling Chinese owner.

"You tourist?" he was asked.

"Not really," in his faultless English. "Came up from Singapore yesterday, I've been here several times before and always come in here."

"Oh yes, me remember you quite well," the smiling Chinese had said. "You like these kind cigars no doubt" – he thrust some fine Havana cigars under Hamilton's nose – "these damn fine cigars, very cheap, how many you like?"

"Well, I only want three for now," Hamilton answered, very pleasantly, and had paid for them and come out with the assurance he could always come back for more, and was certain that, within one hour, Taipan Chin would know that Hamilton was back again in Hong Kong, even if he had not known before, and would visit Chin at the usual place, three days from then, and at three o'clock in the afternoon.

This afternoon he would see Taipan Chin, and as always the time had sped quickly by. This was ever so, the seemingly increasing pace of the passing of time in this teeming city, city of life, and death, cosmopolitan, city of light and city of dark, with a million and more attractions, and as many mysteries, where twenty-four hours in any one day were not really enough for anyone.

It had been a hard night out with Sam Reynolds, the night before, they had visited a lot of places and had a drink in each. Hamilton felt better than he ought to have felt, and finishing his shaving and dressing, his mind was now on breakfast.

He went down to the spacious and cool restaurant of the Peninsula Hotel. It was late really and there were not a lot of people about, but still plenty of staff awaiting the late comers such as he. He ordered fruit juice, toast, scrambled eggs and coffee.

It didn't seem four days since he had flown up from Singapore in the big Cathay Pacific jet, a journey which he had hated, and which had scared him almost stiff. Already, when there was still three days to go before he would fly back to Singapore, he was worrying again at the thought of the flight, worrying greatly in spite of all the other things his brain had to think about.

Hamilton hated flying. He could not explain why, but when he had to fly, he was glad to travel that way on his own, so that he did not have to force himself to make conversation with other passengers. He sat on his seat, bolt upright, with feet firmly braced on the cabin floor, in expectation of any slight deviation of movement of the plane, and prayed for the journey to be over quickly and safely.

He did not know if his fear showed, hoped it did not, and always found it difficult to eat the meal or refreshments provided. But he forced himself to do so, hoping the glamorous stewardesses would not know of his fear. He always treated himself to a couple of brandies, which did help his nerve a little, and secretly, just before take-off, took a couple of travel pills, to ensure he would not be sick en route.

He never looked out – he had tried it once on one of his earlier flights and never got over the shock of the ground so far below him tilted so badly, that he was sure it would never look flat again. He knew why this was, of course, that an aircraft had to bank to turn, but he never looked again.

Not that he didn't envy every other passenger who enjoyed flying, those who could look out, stand up and take photographs, and act so casually about it all, but he hoped they would never try to talk to him. Right from the moment of take-off, after he had said his usual prayer, he sat outwardly content and patient, but inwardly not so, waiting for the precious moments when, with wheels down, they would land, wherever it was, and he could say another prayer to thank God for a safe journey and a safe arrival.

The waiter brought him his order, smiling all over his happy ugly face. Hamilton drank his juice slowly, poured himself a cup of coffee, noting with pleasure how hot it was, then set about his toast, butter and marmalade.

If it had not been for the urgency he would not have flown up this time. He would much rather have come up by sea as he generally did, on one of the cruise liners which called in at both of these major Ports of the Far East, or on one of the big cargo ships which carried just a few passengers and gave such a comfortable and enjoyable journey.

He loved coming up to Hong Kong by sea in this way, no matter how rough it was. Once he had been on a ship caught in the tail end of a particularly nasty typhoon, but Hamilton had loved it, wasn't the least bit worried, and had still eaten all his meals whilst all the rest of the passengers, and half the crew, had been too ill to get out of their bunks. Just let him be on one of those big jets up there in the sky however, and it shudder a bit, or perhaps drop a few feet if caught in turbulence, and he was absolutely frightened out of his life.

The still smiling waiter brought him a large plateful of scrambled eggs. Hamilton pushed his toast to the side, salted the heaped up eggs –

he knew salt was bad for the arteries but it did not worry him, he used lots of it and thought it necessary in the tropics, and started on the eggs. He could eat anything and had the American style of enjoying sweet things with his eggs. His eating was a throwback from that long period when he had been a prisoner of war, held by the Japanese in Stanley, and existing, not living, on the starvation diet they had to exist on, or die. So food was precious to him, and he ate well.

This visit had been an emergency and he had needed to fly. He had known of coming trouble in Hong Kong, and was making plans for a visit when the urgent message had come to him in his office in Singapore. He went in to the office of his chief immediately.

"I think I should go up and see Willis about one or two things," he said, quietly, casually, and after the usual pleasantries had been exchanged.

"Of course, if you must," agreed his chief, and no questions asked.

"I'll get away tomorrow if I can get a plane, be away about a week, I should think."

"Just as you wish," equally as casually, "cable down if it takes you any longer," came the reply, then, as Hamilton stood up to leave – "have a good trip, Ham, enjoy yourself."

Everyone in the hierarchy of the Secretariat called him Ham. He was always Ham when asked out to dinner by a married colleague, and Ham to the wives. Ham on the tennis courts, Ham on the golf course, at all the social functions, and to his friendly chief, who respected him and knew how much real work he did, and his value to the department, even if he only knew some of the story and not all of it, and certainly did not know that Hamilton was the number one British secret agent for Hong Kong, and what Hamilton did not know about Hong Kong was not worth knowing.

He ate his breakfast contentedly, the watching waiter ever ready to move in if required. It was typical of this hotel, a way of life Hamilton very much enjoyed and was now so used to.

It was back in 1946 he had joined the department in Singapore, and now he was the oldest member in years of service. Often he had been asked by people inside and outside the department why he did not think of moving on somewhere else.

His reply never altered – "Wouldn't think of it now, too set in my ways. I like it out here, the climate suits me, it's my home really, and I live pretty well you know. No, I wouldn't fancy a change now, they might send me off to some Heathen place where I might not fit in."

Hamilton was aware his chief must know he was something a bit special, which was why he never asked any questions or put obstacles in his way, but he didn't think he knew any more than that, and didn't worry anyway, as long as he could do what it was his job to do without any interruptions.

Those very few in the know thought it extremely clever that the number one agent for Hong Kong should live in Singapore. Should indeed spend most of his life in Singapore with just the odd visit to Hong Kong for a week or so, or two weeks, and always on a business combined with a holiday, just to keep in touch with what was happening. It was all against the rules that a secret service agent should live so far away, but over the years it had developed that way, and seemed to have paid off well. Hamilton liked it this way, and knew that one person in England, at least, thought it immense.

That one person had been in charge of affairs in Singapore, Malaya and Hong Kong, but when he was promoted and moved on to England to take complete control, he had put Hamilton in charge of Hong Kong, but left him living and working in Singapore.

To the outside world, Hamilton was head of a department responsible for financial liaison with Hong Kong, so it was most essential he visited the Colony from time to time, to keep in touch with the financial department there, and with everything that was happening in that important part of the world.

It was necessary also that copies of the Hong Kong newspapers, both in English and Chinese, should be received in Hamilton's department in Singapore, where a bright and intelligent young Chinese lady was employed to mark – in blue pencil – anything of interest financially, and to type out the necessary English translation for Hamilton, which work she did very well.

She would have been amazed had she known that he could read the Chinese almost as well as she could, and that he did read the papers thoroughly, especially the editorials, so gaining much information of the real thoughts about Hong Kong.

The Hong Kong English papers he saved for the Mess or for his room. They did not attract any attention in the Mess, after all Hamilton was head of a department connected with Hong Kong.

He was nearly finished his breakfast now, lingering over a last cup of coffee, still kept under careful scrutiny by the waiting, and watching, staff.

Hamilton had been born in Hong Kong where his father was a successful businessman. He had been brought up by a devoted mother, and equally devoted amah, and had picked up the Cantonese language as well as the faultless English of his father and mother, with ease. He was away from the Colony at school in England for six years, except for just one long holiday, and, when he left school, had remained in England, articled to a very good lawyer friend of his father, in Liverpool.

The war in 1939 had disrupted everything. He wanted to join an English regiment, but his beloved mother was now quite ill so his father insisted he return to the Colony. Hamilton well understood the need for him to do so, but did think it would keep him out of the war. He was so wrong.

In 1940, after the death of his mother, he joined the Hong Kong Volunteer Force, so he got into the war after all. But not for long. He was wounded on the day before Hong Kong fell, and was a prisoner in Stanley by Christmas of 1941. As much as he cursed his luck, it meant he could continue with the Cantonese language, and during the hard years that followed, he learned a lot of some other Chinese dialects as well.

His father, not as strong as Hamilton, died in captivity in 1943, so he really had no roots in the Colony when those who had survived were released, but the contacts he made took him home to England, then back to Singapore in 1946, to join the Secretariat and to take up his other, more secret, duties.

Hamilton stood five feet seven inches in his bare feet, slim, pleasant features sandy hair thinning a bit on top, and always wore spectacles – tinted spectacles. Hard as he had trained himself not to show anything, emotion, surprise, pleasure, anger, anything, when a Chinese person was talking in his own language, he gladly cultivated the tinted spectacles which did conceal his eyes a little.

He did not look tough, but he was, in spite of the fact that he knew the hard years spent in Japanese activity would one day tell against him. He took regular exercise and liked to do a bit of weight lifting, so there was great strength in his arms and his legs. His wrists were like steel, and if he could have controlled his drive, which he hit very long, but not always straight, he would have been one of the best amateur golfers in the Far East.

It was just ten thirty by his watch as, breakfast finished, he went out of the front door of the hotel, on to Salisbury Road to make his way to the Star Ferry. He was going to Hong Kong to see the island's parade for the birthday of the Queen. Edgar Willis had asked him up to another official parade, which one of the regiments stationed up near the border was holding in the Queen's honour, after which there would be lunch in the officers' Mess. But he had said no. Taipan Chin was expecting him that afternoon at three o'clock, so Hamilton would be there.

Soon he was waiting in a queue to board the ferry. A slight dapper figure in a light fawn jacket, light grey cotton slacks, cream shirt and royal blue tie, beautifully polished brown shoes, with sun glasses to protect his eyes from the fierce glare of the sun and its reflection from the white buildings. He was glad to be in the crowds – just another tourist out to see the sights.

Hamilton was ever careful and a good thinker. There was a danger of being followed always, whilst someone other than Taipan Chin might know of his activities, so everywhere he was watchful and skilful, waiting, watching for anyone who might be watching for him.

Now in the crowds he thought he was all right, but at other times he was conscious of danger. Inside shops he would place himself to watch the door and see out of the windows. When he came out of a shop he very often doubled back on his tracks. If he knew there was a back and front entrance and exit to any shop or place he used, or a bar, he would go in the front entrance, out the back, and then come through the front entrance again, always alert. He didn't think anyone had ever followed him in Hong Kong, didn't think he had been followed these last few days, but he could not be sure. It was so very true how damn clever the Chinese are, and he never took any chances.

But here in the queue he was pushed and jostled by Chinese and by other nationalities, so he pushed and jostled back – except where there were women and children – to keep his place. He felt safe in this squeezing noisy mass of humanity, this was the Hong Kong he knew so well.

As he had left the hotel however, a Chinese man, almost equally dapper as Hamilton, had got up from his seat in the dark cool lounge of the Peninsula, and followed down the hotel steps and along Salisbury

Road, just about thirty yards behind Hamilton. The man had held aside from the crowds approaching the ferry, but was sure where Hamilton was making for, and after a couple of minutes, went back to the Peninsula Hotel, moving quickly now.

2

HER MAJESTY'S BIRTHDAY PARADE

The parade for the birthday of Her Majesty the Queen was almost over with the Battalion lined up for the final march past. Five minutes more and they would be finished.

"Not long now lads," came Sergeant Rankin's low words of encouragement to the men of his company within earshot, "only about five minutes more, give it all you've got lads – not long to go now."

This was Rankin's way. Encourage, always encourage, lead men, don't drive 'em, and right through the parade on this hot humid day, with the blazing heat of the sun beating down, and the humidity bringing the perspiration oozing out of them, soaking their uniforms black across the back and under the arms especially, he had been encouraging, cajoling, helping.

This was typical of Rankin and typical of all the senior men of the Battalion, on parade themselves, and watching how the men were faring, concerned for the young soldiers they had helped to teach and train, helping them as much as possible on a parade such as this.

It was hot, damned hot, the sun's glare terrific, and the men only wearing berets on their heads, whilst it had been a long parade – not easy for any of them. Many were very young, not long out from England doing their national service in Hong Kong, and all of them – national service or regular soldiers – needed all the help they could get, especially now with the salt oozing out from them as they perspired, weakening them fast, so that, as the experienced older men knew, some of the younger men had only just enough strength left to march past as they had to do, and last out the parade.

It was hot for the officers also, and though they wore blue peaked caps, which gave some protection from the glare, they were in long trousers, and not shorts, as the men wore.

Rankin could bet that the General up there on the saluting base had found it hot, whilst it must have been very uncomfortable for the large gathering of spectators, though most of the women – British or Chinese – had sensibly brought parasols to give them some protection from the hot sun.

It had been a good parade so far, well in keeping with the Battalion's very high standard. Rankin had enjoyed it, and knew that it had gone well. He could tell from the sound when the men hit their rifles, and by the way those heels went in together on the turns, and he could see a lot of it from his position at the rear of number three company.

They had marched past once, formed line, been inspected very keenly by the General, who had stopped to have a brief word with many of the men, including Sergeant Rankin. They had advanced in review order – this was a damn good movement – given a royal salute for Her Majesty with what had seemed a near perfect present arms, doffed caps and berets to give the Queen three rousing cheers, with headgear pushed high above their heads as their right arms went up together, replaced caps and berets, and all, as far as Rankin could see, without any serious blemish.

It had been well done, and all on this very rough and ready parade ground, with tar bubbling up from the uneven asphalt, which wasn't suited to good drill and movement, and not a bit like the firm even base of their own parade ground back home in England at their depot.

"Number one company," – the high pitched voice of number one company commander came screeching out, high pitched in good military style, carrying far enough in the still air for his own company, and for all those on parade, far enough perhaps to reach over the top of the peak just north of this military post, and then on to the border with China. Far enough to be heard by some of the Police of the Frontier Division up there watching the border. Carrying beyond that perhaps, and to the Communist guards or sentries, whatever they were, on the other side of the border fence.

"By the left," the screeching voice continued, "quick march."

This was it – the march past, the last part of the parade – what they had all been waiting for, many of them praying for. Just this final march past and they were finished.

The Battalion Band had waited for it too, and now, as they set off to march, the big drummer – Corporal "Beefy" Jacks – took it up –

"Boom-boom-boom-boom-boom-boom-boom-boom" – and with those first eight paces, the men of number one company were in their stride, faultless it looked from where Sergeant Rankin still waited – still at attention, his left hand gripping the rifle hard and firm on to his left shoulder – waited as did everyone else on parade, with the exception of number one company and the band.

"Number two company," number two company commander was bawling out now, less high pitched, but gruffer than the voice of number one company commander, but loud and clear, as befits an infantry major on parade for his Queen –

"Hold it lads – hold it." This was Rankin again, and quite loud, as there was some slight movement from the men just in front of him. "Not us yet – hold it – steady down."

He could understand the tenseness and the movement, every man of them had given of his best, they were still right on their toes, this movement was part of their keenness – but his words had steadied them.

"By the left," went on number two company commander – "quick march."

Immediately number two company were on the move, and their steps – left, right, left, right, were in time with those of the company ahead of them – number one company, now wheeling left and coming into line for the march past the General.

A few seconds only, to get the correct distance between companies, and it would be their turn. Up to their company commander – Major Harry Achingdon – "Old Horace" to all the men of the company out of the earshot of any officers or senior non-commissioned ranks, to set them off on the correct foot and marching in time with the two companies ahead of them.

"Number three company," – here was the splendid voice of Harry Achingdon – calm, composed, with the true unruffled quality of the real professional soldier at any rank – booming out his commands. Better, louder, even clearer, than the first two company commanders. It gave Rankin a great sense of pride to know that his own company commander was this good.

"This is it lads," he said as loud as possible, in the pause before Achingdon's voice came again –

"By the left," – just the right timing as the men of the company tensed afresh, poised for the off – "quick march."

They were away: left, right, left, right, perfect, just perfect, good old Horace. Rankin knew he would do it so right, and now they were in their stride, in time with the band – left, right, left, right, left elbows tucked well in, holding their rifles firm, right arms swinging, straight from the shoulders, heads up, chests out, men – military men – marching, marching to their own band – on parade for their Queen – marching damn well, and proud of it.

Now number four company commander was bawling out his commands and his company set off, in perfect step, with number three company and the rest of the parade. All the company commanders were screeching and bawling, creating a cacophony which could have meant nothing to any but the military. Those on parade were trained for it, had rehearsed this parade over and over again, and though it was difficult with all those voices, screeching, bawling, roaring, over the top of the band, everyone knew they must listen only for their own company commander, act only on his command, so that, in spite of all the din, with added noise coming now from the nearby Royal Air Force airfield where the jets were warming up, it could be all sorted out and all would be right.

The band had changed their music to the regimental march, giving everyone on parade that extra lift which was so necessary at this stage, and number one company had already marched past the General. Achingdon boomed, "left wheeeeel" to number three company, and they were swinging left, a good wheel, the right hand man of each three coming round fast, the inside man slow, and the middle man keeping them together and in line – nice wheel that – and now they were straightening up in their threes, beautifully covered off from front to rear Rankin could see, marching past the spectators, and in front and just to the right of the leading men of the company, he had full sight of the General on the raised saluting base, a splendid upright figure, and, at the salute, as number two company marched past him. In a minute it would be the turn of Rankin's company to salute and go past, and then they would march off and be dismissed – the parade finished.

Sergeant David Rankin was not the biggest man in the company nor in the Battalion, but there was no doubt that he was one of the strongest and the fittest. Twenty three years of age, but most mature in his outlook, he was respected by those above him and those junior in rank to him. He was spoken about as "the tank", and nicknamed "Tanko" because of his splendid build and known strength, and it was sometimes hard for those senior to him to address him as sergeant rather than the nickname everyone knew him by.

He was five feet ten inches tall and just over fourteen stone in weight, all of it rippling strength and muscle. Fresh faced, which long hours in the sun could not darken, for all his size he was an easy light mover, a splendid soldier on and off parade, and an example to the entire Battalion. His drill movements were a delight to the military purists, whilst his pleasant nature, unfailing good humour at all times, and athletic prowess, had made him the best known man in the Battalion, and the best liked.

He was well known in sporting circles throughout the Colony, captaining the Army football team in addition to his own Battalion team. He boxed for the Battalion, and had never been beaten in Hong Kong, threw the hammer and the discus far enough to beat all comers in this part of the world, and as anchor man on the tug-of-war rope had helped the Battalion team maintain an unbeaten record during the eighteen months he had been in Hong Kong.

He loved Army life. He enjoyed a parade such as this, and was sorry it was coming to an end now, the pomp and splendour of the occasion thrilled him and brought the best out of him. Parades, military training, drill instruction, and sports, were an equal joy to him, and it was a happy life in the Battalion with always so much to do. He fitted in well in the sergeants' mess, where they called him the most eligible bachelor in Hong Kong, and his motto was life is for living, so he worked hard, kept himself fit, enjoyed his sports and his off duty pleasures, to the full.

Born in Swansea, the youngest of a family of four, he had an elder brother, who owned a thriving little electrical business, and two married sisters, he had been well and carefully brought up, had done well at school, and had been encouraged by a doting father to take part in as many sports as possible, even though he had preferred football to rugby, and, then at the right time, to join the Army. There was a letter from home giving him all the news once a week, with photos and cuttings from the local papers, and he set one night free each week to write a long letter to his mother and father, and to keep up his correspondence with special friends.

The jets were taking off now, the fighter aircraft which was all there was to offer resistance to whatever might come against Hong Kong from the air. They were to dive past in salute just after number four company had marched past the General. They've left it a bit late, Rankin thought, they have to climb and get into formation yet.

The command, "By the right," from old Horace brought him back to the parade – they were dressed by the right now, each three by the right hand man, almost ready to go past the General –

"Nearly there now lads," Rankin shouted as loud as he dared, "Give him a good one lads – throw that head round." –

"Number three company," boomed Achingdon –

"This is it lads," Rankin urged –

"Eyeyeyeyeyes," – long drawn out – not too long Horace, old lad, Rankin thought, don't have us hanging on too long –

"Right." – Short and sharp and loud from Achingdon, and right it was, on the correct foot – the left foot – with the right foot coming down again, and then on the next left foot over went the heads of the men of the company, all together as far as Rankin could see, as he jerked his head and shoulders right.

He was passing the blur of the colour of the spectators, the wives and children of officers and men of the Battalion, the many visitors who had come up from Kowloon and over from Hong Kong, the Chinese staff – very interested and very noisy, with the raised parasols of the women, and the flags behind the stand, which had been specially built for the occasion.

It's a good eyes right he told himself. It seemed so, but his view out of his left eye was not as far as the front men of the company. The perspiration was coming down his forehead into his eyes, and down his nose, so that, as he licked his lips, he could taste the salt. He could feel the perspiration oozing down his back, down the middle of his body, and down the back of his legs. Cripes – it was hot, and sticky.

Then he was marching past the General. Rankin pushed even harder, to get his chest out and his head erect, looking the General straight in the eyes for a brief second as he went past. That's a damn fine salute the General is holding, he thought. It had been a long parade for him too, and just as hot, but he, like the men of the Battalion, was giving all he had to give. This was the Queen's birthday parade, and only the very best was good enough.

Rankin caught a glimpse of the Union Jack above and behind the General, flying limply in the still air. Beyond was the far hills, the blue sky, and the puffy white clouds. Just a few clouds, but puffy and white. He could hear the jets over the music of the band, they were still high up, but the noise was coming closer very fast. They'd be down on time.

Achingdon gave them the eyes front, and, as he brought his head and shoulders round to the front again, he could see the men of the company had held a good line. We've done well, he told himself, damn well.

"Keep it up lads," he shouted – "keep going, keep marching." He could shout louder now, they were well past the General, and he had to shout loud to get above the sound of the fast approaching jets.

He knew how many of the men would be feeling, how glad that it was nearly all over. Days and weeks of rehearsing, culminating in the actual parade today, and, for many of them, it was damn hard work. For himself, it had been a joy, an occasion to be proud and act proud, stick his chest out, hold his head up, be a man and look the part. But, then, he was a professional soldier and this his chosen career. A great number of those on parade were not professionals, though they had all done well today.

They marched off the parade ground through the line of hutments to where they would be dismissed. Now there came a fiendish roaring and snarling from behind. All Hell was let loose as the jets – three by three by three – came swoosh – swoosh swoosh, as they dived past the General in salute. They were down very low, not much above a hundred feet, as they levelled off, swooshed by, then up and away again. The bushes, the hutments, the ground even, shook and vibrated in the aftermath of that dive, whilst many of the men, who had involuntarily crouched down as they marched, because of the fear of that awful noise behind them, straightened up again as they marched on.

Rankin's bearing and marching had not altered, but cripes, that noise had been really frightening. Those jets had been moving very fast, they had come lower than he thought they would have done, and he had never heard anything quite like that noise before.

He was prepared to bet though that they had been right on time, and not kept the General waiting.

3

LEE KYUNG KOH

At eleven o'clock Ai Fah, the number one amah, opened the door of the bedroom. Her timing was exact, eleven was always the time she woke her mistress, and everyone on the large staff knew how important punctuality was in the household, especially for Ai Fah who ruled the servants, both male and female, with strict impartiality and firmness.

She opened the shutters carefully, and without noise, draping the white ruffle nylon curtains back into place, to soften the severe light from the sun streaming through the large windows. Her movements, though quiet, were awkward, she had been born and brought up in a province where it had been the custom to bind the feet of the female children.

The room was cool. The air conditioning plant had cost a great deal of money, and the men of the household, who looked after it, were experts.

Lee Kyung Koh awoke when her amah first entered the room, as she always did, but did not move or speak, letting her eyes become accustomed to the light and waiting for Ai Fah to approach the bed to make the first greeting. This was the way it must be – the servant must always greet the mistress, and Ai Fah, herself, would have it no other way.

She glided to the side of the bed. "The day is good," she said, "I trust my lady feels good to enjoy it." The voice was pleasant, the Cantonese melodious and sing-song.

Her face took on a great softness as she looked down at her mistress. She had been present when Lee Kyung Koh had been born, had looked after her as a child, brought her to Hong Kong when the need had first arisen, and graduated to become the senior female servant of the large household, serving her mistress with a loving, yet fierce, devotion. She would gladly kill, as she had killed one man, anyone who dared to attempt harm Lee Kyung Koh in any way. There was another man, now sightless if he still lived, his eye balls gouged out by Ai Fah, who had tried to molest Lee Kyung Koh when she was only twelve years old.

"I am well Ai Fah," the Cantonese was the same sing-song, though much more melodious, "it is going to be a good day."

"My lady has slept well and is refreshed?" Ai Fah asked.

"Yes, I am so and ready for the day," came the reply.

The amah drew back the white bedspread, which was appliqued with a small deep blue orchid, the flower emblem of the Triad of which Lee Kyung Koh was the head, and the snow white quilt – there was no top sheet on the bed. As the naked Lee Kyung Koh stood up, her amah handed her a light blue dressing robe, which also bore a flower emblem, identical to the one on the bedspread. Lee Kyung Koh slept without nightdress or pyjamas, and only wore a robe when she was out of bed.

Ai Fah watched her mistress disappear through a door at the far end of the room before piling the pillows up against the bed head, and waited patiently until she appeared again to climb back on to the bed and sit back against the pillows.

When she was comfortable and settled, Ai Fah clapped her hands. As if by magic, the main door opened and another amah, a youngish girl, came in to the bedroom, pushing a high wheeled trolley carefully and quietly to the side of the large bed. The trolley placed to the satisfaction of Ai Fah, the young amah kowtowed to her mistress, and then to Ai Fah, and withdrew, leaving Ai Fah to help Lee Kyung Koh with the important business of breakfast.

First, a glass of orange juice, cold, and from a large silver jug, the handle of which was a dragon with a very large tail. The juice had already been tasted by Ai Fah, as was everything of such nature before her mistress could be allowed to partake of it.

As Lee Kyung Koh slowly drank the juice, Ai Fah buttered a slice of thin brown bread toast, and then placed one poached egg from a silver platter on to a delicately patterned plate.

The fruit juice finished, Ai Fah took the glass, then spread a large white serviette, again with the deep blue Hong Kong orchid appliqued, on the lap of her mistress. Next she placed a light tray with the poached egg, toast, knife, fork and silver salt cellar, gently on top of the serviette.

Lee Kyung Koh used just a little salt and began her breakfast. Ai Fah watched patiently and happily. She knew better than to interrupt her mistress when she was taking breakfast. Only when that was over could the day's business begin.

At thirty two years of age, and even without make-up of any kind, the great beauty of Lee Kyung Koh was obvious. Her dark hair was held in place by a light blue silk head-scarf, her skin very white, the features most regular, and the eyes large and sparkling. All her life, since she was a young girl, Lee Kyung-Koh had trained and worked to be a beautiful woman, and though she would not have admitted it, she delighted in reading the eyes of the many men who looked at her, knowing that they enjoyed, in their different ways, what they saw.

She ate slowly and carefully, being well aware that the digestive organs play a great part in the art of beauty, looking around her room the while. She was proud and entranced with the room, her boudoir, her holy of holies, and never failed to find pleasure in what she saw. The carpets, curtains, the silk brocade, the lighting and every piece of furniture, had been her own choice.

For the day time the lighting, when required, was normal, but at night, when retiring to bed, she could switch on a different set of lights, or, sometimes, Ai Fah would have them switched on, so that the room would reflect the gentle blush of dusk with a pale pink glow on the far side from the windows. In the wall, high up, were two bright lights to give the effect of two stars in the night sky. She thought of them as her own guiding stars.

The room was large and luxurious, with the windows running almost the full length of the end wall she faced. The wooden interior shutters were painted a light blue. Her large four-poster bed had intricately carved bed-posts, and was draped in white ruffle nylon matching the curtains.

The room was carpetted from wall to wall in a thick white pile, and the walls covered with brocade. An elegant chaise-longue, upholstered in rich white and blue brocade, and heaped with deep blue scatter cushions, to the left front of her bed, would have driven any good furniture dealer mad with desire, and this, her dressing table and bedside tables, were the only pieces of furniture in the room.

The large white laquered dressing table had a huge centre mirror and two wing mirrors, with the dressing table stool in blue leather. The four-poster bed was flanked by two bedside tables completely matching the dressing table.

It was a luxurious room, and one of great privacy, with the beautifully designed blush pink tiled bathroom at the near end being an interior room, so that the only entrance to the room itself was the door at the far end near the windows. Apart from Ai Fah, Lee Kyung Koh's personal staff numbered four amahs and a masseuse, but none of these were allowed in unless brought or ordered in by the number one amah. Outside the door was a long passage, off which was her private saloon, which she also used as an interview room, and Ai Fah's quarters. At the far end of the passage was a very strong door, with a Japanese designed television screen so that anyone inside could see anyone and anything outside, whilst outside, day and night was an armed guard, changed in military style every two hours. The security of Lee Kyung Koh was of the utmost importance, and the guard system would have done credit to the top unit of any army.

It was often a source of sadness to Ai Fah that, apart from the architect, the builders and decorators, who had finished the room to Lee Kyung Koh's personal instructions, and then the men who had fitted the bullet proof plate glass windows, no male person had ever entered, or been invited, into the room.

The whole of the vast block, which took up an entire street on Hong Kong island, was owned by Lee Kyung Koh, and the block housed her personal servants, her guards, and some of the higher-ups of the Triad she ruled. The block was fortress strong, the interior rooms large and of good standard, and very well furnished. Her personal kitchens were on the same floor as her bedroom, the fourth floor of the five storey block, with her cooks, all females, known to Ai Fah since birth, and chosen by the number one amah personally.

There was only one main entrance to the block, but there were six other entrances and exits, two of which passed through underground passageways to emerge two and three blocks away. All were constantly guarded.

Lee Kyung Koh was a Nationalist, many people called her a fanatical Nationalist, and all her personal guards were recruited from Taiwan. All had served in the Nationalist military forces, and all, like Ai Fah, would serve her faithfully until death, and would gladly kill for her, should that necessity arise.

Rich by birth, her riches had increased in spite of the Second World War, and in spite of the final overthrow of the Nationalists, and the coming to power of Red China in 1949. Long before that, her wise father had known it was time to get his wealth and his daughter out of Shanghai to the comparative safety of Hong Kong and the world beyond.

The family businesses had been set up in Hong Kong and America, and Lee Kyung Koh was in America with her father, before the Japanese troops had overrun and captured Hong Kong in December 1941. The war, in fact, helped to greatly increase the already large fortune of the family Koh, and her father had been quick to return to Hong Kong towards the end of 1945, and almost as soon as the British forces had begun to restore law and order.

By then her father was failing in health, and in 1948 had been forced to return permanently to America for the medical treatment he could not obtain in Hong Kong. This treatment prolonged his life until 1953, five long weary years for him, and it had been a great relief when he had passed to his ancestors in the great beyond in the October of that year.

All this time, as the power of the father had waned, that of the daughter had increased, and her influence was such that there was never any doubt but that she would succeed to her father's position at the head of all the industries, and, more important, succeed him as head of the Triad.

The interests and industries of the family had not suffered. The wise old man had seen that his daughter should have the best possible advisers, and the wise daughter had always sought their advice, whilst the increase in the prosperity of Hong Kong after the war had seen the same increase in the fortunes of the family, so that Lee Kyung Koh was now the richest woman in Hong Kong, if not the richest person of all.

Her activities were many and she supported, mostly anonymously, all the proper social activities of the Colony. She gave considerable help to such places as Rennie's Mill Camp, and caused her treasurer to donate sums of money each year to all the hospitals, whilst the people of the Triad, in all walks of life, were well looked after in sickness and in health.

It was essential they should be in all walks of life, for it was from these sources that much information was gathered, little by little, piece by piece, and put together by her intelligence section. Information was necessary in this city of intrigue, of politics, of international strife.

Information to keep that one jump ahead of other Triads, not so well organised, and not so well purposed as hers, and information to keep ahead of the Communists and the many agents of Red China.

She was very loyal to the Nationalists, and a large part of the yearly income from the industries and activities of the Triad were devoted to the Nationalists' cause. Agents had to be kept in China, large sums of money had to be found for Taiwan, and from Taiwan she could ask for anything. Her activities and her Triad were the outlet for many gallant young Chinese who, otherwise, would have been bored to death with the inactivity of waiting for an invasion which never came.

Lee Kyung Koh hated the Communists for what they had done to her father, to his estates, to his properties and industries, but mostly for what they had done to her country. Her Triad was law-abiding, and their warfare, which they waged whenever they could, was against the Communists and not against the law. She detested all the bad things other Triads helped to prosper, the drug trade and all its evil, prostitution, and other vile things other Triads rejoiced in, but she was militant and encouraged to her utmost the continual war her Triad waged against the Communists, and all other evils of the Colony.

She was well known to the Colony's police force, whilst the help her Triad gave to the lawful running of Hong Kong was known to all those in high administrative positions. The Triad always passed on some warning of Communist and anti-Communist activities. The senior police officers knew that her life was constantly in danger, because of the help she and her Triad gave them, but it was high amusement to Lee Kyung Koh that she was guarded more closely than was the Governor, but this was essential as she was in much more peril.

The Triad in liaison with Taiwan had their network throughout China, and knew much of what was happening across the border. Most of this information was passed to the Colony government, and then to the outside world. Her activities and influence were widespread through Hong Kong, Kowloon and the New Territories, and everywhere she was known just as Lee – known, loved, respected, feared, and hated.

To her own Triad she was their Lady, and she was served loyally and most devotedly. In return she gave her best, saw they had the best of conditions, even though some had to be in low positions. It was her great pride that none of her Triad ever became a burden to the hard pressed social services of the Colony. When medical treatment was needed for any of her people of the Golden Lotus Triad, it was readily available and paid for.

There was one weakness, a night club – the "Golden Lotus". This was Lee Kyung Koh's own project, her link with the outside world she determinedly called it, but it was the one weak link in the armour of her Triad. Known generally in Hong Kong as a gorgeous establishment, richly decored and excellently organised, with the best possible cuisine, it was a place she took a very personal interest in. It was her showpiece, and she was there every night.

Those close to her knew the danger, and had warned her of the personal danger to herself, and so to the Triad. She was well aware of it, but because of the quality and loyalty of her personal guards, and her own vanity, chose to ignore their fears and their advice.

At first the night club had been an expensive whim, and she had not been so well known in those days when it had all started. At first it had been a useful part of the Triad's activities, and from there much information had been gathered. It had flourished to the present success beyond all expectations, and now was amongst the very best in Hong Kong, but none of the senior men of the Triad had been able to convince her that, with its success, had come more danger to her, and as she was their head, to the Golden Lotus Triad.

The very wise Ai Fah had not advised against it. She knew the danger, but she also knew the real reason for the Golden Lotus, and that it was the outlet for the sex of her mistress. Ai Fah was perfectly aware that Lee Kyung Koh had never really known a man. Knew that she had never enjoyed a man's love and passion, had never thrilled to a man's dominance and personality, and never known suffering because of a man. The ownership of this famous night club was her only thrill and passion, and her one way of showing she was a woman.

But this was all wrong to Ai Fah. To be seen from near or afar, and be admired by many men, was not Ai Fah's idea of being a woman. To her a man must own a woman after conquering her, must love her, thrill her and enter her, and not just look and imagine, which was all men could do when they saw Lee Kyung Koh. To Ai Fah it was very sad, and she was pleased it was something she did not suffer from, even at her age.

Lee Kyung Koh refused a second egg, but accepted another thin buttered slice of the brown bread toast, and only when that was eaten would she have coffee. Liquids were not meant to be mixed with solids in the mouth. Ai Fah served the coffee graciously, in a gold handled cup.

Lee Kyung Koh handed the cup and saucer back to her amah, wiped her long slim fingers on the serviette and left it on the tray, which Ai Fah deftly removed and placed back on the trolley. She clapped her hands and, in the same magic way as before, the door opened immediately. Into the room came the young amah, kowtowed to her mistress and to Ai Fah, then silently wheeled the trolley out of the door, which closed at once behind her.

As the door closed, Lee Kyung Koh came off the bed with the litheness of a gazelle. She unbuttoned and took off the robe, handing it to Ai Fah, as she moved past her and forward to stand centrally in the room, and about three paces from the windows. Nakedness was a delight to her in the privacy of her room, and she knew that she could not be seen through the windows, even if the curtains had not been carefully draped. The block opposite belonged to her Triad, and her guards ensured her room was not overlooked.

Feet wide apart, she began a gentle trunk rolling hands forced down hard behind her back. Gentle, but a full sweep round, so that her head brushed the carpet quite firmly as she brought the upper part of her body down and round. Three times right, three times left, then back to the upright position.

She was five feet ten inches tall, so that, even when wearing flat heeled shoes, she was taller than most of the men of her Triad. Such height is not unusual for a Chinese woman of good class.

Her breasts were big and firm with very large nipples. Though slim waisted, she had large hips and buttocks, but not too large, and not so that it spoiled the symmetry of her lovely figure, and her legs were long and perfect. She had not suffered the old Chinese custom of having her feet bound as a child. This was something her father had always been against, and had not permitted be done to his daughter.

Except for the large splashes of red of her nipples, her body was white. In common with most Chinese she was not a sun lover, and protected her face and body from the sun. She could not understand the sun worship of the English and other white nationalities, who exposed themselves to the excessive heat of the sun to brown and bronze themselves at all the big bays of the Colony, and at every available opportunity. High caste Chinese, especially the females, retained their porcelain whiteness and did not wish to become bronzed. It was only the low caste who were that way because they worked in the open air in the sun, so could not avoid its rays.

The whiteness of Lee Kyung Koh was all the more striking because there was no hair on her body. Long years before, in America, she had been friendly with a lovely Parsee girl, and had learned that high caste Parsee women only allowed hair to grow on their heads. She adopted the custom and, thanks to members of her Triad in Bombay and Calcutta, had never used any other oil or spirit than that provided from Parsee friends, so she had no hair under her arms, on her private parts, or on her legs.

Ai Fah had never understood this. She had often thought it might have something to do with the fact that her mistress had never really known, or encouraged, a man. She dared not have said so, but she thought it a silly custom. Pubic hair was natural, and had never upset her many lovers. Quite the opposite, as all her sort of men expected to find a woman as a woman, and enjoy her.

Lee Kyung Koh began some harder exercises. Legs still apart, she forced her trunk down, forward and down, until again her head was touching the carpet. Down and up six times.

Ai Fah admired the exercising of her mistress, and never failed to appreciate what a magnificent woman she was, even if she didn't have any pubic hair. She was spellbound as her mistress changed the exercise, and began to kick her left leg high in the air, higher than her head. The left leg, then the right leg, six times each alternately. This finished, the left leg was brought up high behind the body, doubled at the knee, and her head and upper part of the body forced back, until the foot touched her head. Six times the left leg, six times the right leg. Exercises, like good eating, were necessary for loveliness.

Ai Fah's expression softened as Lee Kyung Koh changed from the violent exercises to the slow and graceful movements of the "tai chi chuan", a series of lovely movements, the knowledge of which had been handed down from generation to generation from the most ancient of Chinese times. Movements both beautiful to look at, and, if done properly, very beneficial to the performer.

Ai Fah loved to see her mistress in these glorious movements, and was so proud when the grace of the "tai chi chuan" brought out all the exotic charm of the woman she considered the most lovely in all the world. What prayers she offered for her wonderful lady, and how sad it was they were so slow to be answered. Ai Fah was a Christian following the lead of her mistress, but still had memories of some of the Chinese Gods which had been so much a part of her life prior to her conversion, so that, in addition to her prayers to God in Heaven, she secretly prayed to some of the Chinese Gods as well, not that she would have confessed it, even at the pain of death.

Her prayers were mostly for her mistress and never altered. She prayed for a virile and handsome prince to come along, to conquer her, and carry her off to his kingdom, taking Ai Fah along to look after her mistress still, of course. This happened to the heroine in almost all the many Chinese films Ai Fah saw, though the films never showed the faithful amah being carried off as well.

Ai Fah had so much in life that she knew her mistress did not possess or enjoy. She was fifty two years of age, but still very much enjoyed the worldly things she considered a woman was entitled to. She lived well and comfortably, and none of the higher-ups of the Triad dared question her activities. In her comings and goings about the household, and outside amongst the other businesses of the Triad, she never missed the chance to look at a man, and not a quick glance at that. She could take her pick from the senior men who served Lee Kyung Koh, and who lived in this very block.

She was still bubbling with energy and, like her mistress, ate wisely and well. The masseuse of the household served only Lee Kyung Koh and Ai Fah, but, in truth, spent much more time massaging Ai Fah than she did her mistress. When she was entertaining a man she had chosen, she could banish all the severity of her normal manner, so that she was just a woman, and a very passionate woman still.

She was well built and the wisest of women where a man was concerned. She could tell instantly by the way a man looked at her how much he was desiring her, and, from her own feelings, she would know whether she would be suited to him, and he to her.

There was a man now, an officer in the Chinese Nationalist Army, who had been seen and selected by Ai Fah within one week of his arrival from Taiwan, to serve in the personal bodyguard of Lee Kyung Koh. He was about forty years of age, fit and well disciplined, which was a special characteristic of selection for personal service to her mistress, and had looked, at first glance, as strong as a bull. So he had proved, much to Ai Fah's satisfaction.

Because her mistress was out at the Golden Lotus almost every night, and until the early hours of the next morning, Ai Fah was able to dine and wine her suitors in her own apartment, where, when they had partaken of the fine food and wine which was offered them, it was their turn to provide something for her. But she continually prayed that this could happen to her mistress as well, praying every night, as she was praying now, that the prince would come along very soon.

The exercising was nearly over and Ai Fah came out of her reverie. Without disturbing her mistress's movements or concentration, she went to the door, opening if to let in two amahs, the young one, who earlier had been in charge of the breakfast trolley, and another, who also was quite young. They were dressed in the two piece tunic and trousers worn by all the amahs, except Ai Fah, and were carrying a long roll of canvas. They made a small kowtow in unison to their mistress who took no notice of them, and another kowtow to Ai Fah, and waited just inside the door which had closed after them.

Ai Fah was ready with the robe as Lee Kyung Koh finished the movements. Apart from a little colouring of the cheeks, there was no other outward sign of the exercises and movements she had been performing, and no increase in the strength of her breathing. She sat down on the chaise-longue, her long legs stretched out in front of her.

The two young amahs were well trained. They spread the canvas squarely on the carpet, turned to the door which opened as they turned, and went out to bring in at once a long narrow table topped with thick white padding. This they placed exactly central on the canvas, kowtowed to their mistress and to Ai Fah, and left the room. The door this time did not close behind them, and remained open until another amah entered. This one, dressed in the same manner as the other two, was both older and taller. This was the medical amah of the household, who now came to the side of the narrow table, waiting for her mistress.

Ai Fah went into the bathroom. This was one part of the day she did not like, this application of the "Indian muck", as she called it, on her mistress. Under the arms, on the private parts and on the legs. She could not bear to watch it, and was glad to be busy in the bathroom, where it was her task to prepare the bath, to ensure it was the correct temperature and properly scented.

Lee Kyung Koh lay on the table and submitted herself to the fingers of the medical amah. First of all, under the arms, then just above where the legs joined the body, then the legs themselves. The strong and supple fingers kneading in the secret oils. After some minutes, the oils were washed off by a clear white spirit. It was all done without a word between mistress and servant.

It was protocol of the highest order. The orders of the mistress were only given to the number one amah and passed by her to the amah concerned.

The medical amah kowtowed to show she was finished, and, this time, Lee Kyung Koh stood up to make a little nod of acknowledgement in return. It was enough.

In the bath Lee Kyung Koh belonged again to Ai Fah. Her back was scrubbed and sponged, each dainty foot washed in turn, and then Ai Fah, breathing a little more heavily, stood patiently waiting whilst her mistress soaked her lovely body in the fragrant water of the bath.

For both, though they might not have known, it was the same for each of them, it was the most peaceful and loving time of the day. Lee Kyung Koh loved her number one amah, and knew how much she was loved in return. She could not remember a day of her childhood when Ai Fah had not been with her, and could not remember a day without her since she had returned from America. The one thing that had spoiled her stay in that country was the separation from Ai Fah, and it had been a wondrous and joyous day when she had returned to Hong Kong, and they had been re-united.

The older woman was devoted to her, she knew, and she could not think of life without the patient, loyal Ai Fah, who was always there to serve her at all hours of the day and night. Lee Kyung-Koh knew she was a fortunate woman to have such wonderful servants and such a splendid number one amah, and though she knew that Ai Fah was strict and severe with the other servants, she was not cruel. It was her task to see that all the chosen personal servants were well looked after, and Ai Fah had always held the loyalty and affection of those under her.

A cold shower to finish the bath, then a brisk rub down, and it was time for the massage, with the masseuse waiting for her in the bedroom. Lee Kyung Koh enjoyed her massage, it was a necessary part of the day for her, with the skill of the masseuse helping to keep her fit for the long hours ahead of her. Ai Fah could bear to watch the massage, she knew what the skill of the masseuse could do, and how it helped the suppleness of the body.

When the masseuse had finished and left the room, Lee Kyung Koh put on her robe and resumed her seat on the chaise-longue. The two young amahs carried out the long table, then rolled up and carried out the canvas. With their going, Lee Kyung Koh could begin her make-up and then dress.

She did not waste a lot of time on make-up at this time of the day. A little blue eye shadow, a tough of rouge, a slight application of lipstick, and a small blob of cream in the palm of one hand to use on the hands and wrists. Later on at the Golden Lotus, the preparation would take much more time, with Ai Fah and a manicurist in attendance, but now, when she was soon to be occupied with members of her staff on Triad business, this little was sufficient.

But she was never in a hurry when it came to Ai Fah doing her hair. She took off the headscarf, letting her hair fall down her back in a glorious cascade of black, and Ai Fah began brushing it at once. It was not Lee Kyung Koh's custom to keep the pigtail, and though Ai Fah ensured that the young unmarried girls of the household kept faithful to the Chinese custom, the head of the Triad wore her hair as she wished, in modern style.

Hair, brushed and pinned up, making a splendid crown of black for the white of her body, Lee Kyung Koh stood up taking off the robe. She put on a pair of panties and a brassiere, her movements full of grace. Then came trousers in white, slim fitting, but flaring a little at the bottom of the legs, and a matching jacket edged with light blue silk, appliqued as all her personal possessions were, with the small deep blue Hong Kong orchid.

Ai Fah removed the pins holding up her mistress's hair, and stood back to admire her.

Lee Kyung Koh was ready for the busy day ahead of her, looking proud, beautiful and regal, her black hair spreading down almost to her waist at the back over the white jacket. The look on Ai Fah's face was appreciation enough of her majestic appearance.

Lee Kyung Koh said simply – "thank you, Ai Fah." The first words she had spoken since she had greeted Ai Fah on waking. Her voice was very sincere.

Ai Fah kowtowed deeply and gracefully, such words were both thanks and praise.

As Lee Kyung Koh approached the door, it opened, and even when she had left the room, the look on Ai Fah's face did not alter. Her face was still aglow two minutes later when the two young amahs came back into the room, but then the look changed, back came the severity and discipline. The room had to be cleaned now, to Ai Fah's complete satisfaction.

4

RANKIN'S 48 HOUR PASS

The two sergeants marched briskly through the camp towards their living quarters near the sergeants' mess, the long swinging stride of their profession evident in both as they marched, in perfect step, and right arms swinging exactly in time. Their company had been dismissed and rifles handed in to the armoury, so the day was now almost their own. In spite of the great heat, they marched as if still on the parade ground, their uniforms glistening black with their perspiration right across their backs, in front at the waist, and under the armpits.

The sun beat down from an almost cloudless sky, and reflected back with even greater heat from the asphalt roads and concrete pavements of the camp. They passed the tennis courts, where the Hong Kong orchids had raised themselves rampant high up to the wire fencing, a glorious mass of colour, hiding the red shale of the courts from view from the outside of the wire.

"Cripes Tanko," Bob Denton said, without turning his head, "I'm glad that little party's over."

David Rankin grinned – he had been whistling "Men of Harlech", as they marched together, but broke off now – "it was great Bob," his voice full of pride in his Battalion and the Army – "just great, we must have looked good."

"Aye, it's all right for you," Denton's voice had not the same pride. "You lap up these blasted parades, I find them damn hard work."

Rankin turned his head to look up at the other man. He was five feet ten inches and broad, so that most of the Battalion called him "The Tank", or "Tanko", but he was still five inches shorter than the more slimly built Denton. "That's a laugh Bob lad, you've got to like it, it's a part of our job. Of course I lap it up, it's a tremendous feeling when you're out there, it makes you feel what you are – a man."

Denton did not reply as they turned left past Battalion headquarters, and then marched along Cambria Avenue, at the top of which was their mess. Far away to their right, on the airfield, one of the aircraft which had taken part in the fly-past was still being revved up, the high piercing whine shrilling through the still air. All was quiet apart from this. In front of them was the high peak which lay between their camp and the border, but all this part of the camp was deserted at the moment, and they seemed to be the only two human beings about.

"The band was marvellous, just marvellous," Rankin's voice was still full of pride – "say what you like Bob, old Jonesey does a damn fine job. Even a cripple could march to our band."

A wry little grin spread over Denton's face. "Yes, they're good, but I like 'em best when they start up the regimental march, then I know it's nearly over."

"Funny enough," Rankin came back at once, "I don't. I tell the lads to give it all they've got – this is it, only a few minutes now, head up, shoulders back, chest out, look the old blighter right in the eye as you march past, but I can't help thinking that's another parade we'll never do again." He paused a few seconds, thinking, then – "But it was a good parade today, reckon it was the best we've ever done, I'll bet the old man was proud of us."

"I'll bet he was," Denton interrupted, "and when they give the bloody medals out he'll get one, but you and me won't."

Approaching the large building which was their mess and their home, at the top of the Avenue – a long low brick building, set back in the gaudily flower spattered green bushes of the gardens – they turned left to a line of hutments.

"Come off it Bob," Rankin said, "who wants a flippin' medal for a parade? I don't, I'm right happy to be on it and for it to be a good 'un."

They went in through the door numbered Seven, Rankin allowing the taller Denton to lead the way, down a long passage, dark and cool after the glare and heat outside, a long strip of matting deadening their footsteps, into a large room right at the far end.

The room was neat and tidy in typical Army style, an iron single bed with sensible, but attractive, bed covers on each side of the room, a small highly-polished table, two chairs, semi-comfortable but suitable, a wash basin and a large mirror above it, with glass shelves on either side, and down one side of the room, a big cupboard with sliding doors. There were two windows at the far end of the room, one on either side of the wash basin.

Rankin commenced stripping off his clothing at once, but Denton took off his bush-jacket only, and sat down on the bed to remove his hose tops, gaiters, socks and boots.

"I'm ready for a cold splash," Rankin said, his shorts falling down to his feet, revealing the great strength of his thick thighs. He sat down on the bed, a really powerful man in the pink of condition, and it was obvious why he was nicknamed, "the Tank". He quickly shed himself of his hose tops, gaiters, socks and boots, stood up in his brief under shorts, and commenced a few trunk rolling exercises.

Denton, now with just his Army shorts on, lay back on his bed, his hands clasped behind his head.

"Cripes, Tanko, is that how you feel after that flippin' parade? I'm just about beggared," – the admiration was marked in his voice. "You're a strong beggar you are, I pity anyone that has to tangle with you, I wouldn't care to try it on."

Rankin stopped his exercises, "Reckon you'd want a bit of stopping yourself Bob, with that long reach you've got. You should have been a boxer." He took off his briefs and wrapped a towel around his middle., "Come on lad, let's get under those showers before the other chaps come in," he urged.

The ablutions room was halfway back to the door along the passage, and Rankin was soon enjoying his shower. He grimaced at first, and gasped, it was cold once the pipe-warmed water had been quickly run through, but after a few seconds of the really cold water, it was lovely. He began to soap himself, head, hair, body, under the arms and legs, spluttering and splashing, half whistling "Men of Harlech," as best as he could. He heard footsteps coming down the passage, some of the other sergeants coming in off the parade, as Denton moved in to the next shower to him.

"Cripes Tanko, it's cold," he heard Denton gasp.

"Lovely, Bob lad, lovely," he shouted over the hissing of the water, "nothing better than this." He let the cold water run down all over him, washing away the soap, still spluttering a bit himself.

He was back in his room, dried, and with a clean pair of shorts on, when Denton came back, still towelling himself.

"What say, Bob," he asked, "shall we go over and have a game of snooker before lunch?"

Denton sat down on his bed, his towel around his middle, and reached for a cigarette – "not just yet, Tanko," he replied – "it's a bit early really, and we'll only be having too many pints if we get over there too soon."

"Not me," Rankin said emphatically – "one or two gills at the most for me, and only because it's a special occasion. Must have a gill to toast her Majesty, of course. You have as many pints as you like, but I don't like the stuff really."

He went over to the cupboard, searched around until he found some clothing he required, then came back to sit on the bed –

"What time will the CO and the officers be in, do you reckon? We'll have to have one drink with old Horace for sure."

"We can take our time, we've half an hour and more yet," Denton said between contented puffs of his cigarette. He lay back on his bed, stretching himself – "cripes, I'm tired," he continued – "take it easy Tanko, I can always beat you at snooker some other time."

Rankin grinned. "That'll be the day," he said. He too lay back on his bed.

There was quiet for a while in the room, each of the two men relaxed and with his own thoughts, and Denton occasionally blowing perfect smoke rings in to the air, it was warm in the room but peaceful, with just the faint sound of music from either a wireless or a record player from the room next door, and now and then sounds down the passageway from the occupants of other rooms.

Rankin was thinking of home – would it be such a day as this in South Wales, and, if it was, would his dad be at the county ground watching the cricket? He had lost touch with cricket and didn't know who, or where, Glamorgan might be playing, but if they were at home, and it was a nice day such as this, he was certain his dad would be there. He was as keen on cricket as Rankin himself was on football, and that was saying a great deal.

He was dozing, almost asleep, when Denton's voice brought him awake again.

"What time are you off this afternoon?" Denton asked.

"Three o'clock," Rankin told him. "And that reminds me, you know

I've got a forty-eight hour pass this time, so just you make sure nothing goes wrong while I'm down in Honkers."

He slowly brought his legs up, stiff and straight, until they were at an angle of ninety degrees with the rest of his body, then began to move one leg at a time, alternately, in circular fashion.

"You don't sound a bit sorry to be missing the Mess Ball then?" Denton made this more a statement than a question.

Rankin lowered his legs to the bed. "I suppose I am in a way, Bob, after all, I enjoy these functions really, and it should be good tonight – but then I'm not." He paused for a few seconds in reflection, then went on. "The RSM's been decent about it, he even said I deserved the break, so now it's on I am really looking forward to a bit of the old bright lights."

"You can enjoy yourself this time," Denton assured him. "The football season's over, and you're not in training now, are you?"

"Not really," Rankin replied, "though I like to keep myself fit all the time – but I can do with the break, it will do me more good than harm."

"Course it will," Denton was quite enthusiastic. "You make sure you have a bloody good time."

They were quiet again for a time, but this time Rankin was thinking about Hong Kong and not his homeland.

"You'll try to see what's her name?" Denton asked eventually.

Rankin smiled. "You mean Lee?"

"Who else?" Denton asked.

"Well, I shall go to the Golden Lotus," Rankin told him – "and hope to see her, but she might not be there."

Denton sat up to reach for another cigarette. "I'll have to come with you one night, Tank, and see if she's as smashin' as you say."

"She's gorgeous, Bob," Rankin's voice had come alive. "There isn't any other word for her – but she's a mystery all right, I wish I knew more about her."

"She must have plenty of dough, if she owns the place," Denton said.

"The first night I went there – when they took the Army football team," Rankin was thinking back as he spoke – "they said she was the owner, and ever since that night, though I've only been in three times, I've never had a bill, everything's been on the house and with her compliments."

"That's nice, Tanko," Denton said. "There's not a lot of sergeants in the British Army that can afford the Golden Lotus."

"I suppose not," Rankin agreed. "I sometimes wonder if I ought to go, but I like the manager there and he seems to like me. He's a fanatic on football, knows all about the teams at home, so we have a good talk when I'm there. As a matter of fact, I'm taking him down some papers today, so I have a reason for going" –

"You go and enjoy it," Denton said. "I don't reckon it'll cause them to go broke what you eat and drink."

"Well, I eat well enough, but I don't drink a lot. There's plenty of drink if I want it, and that manager looks after me wonderfully well. Always tells me not to worry when I offer to pay the bill – it's all on the house, and with her compliments, and to come anytime I'm in Hong Kong."

"An' does he say anything about who she is?" Denton asked.

"Very little," Rankin replied. "He's told me her name of course, and that she owns the joint, but he's much keener on talking football."

"Aye, it must make a great change for him to talk to someone like you," Denton agreed. "You just make the best of it, it's your good luck and you enjoy it. Don't get frightened if she offers to take you home and show you her etchings one of these nights," he laughed. "They're supposed to be very nice, and different."

Rankin joined in the laughter – "I don't think she's likely to do that, but she's been friendly in a way, always smiles graciously. She really is a terrific looking woman – a bit out of my class though."

"Don't you kid yourself," Denton told him. "If a hen fancies you, she won't worry about your class. You just remember you're a heck of a lot different to the sort of fellows she has to mix with." He looked hard at Rankin. "You're not a bad looking chap you know, Tanko, nearly in my class."

"Thanks, Bob," – Rankin was amused. "Praise from you is praise indeed as they say, I wish I could dance like you though – I did have one dance with her on that first night, but that must have been a special night when they took us there after the football match. I think I must have been a bit tiddly that night, I haven't dared to do other than nod and say good evening since then."

Denton stood up, "That's the time, Tanko, when you're dancing with 'em. You take a tip from your old Uncle Bob himself – hold them nicely at first, keep away from 'em a bit – make them think hey what's up with me, this lad doesn't want to feel my body against his. So they move in themselves, closer and closer, you just let 'em, and when they do, you've got 'em – see what I mean?"

"Sounds easy, Bob, but I didn't have much chance really."

"It is easy," Denton interrupted very enthusiastically – "dead easy."

"That's what you say," Rankin said, "but all women aren't alike."

"Oh yes, they are," Denton replied – "once you've got them in close, they're all the same, they're on the chase, and once you've got 'em on the chase, there's no stopping 'em."

"Well, you ought to know, Bob."

"Course I know," Denton went on, "then you can try a bit of the old body game yourself – that's what they want. Hold 'em against you all the way down, they like to feel what you've got, no doubt about that, and you make sure you hold 'em close enough to feel their buds against you – they like that too, then you just push your face up close against theirs, and start whispering in their ears."

"Whisper what?" asked Rankin. He was enjoying the other's performance.

"Anything, Tanko, anything and everything – they love it, that's for sure, and they fall for it in a big way. Tell 'em how nice they are, that they smell lovely – that's a good line and they always go for that – tell 'em that, even just dancing with 'em is getting you in the mood, and give 'em an extra bit of a press low down to convince 'em. I know what I'm talking about, had long years of practice, and it never fails." He lowered his voice, "that's what I do with Natalie in the mess, an' she just laps it up."

Rankin sat up on his bed – his face was serious now. "That's something you should watch your step with, Bob lad." There was a strong note of warning in his voice. "Old Gerry Hibbert'd kill you if he thought you was messing about with Natalie."

"Not messing with her, Tanko," Denton's tone was heated. "That's a bloody crude way of putting it. I'm just trying to keep her morale high, like I try to do with all the hens in the mess. I'm playing me social part and helping to entertain the wives – not like you, dashing off to the bright lights and the Chinese birds."

"Well, you just watch yourself," Rankin was still very serious. "If Gerry Hibbert ever had the slightest suspicion about it, there'll be a funeral in this Battalion, and you'll be the one we have to carry in the box."

"Oh nuts, come off it, Tanko," Denton argued – "anyone'd think you never had a bit of a gallop in your time. Besides, she likes it, looks forward to it, says that's what mess dances are for, so old Gerry can get himself well sloshed and I can do her a bit of good."

"That's your affair," Rankin said, "But I don't agree with it, old Gerry is our own sergeant-major, so all I hope, for both your sakes, that nobody else has any idea it's going on."

"There's no danger of that," Denton seemed very sure. "Natalie nor I are stupid, and we're damn careful none of the other hens suspect it. We really only meet on such occasions like tonight. But Tanko, what can we do, it's something that just happened the first time – you know how these things do happen, but I'm bloody sure you're the only one who knows, and you won't say anything."

"Of course I won't," Rankin replied. "Even though I don't agree with it, but I am telling you to go careful – once you start an affair like this, you can't know what'll happen."

"You're right there," Denton agreed, "and I would like to see more of her, but, of course, we can't meet only at the mess like tonight."

"Well, keep it that way," Rankin told him. "Don't get in any deeper, you're in deep enough already, and like I've told you – watch your step."

"We always do," Denton was very thoughtful. "Never anything wrong in the mess. I dance with all the hens, not just with Natalie, you know that, and I do it purposely, I do my best to dance with everyone of 'em even though I'd much rather be jazzing round with Natalie."

"I know that, and it's a good thing, Bob."

"That's why I do it, and Natalie understands," Denton went on, "But all old Gerry wants to do is sup his pints – silly beggar never dances himself, and he ends up getting well sloshed. Then Natalie and me have to get him home, nobody else wants to get him home, he's such a bloody obstinate beggar when he's on the booze."

"He is that," Rankin agreed.

"An' I'm the only one who seems to be able to handle him right. They say you help Natalie get him home, Bob, so that's how it happens. We get him back to their place, get him to bed – by then he's pretty well paralytic, and that just leaves the two of us, and after we've both been struggling with him for half an hour or so, what do you expect me to do,

Tañko, just say goodnight and leave her?"

Rankin smiled a little at that, "No, I'll be honest, Bob lad, it takes two to make a bargain, and I must say she's quite a hen is that Natalie."

"Quite a hen," Denton's voice was thick and his eyes alight, "she's a real beaut is that woman, and just bloody marvellous, and by that time, she's right in the mood for it, and me – well, I'm just nuts about her."

"That's the trouble," Rankin said, "Of course you're nuts about her, and I can't say I blame you. She's here and she's damn nice. But can you stop at that? Isn't there a danger if you continue the association?"

"Of course there is," Denton agreed. "There always is danger in these sort of things, but we keep it for mess dances, Tanko, there's no other meetings much as we should like it more frequently, we know it wouldn't be a good policy. So, we make the most of it whilst we can."

"I'm glad, Bob, I should hate it to be otherwise – I don't agree with it but it's really none of my business. It's safe with me, but just let one of those other hens get it into her sights that there's something going on between you and Natalie, and it'll be curtains for you both."

"We know that, we both know that," Denton said – "we've talked it over a lot, you know, Tanko, we both know what we're doing, we both know the risks, and I agree with you about old Gerry – I'd murder anyone myself who was associating with my missus – if I had one – but I can't help it, and she can't help it, so what?"

"Like you say, Bob, so what," was Rankin's reply. "I think you're right, what can you do when it starts? I suppose it's wishful thinking really, but you know the reason I go to the Golden Lotus – it's not to talk football, and it's not for a free meal and that – it's just to see that woman."

"There you are then, Tanko, so how can you blame me for what goes on with me and Natalie?"

"I'm not really blaming you," Rankin told him, "but I am telling you very seriously to watch your step."

"We do, Tanko, don't worry about that, and Natalie'd be the last one to want it any other way." Denton assured him.

Rankin got up and went over to the cupboard. "Come on Bob," he said, "time to get dressed, we'll have to be in before the officers get there". He turned from the cupboard to look hard at Denton. "But you just remember what I've said, there'd be murder done if Gerry found out, make sure for both your sakes that you're not caught."

"I won't forget," Denton replied. He was now starting to dress and was pulling on his socks. "You can bet your bloody bottom dollar on that."

Rankin was still searching in the cupboard for the uniform he wanted, and had bent down to sort out his shoes.

"And don't you forget, Tanko," Denton went on, struggling to get a sock on his left foot, "enjoy yourself tonight, and if that Lee girl offers it to you, don't turn your nose up at it, they say these Chinese birds are terrific."

He just managed to dodge the shoe which Rankin hurled at him, and in doing so, fell off the bed with a tremendous crash.

Rankin was highly amused as he moved over towards the door to collect his shoe.

5

THE GOLDEN LOTUS TRIAD

Lee Kyung Koh's Treasurer was waiting for her in the salon. Kowtowing as she entered, he stood head bowed as she passed him to take her place at the large desk at the far end of the room. The salon was a place for business, but it was beautifully furnished in the same luxurious manner as the bedroom, as befitted a person of such riches as the head of the Triad.

The Treasurer had known Lee Kyung Koh all her life, as he had steadily progressed to the important position he now held. His father had served her father, and this man had always been a part of the household. Like many of her staff, he had been educated in America, and held her complete confidence. She appreciated his modern approach to all the problems. Business with the Treasurer was not so irksome as it might have been. He was pleasant, efficient, and his appreciations and explanations were always very clear.

She spent well over an hour with him. There was much to be done, accounts to be seen, payments to be authorised, incoming sums to be told about, grants to be made, and decisions to be taken.

The Triad owned factories in Hong Kong and in America, businesses in many parts of the world as they spread members seeking both trade and information; many farms over in the New Territories, and a great deal of shipping. The shipping ranged from large ships which plied the oceans of the world, to the picturesque, and very profitable, junks which operated in the home waters of Hong Kong, and down to sampans.

It was a large business empire, and though Lee Kyung Koh could not possibly deal with everything, she was a keen business woman, who would authorise the spending of a million dollars on something, or some project she thought worth while, yet quibble about a single dollar if it was not. Much as she trusted her Treasurer, she still ensured she knew as much about the financial side of affairs, and the final decisions were always hers.

At last, the Treasurer made his kowtow and departed, and it was time for Ai Fah to usher in the young amah with a trolley. One cup of tea only for Lee Kyung Koh, weak with a slice of lemon and no sugar, served in the delicious cups used by the household, and made specially for the head of the Triad by one of her factories. Like the coffee cups used at breakfast, the handles were made of gold. At this time, Ai Fah was permitted to take a cup of tea with her mistress, also weak with a slice of lemon and no sugar, and they could discuss any household problems. Such times as these were precious to them both.

But there was nothing of great importance to discuss today, whilst idle chit-chat could not take place between mistress and amah, so soon the young amah was back to remove the tea trolley, and Ai Fah left the room. It was now the turn of the medical advisor to be granted audience.

The Triad was run on very modern, yet ancient lines, with Lee Kyung Koh at the head, supported by a council, all of whom were males. The council met once each week, or more often if there was important business to discuss, while different days were set aside for the business of the individual members. Only the number two of the Triad, the Minister, as he was called, would see Lee Kyung Koh every day.

The medical advisor brought news of the health of the household and of the Triad locally, and of a birth just that morning to the wife of a member of the council. He had already sent greetings and a gift on behalf of Lee Kyung Koh, who would no doubt take early opportunity to see the child – a boy, herself.

This part of the business was as important to her as any other. There was so much sickness, some of it hereditary, and so much danger to those lower down in the order. Recently there had been a lot of fighting in which some of the Triad's ricksha boys, and men of the junk fleet, had been involved. It was part of the general disturbance of Hong Kong in the past few days, and to the trained observers, the first evidence of trouble to come. She was saddened to be told that one of her men had died of a stab wound received in a street fracas, but did not need to give orders that his wife and family were to be taken care of, that was understood in the Triad.

She was pleased, however, to be reassured that there was never any evidence of any member of the Triad being involved in drugs. This wasn't really correct as she knew, for some of the older men, including one or two of those most senior, still partook of their opium. But she knew all about opium from her father, as he had smoked more and more towards the end of his life.

She remembered how he described the effects, "No dreams, my daughter, no dreams. An increased sense of physical well-being, with no thought or interest in the passing of time, and no thoughts of women or erotic pleasures."

Opium smoking was illegal, but the authorities did not really worry too much about it. Far worse, and the real worry, was heroin, which was a killer and known as the "living death". Heroin is a by-product of opium, and is converted speedily and cheaply in Hong Kong. Hong Kong's number one problem, heroin, was well known as the root of all things evil, of crime and of violence, but, as even her Triad would acknowledge, it was something for which the cursed Communists could not be blamed. The Reds fought as hard as the Hong Kong authorities to put down the drug, but the free world, especially America, required heroin, and it was certain knowledge that half of Hong Kong's criminals were heroin addicts.

The medical advisor was an expert on heroin and the evils it conveyed, but he was sure there was not one addict among the men of the Triad.

Lee Kyung Koh took a very great interest in all the activities of the Triad, and was happy to devote as much time as necessary to each member of the council, but she was glad today when the medical advisor had taken his leave of her. It was time for her to see the Minister.

She knew he would wait for just one minute after the medical advisor had left before coming in to the salon. This had ever been his custom, and it was so today.

He was a great man in height and girth, six feet four inches, and the only member of the council taller than Lee Kyung Koh. A strong serious face, with a short clipped beard, which he had always worn as far back as she could remember. The room came alive when he entered, and her interest quickened. Here was a great man in every sense of the word, as she had always known, and as her father had known before her, and here was the strength of the Triad. She often thought of the Triad as a clock, with herself as the pretty face, but the real works and the strength out of sight.

She knew his name, but called him Minister, but always with a softness and care which was not known by any other member of the council. Nothing she could ever do was as important as the work this man did for the Triad and for her, whilst she recalled with pleasure every time she saw him how well and faithfully he had served her father.

He kowtowed as deeply and properly as any other member of her staff did, then came to stand before her table until she asked him to sit down. He retreated a little to sit on a large upright chair, placed near to the right hand front edge of her table. This chair was reserved for him, and no other member of the council was allowed to use it.

He came straight to the point, he was not a man to waste words or time.

"There is important news, my Lady, and the action will be soon – perhaps even tomorrow."

Lee Kyung Koh waited, knowing well that this was not the time to ask questions. There was more, much more, to come.

"I have definite information that three of the heads of the Ninety Seven are in Hong Kong, and perhaps twenty or more of the second heads. There is to be a meeting. It must be – will be – in Kowloon, and very soon. Then will come the action."

Lee Kyung Koh listened and nodded her head.

"The action will be exactly the same as before," he continued – "skirmishes to start at various places, to develop into full rioting, and then will come all the things we know are associated with such disorders – pillage – looting – killing – everything. As before, the low Triads will be paid, and will do what they are paid to do. There will be much, much trouble."

Still Lee Kyung Koh did not speak – it was not yet time for her to do so.

"I have information that Mong sees such action here as a manner of discredit to Mao, and I have information that similar action will take place in Taiwan."

The surprise of Lee Kyung Koh could be seen in her face, and in the lift of her eyebrows, and now she could speak at this surprising piece of news. "That is hard to believe," she said.

"But it is not, my Lady," he countered, "We know that infiltration can be accomplished anywhere. Here – in Hong Kong, in London, in

Washington, if the effort is high enough, it can be accomplished anywhere, and it is not impossible in Taiwan."

Her thoughts were racing – he is right, of course he is right. How cleverly he organises our information services, and how well he puts it all together. An accomplishment he had spoken of depending on the strength of the effort and the skill and bravery of those selected to make the effort, was possible even in Nationalist held Taiwan. But she did not interrupt, and let him speak on.

"You will agree, my Lady, that if Mong can cause disorder in Taiwan, it will he a big feather in his cap. It is something which Mao has never been able to do."

She nodded her agreement, wondering how much the members of the party they knew as the Ninety Seven had infiltrated into the Taiwan she knew so well. If they had infiltrated there, they could even infiltrate into her Triad. It was an alarming thought, but one which no doubt her Minister had constantly in his mind and guarded against.

"The action here is much easier," he continued – "it is what we expect, the attempt to gain favour in China and belittle Mao. The age old shout of retaking Hong Kong for China—"

"But that is ridiculous," she interrupted.

"Yes, it is ridiculous to us, my Lady," he agreed, "but not to the simple people who will believe what they are told to believe. They are not thinking persons as you and I, they are not allowed to think, only to believe what is told to them."

Her thoughts fully agreed with him about this.

"The fact that China will lose so much by retaking Hong Kong is not understood by the simple people, the fact that China does not really want to retake Hong Kong – yet, is not known to them. What they are told by Mong and his swine the simple people will believe gladly, as you and I well know."

"You think Mao is losing favour then?" she asked, deeply thoughtful.

"Perhaps a little," he said. "Perhaps a little, perhaps a lot. Times in China have been hard, and there has been a great and surprising easing up on Hong Kong. There are those who do not like this easing up. There are those who know that riots and affrays in Hong Kong will please the simple people, even if a great deal is not accomplished."

He paused a few moments to let her thoughts grasp this, and she knew the reason for his pause.

"It will be an attempt, a happening," he went on. "And the simple people will know that Mong has tried something. You know that Mao has not spoken one word against Hong Kong for many moons."

"But how can Mong's followers make trouble here in Hong Kong where everyone supports Mao?" she asked.

"A good question," his tone of voice showed his approval of her thinking. "But these so-called followers of Mao here are simply swine and vermin and vagabonds. They will be paid for their work, but they will not realise the way the news will be released back in China. They will be happy to riot and fire the place, to loot and kill, thinking it all for Mao. But, of course, it will not really be for Mao – it will be for Mong and against Mao."

"Government will know, of course," she said.

"Yes, they will know," he replied. "The British are far from being the fools they like to let others think they are. The Englishman, Hamilton, is visiting Chin this afternoon, so they will know."

"What about the Americans?" she asked.

"Nothing to do with them – it will be if Taiwan erupts, but they will not want to cause any problems. As we look at it, the Americans are slowly moving to a better understanding with Mao, though they do not want to be against anyone."

"The Police will be better prepared this time when it comes," she said.

"They will," he agreed. "And that much will be appreciated by the Ninety Seven, not that they will care. They will only promote the action, none of the high-ups of the Ninety Seven will be in it. It will make an interesting trial of strength – the Police learned much in the double ten, and have worked and trained on what they learned ever since. This time they will surely call in the Army much quicker, they will not make the mistake of last time."

Lee Kyung Koh remembered the double ten riots of three years before very vividly, even though her guards had seen that she was never in any danger. But it had been a bad time in Hong Kong, and for Hong Kong.

"I cannot understand," she said, "why there are so many heads and second heads of the Ninety Seven in Hong Kong. Surely all this could have been left to one man to organise."

"It could." The Minister nodded his head in agreement, "but there is no real danger for them in Hong Kong unless we put them in danger.

The Police will know they are here, but will not know who they are, whilst the Communist swine will be only too glad to take the money they offer, and while they are providing the money to cause disorder, they will not be in any danger from the Reds.

"In any case," he continued, after a short pause expecting a question from her which did not come, "the heads will be away after the meeting, but long before the action commences – they also are not fools. When news of the disorders are known, it will be good for them to say they were in Hong Kong. Their followers will think they are the brave ones, brave enough to go to Hong Kong, or Taiwan, and even if it does not succeed this time – and they know it will not, it will be something, a start only perhaps, but something to talk about in their avowed intentions to release Hong Kong from the barbarians, and Taiwan from the Nationalists, and restore them to their rightful owner – China."

"And Mao," she asked, "what of Mao?"

"We must wait and see," he replied wisely, "but if the action drags on for a few days, if the Police do not stop it quickly, it can only help Mong and discredit Mao."

"The money, where do they get the money?" Lee Kyung Koh knew it cost a lot of money to bribe the low Triads, as they called them. The Triads which specialised in vice and drugs, and thrived on riots and disorders. Low Triads they were, and, without the intelligence and virtues of her own Triad, but they were hard bargainers when it came to money matters, and would have to be paid well.

"From Russia, of course," her Minister told her. "That is our information, and where else could it come from? Not from America, nor from Britain, and hardly from Japan, and who else has money for all this?"

Lee Kyung Koh screwed up her beautiful nose a little at the distaste she so obviously gave to this information. "It's so stupid, all this money being spent, wasted, on such hateful things, when there is so much good it could be put to."

The Minister almost smiled. "True, my Lady," he agreed, "but these are the activities of men, and have been so since the world began, will continue whilst there is still a world. Men, certain men, must have power, power is helped by intrigue, and intrigue needs money. It is surprising there is always so much money for wars and warfare, but there always is."

"You have told me that the information about Mong is of his increasing stature, will he eventually be able to oust Mao?"

"You ask wise questions," the Minister was pleased with her. "And your memory is good. Our information says yes to your question, and it must be remembered that Mong is younger than Mao, and young persons are dynamic." Again he almost smiled. "We know that in our Triad." This time he did smile, and her face softened as she smiled with him, sharing this little confidence with him. "Mong is Russian trained – Mao is getting older, as we all are. It will be a pity in many ways, but I agree with the information we receive, and, yes, barring accidents, he will oust Mao."

Lee Kyung Koh was puzzled. "Why, when we hate Mao so much, will it be a pity if Mong takes over from him?"

"That one is easy, my Lady." The smile had left his face. "You know the age old saying – better the devil you know than the devil you don't – that is true of Mao and Mong, of that this person is very sure. Mao is becoming more co-operative as he ages, he sees that China must live and be like the other nations, must put their hopes in trade, and live in peace with their neighbours."

He paused again awhile, collecting his thoughts, but she remained quiet.

"This is what we have known about Mao these past three years," he went on – "He is more sensible as he ages. The time is coming when he must – China must – be accepted into the United Nations. Wars are fast becoming outdated. Intrigue will stay, but a country can be peaceful and continue to use intrigue to further its aims. It is already obvious that America will continue to support Taiwan and, yet, will not block the entry of Red China into the United Nations." –

Another pause, and a wry smile, "It is now accepted, my Lady, that one side of your face may smile, whilst the other side still wears a look of hatred."

"So it would appear that Mong, if he gained control, could spoil all this?"

"That is most certain," the Minister's tone was definite – "it would take many years for Mong to reach the stage again which Mao has reached now, so any success for Mong and his followers would really put China back many years."

He stopped again, for almost a minute, but she was wise enough to know she had not to talk, or ask questions, whilst he was putting his thoughts together.

His eyes were closed, as he continued. "Mao is seeking and will gain the peaceful way into world affairs, but Mong has vowed to restore both Hong Kong and Taiwan to China. He knows, as we do, that it is impossible, and he knows also that it would be wrong for China, even if it was possible. But he will not care about that, and will not care for China, only for himself, and the power he is lusting for."

She gave her full attention to him, appreciating that, above all else, he was still Chinese. It was his country, still China, he was thinking about, talking about, no matter what others had done to it.

"Mong knows – must know – that Hong Kong is worth untold gold to China," his voice had taken on a different tone, she knew the inspiration it conveyed was deep and real – "but he must carry on with his vows, or pretend to carry on with them, if only to discredit Mao. Mong will not worry what harm it will do immediately, and it will do great harm this action when it comes, and if it succeeds."

Another pause – his eyes remained closed.

"Mao, on the other hand, is within sight of gaining the recognition which China must have. We have sure information that all is not well in the interior, but we know the outside world is not really aware of this. Mao has gone to great lengths to give the outside world the impression that all is well with him, and with his planning. In spite of all the difficulties within, and they are many, it will not be long now before China has its own atom bomb, and then it will rank equal with any country."

There was no mistaking the deep pride in his voice. He is such a good man, she thought, in spite of the fact that he has had nothing to do with it, he is so proud that China has progressed. How great a pity it is that such brains and leadership as he possesses have not been used for China. She could not think, however, what the Triad would have done without him , but that was not really the point. Here was a man who was fit and suited to lead his country, and what a different China it would have been.

The Minister carried on speaking, but now the pride had left his voice and there was scorn, and a little fear, in the tone.

"We do not want Mao, my Lady, but we want Mong far less. From what information I have, he is truly a vile person, and would be as ruthless as any man known to history." He paused again, then his voice rose to the loudest it had been during the whole of their conversation. "This Mong, if he is not stopped, will plunge the East into the turmoil from which it is emerging – from which it must emerge. It is essential that he is stopped."

She sat watching him for a while. Often she had seen him talk with passion, and with pride, when he spoke of the country as progressing, but never had she seen him in such a fierce mood as this. She realised that the danger must be very great indeed.

"You are so wise, my Minister," she told him. "I find my time with you so interesting and instructive, but you have much to do, I know."

"There is just one more word," he interrupted, looking straight at her, his eyes now wide open.

"I know it well," she said, with a trace of a smile across her beautiful face. "There is danger for me, and I must take care."

"There is very great danger," she could not but note the concern in his voice. "We must never underrate these people. They are, we know, Russian trained, and would stop at nothing. I cannot even think of what would happen to you should they get hold of you. We must always think them better than they perhaps actually are, and we must always think and act to protect ourselves, and, most important of all, to protect you."

It was a grave warning, and she knew exactly what he meant. But her pride was also a danger – her pride, and her great belief in the security built around her. "But my guards are most capable and trustworthy," she said, and he knew of the arrogance and feeling within her.

"They are so," he agreed, "otherwise they would not be your guards."

"Then all should be well," – she was winsome now – "unless, of course, you order me not to go out."

"We wish you to take the greatest care," he told her, and realised he had failed to convince her how great the danger was, "and we wish that you do not attend the Golden Lotus for a while."

"But, I am sure, my Minister," said with great charm, but still the arrogance was there. "You would order me not to go, not wish me not to go, if the danger was that great."

If he was annoyed, he did not show it. "I may not order you, my Lady," he made a little bow of the head as he spoke – "it is for me to advise, to wish, to ask. It is for you to decide. I can only repeat that there is great danger, much more perhaps, than ever before."

"Then I will take great care," she replied simply, "and if tomorrow the position has worsened, you must tell me so. But I retain very great confidence in my guards, and I am sure I will come to no harm."

"We all pray not, my Lady." He said, speaking very slowly, and she knew how much her decision had affected him. This was an old score between she and him, though she knew he represented her council and their thoughts. In her opinion, they erred too much on the side of safety, and made the dangers of her appearance at the Golden Lotus much greater than they actually were. A leader such as she must take some risk, could not always be hidden away – this was so in any country, and applied to any leader. She appreciated his concern, their concern, but she was not afraid, and she would not be hidden. There were other places she had to go, besides the Golden Lotus, where her appearance was so necessary, and she could be seen by the lower members of her Triad. It was a way of keeping up morale, they had always told her, and surely there was as much danger on these occasions as there was in her own night club, with her own guards around her.

The Minister had failed this time, but he thought he had moved just a little closer to final victory. He knew the dangers, but he knew her also, and knew she was a true daughter of her father. Fear was not in their make-up, perhaps he was wrong to go about it the way he did, perhaps he was making it too much of a challenge, a challenge she must accept. In his innermost thoughts he agreed with Ai Fah, that this was the only outlet Lee Kyung Koh had for her sex.

It was a weakness in the security of the Triad, but she had made her decision, and he admired her for that. She was not afraid, and she had trust and faith in her guards.

He would make very sure the commander was well warned, so that all should be at their very best and most alert tonight. He was not stupid, and did not think his Triad were the only clever people. There were other Triads as clever and as cunning, and perhaps as well informed, and certainly more ruthless. He had genuine respect in this way for the Ninety Seven, as yet really an unknown quantity, and was sure they would be as intelligent, and as cruel, as the Russian masters who had trained them.

He rose from his chair as Lee Kyung Koh rose to leave. The arrogance had left her. "We shall meet again tomorrow, Minister," was all she said in parting, but there was warmth and friendliness back in her voice.

His kowtow lasted until she had left the room, and he could not see the affectionate look on her face as she passed him. But he well knew of her respect for him, and was content.

6

TAIPAN CHIN

Hamilton crossed Connaught Road Central, and five minutes later joined the queue at the Star Ferry Pier for the return journey to the Kowloon side.

He was in good time for his appointment with Taipan Chin, and he had the same tense feeling within him that he always knew when such a visit was close.

He didn't know if he had been followed, but thought not. He had been his usual careful self, and it had been a quiet peaceful morning for him. After the Hong Kong parade to honour the birthday of her Majesty, at which the Governor had taken the salute, he had thought about going into the Hong Kong Club, but had decided against that knowing how crowded the club would be, so he had walked slowly, content to amble as the day grew more hot, to the Star Ferry area.

He had eaten a nice shrimp sandwich, washed down by a glass of milk, in the window seat of a pleasant little restaurant, and that would be sufficient for him until the evening. He took his time over the sandwich and milk, gazing now and then at his 'Cricketer' magazine, but keeping a good look out through the windows for anyone who might be following him, and could be waiting outside for his reappearance. If there was a 'shadow', he was a damn good one, and too good for Hamilton to spot.

He was anxious to see Chin. There was something big going on, that was obvious, and he was sure Chin would know what it was.

Sam Reynolds had talked about it last night, "It could be something like the double ten riots all over again," he told Hamilton, "and even bigger."

Ham was a cautious individual who liked to know all there was to know, hear everything, think of everything, sift all the facts and put it together, take it apart again, and then put it together again. He would take his time in doing all this, but then would give his opinion to the best of his ability. But he could not confide in Sam Reynolds who knew Hamilton only as a Government official, and a friend.

"It could well be," he agreed thoughtfully, "we know the double ten didn't really finish anything, and there is always danger of that sort of thing up here – this is a highly explosive place."

"It is indeed," Reynolds said, "and we know something big is about to happen again. Personally I can well do without it."

They both remembered the double ten riots well. Hamilton had come up to Hong Kong three days before the riots started on 10th October 1956. This was the anniversary of the formation of the Chinese Republic – 10th October 1911, and the name – double ten – was a natural as it was the tenth day of the tenth month of the year. It was always a risky time, as 10th October followed so closely on the celebrations of the birthday of Red China – lst October each year.

The riots had been very bad. They had started in upper Kowloon, then spread to the New Territories, and down to near Kai Tak Airport. Everyone had been in the fighting – the Communists of Red China and the Nationalists, whipped up as every riot, or demonstration of public disorder, was by the Triads, which is the Chinese name for the Tongs, or Chinese secret societies.

The double ten riots had flared up in many places. At first, they were considered solely communistic troubles, with the thugs of the Communist Triads behind them, as they always were. But the riots rapidly worsened as the Nationalists joined in, with these two great and natural enemies fighting and killing each other.

It was a very anxious period as the Police fought both sides to restore order, but it wasn't until the afternoon of 11th October, when the Army was brought in, that authority commenced to regain control, and by that time there had been everything – murder – pillage – arson – rape – looting, and over fifty people had been killed, with hundreds more injured, many of them seriously, and many thousands homeless because of the fires. The fire engines and ambulances even, had been wrecked and set on fire by the rioters, but it had eventually been got under control, leaving Hong Kong and Kowloon badly shattered.

Reynolds had been in the thick of it most of the time, and had earned high praise for the work he had done at Mongok. Hamilton had been confined to the headquarters building on Hong Kong itself, and had seen little, or nothing of the actual fighting, but at night he had seen all the fires burning, and he knew from all the reports he had sifted through for a year and more after it was all over, how bad it had been.

"Up to a couple of weeks it had been very quiet," Reynolds said, "too quiet really, then there's been this burst just recently which is always a bad sign. We hear there's a lot happening inside China again, so someone else must he having a crack at our friend Mao."

"That could well be," agreed Hamilton, who was more aware than Reynolds about what had been happening in the interior, though he could not say so. Relations with Red China had improved greatly in the last two or three years, and as Reynolds had said, things had been very quiet. Recently, however, there had come news of an anti-Mao movement, which wasn't Nationalist inspired, and this was puzzling. But he would have to wait for the information Chin would surely give him before he could frame the real answer.

On the ferry, he sat next to two young attractive Chinese ladies, very smartly dressed in their almost matching cheongsams, split thigh high. They came and placed themselves alongside him on the wooden bench seat. The fragrance of the scent worn by the nearest one to him betrayed an extravagant taste, which matched their appearance.

Quite sure that Hamilton was English, after a very thorough and searching examination of him, and therefore could not possibly understand what they were talking about, they jabbered away to each other in Cantonese. Hamilton was certain they would have been shocked to know that all their secrets were being revealed to the harmless looking, and very mild, Englishman, sat next to them.

His expression never changed, and his eyes did not even flicker beneath his sunglasses, but inwardly he was most amused. Their conversation, of course, was about two men, two young British Army officers, and mostly about their highly amorous adventures the previous night. A night, which had commenced with a sumptious dinner at the Mirimar Hotel, and had ended up many hours later in the flat of the lady furthest away from him. It seemed to have been quite a night, full of good things for all four, with many promises made about more such nights to come, and possibly a trip to England for one of them.

To Hamilton, it was in a way, amusing to hear how wonderful British officers were, how handsome, how virile, how gentlemanly, and how keen they were to take the ladies to their officers' mess. It couldn't be done just at present, because the old man was a bit sticky, but there was to be a new old man soon, and things could change for the better. The Chinese ladies appeared to well understand this, and the mess wasn't really any attraction for them, but a trip to England certainly was. Hamilton hoped the ladies would fare better than he thought they might, but he was a cynic and had heard such stories before.

As the ferry slowed and bumped to a stop, rather more forcibly than usual, the lady nearest to him, standing up too early, half fell back on him as the boat bumped the side of the dock. She turned round to him, with an exclamation which he knew not to be really polite, but she recovered at once, smiled most pleasantly at him, and said, "Very sorry."

Hamilton could not help but admire the quick reaction, and had put his arms out to hold her, and prevent her from falling. He released her and helped her away from him. "It was my pleasure," he told her with great courtesy, and wondered if she, or both of them, appreciated the remarks.

He thought they did, because they were both laughing and still jabbering away twenty to the dozen, as they preceded him off the ferry.

He was still not in a hurry – he had just over half an hour – so he sauntered slowly back towards the Peninsula Hotel.

Outside the Peninsula, he saw the ricksha boy he was looking for, stood just a little apart from the other boys with their rickshas. He had not seen this man for six months, but recognised him at once and now, that last journey with him seemed only yesterday, so strange is time on such occasions. He felt well when settling into his seat, all was going according to plan.

The ricksha boy settled quickly into a jogging stride, and turned right into Peking Road, then left when he reached Nathan Road. Hamilton did not look around to see if he was being followed, he had no need to do so as he was in Taipan Chin's charge. He sat relaxed, the man pulling the ricksha had surely been well chosen for his task, and Hamilton was content to be taken where he had to go. At Austin Road the ricksha turned left again, then a few minutes later right into Shanghai Road. It was ten minutes to three.

Two hundred yards or so up Shanghai Road, the ricksha man stopped and let the shafts down. Hamilton took a quick glance around, stepped down, and went immediately into the shop outside which they had stopped. There were two tough looking Chinese men standing alongside the door of the shop, but they drew aside to let Hamilton past them and through the door. Inside the shop he was safe, the two men outside would see no one else entered, and he could be sure other men would be at hand should they be needed.

The front room of the shop was full of artificial flowers, with two women putting bunches together, and a third woman arranging the bunches on the shelves. Hamilton went through into a rear room, empty, except for an old strip of carpet on the floor, a battered old chest in the centre of the room, and three old chairs. There was a door at the far left hand corner, at which a man was waiting. As soon as he saw Hamilton, he turned, and went out through the door, with Hamilton following him.

Three minutes later, at five minutes to three, he was in Taipan Chin's parlour.

This had been the way of all their meetings for several years past. The day and time set by Hamilton's visit to the tobacco shop, as soon as possible after his arrival in Hong Kong, the ride with a ricksha boy, the approach through the artificial flower shop, then quickly guided down several back alleyways, to the amusement arcade in which Taipan Chin had his stronghold.

Taipan Chin – Taipan means great manager – lived up to his name. Everything was well organised and beautifully managed. It never seemed difficult, even though it was a tense time, with the chance of some sort of ambush somewhere, sometime.

The arcade had been very busy as they passed through, even at that time of the afternoon, but Hamilton knew this was as artificial as the flowers in the shop. All the men engaged in the activities of the arcade, with the many different games machines and flashing lights, were Taipan Chin's men, highly capable, and well trained. It would have taken a company of British paratroops to have forced a way into Taipan Chin's parlour, and it would have been many hours before they got in.

The parlour, which Chin used as an office, had no windows, but was air-conditioned, and very cool after the heat outside. The walls were hung with a deep blue velvet, the floor tiled and highly polished, with two huge rugs matching the velvet hangings in colour. Almost central was a long black-laquered table, and behind it was a high wooden armchair. In front were two matching chairs in the same wood, but with leather seats. The room smelt very strongly of incense.

Hamilton stood waiting patiently, just in front of the table, carefully polishing his sunglasses.

He did not look at his watch when Taipan Chin came into the room, but knew it would be exactly three o'clock. There was a slight rustling noise at the back of the room behind the table, where the hangings were held back to allow Chin to enter through a door, which was otherwise hidden by the hangings.

He was old, tall and slight, clean shaven, and almost bald, with keen sharp features and piercing eyes. He could have been anything from sixty years upwards, and Hamilton, for all his knowledge of the Chinese, could not have guessed his real age. He was dressed in a mandarin robe of vivid colouring, and came shuffling forward, past the table, to bow slightly and shake Hamilton's hand, his wizened old face easing into a smile.

"Greetings, most respected sir," Hamilton said, his voice very correct and his manner faultless, "you look exceptionally well " – but he waited till the old man had gone back round the table, and sat down in the high wooden armchair, before he himself sat down.

"You also, my friend," Chin's voice had a slight American accent. "You age not at all."

Hamilton nodded his thanks. It was his great care and habit to choose his words well, and use them sparingly, when he was with Chin. He never used a Chinese word to anyone, and was not one to interlard his speech with any Chinese word or phrase. He was aware of the cleverness of Taipan Chin, and never failed to be at his best in his company, to keep up to the cleverness and the standard of the old, but most sincere man, across the table from him.

The hangings were pulled aside again, to allow two Chinese girls into the room. They were both dressed in a deep blue pyjama suit top and white trousers, and each carried a tray. On one tray was a large pot of tea and two delicate china cups. On the other, a large cut glass decanter, two thirds full of what Hamilton was quite certain would be Martell brandy, and two glasses. The girls arranged the trays on the table, their pigtails denoting their unmarried status swinging behind them as they moved. They kowtowed to Chin, and left as silently as they had entered, without one glance at Hamilton.

"Brandy, Mr Hamilton?" asked the old Chinaman, and did not wait for the acceptance, pouring out two full glasses. Hamilton rose from his chair to take one of the glasses, and raised it in silent toast to the old man, then took a small sip of the liquid. He was right of course, it was Martell as always, and there was a lot to be sipped so it would last all the meeting.

Then came the tea poured by Chin with a very steady hand. Hamilton much appreciated the beauty of the pot and the cups, their quality was a great deal better than the tea. Typical Chinese tea, weak, and not too hot, and really too weak for his taste. Two cups, each drunk slowly, and without a word being spoken. A sip of brandy after the first cup, and another after the second cup, then they could begin the conversation.

He was well aware these preliminaries were essential. Taipan Chin insisted on the necessary and correct hospitality to his guest – the tea and the brandy, but now it was time for business. Neither wanted to waste the time of the other, and the information would be passed, and nothing unnecessary would be said.

Hamilton put his glass carefully on the tray. He was ready to listen and Taipan Chin could commence.

"Since you were last here, Mr Hamilton," he began, "there is much information from the Interior. Had you not come this week, I would have intimated to our master that he should send you once more to Hong Kong."

He is right, absolutely right, Hamilton told himself. I should get up here more often, at least every three months, and not leave it as long as six months. The old chap's handing me out a mild rocket to start with, but he's dead right.

"We are informed that Mong Lin San had made much steady progress. It would seem the Russians chose him well, and have trained him well. He is intelligent and has been given every encouragement, whilst – equally important, if not more so – he has been kept well supplied with money. All in all, Mr Hamilton, he is reputed to be a good leader."

Hamilton, still wearing his sunglasses, because of the bright electric light of the room, was listening and thinking.

"Mao Tse Tung has made progress also," the name he spoke seemed repulsive to him, and Hamilton recalled that Chin's voice always took on this tone when he spoke of the present leader of Red China, was aware that the hatred must be very deep – "but his progress is with the outside world. All goes well with China's atom bomb, but at great expense. The elements have not been kind, and the crops not as big as they might be. Splitting the atom will not feed the people, and we are informed – and have no doubt it is true – the red guards have been at their most militant to suppress the people."

He paused to take a little drink from his glass. This was his way, his manner, as Hamilton well knew, of making sure everything was carefully noted and thought about.

Chin put down his glass, and continued, "Mong, in the meantime, has done, or tried to do, all the things he should do. He must wreck the plans, and the progress of Mao, to have any chance of supplanting him. He is not yet powerful enough to wreck the atom structure, but he could well wreck the human structure, and this, of course, is what he has been doing in the Interior, hence the reports of trouble, and the activity of the red guards."

He paused awhile again. Hamilton did not interrupt. He was listening intently and thinking carefully, getting the broad situation of it all in his mind. Chin knew this of him, and it was one of the reasons he respected the Englishman so much.

"Now Mong considers it really time to put the clock back for Mao. We are told he is strong enough inside China to come out and show himself to the outside world. Very soon – within two or three days – there is to be a double rising here in Hong Kong, and in Taiwan."

Hamilton knew the sunglasses he wore helped always to hide any surprise he may otherwise have shown. The news of Taiwan was a surprise and big, even though anything and everything was possible in the East. He had never been to Taiwan, but had read a great deal about it, and was aware, like every other place in the world, it was opening up to tourism. No doubt, in spite of all the precautions of the Americans, the Reds had been able to infiltrate into Taiwan, as they had done into Hong Kong.

"If Mong and his followers can cause the riots they plan," Chin went on – "both here and in Taiwan, it will bring them great success in the interior, where, of course, the ignorant are told they must have Hong Kong. The foolish apes," – he was most scornful – "it would be damnation for them, as Hong Kong is so vital to Red China, as Mong knows so well, so there will be riots only, but very nasty, and they will serve his cause well, but do great harm to Mao."

His voice grew more intense. "It will show the outside world there is again a serious rival to Mao, and this is what Mao does not want." A short pause for effect, then: "Oh yes, Mong is wise to do this, it is nicely timed, whilst, if they succeed in giving the authorities here, and in Taiwan, a great deal of trouble, as they surely will, it could mean much more trouble inside China, and a serious setback to Mao's world plans."

Hamilton took his glass from the tray and held it to his lips to take just a sip. He liked Martell brandy, liked any good brandy, enjoying to sip it slowly. He considered it helped the thoughts racing through his mind. Chin was quite right, there would be very serious trouble for Mao within China. There would be trouble in Hong Kong also, which would exercise the Police, and perhaps the Army, but he thought this time they will be ready for it, quicker to deal with it, than previously in the double ten riots. This may not, however, be the case in Taiwan, where a quick and carefully planned uprising could bring some good success for Mong.

Chin was not finished. "The information we have is that the followers of Mong now call themselves the Ninety Seven. This because, as you know, Kowloon, or some of it, and the New Territories, are due to pass back to China in 1997, if they want it then."

Chin paused again, to let this part sink in. It was something Hamilton had often thought about, and knew many other people thought about it also. 1997 was thirty eight years off yet, but when it came, would China take back the land they had ceded to Britain long ago, or would they grant another lease? It was interesting to think about it and consider it all, even if he would not be around when it happened.

Chin would know what his thoughts were, and Hamilton would have liked to have known how Chin summed it all up. Because of the present trading through Hong Kong, China would not want to spoil anything at the present time, but in the future, and, with China established as a big world power – who knows or who could really guess.

Chin had given him long enough to think that one over and was speaking again. "The popular cry of Mong is Hong Kong now, and Taiwan as well, but only to disturb Mao. It would harm him greatly in the Interior if Mong has any success in Taiwan. It will be of great interest to you that Taiwan is more dear to the true Chinese than is Hong Kong. To the modern Chinese, Hong Kong has always been ceded to Britain, but Taiwan is China."

Another pause so Hamilton could think about that, and again Chin was absolutely correct.

"Not of course," Chin was very sure, "that anything can throw the Americans off Taiwan short of one of their own atom bombs, but a riot there will gain great publicity in the Interior, and will be magnified out of all proportion, as everything always is of this nature."

He paused yet again, this time to take another sip of his brandy, and in doing so, purposely opened the way for a question.

Hamilton, still holding his glass, and still very thoughtful, took the opportunity.

"Then this is another Russian throw," he said – slowly, gathering his thoughts, making sure he had everything in the right order – "perhaps their last throw, their last effort to stop Mao," He saw Chin nodding in agreement – "As you say, Mao is going from strength to strength in the outside world, no matter how hard he finds it to hold the Interior secure. I agree with you that the day is fast approaching when he will be invited to take China into the United Nations. America will not – cannot – oppose him. It must come, if he behaves himself as he is doing, and when he has the bomb he will be level with Russia, level and equal, and we can be very certain that Russia does not want that."

Chin had continued to nod his head right through. He agreed completely.

"You are wise in your thoughts, Mr Hamilton," he almost purred – "what you say is true. The world is levelling out – this levelling, this easing, will continue, and China will be a part of that world. In our time, Mr Hamilton, though it may seem hard to believe, China and America will be near friends. Mao, who I hate," – the bitterness had come back into his voice – "knows there is more to be gained by being part of the world than by being out of it. Russia knows this also, but they try to delay others, as they are trying to delay Mao, whilst they make progress themselves to being masters of all. This is really trying to deal yourself all the aces and having the joker as well."

Again a pause, and a few moments silence.

"May we come back to the Ninety Seven?" Hamilton asked. Much as he was interested in the affairs of Red China, his job was to find out what was going to happen in Hong Kong. "Do you think they can cause trouble here, and in Taiwan?"

"Certainly," Chin was adamant, and his reply immediate, he had no need to think about this one. "We have seen it happen before in Hong Kong, and what has happened here can happen in Taiwan. They will do the right things, pay the right price to the right people, and the result will be as before. Soon, within two or three days, the troubles will commence."

Hamilton wanted something more definite – "what information is there of the Ninety Seven in Hong Kong?"

This was the real criterion, and what really mattered. No strength in the interior would be of much use without a good organisation here, and in Taiwan, so that, when Mong gave the orders, the matches could be applied to the waiting firecrackers, and the eruptions would commence. Without a good foundation to work out on, the firecrackers could fizzle and die like damp squibs.

Both Chin and Hamilton knew this. It was the organisation of the Ninety Seven here in Hong Kong, and in Taiwan, which would be the deciding point.

Chin thought for a while before answering, and Hamilton waited patiently. What was required now was a brief, but accurate, summing up of all the probing Chin's men had done, as Hamilton knew they would have done, because Chin had to know everything that was likely to happen in Hong Kong. If he did not know, then he was of no use to the British Secret Service.

He would know, of course, both about Hong Kong and Taiwan. It was Hong Kong Hamilton wanted to know about first, and he could be sure that the important information about Taiwan would be passed by Chin to where it was required.

"We know enough," the old Chinaman said finally, "to class them as very good, and can really fault them on one point only." His eyes were closed as he spoke, his hands tightly clasped together in front of him, high on his chest, as if in prayer. There was no outward expression on his face other than complete serenity, the voice quiet but full of purpose.

"The number one man here is by name Lin Poh – he has been very well trained in Russia. He is different to Mong, younger, and perhaps even more ruthless. Certainly he will prove to be more clever than Mong." A pause. "He speaks English well. He has spent several years in England to study the English, the English ways and their thinking – if such a study is possible." Hamilton noted just a trace of a smile on the old man's face as he said this.

"He has plenty of money," Chin went on, "the Russians must have an everlasting spring which flows sterling and dollars, and he has spent it well here. He will be able to call on all the Tongs except one." Hamilton knew that one exception would be the Golden Lotus – "and when Mong tells him to commence, all the thugs of Hong Kong will be let loose, but," – another pause, again for effect – "this time to a better plan than at the time of the double ten. This time the rioting will be better planned, highly controlled and wider dispersed. It will give Government and the Police much trouble, though I trust they also, because of what they learned in the double ten will be better prepared."

He stopped, opened his eyes for a minute, looking straight at Hamilton, the fingers of his right hand tapping hard on the back of the left hand. Hamilton did not interrupt, he realised that Chin had not yet finished the summing up.

"The preliminaries have already begun, as you have probably heard from your police friend," Chin told him. Hamilton kept his face blank – of course the old man would know he had been out with Sam Reynolds. "There has been much, shall we say petty skirmishing already, and all against the Golden Lotus, none of it yet against authority. Mong sees it as an affair to discredit Mao, but Lin Poh sees it as a battle for the supremacy of the underworld of Hong Kong, and he means to exterminate the Golden Lotus – once he does this, if he can do it, Hong Kong is his."

"Which will be a damn bad thing for Hong Kong," Hamilton could speak now. "But the Golden Lotus must know it is coming, and will be prepared for it. You have often told me how well organised they are, so must be ready themselves."

"Indeed they must," Chin agreed. "And they are prepared. They will not give up their control without a great battle. They know it is they against the Ninety Seven and the other Tongs, but it is the Ninety Seven who are the danger – the others without a lead will be just as hounds without a master."

"Are the Golden Lotus strong enough?" Hamilton asked.

Chin's eyes remained closed, his hands were now still – "They are strong, and, of course, knowing this is coming they are reinforced from Taiwan, but they, like the Ninety Seven, have one great weakness."

He stopped, opened his eyes and reached out for his brandy.

Hamilton had retained his glass in his hand all this while, and drank now at the same time as Chin, waiting for the old man to continue, and knowing full well he would explain some of the remarks he had just made.

"Yes, the Golden Lotus are strong," Chin repeated, "but what should be their great strength is their weakness." He was looking only at his glass, at the liquid, as he very slowly sloshed it around in the glass.

"Lee Kyung Koh is the weakness – she and her vanity. It is well known to all in Hong Kong, and it will be well known to Lin Poh."

Hamilton knew of Lee Kyung Koh and had seen her at her night club. He knew of all her activities from the Chinese newspapers he read, and that she was the head of the Golden Lotus Triad. He knew also there was some bond between Taipan Chin and the Golden Lotus, which was again obvious in the deep feeling in Chin's voice. He was certain Chin and the Golden Lotus worked together, and they shared a lot of the information they gathered from their own various sources. After all, they worked towards the same ideal – law and order.

"If the Ninety Seven can take Lee Kyung Koh," Chin continued, "as they could well do, because she exposes herself to that danger so much, then the Golden Lotus are lost."

"Why then," Hamilton asked at once, "do they allow her to frequent her night club so often, and place herself in this danger?"

Chin had the immediate answer. "Because she is the daughter of her father and she is the leader. I knew her father well, and his spirit, his soul, lives on in her. She is decisive as he was, and she thinks she is right because she is a woman, and being a woman without a man, she is vain and headstrong, such is the way of women. As she has no man of her own, she must show herself to all men, it is a way of self-expression and self-satisfaction."

Hamilton could sense his indignation, yet there was more than a trace of admiration in his voice also.

"Let us hope then," he said, "that she can take care of herself. I should hate to think of the Golden Lotus losing their place in Hong Kong."

"You are right, Mr Hamilton, very right," Chin was again nodding his head in agreement – "I would hate it also, so would the Governor, and the Police, but if the Ninety Seven take her, and they will surely try to kidnap her from that night club she runs, Lin Poh will run Hong Kong."

Hamilton found this hard to believe, even though Chin knew his Hong

Kong so well. It would be a serious blow to the Golden Lotus Triad for a while, not a doubt about that, but the Chinese were hard people – he knew this from the Chinese history he had read – Chinese fathers had sold their daughters from the beginning of time almost, so why should not a Chinese Triad recover quickly from the loss of a female leader, and surely there must be someone next in line as the leader to whom they would rally?

But he was concerned more about the Ninety Seven just at present, and must know more about them.

"I do not doubt you speak the truth about the Golden Lotus and their leader," he said, "she is a serious weakness, although she must be very well guarded, but that is their affair. May I bring you back to the Ninety Seven? You have said they can be faulted on one point. May I, respected sir, know more of this?"

"I was coming to that," Chin's voice might have contained just a touch of reproach. "Actually there are two weaknesses." He paused a few moments. "The first is that they are in the heroin business, and are, therefore, down to the level of the other worthless Tongs."

Hamilton well understood the reason for the scorn in Chin's voice. The heroin business was repulsive, and those who took part in it were swine. To the decent Chinese, especially the elders, there was no harm in opium, but heroin was a scourge. Nevertheless, there was vast money to be made in the sale of heroin.

"It seems strange that Mong allows this, especially as the Communist pigs themselves are so much against heroin," Chin's eyes were closed again, and he was deep in thought as he spoke. He had put his glass down on the tray a few moments before, and his hands were clasped high on his chest again. "Perhaps he does not allow it – perhaps he does not know of it yet, know that the Ninety Seven are in this foul business here in Hong Kong. There is no need for it, they have ample money without this trade," – another pause – "and this leads me quite naturally to the second weakness, which is really the main one."

Again he paused; Hamilton knew the reason – more effect, leading up to the big point.

"Our information is that Mong is a good leader. He is, as I have said, well chosen in the first place, well trained, and ruthless. We know the same of Lin Poh. He is a good leader, well chosen, well trained and ruthless, but he – Lin Poh – is the weakness."

A further pause – to let Hamilton think about that, then –

"Yes, he is the definite weakness," his eyes were still closed, his voice quiet, but very concise. "In my opinion, Lin Poh is not really content to serve under Mong. There are some who cannot serve under others, and Lin Poh is such a man. We are very sure of this. Now, with Hong Kong still to win, he bides his time, patient, content to wait. But, if he wins Hong Kong, then he will not be content. He will want more power – it is often such as this – power wants more power. Mong himself must be aware of this, of the danger of Lin Poh to him, and we know it – know it well."

He was almost finished, Hamilton knew this well and kept silent – there was still a little more to come.

"This is a typical Russian ploy," Chin had opened his eyes now as he spoke – "train a man, train him well, let him think he is the number one, then train another man to oust the first one trained. Not one is to be trusted – yes, so typically Russian, and sometimes not in accordance with their other clever ways."

He stopped, reached over and took up his glass again. This time he drank a lot of the brandy, leaving just a very little at the bottom of the glass.

Hamilton well understood the action. Chin was finished, except for answering any questions which Hamilton put to him.

"I gather," Hamilton said, "that the Ninety Seven have made good infiltration into Hong Kong life?"

"That is so, they are in everything, even in Government service."

"The skirmishing you have told me of, that is a sure sign that the action is near?"

"Most definitely so," Chin was certain of this, "it is there for everyone to see."

"Is this not a mistake?"

"Not in Hong Kong, where it is the start of the real trial of strength between the Ninety Seven and the Golden Lotus."

"And in Taiwan?"

"Nothing yet," Chin replied, "or nothing we have heard of. There it will he a case of sudden uprising."

Hamilton agreed that, and thought a minute before continuing – "But this skirmishing has given the warning to the Police and Government."

"It has," agreed Chin, "and purposely so. The riots are not meant to succeed, even if that were remotely possible. Mong is seeking the publicity, not the finality, whilst Lin Poh seeks to conquer the Golden Lotus. They will not care who is hurt or trampled on in this action, they are only out to attempt their own separate and different aims."

Hamilton was well aware of that, but continued his probing – "Then the Police and Government know it will come, but do they know of the inward battle for the control of Hong Kong?"

Chin was not so quick with his answer this time – "Perhaps not," he said, after a while, "though they are certainly aware of the progress of the Ninety Seven, and will know of Lin Poh."

"This battle for Hong Kong is really more important than the riots?"

"A difficult question to answer, my friend, very difficult." So difficult that Chin took his time in answering, and thought for quite a time.

"Yes, it is," he said at last. "It will not seem so at the time, and a successful riot could badly put back Mao's plans, so will help Mong. But if Lin Poh gains control of Hong Kong, he will want to control the Ninety Seven, and so there will be a great problem for Mong. Lin Poh will run true to type, if he ousts the Golden Lotus, he will then seek to oust Mong, and that is the weakness I have told you about. A battle within the Ninety Seven can only help Mao," – a slight pause – "difficult, complicated perhaps, but you are right, Mr Hamilton, the battle for Hong Kong is the important matter in the long run."

"There is nothing Government can do to stop it?" Hamilton felt he had to ask that, though he knew the answer before it came.

"Nothing, absolutely nothing," Chin was so very sure of this. "It will come soon, in two or three days. The vultures are gathering – flying in, in a manner of speaking. First there will be the big meeting, then the orders will be given, and it will start. The format never differs."

He drank the last of his brandy, draining his glass. Hamilton waited for what was to come – something big. Taipan Chin never altered, it was true of him also that the format never differed. The finale had to be the best part of it all.

"The vultures are very big vultures," – slowly, evenly, then a pause – "We are informed that one of the vultures will be Mong himself."

Hamilton's eyes blinked sharply under the sunglasses. This was as important a piece of information as Chin had ever given him. He was quite sure of the truth of it, the old man had never given him the wrong information.

"He is taking a big risk," he said simply.

Taipan Chin did not agree. "Not at all, he is not known to anyone in authority here – he is just another Chinese male, and we are so much of a muchness." His face eased to just the slight trace of a smile, and Hamilton knew what he would he thinking. "No, there is no risk."

Hamilton asked the obvious question; "Are there no photographs of him?" If there were any, he had not seen them.

"Yes, one we know of," Chin said easily, "taken in Peking only last year, but it is nothing, a man can alter his appearance quite easily, as you well know."

Hamilton did know, but a photograph was something to go on, and it might have helped to see a copy and pass it on to the right quarters.

"You surprise me," he told Chin, "and yet you do not. Mong has really a great deal to gain by coming here, if only to sense the backing for Lin Poh. He will be gone again, I should think, before the actual trouble commences."

"Of that there can be no doubt," Chin was very positive about this. "It is always the way. He has a great deal to gain, as you say, by coming here. He will gain first hand knowledge of Lin Poh, and you can appreciate that his own trusted men will be busy in Hong Kong whilst they are here."

Hamilton could be very sure of that.

"Further, it will be known in the Interior that Mong is in Hong Kong, it will be something to make very big, and those it is told to will not know that he will be gone long before the action starts. Just like your Scarlet Pimpernel, who was, so I have read, here today but gone tomorrow."

"How right you are, just like the Scarlet Pimpernel." Hamilton found it amusing that Chin should liken one to the other in such a way. But it was time to end the conversation, he still had much to do.

"You have given me much information," he told Chin, "and of great importance. Now I must write my brief report to the commissioner – you will deliver it for me, as always?"

Taipan Chin nodded. It was the usual custom after such a meeting between these two. Hamilton would write his report, and it would be delivered by one of Chin's most trusted men to Police headquarters. The report had never failed to reach the commissioner, whilst it had long ago been agreed this was the best way to send the information.

The writing paper was waiting on Chin's table, and Hamilton drew his chair up closer to the table to begin the writing. Brief as it would be, it would contain sufficient to put those for whom it was intended well in the picture, and add something to what they must already know.

The old man sat patiently as Hamilton wrote. It was he who had suggested this method in the first place, at a time when it was thought Hamilton could be well known, and captured or killed by the increasingly powerful Chinese Communists. They had never thought to alter it over the years, and Chin would guarantee the safe delivery of it within one hour.

Hamilton looked up a moment at Chin. "I shall mention, of course, the grave possibility of a sudden uprising in Taiwan, they will pass it on."

Chin again nodded his agreement. He was sure this information would be passed on immediately, and long before Hamilton, in the morning, would receive a message in some form and be summoned to a meeting, perhaps at police headquarters, perhaps elsewhere, to discuss his report with the commissioner.

Hamilton finished his report and took up an envelope. This would be addressed in such a manner so that it would be instantly recognised on delivery. He had just begun to address the envelope when Chin spoke.

"You will wish to send this no doubt."

Hamilton took the photograph from Chin's hand. He looked at it carefully but, because of his sunglasses, it was not as clear to him as it would be perhaps tomorrow, when he would be able to examine it through a magnifying glass, or when it had been enlarged by the police photographic experts.

He could see, however, that it was of a single Chinaman. It had been taken in the open air, and in very good light. The man, dressed typically in a dark tunic and trousers, was without a hat. His face, very serious, showed up clearly. It was also obvious that the man was big and heavy.

So this was Mong Lin San.

Holding the photograph until almost the very end of their conversation was typical of Chin. Among the many activities of the man Hamilton and the British Secret Service relied upon for so much information, was the ownership of the second largest cinema company in the East. Taipan Chin played a major part in the organisation which produced so many films for the Eastern world, and so much information for the British cause.

Hamilton had always known that Chin was a supreme showman, even in the most serious of times.

7

DEATH ON THE ROAD

Rankin arrived at the transport lines shortly before three o'clock to find two young privates with the driver of the waiting three-ton truck.

It had been a good lunch in the sergeants' mess, and the General, with their commanding officer and the company commanders and the adjutant, had spent about half an hour in the mess before the lunch, and before going on to their own lunch in the officers' mess.

It had been a pleasant half-hour. The General had spoken to Rankin about the football match several weeks previously, when the Army had played the Chinese in their annual match. This had been a great encounter in which Rankin, captaining the Army team, had excelled. The Chinese had won by two goals to one, but only after a very hard game, and one which had pleased and thrilled the thousands of spectators, and had not really upset the Army team, who had done much better than they were expected to do. It was the sporting way in which it had been played which pleased the General, and had been very good for public relations.

There had been high praise from the General about the parade, with the regimental sergeant major coming in for many congratulations, so the lunch after the officers had left had been a good one. Rankin, true to form, had drunk very little, and had got away as soon as he could reasonably excuse himself.

By then the regimental sergeant major was in jocular mood –

"Take it easy, Tanko," he told Rankin, "leave some of those Chinese birds for the Yanks."

It was always a great joke in Hong Kong, the goodwill visits of the American Navy, with many of their ships often sheltered in the great natural harbour, and thousands of the sailors who manned the ships enjoying the delights of Hong Kong and Kowloon.

If goodwill was stuffing all the Chinese birds they could get hold of, or getting sky-high plastered on the spirits they were not used to, or brawling with all and sundry, then Rankin thought these goodwill visits were very successful indeed.

The number of American Navy shore patrols was evidence of the general conduct of the Yanks, and Rankin had never seen anything like the same number of the Navy's own patrols around, but this was because, to him, and to any British soldier, they did not make themselves as conspicuous as the Americans seemed to do.

Rankin was pleased to be able to travel in the front seat of the leave truck. With nobody senior to him on the truck, this was his privilege, and far better than sitting on a hard wooden form in the rear of the truck. A general holiday had been declared for today after the parade had finished, except for the normal police and guard duties, so very few men had been interested in taking a pass. Far better to leave their entitlement to a normal working day. In any case, there were special meals laid on to celebrate the birthday of the Queen.

Rankin knew the young lance-corporal who was the driver of the truck, as he was a good footballer, and had played several games in the Battalion team towards the end of the football season which had recently finished.

"Climb in, serge," he said, "there's only you three, and I'm ready if you are."

Rankin swung lightly into the front seat of the three tonner. His grip, which had his best civilian suit in it, he had entrusted to one of the young soldiers in the rear of the truck.

The driver made sure all was in order at the rear, tail board securely fastened, and they were away.

They stopped at the guardroom, where the corporal in charge of the Battalion police who were on duty until the guard came on, ticked off their names in the leave book before the gate could be opened. He had much the same advice to offer to the two young privates sat in the rear as had been offered to Rankin in the mess about an hour previously.

"That's all these nits think you go to Honkers for," the young lance-corporal growled as they drove off through the gate. "Anyone'd think they'd never seen a woman, let alone a Chinese bird – personally I'm a bit fussy what I do with my old man."

Rankin laughed. "Well, there's not actually a lot of female company up this way, and I suppose it's classed as the Army's favourite pastime – you have to admit there's some damn smart Chinese birds around Honkers and Kowloon."

"Oh, I agree," the young lance-corporal answered, keeping his eyes on the road in front of him, "but not what you'd say at our sort of level. I'm not interested myself, I've got a smasher at home so I'm not bothered about these ten dollar bits of crumpet."

Rankin was warming to the driver, he was a very pleasant young man.

"You're national service, aren't you lad?" They were all 'lads' to Rankin.

"Too right I am," came the answer, "and I can't wait to get my two years done and get home."

Rankin was surprised at the sudden bitterness in the other's voice. Regular soldiers found it difficult to understand why those doing their national service spent so much time in wishing their lives away in this manner.

"Don't you like Hong Kong then?" he asked.

The driver did not reply for a minute, concentrating on passing a group of Chinese workers, who had been spread across the road prior to hearing the truck coming up behind them.

"Yes, I do, it's not at all bad," he replied, when the group had been safely passed. Rankin noted the bitterness had left his voice. "I find it interesting and, in any case, it's better to do your service in a place like this, where you can see a bit of the world like, than waste your time at home in some damn depot where there's nothing to do."

"That's something you're dead right about." Rankin was quite pleased at this. If he had his way, all national servicemen would be in Hong Kong, or Singapore, or overseas in some place, but certainly out of England.

He watched the road for a minute or two, then asked, "what's your name lad?"

"Anderson, sergeant," came the immediate reply.

"You drive this truck well," Rankin's tone was very complimentary, "are you a driver in civvy street?"

"No," the driver kept his eyes straight ahead as he spoke, which pleased Rankin, "but I learned to drive trucks and tractors on me dad's farm – we had a couple of cars as well, an' I could soon drive 'em all."

"So you're a farmer eh," Rankin was impressed, "where from?"

"Lancashire," Anderson replied, "I thought you might know that from me accent. Not far from Southport, if you know that part of England."

"No, I don't," Rankin said, bracing his feet hard down, as Anderson changed gear twice in the space of a few seconds, slowing the truck – "I can't ever remember going up north, and you haven't much of an accent."

Anderson did not speak, he was busy negotiating a bad bend in the road. Some distance before the bend, Rankin had noticed the big sign, typical of the many the Army had erected on the roads, giving good warning of the danger. This bend was a particularly bad one.

Then they were on a straight piece of road, slightly downhill, and cutting across a fertile plain. The land lay below the level of the road, and was all rice fields with, here and there, a few Chinese, mostly women, working bent double, and up to their calves in water and mud.

Anderson could now resume the conversation – "Well, I can tell you're a Welshman," he was grinning broadly, "not that I didn't know already. How come you're a footballer? I thought all the Welsh played rugby with that flat ball," he was grinning hard and thought that a great joke.

Rankin was used to it and had stood this sort of banter for years, wherever he had served. "Not all of us," he replied, "and not all Welshmen sing in choirs either."

They were silent for a while, letting Anderson get on with the driving. He did not attempt to continue the joke about rugby. Rankin had been decent about it, but enough was enough, after all Rankin was a sergeant, and he only a lance-corporal.

Rankin watched the countryside. What a life these people have, he thought, "I can't understand why they have to do everything by hand out here. Why don't they use a few tractors?"

Anderson was interested. "You can tell you're not a farmer,' he said, "they couldn't use tractors, all the plots are too small like. Those bunds are all built by hand to keep the water in. Tractors just couldn't operate in this stuff, and them water buffaloes do all the work a tractor could do, and better."

Rankin appreciated the superior knowledge. "I suppose they can only grow rice, that's all there seems to be."

"You'd be surprised what they do grow." Anderson enjoyed talking about farming. "There's a damn nice farming community just near our camp, and the old Chinese fellow in charge is a friendly old type. He's shown me around, me and the education sergeant, and he speaks good English. They do a fine job really, and nowadays they grow a lot more vegetables than rice."

He changed down again to third, slowing down as they reached the end of the straight piece of road. His handling of the big truck was excellent. Slowly they took another long bend, where there was a splatter of low buildings just off the road. Rankin could see some water buffaloes sat deep in water, in one of the small plots of land, so deep that they were almost completely submerged. Over to their left was a big village, completely walled around in the typical manner of the country.

"Beats me how they put up with it," he said, "they don't seem to have made any progress at all."

"It beats me too," Anderson agreed, "they get practically nowt in the way of pay for all the hard work they do, they have to pay a big rent for using the land, and barely eke out enough to live on – then there'll be a funeral or a wedding in the family, an' the bloody fools I'll go and spend more than a year's pay on it, whatever it is – seventy quid on a wedding, and forty or fifty on a funeral – it's bloody stupid, it really is."

Rankin could understand his feelings. What an existence it was for these poor farmers, living as their ancestors had done for centuries. They just lived and worked and died. It was pitiful, and, as Anderson had said, stupid, but it was their way of life.

The truck slowed again to let a big black limousine pass and go speeding on its way towards Kowloon. It swayed badly as it passed them, offside wheels biting into the dry mud at the side of the road, and spraying a lot of it high and sideways, so Rankin immediately thought it as well the road was dry. There seemed to be four or five men in the vehicle, all Chinese, and it was travelling far too fast for safety. He felt glad he was in the truck with a driver such as Anderson. It was a well known fact that the driving of many Chinese was terrible – they didn't appear to care for their own safety, or that of any other road users.

"Flippin' heck," Anderson ejaculated, "he's bloody well motoring."

A minute or so later he again eased more to his own side of the road, this time to let a Police truck pass him. This was travelling fast, but under much better control.

"Well, I'll go to our house," Anderson was puzzled, "what do you make of that lot?"

Rankin thought awhile, he did not really know.

"Could be anything," he said eventually, "could be a chase, could be the Police are guarding 'em, but it looks more like they're chasing the Chinks, whoever they are."

"Bet a dollar they've got a car full of drugs and the Police are after them, but they won't bloody well catch 'em," Anderson was quite sure he was right in his assumption. There was always so much talk of drugs in Hong Kong, and in the Battalion, and most of the men knew of the dangers of drug taking, and also the high cost of the stuff, which led to a lot of fancy tales as they spoke between themselves about drugs, as they often did.

Rankin knew better – "I don't think so," he said thoughtfully, "the Reds are against drugs as much as anyone, and it isn't likely they bring drugs in this way. Those lads in the car looked important, an' it was a damn nice car. They must be visitors from across the border, but whoever they are, they're in a hell of a hurry."

Anderson settled back to his driving again, that little flash of excitement now over. After a while he came back to the subject of farming –

"You know serge, the climate's so good for growing out here, these farmers have that advantage. They get two crops of rice a year, which is bloody good, an' this fellow up near our camp says they get eight crops of vegetables, an' that's bloody marvellous. He says vegetables never stop growing out here, not like at home where we get only one crop a year. They're using some good fertilisers out here now, so add that to the sun and to water and anything'll grow."

"But you still have to work hard, just the same." Rankin knew that much about farming.

"Too bloody right serge," Anderson agreed, "they're damn fine workers all right. Have you seen that big hill near the camp, where they've terraced it all the way to the top almost. They don't miss a trick these chaps, and they don't waste an inch of earth."

Another change of gear down to third, slow for about thirty yards, round another long bend, change up to top again, and he could continue to expound on his local knowledge.

"These fish farms are bloody marvellous an' all. We went to see one, just a whopping great pond, about five feet deep, fill the pond with young fish, feed 'em on rice or bran or soya, or anything like that, wait a few months an' they drain the pond, and there they are, hundreds of fat fish, fat and juicy – say what you like, it's bloody clever."

Rankin had heard of the fish farms, but had never actually seen one.

"Course, buildin' up these hills with earth is a bloody sight better than using 'em to keep dead bones on" – Anderson was in full voice now, but still had his truck under perfect control, still keeping his eyes straight ahead, but with a glance through the wing mirrors from time to time – "That's bloody daft if anything is."

He slowed the truck and stopped talking, as another three ton truck from another Army unit passed them in the opposite direction. "About seven years after someone in the family has died, along come the rest of the family, open up the bloody coffin, sort out the bones, polish 'em up, put them in a big earthenware jar they've had to buy, then carry this flippin' jar up to some hill, an' what do you think serge?" – he was really scornful now – "they have to find old Grandad's bones a nice view up on that bloody hill, if not, he'll he flippin' upset – talk about bloody stupid."

Rankin did know something about the Chinese custom Anderson had described so vividly – the Ching Meng festival of late March or early April, during which time the Chinese honoured their ancestors. But it was their custom, and he didn't think the Chinese considered it flippin' stupid. He kept silent about it, however, as Anderson changed down again, slowing carefully as they came to another bend in the road.

Then they were in a small village, with the town of Tsuen Wan over to their right, and now there were crowds of Chinese to pass in the narrow road. Anderson eased through carefully, as the pedestrians reluctantly gave way to his approach, with none of them really taking any notice of the truck and its occupants. Men, women and children of all ages, dogs, ducks, hens and pigs. Most of the women, and some of the men, were carrying the big double baskets full of fruit and vegetables, staggering under heavy loads, whilst many of the women had young babies strapped to their backs. The older children also had younger children strapped to their backs, and those who were old enough to walk, but yet not strong enough to carry, were holding on to the baskets the men and women were loaded with.

Rankin appreciated the care of the driver, as he stopped several times to let women past, or to avoid children.

At one point, there was a big crowd, adults and children, around a brazier on which a man was cooking something in a big metal pan. They had to stop here a few seconds to let another vehicle approach and pass them, and the aroma of what was being cooked filled the cab.

"Smells like a bit of sweet and sour," Rankin said.

Anderson did not reply, he was too busy with his driving.

Then they speeded up a bit again, and came to another straight piece of road. They were not far from Kowloon now.

It was hot in the cab of the truck, had been very hot when they had been stopped back there in the village, or been moving only slowly, so they were both glad of the flow of air as they speeded along. Rankin was now looking at the sky – it was very colourful. "We'll have a storm tonight, I reckon," he said.

Anderson kept his eyes straight ahead, they were approaching another bend in the road,"Shouldn't be surprised," he replied, "they say it's the start of the typhoon season." He changed down into third gear. "It's been bloody hot all day, and we haven't had any rain for a while, so – whoops – what's this?"

A quick double de clutch, and he was in second gear, slowing the big truck evenly, then braking to a stop. It was as well he had been driving carefully.

Just around the bend, and far too close to the bend for safety, there was a crowd of Chinese in the road. Had Anderson been going fast he must have ploughed through them. Rankin could see vehicles on the road, on the other side of the crowd, and stretching away from them. Looking left, he could just see the reason for the crowd – a car off the road, down in the paddy field, and on its side.

He was down from the cab immediately, and dashed round to back where the two privates were stood up, looking round the side to see what had caused the truck to stop.

"Quick, you lad," to the first one, "down you get and to that bend back there" – he shot out his arm to give direction – "stop any vehicle coming up, and keep your eyes on the back of this truck, we don't want anything pinched. You " to the second private, who was climbing out over the tail board of the truck – "you come with me."

He went back to the front of the cab, where Anderson was still sat, trying to see what was happening down in the paddy field.

"Stay in the cab," Rankin ordered, "you can't move up any more at present. I see the Police are down there, they'll got around to sorting this lot out soon. Keep your eyes skinned – move if you have to – I've got one of the lads at the back stopping anything at the bend back there – told him to watch the back of the truck too, my best suit's in there, and I shall want that tonight, so you make sure nothing's pinched as well."

He had seen the police truck as he came to the front of the vehicle to speak to Anderson. It was parked on the side of the road about fifteen yards in front of them with the crowd of Chinese onlookers almost surrounding it.

Three of the police were down in the paddy field besides the badly damaged vehicle. At first glance, Rankin thought it must be the limousine which had passed them a while ago. A fourth policeman was stood by the police truck, and in amongst the crowds of Chinese.

None of the Chinese had ventured down into the field, and Rankin could now see that traffic coming out of Kowloon was being held up on the other side of the crowd. From the hooting of horns further away, he could guess that some of the waiting drivers were already impatient. He knew that the patient Chinese could be as impatient as anyone else when they chose to be.

Followed by the young private he had detailed to accompany him, he jumped down into the field – quite a drop at this point. He reckoned that the crowd of Chinese had come from the largish village not far beyond, where the damaged car was lying, and there were more and more onlookers coming out to join the throng.

It certainly looked a very bad smash, and the limousine must have been travelling very fast when it shot off the road. It was well out in the paddy field, and had obviously slid forward in the slimey mud across the field, hit a bend at an angle, and turned over. Rankin was now certain it was that big fast-driven limousine they had seen earlier.

There were three policemen around the vehicle, an English inspector, a Chinese sergeant and a Chinese constable.

Rankin moved straight to the inspector, who was trying to force open the rear door to get into the back seat.

"Want some help, sir?" he asked.

The inspector pulled himself back from halfway inside the back of the crashed vehicle. His eyes lit up as he turned and saw Rankin and the young private.

"My God, we do," he looked down at Rankin's sleeve, "Sergeant, this is nasty."

Rankin took in the scene quickly and thought that an understatement. It was more than nasty – it was terrible.

In the limousine there were still two men, both in the back seat. A third was lying a little away from the front of the car, quite motionless. All three were dressed in the same style of black pyjama suits. There was broken glass and blood everywhere, and the vehicle was badly damaged.

"We got him out, luckily," the inspector said, nodding to the man lying in front of the car – "he's the driver, and I think he's a gonner, and these two blighters in the back must be in a bad way."

It was quite plain he was correct. The two men in the back had been thrown on top of each other when the car had tipped over, and both were moaning pitifully. Rankin could see a tangle of arms and legs, but could not see either of their faces.

"Let's get them sorted out, sergeant," the inspector went on, "as quickly as we can."

Rankin gave the vehicle a few hefty pushes to see if it was steady, then climbed on to the side, leaning right in through the opening at the back where the inspector had managed to force the door back and nearly off.

Hanging right down, he managed to get his arms under the top man of the two and, as gently as he could, with the inspector keeping him steady from the back, began to drag the man out. He was completely limp, and Rankin thought, "he's almost a gonner too", when he heard the young private shout from the front of the car, "there's some more police coming." They'll be needed, Rankin told himself, and kept gently easing upward and back, lifting out through the rear door opening, what he was certain was now a dead body.

"I think this lad's broken his neck," he said, more to himself than the inspector.

The young private had got on to the top of the vehicle from the other side, and was able to reach down inside the car, and untangle the legs, as Rankin slowly eased back. "Gosh, these feel funny." Rankin heard him mutter.

Slowly, carefully, they managed their task. The man was big, plump and heavy, seemed badly injured low down in the body, where the trouser legs were saturated with blood, and heavily injured about the head, hanging limply from the shoulders.

The inspector helped them as much as he could, as they carried the limp figure to lay beside the other man in front of the car. Other police were around now, and ambulance men.

Anderson told Rankin later that the police reinforcements had soon cleared the crowd on the road, and got the traffic moving, but it was a good half hour before they got the third man out of the car, so badly had he been crushed and jammed in the rear seat, and it was going dusk before Rankin and the other three set off again for Kowloon.

Rankin had been right about the heavy man they had lifted out from the back. His neck had been broken, and there were some terrible injuries to his legs and the lower part of his body. The man the Police had got out from the front seat was also dead, but the third man, who had taken so long to get out, was still alive, though in a very bad way.

It seemed to Rankin that the Police had paid a lot of attention to both the bodies and to the badly injured man, more than was usual, he thought. Two young Chinese men, obviously police photographers, had taken many flashlight pictures of the scene of the crash, the badly wrecked limousine, and each of the men.

The police inspector who had been at the crash when Rankin got to the car was profuse in his thanks. He had taken all their names.

"Sorry about the uniforms, sergeant," he said, "but I'll have an official report and a letter of thanks sent to your commanding officer, so I'm sure they will let her Majesty pay for the uniforms being cleaned for you and Private Walker, or provide new kit for you both."

"Not to worry," Rankin replied as cheerfully as he could, "glad to have been able to help."

But he was very puzzled about it all, thinking back to the way in which first the limousine, and then the police truck, had passed them on the road, and to the fact that, though a lot of Chinese had been watching, none had been down in the paddy field, or had attempted to help the Police. He asked why?

"Perhaps it's because these people are scared of us in a way, but in any case, they would not have known what to do. They'd have been down all right if we hadn't been here."

Then another thought flashed through Rankin's mind. "We saw the car, and then your truck, pass us way back there. I thought then they were travelling too fast. What was it, inspector, were you chasing them, or escorting them?"

The inspector grinned a little, "Let's just say we were chasing them."

"Who are they then," Rankin asked, "VIPs?"

The inspector was giving nothing away. "I don't really know yet," he answered quietly, "let's just say they were visitors."

Rankin wasn't finished. "Another thing, inspector, I swear there were more than three men in that limousine when it passed by us. What happened to the others?"

The inspector didn't really want to answer that one either, and thought carefully before he did so.

"Between we two, you are right," he agreed, "there were five, so two must have been unhurt, or not badly hurt, and they got away."

Rankin looked around. "To that village?" he asked.

"Of course, where else? And now they'll be in Kowloon, or wherever it is they were bound for."

"Couldn't you have gone after them?" Rankin persisted.

"We could," the inspector agreed, "but we wouldn't have found them, they'd either be away fast from that village, or well hidden."

Rankin knew there was a lot more to it, but the inspector couldn't say any more, even if he must have a good idea of what it was all about. They must have been special people because of the police truck following them. Then there was the large number of police, who were very quickly on the scene after the accident, and the photographers, surely they did not need those after every accident. If they did, it must keep them all very busy in this accident ridden Colony. Yes, they were somebody special these three, hence the reasons for all the photographs.

Back in the cab of the truck again, after making sure his grip was safe in the back, Rankin realised Anderson was bursting to ask questions, but didn't give him any encouragement to do so. It was none of their business, and in any case, the driver needed all his concentration, as they drove slowly down the steep hill towards the outskirts of Kowloon, where the lights were already ablaze in a myriad of colours. Away, far to his front, Rankin could distinguish the lights on the houses on Victoria Peak on Hong Kong island itself.

It was always a glorious sight this approach to Kowloon. In the daylight, so much to see, with Stonecutters island below them, and to their right, whilst beyond was the far larger Lantau island. At this time, with the night closing in, it was equally glorious, and as they reached the fringes of Kowloon, the blaze of light and colour appeared to reach out and engulf them.

Soon they were in the crowded streets, the hurrying, scurrying Chinese, as always, occupying as much of the roads as they could, as well as the pavements, and only scattering from the front of the truck at the very last moment.

Anderson drove very patiently, easing carefully through the crowds in low gear, always alert, and stopping when he had to stop, to avoid other traffic or the rickshas, or the almost solid mass of pedestrians doing their best to mar his way.

"Flippin' heck," he said at last, "it's worse than going to Old Trafford to watch United."

Rankin's thoughts came back to football, the game he loved so much, and played so well.

"Manchester United?" he asked.

"Who else?" There was a wide grin on the young lance-corporal's face, "There's only one United." Then, as they stopped for a minute at a busy traffic crossing, "Can't understand why you don't buy yourself out an' take it up as a pro – you're bloody good enough like."

"Thanks, lad." Rankin was pleased. Praise from a fellow player was praise indeed, especially from someone who could watch Manchester United, and knew what he was talking about.

"Damn good money too, serge," Anderson went on, still waiting for the Chinese policemen on traffic control to wave him on, "more than you'll get in the Army."

"Perhaps you're right, lad," Rankin agreed, "but I'm not sure about turning pro. I did have an offer of a trial from Swansea, but I fancy the Army myself, it's not a bad life really."

"Well you have it your way," Anderson said, "I'll stick to mine, course you're a regular, but I know what I'd do if United offered me a trial, I'd bloody well swim back home."

They moved on again, down Nathan Road, and Anderson was all watchful as he well needed to be. Rankin thought he would never tire of seeing Hong Kong and Kowloon at night. It was always so busy with so much going on, the shops never seemed to close, and the streets were always crowded. The glow from the coloured neon signs added to the fantasy of the scene.

"Drop me at the Kowloon Hotel, will you, lad?" Rankin was in a happy mood – "it's not much out of your way, and I don't want to be seen walking around like this." His uniform was in a bad state, smeared with blood and oil, and torn in places. His need now was a good bath, a cold shower, and change into his best civvy suit – the suit he had been so concerned about up there where the accident had happened.

"No trouble, serge," Anderson told him, "we can go straight down Nathan Road, and I can nip round the block there."

"You know I'm not coming back with you tomorrow. I've got a forty-eight hour pass this time." Rankin was pleased about the extra day he would have to spend in Hong Kong.

"Take care of yourself, serge," Anderson was cheerful also now as they were moving quite well down Nathan Road, "don't do anything I wouldn't do."

"I won't," Rankin's voice was definite about that, "I'm one of the quiet lads."

He was looking forward to his night out. Now he was in Kowloon, his thoughts were just across the water that divided Kowloon from Hong Kong, and on that very lovely night club – the Golden Lotus. On the most elegant Chinese lady, whom he knew owned the place, at which, since the night of the Chinese and Army football match, he had been such a welcome visitor.

"Drop me just here on the corner," he said, "I'll be all right from here, an' you can turn right, you know the way?"

"Yes, serge, don't worry about me, I know where I am," Anderson replied, "I may be a farmer's lad but I like the big cities." Down through the gears he went, slowing carefully, and stopping exactly where Rankin had indicated.

"Cheerio, serge," he called, as Rankin got down from the cab, "have a good time."

"I will," Rankin said, holding the door open, "just a minute while I get my things from the back. Thanks for a good run down, lad. It's nice to be with a good driver."

8

MEMORIES – MEMORIES

Hong Kong sizzled. As dusk fell and afternoon became evening, the beat and the humidity increased, whilst far away to the south west, lightning flashes repeatedly pierced the rapidly darkening sky.

The first typhoon of the season – "Judy", they christened her, was fast approaching. "Judy" would miss Hong Kong, the radio stations were telling the world, but would pass near enough to bring strong winds and heavy rains, as many of these near miss typhoons often did.

The small craft had either gained, or were making for the shelter of the storm harbours, whilst the large ships to the west of the Star Ferry were stopping loading or unloading, and preparing to meet whatever the elements would throw at Hong Kong. These large ships were safely anchored to gigantic buoys, strong enough to-hold them securely in winds up to one hundred and fifty miles per hour, and allowing them to swing full circle without touching another ship, unless that ship had broken its own moorings.

The naval ships to the east of the ferry were making themselves equally safe, and some had already up-anchored to steam away out of the path of this "Judy", who would be making her presence felt in the course of the next few hours.

The red sun sank down below Lantau island, the colours kaleidoscoping to all those of the rainbow in turn, and, finally, to a vivid purple as the sun vanished, leaving only its rays purpling the sky for a brief while.

The day workers hurrying home, after their day's work sweltered in the heat, the women fanning away at themselves as best they could with fans, magazines or newspapers. They poured on to and off the ferries, the buses and the trams, in their thousands – hot, sticky, tired – and all going somewhere, wherever home was.

Those who had to work the night, in the night shifts of the factories, in the shipyards, the shops, the bars, the night clubs, were leaving home, and soon were as hot and sticky, if not as tired, as those jostling and scurrying to get home.

The streets and the sidewalks were brighter in the artificial lights than they had been in daylight. The emporiums and the shops were ablaze, offering their wares – jewellery, silver goods, cameras, furniture, carpets, jades, silks, antiques, cottons, costumes, furs, textiles, plastics, watches, clocks, cultured pearls, leather goods, toys, and food of every kind.

The tourists in the hotels were getting ready for the evening excursions, brave enough to risk a night out, in spite of the coming typhoon, which would take them around the crowded streets, to some of the shops, to some of the bars, for a cable-car ride up to Victoria Peak, to the Chinese opera, to the night clubs, or to a typically magnificent dinner on a floating restaurant at Aberdeen, or some such place.

So the night chased in with a rush, the bright lights of Hong Kong and Kowloon becoming brighter with the oncoming darkness. The multi-coloured nonflickering neon signs stabbed out their beauties, whilst the light haze reached up to embrace the night skies, and the waters of the harbour reflected back the colours in shimmering profusion.

Hamilton's report had reached police headquarters less than an hour after he had sealed the envelope. It had been passed quickly to the commissioner just as he had been about to leave his office, and he at once called in his deputy and three of his senior officers on duty. The commissioner knew Hamilton was in Hong Kong, had been expecting a report at any time, and now it had been received, was well aware of its importance.

Hamilton had not wasted space in the report telling the Police what he was sure they would already know. Police intelligence would be well aware of the growing activities of the Ninety Seven Triad, and of their increasing fighting with the Golden Lotus. They would know of various visitors coming in from China, but, from the way Taipan Chin had spoken, probably not be aware of the visit of Mong Lin San himself.

Mong Lin San was important, but not as important, in Hamilton's opinion, at this time as the conflict which would be the main purpose of the uprising soon to be started by the Ninety Seven, and be a battle for the control of Hong Kong. So this was the gist of the report, and Hamilton had stressed that, if Lin Poh won this internal battle, things would alter quickly, and for the worse.

The photograph of Mong Lin San was a triumph for Taipan Chin, but his visit was not the real problem. The threat very definitely was Lin Poh, and there was no doubt in the minds of all these senior police officers, after reading and discussing the report, that this man – strong, ruthless, well trained and ambitious, was a tremendous danger to them, and to law and order, in the Colony.

Hamilton's report added a lot to what the Police knew of the Ninety Seven and Lin Poh, but the commissioner and his officers were sure they could deal with the threat when it came. They had learned a great deal from the Double Ten riots, and all police training since then had been based on suppressing another rising of the same nature, but with a lot of forward thinking of what could happen if the rioters were better prepared, and had also learned lessons. Much as they hated the thought of this new trouble ahead, it's what was always expected in this trouble spot of the East. The commissioner was certain the Police were as ready as they ever could be, they would move immediately they had to, take whatever action they could beforehand, and were confident of maintaining law and order, and quickly putting down the rioters.

The commissioner thought it unnecessary to worry the governor at this point. The governor knew all they knew, except for the new information contained in Hamilton's report, and knew of all the preparations and plans made by the Police and the military. In any case, the commissioner, and the military chiefs, were dining with the governor that night at an official function in honour of Her Majesty's birthday, and the commissioner would find time to put them all in the picture.

He was satisfied that his headquarters had already swung into action, and all that could be done was being done – messages being sent out, messages being received – officers off duty being warned to stand by – a certain code name was sent off to Land Forces headquarters. Let the Ninety Seven commence – the Police were ready.

It was at this time that the first news of a serious road accident, near the northern outskirts of Kowloon, began to come in, and soon the first trickle of news became a flood. It was passed to the commissioner and his senior officers at once. Quite rightly, they considered it big news and most important, and it confirmed much of the information Hamilton reported.

In the meantime, Hamilton had been returned to the Peninsula Hotel, in the same careful way as his journey to see Taipan Chin – first by ricksha, then by taxi. Taipan Chin's protection was most thorough and, only when Hamilton alighted from the taxi at the main door of the hotel, did he feel that he was on his own again.

He had so much to think about and was very disturbed. Disturbed about the news he had heard from Chin, and which he had passed on to the Police, and disturbed because some inward feeling gave the definite impression that all was not well for him.

"You must be getting old," he told himself, but treated himself to a gin and tonic – a large gin – in the large, cool lounge of the hotel, where he made himself comfortable to spend a half an hour before going up to his room. The gin wasn't really a good thing after the brandy he had drunk earlier, and he knew he should have stuck on the same drink. But he had plenty of time to sit and think, a lot to think about, and there was a long evening and night in front of him.

He watched the comings and goings in the lounge, always a place full of life, a place where one could sit and watch most of the world go by. People of all the nations, people of all types, the young and the old, the rich and those not so rich, and one could look at them and wonder who they were, why they were here, where they were going, what did they do. He had always been interested in people, and wise enough to tell one nation from another, whilst he was sure he could pick out the tourists from the purely businessmen, and he still liked to look at a pretty woman as she passed by, whether she was foreign or local. It was a good spot to sit and rest, to think, or think you were thinking, and he wondered who of those sat around, or passing to and fro, was watching him, if anyone was.

The hotel lounge was much the same style now as it had been long ago, and as he first saw it. Whatever other changes there had been in Hong Kong, and there had been many, this grand hotel had remained much the same, and a central feature of life in the Colony.

He had often been brought here in the old days by his parents, sitting dutifully in this lounge, whilst his mother and father had tea with friends, whilst now and then they would bring him for a special treat, which would mean a meal in the dining room. His own taste was similar to that of his father – Chinese food – with such things as fried prawns in chilli sauce, chicken and walnuts, Tien-Tain cabbage with cream – he had adored that – and Peking duck, but his mother had been more conservative and content with good old roast beef, with the usual trimmings, which she had never failed to say was better even than you could get at home, meaning – as Hamilton came to realise as he grew older – England, and not the fairly luxurious, and very comfortable, house they lived in here in Hong Kong.

In his teens, especially during that wonderful time he had enjoyed a long holiday with his parents, which brought him such happiness, after being away from them so long at school in England, he had several times accompanied his parents to the hotel for festivities with his father's Chinese friends and business colleagues, and he had been lucky that holiday had coincided with the Chinese new year, the principal festival of the people, and lasting for fifteen days really, though the shops generally only closed for two or three days. This was a time of great gaiety and party giving, the exchange of presents, the distribution of "lai-she" money to children, and other old and lovely Chinese customs. This was the supreme time of the terrific fire-crackers, with the famous lantern festival, to bring it all to a thrilling climax.

What days those had been for a young and impressive boy, back home with his parents, after an almost three year absence, back home in the Hong Kong he knew and loved. How different then, when life had seemed so good and overflowing with pleasure and the love of his parents, to the hectic hard life of today. Why did one have to grow up, he asked himself, and that, he told himself, is a very sure sign that you are growing old and getting past it.

Was he really getting past it, was it becoming too much for him? He had been a long time in this game, had been lucky really to have survived without serious trouble of any kind. He had had minor problems in the past such as this, but had shrugged them off without worrying too much, but now he didn't seem to be able to do that – all of a sudden things had got on top of him. It was perhaps time to take a rest from it all.

He hadn't quite finished his gin – he shouldn't have had gin after brandy and wouldn't have another. The thing to do was to get up to his room, have a shower, a change of suit, and get out somewhere for the night – jigger the oncoming typhoon, he wasn't worried about typhoons, he had seen plenty in his time, and this "Judy" one could be no worse than some of the real ones he had experienced, and which had actually hit Hong Kong.

He watched a new party come through the lounge – a BOAC crew obviously – with two of the males going off to reception, leaving another male and three very attractively uniformed girls waiting just across from where he was sitting. How well they looked, and what a life it must be for them, even if it meant being up there in one of those jets in the sky which he hated. One of the girls perched herself against the arm of a settee, sitting half on and half off, and showing a lot of thigh in the process. It was most attractive, and, my gosh, these British girls really were beauties. He looked across at her, she was a stunner – nice smile, good teeth, lovely complexion, and gorgeous legs. She knew he was looking at her and smiled at him, or he thought she did.

Now, that's what I ought to do, he told himself – get up, go over, and introduce myself to this charmer, and take her out for the evening. They're obviously here for a stop-over night, and it would be simply great to take this one out, and all the rest of them, if they'd come – girls and men, and he was sure that would lift him out of his gloom.

But he couldn't do it, he wasn't the type, never had been and, like the leopard, he couldn't change his spots now. He wondered why – perhaps because he had led such a sheltered life with his parents, and, after all, that sort of upbringing was life in those days, but it had been a wonderful time, and he had no regrets about that.

The BOAC party were soon on the move again. He watched a couple of the hotel bell boys collect their luggage, and they went off to join the other two males who were awaiting them at the far end of the lounge.

Oh well, that was that, but the one he was sure had smiled at him was really luscious. What a pity he was such an old stick-in-the-mud as far as women were concerned. That supreme delight of English loveliness would have been a pleasure to meet, and take out for the evening, whilst judging by the way she had looked his way again, straight at him, before they went off, it could have been possible if he had made the effort, as he should have done. In these modern days of 1959, an introduction wasn't necessary, especially in a place such as Hong Kong, and as long as one was decent and respectful about the approach.

But it had always been this way with him, always seemingly sheltered by his mother and father, and he really had been brought up in a very protected manner. When he had attended those functions in this hotel and other restaurants with his parents, he had always sat at table on his mother's left hand side, with his father at her other side, and always a Chinese male, generally old and venerable, on his other side, whilst he could never recall meeting Chinese of his own age, or any English girls. It had never been anything for him to think about then, but he had long realised how carefully his parents had protected him from what he presumed they thought were the evils of the world they lived in.

Not that he had any resentment about his parents, or about the way they had brought him up. Quite the opposite, in fact, and he had enjoyed his youth and his life at home, whilst his mother and father were entitled to their manner of care for him, until such time as he could fend for himself.

He had very much enjoyed also the huge Chinese feasts, which had been a part of life in those days, and which he and his father revelled in, but were such a great trial to his mother. Shark's fin soup, roast suckling pig, steamed fish – and you selected your own fish live from a huge glass tank, and always thought, when it was placed on the table for you, that it was the one you had selected, sweet and sour pork, Mongolian hot-pot – this was delicious, and his favourite of them all, fried rice, which was much better than fried rice anywhere else in the world, prawns, lobsters, all the vegetables you could think of, everything and anything, with some of everything cooked Cantonese style – not salty and not greasy, or Shanghai style – saltier and more oilier, but sweeter as well, or Peking style – saltier and more spicy still, because some of the guests would originally have come from those parts of China.

Then there would be preserved duck eggs, said to be many years old, and a must for everyone including his mother, though she really hated them. He helped her by taking most of what was on her own plate, as well as what was on his plate, as he did with most of the Chinese dishes. It was a good thing he enjoyed the normal healthy appetite of youth, but he often wondered how his mother managed at such a meal when he was not there to help her.

The sweets were delicious, though, by the time they came to the sweet course, many of the guests were past eating, and some, past drinking. Hamilton always had room for the sticky sweets, the fancy pastries, and the fruit, no matter how much he had eaten previously, whilst his mother liked this course far better than any of the others, so there would be no need to help her by taking things off her plate now.

The wines came from France and Germany, of course. These Chinese could afford the best, and wanted the best, so the red and white wines, and the brandy, would be as plentiful as the food, even though the young Hamilton, like his mother, drank very little of them.

His father, as a dutiful guest, had to keep up with the hosts, so the morning after such a feast would be an aspirin morning for poor father, with a vinegar and cold water pad on his head, kept cold and damp by his mother, and the blinds of the bedroom drawn.

He had often heard his father moaning, "Never again," which he and his mother well knew would mean, never again until the next time, and, when his father had recovered, he would explain it was a matter of honour and national pride to be able to keep up with these Chinese, who appeared to be able to drink anything, so that Hamilton was proud his father could match the hosts for drinking, and then manage to get home, without staggering too much, or slurring his speech even, though it always did mean a very bad morning the next day.

At these feasts, the food was served in large bowls, or in baskets, from which all the guests helped themselves, many trying to dip into the bowls at the same time with their chopsticks, which all seemed to add to the fun. Hamilton, like his mother and father, could use chopsticks as well as any of the Chinese, so they were never out of place at a Chinese feast, but it amused him nowadays, when eating out in restaurants, to see the English, and other foreigners, trying to cope with chopsticks, not being able to master, what to him was a simple manipulation of the fingers.

He never remembered any violence, though it always seemed possible, with the atmosphere becoming more hilarious and adventurous as the wine flowed, and as more bowls and baskets, filled to overflowing with the chosen delicacies, were brought to the table. Chopsticks worked overtime, whilst the wine glasses were refilled the moment they were emptied by the attendant wine waiters. If one didn't want to drink much, it was policy to leave your glass filled. Empty it, or half empty it, and it would be refilled at once.

Custom decreed that the bowls, the baskets, the plates, and the empty bottles, be left on the table as proof of what had been eaten and drank, and, as the stacks grew higher, and the empty wine bottles more heaped, so the chatter and merriment rose to a loud crescendo of noise, whilst it was not possible to see across to the other side of the table, but he had seen guests, both male and female, stagger away, or even slip gently under the table where they would perhaps be left to sleep it off, until a wife or a friend, or a couple of the wine waiters, or the captains, gathered them up and took them away.

That long holiday was really the end of the good old days for him, but he had enjoyed it until just the last two or three days, before departing for England and school again, not caring till then that he would not be with his parents for at least a couple of years, and not knowing that these times would never come again, that world events were stirring, which would terminate such activities for a long time, and would bring to Hong Kong the cruelest of foes and conquerors.

So his memories were mostly of the good times, and he didn't often think back to the days when Hong Kong had been beseiged, and had eventually fallen to the Japanese, with all the horrors that had brought. When he did think of those years, he had never failing memories of the cruelties and atrocities, but he knew also it was typical of the race.

In his early days as a prisoner of war, he had been in a labour gang on the dockside, and had seen Japanese troopships arrive. Working away, as he and the other British prisoners in his particular labour gang had been forced to do, he had still been able to watch the ships disgorge their human cargoes, the dumpy soldiers form up into units, and load their kitbags and other stores into the light styled transport they had for each unit, which he judged to be about the strength of a British Army platoon. This transport would have to be pulled with ropes by the Japanese soldiers themselves, and the non-commissioned officers and the officers even would ensure the soldiers pulled hard enough. If not, out would come whips and sluggards would be cruelly whipped and beaten.

Hamilton had not known much about the Japanese until then, and they had never really interested him. But he was to learn a great deal about them in the years they held the Colony, to know of their sadistic ways, harsh to the extreme, and cruel enough to equal any of the doings of the dark ages he had read about in his studies at school. He knew he had been lucky to survive the captivity when so many others had not, and it had been a relief, as well as a great sorrow, when his father had passed away.

At that time, it had looked as if the Japanese would hold Hong Kong for ever, though to the observant eye, it would not have been thought so the way most of the conquerors were sacking it, but Hamilton, ever an eternal optimist, never lost faith, kept as fit as he could, in spite of the miserable diet they all existed on, thanked God for his good health, and for his slight frame, which he was sure helped a lot, kept cheerful in spite of everything, through the bad news, the lack of news, the terrible conditions forced on the prisoners, the deaths of his comrades, and he had come through it all, and was here now in the hotel the Japanese had used when they held the Colony, and really he was as worried now, and more worried, in some ways, as he had ever been in those awful days of captivity.

He finished his gin, knew he should not have another, so went over to the reception desk. The young Chinese male on duty knew him well.

"Can I help you, Mr Hamilton?" he asked.

"You can indeed," he replied, "I'm thinking of going to the Golden Lotus tonight. Can you get me a table?"

The young man's face did not lose its smile, even though, as Hamilton well knew, it was a bit late to be thinking of booking a table at such a popular place, and a day such as this.

"It may be difficult," he said, "but we can try. Perhaps they will have had some refusals with this typhoon around us. In any case, I know them very well at the Golden Lotus. Will you please wait a while, sir?"

Hamilton knew this young man had been at the hotel a long time, and actually remembered him as a bell boy on one of his earlier visits, so he was glad to note the progress he was making. He waited patiently, reading, but not really being interested in the various notices adorning reception, whilst he could see the young man in the inner office, and obviously telephoning to the night club.

He was smiling even more broadly when he came back to Hamilton.

"Yes, sir, they can do a table for you – it's a table for two, honestly, but they hardly think they'll get another single, and they're not taking anyone at the door tonight. It's a special day today, so it is a special night as well. I've told them who you are, and I am sure they will look after you very well."

Hamilton thanked him, pleased at the service, and the young man's perfect English. He knew better than to offer a tip, a courteous thank you was quite enough, and the young man would have been offended with an offer of money. He was an executive of the hotel, on his way up, not a waiter or a captain to be tipped. I'll bet one day he's the manager of this hotel, or one like it, Hamilton told himself.

He went up to his room, glad to have made up his mind what he would do. In a way, it would be better if he had been in company, and he regretted now, more than ever, his inability to get up and talk to that BAOC honey, who, he was sure, would have shared the table with him. Earlier he had been regretting that he had turned down an invitation Sam Reynolds had given him last night, to join a party some of the police officers and their wives were planning, to celebrate the birthday of their young Queen, but in spite of his regrets, he was glad to be going to the Golden Lotus. It was the Golden Lotus Triad he was concerned about, and he would feel nearer the heart of it by being at the luxurious club owned by the leader of the Triad.

But he could not shake off the feeling that all was not well, and this became worse, as he realised that his room had been searched. He could not really have explained why he knew, perhaps it was the sixth sense he was sure he had developed. More likely, it was because he was meticulous in arranging his shirts, underwear and socks, in the drawers of the dressing table, and he was sure these had been searched though as carefully as he or she who had done it, had replaced them in the right order. In the bathroom, he was sure his toilet articles had been inspected by someone, even though these also had been replaced in the orderly way he had left them.

The wardrobe had been rummaged through, and his shoes looked at. This, he was certain of. The toilet articles could have been disturbed by the room amah, but she would have no need to look into the wardrobe, and certainly had no need to take up and put down his shoes, as someone had done.

Whoever it was had not obtained any information. His briefcase was unlocked, as he had left it, but that contained only a few harmless official papers, and he never was one to leave anything important in any room, let alone a room in the Peninsula Hotel. But he could tell the briefcase had been opened, and the papers taken out and looked at. Ah well, if they had taken photocopies of them, it was of no harm, but it was worrying.

Such a thing had only happened to him once before, many years ago, and in this very hotel. From the enquiries he had made then, he had learned that several other rooms had reported the same thing, so he presumed it had been some member of the hotel staff, and though nothing had been taken from his room, some of the other guests had reported losses of watches and cameras, as well as some jewellery, and whoever it was who had done it, had never been discovered. It could be the same now, he would ask about it in the morning, but for it to happen at this time added to his general disturbed feeling.

He undressed slowly, his brain busy with his thoughts. He certainly was worried about the Golden Lotus Triad. They had been the most powerful Triad in Hong Kong for many years, and, because of their law-abiding outlook, had been a great help to the authorities. He knew from what Chin had told him in the past, and what he had learned from the Police, how much they had done to help maintain law and order by the information they had passed on, and by action they had taken against evildoers, and also how much financial aid they had given to the many worthwhile causes in the resettlement of the hundreds of thousands of refugees, who had flooded into the Colony from China in recent years. For them to be overthrown by this new Ninety Seven lot would be a very bad thing in every way.

It could happen, of course, and such things had often happened before in history. He thought over what Taipan Chin had told him about the youngish man, who was the leader of the Ninety Seven in Hong Kong. He would certainly want to control the Colony – this would be a step towards control of the whole of the Ninety Seven, and perhaps a step towards the control of all China, and that was something big enough for any man to aim at, and to take great risks for. The Golden Lotus were well disciplined and very strong, but they had been in control in Hong Kong for a long time, and this, as history had often proved, was not always a good thing. He hoped they would be equal to the task which was obviously in front of them now.

As he showered – luke warm at first, then as cold as possible, and most refreshing – he thought over the great deal he knew about the Golden Lotus, their organisation, and the man they just titled the Minister. He wondered, as he had often done in the past, how very close to the Golden Lotus Triad Taipan Chin must be. Was he perhaps a member of the Triad? It could be so. If he was, then it would be a bad blow if the Ninety Seven were able to wrest control of Hong Kong from them. This trouble which was coming could only be the start of an internal war, an internal war which one Triad would win and the other must lose. He hoped the Golden Lotus were prepared, knew it was a war for survival, and would win.

Dried after his shower, and dressed only in fresh underwear, he spent a few minutes at the open french windows, looking out across the water. There were still a lot of ships in the stretch between Kowloon and the island of Hong Kong, and he knew those big ships out there must be securely anchored. Oh yes, they were going to get a bit of that typhoon at least, and he knew he must get on and get over to Hong Kong, if he was going to the Golden Lotus that night – soon these ferries would be forced to stop running.

The night had come in black and ominous, but, because of the blackness, the lights shone brilliantly – on the ships, on the ferries, still plying busily between Hong Kong and Kowloon, and on Hong Kong island itself, which looked so clear, and so near, across that stretch of water, with the neons as colourful as he could ever remember them, and the whole front of the island, right across from him, ablaze with lights, thick and dense low down near the water, and still in great profusion up and up to the top of the Peak, its black hulk outlined more prominently now and then by the sheet lightning far away behind it. What a glorious sight it was, man's work and nature's work, combining to give this tremendous spectacle.

Back came his thoughts to Lee Kyung Koh. He had seen her in the flesh only three or four times over the years, but her lovely photographic face, and her wonderful figure and dress sense had appeared many hundreds of times in the Hong Kong newspapers and magazines, which were so much a part of his life and his studies, so he knew her to be a very lovely woman, as graceful as any woman he had ever seen. He had learned she was very intelligent, and she was much beloved by all her Triad. She was also well respected throughout the Colony, because of the many charitable acts of both herself and the Triad, but he thought her vanity had conquered her intelligence, there was something lacking within somewhere, hence this night club, which seemed to be her ruling passion, so she was the weakness, and Taipan Chin was absolutely right – the weakness which could bring down the Golden Lotus Triad.

If Lin Poh was the leader Taipan Chin judged him to be, and as well trained by the Russians as was thought, then he would know she was the weak link in the otherwise so strong Golden Lotus Triad. It was most obvious to Hamilton that the first move would be against Lee Kyung Koh, and he had no doubt about the place being the night club where Lee Kyung Koh was reputed to be every night, and where she would almost place herself at the disposal of the Ninety Seven.

Surely the Minister, as wise as anyone in Hong Kong, according to Taipan Chin, would stop her public appearances for a while. Surely he would know this was a dangerous time, and surely Lee Kyung Koh would realise it also. They must know that, if she was kidnapped, it could be a mortal blow to the whole structure of the Triad she ruled.

They all knew the confrontation was coming, and could have no doubts where the danger lay, and where the enemy would strike. A kidnapping was such an obvious move, so they must keep Lee Kyung Koh away from that danger. If they don't, he told himself, if she is taken, they will never recover from it, the ransom demand will put an end to the Golden Lotus, he was certain of that. Then soon, Hong Kong would belong to the Ninety Seven, and from what Chin had told him of them, this was a terrible prospect to think of.

How frustrating it all was, the more so, because he could do nothing about it, other than what he had already done. His purpose in coming to Hong Kong on this occasion was over, he had made his contact with Taipan Chin, made his report to the Police, and now he was out of it, could only be patient, watch and see what happened, and worry that it might all go wrong.

Come to think of it, he told himself, I'm not really necessary at all. It is such a farce really. All I do is to act as the contact between Chin and the Police – why cannot the Police deal with Chin direct? They surely know who he is, and they know I get my information from him. I come all this way up here, take all these precautions, worry myself sick, make my report, and that's me finished. I have no further part to play in it at all. There's no sense in it.

Then – don't be stupid, of course there is sense in it. You have done your part, and it must be of use. Perhaps Chin would refuse to deal direct with the Police. Perhaps it's only because he knows you well, trusts you – and that's a must with the Chinese, and with a man such as Chin – that he gives you the information, not the police. What you do with it is your business, and you know damn well that, if all this wasn't necessary, that very astute gentleman in England would be the first to say so.

Of course he would, he's no fool, he knows what is necessary, knows there is a reason for all this, and knows you have a part to play in it, even if it seems such a little part to you. Besides, without that information you get from Chin, and pass on, the task of the authorities here would be very much more difficult. So don't get upset, keep trying, chin up, and don't worry. Go on, get over to the Golden Lotus and enjoy yourself – you deserve it.

He finished his dressing, trying hard to reassure himself he was an important cog in the wheel. A light oatmeal coloured suit, accentuating his slimness, a blue shirt, brown knitted tie, and brown shoes, very highly polished. Better get going, Hamilton, he told himself, before that typhoon breaks, and before those ferries stop.

He took a careful look around the room, noting and remembering the placings of all the furniture, then turned out the lights, and stood in the semi-darkness for a while. It wasn't really dark, he had purposely left the curtains partly open, and he could see everything in the room quite clearly. He could see the lightning flashes, but that storm seemed still quite some way off. He stood for some time before letting himself quietly out of the door.

At the main doors of the hotel he nearly decided not to go. He had been wrong in his room thinking that the storm was a long way off – it was blowing hard, very black indeed to the south-west, and the lightning flashes much nearer, and the noise of thunder very loud. Oh lor, he thought, the rain's not far away, and you'll get drowned without a macintosh – not that a macintosh would be much use in the sort of rain that's coming. But he moved on towards the ferry, quickening his pace. Keep going, he told himself, you're not worried about a typhoon, you've been in them before, but it'll be a bit rough going over on the ferry. Go on, get moving, it really is a night for a celebration, and they've gone to a lot of trouble to get you a table.

9

A MAN FOR EVERY WOMAN

It had been a busy day for Lee Kyung Koh. Not long after the Minister had left her, she went out to visit the new baby her medical adviser had told her about, born that morning. Though the father was only a junior member of her Council, he was still an important man, and one to whom respect must be shown by this visit.

The mother was in her early twenties and this was her second child. Both were boys, so the wife would be in high favour with her husband and his family. She had recovered well from the birth, and had been able to talk proudly to Lee Kyung Koh, as well she might having produced another son for her husband, and another young man for the Triad. In any case, she had been known to Lee Kyung Koh all her life, so there was no strangeness between them. Lee Kyung Koh was happy to see mother and son so well, and to hear how excellently the mother had been looked after prior to, and during, the birth.

Lee Kyung Koh returned to her own premises very thoughtful, as Ai Fah quickly discovered, even though Lee Kyung Koh was enthusiastic about the event, the state of health of mother and child, and the medical care the Triad provided. There could be no doubt that the medical adviser made the fullest use of the monies put at his disposal, for those in high office, as well as for those of the lower orders, and this pleased Lee Kyung Koh greatly.

Ai Fah listened with great attention, as she always did to her mistress, but could not fail to be aware of the sadness in her voice, and perhaps more than a trace of envy, even though the story of the visit was told with such great enthusiasm and pride, but she was very surprised when

Lee Kyung Koh spoke about her own state, something she had never previously discussed with her amah.

"I am sure my Council must often wonder who I am to marry, if I am to marry," she said.

Ai Fah could not conceal her surprise.

"Well, who am I to marry," her mistress continued, her voice rising, "who is there for me?"

Ai Fah's thoughts raced – indeed, who was there for her mistress to marry, but she could not say that.

"There is a man for every woman, my Lady," she replied quietly.

Lee Kyung Koh was not of that opinion.

"There is – you say there is – then who is there for me? Tell me that. All my Council members have their wives, so who is there for me here, and," quieter now and very pointedly, "Who is there on Taiwan?"

This was an entirely unexpected conversation and topic as far as Ai Fah was concerned, and she could not cope with it. Wisely she kept quiet.

"Oh, yes," – Lee Kyung Koh's voice had risen again, well above her usual calm, "there are men on Taiwan – but not for me – for others perhaps, but not for me."

Ai Fah's eyebrows raised high in astonishment. Who could have told her about the men from Taiwan, she asked herself. She is referring to me, she must know, she does know. But, who could have told her?

Lee Kyung Koh had not finished, "And there can be no man for me in China where now they are only pigs, so where is there a man for me – is it to be a foreigner?"

There was silence for a minute, and when Lee Kyung Koh spoke again, she had recovered her composure. "You see, Ai Fah, what a visit to a young mother and her new born son can do to a woman. If, as you say, there is a man for every woman, where can there be a man for me?"

Now she was sincere, and Ai Fah knew they were talking as woman to woman for the very first time, and not, as always before, as mistress and servant. Ai Fah was aware, if she was to speak at all, it must be great sense and the truth. Her mistress did not want sympathy. She had been stirred today, obviously in a way she had never shown before, and she wanted a man, at long last, Ai Fah thought, but she wanted truthful advice also, and she wanted it from someone she knew to be a real woman, and would well know the inner feelings of her soul and body.

Ai Fah had to be at her very best and she must speak without fear.

"I know, my Lady," she said quietly and carefully, "that many men have desired you, but, because of your birth, none have been able to reach you. Perhaps there is such a man in Taiwan, a man for you, but you are so far above all." She paused, and Lee Kyung Koh did not interrupt.

How much more dare I say, Ai Fah asked herself – and then – yes, say it all, it is the truth – "You are much to blame yourself, my Lady," she continued, and was pleased that the expression on Lee Kyung Koh's face did not alter. "You deal only with men in the Council, you are too high, too mighty, and you well know you have always kept yourself at a high level, you have never placed yourself where a man could take you."

She had said it, most all of what she had thought for many years. After all, a woman must do some chasing, even though she pretends it is not. That, to Ai Fah, was the art of love. A woman must never seem too far distant, she must offer some hope, some chance, to those who could chase, and Lee Kyung Koh had never done this, as far as she knew, but she was relieved when her mistress agreed with her.

"You are right, Ai Fah," she said simply, "very right, but what can I do now?"

"It is written in the stars there is a man for every woman, my Lady," Ai Fah was sure of this even if Lee Kyung Koh was not.

"Then we must find him soon," Lee Kyung Koh replied, "or he will only find me an old crone."

"Oh no, my Lady," Ai Fah would not have that – "that is not the truth, you are the most beautiful woman in all the world."

Lee Kyung Koh smiled. She could see her amah was sincere, and was truly pleased. "Thank you, Ai Fah, though you flatter me greatly – but what good is beauty, what good being a woman, if there is no man to enjoy me? Better my father was given a son than a daughter. I know he often thought so, as I do now."

"You wrong your father, and you wrong his memory," Ai Fah was indignant and still bold. "It is well known your father loved you greatly."

"I am sure he did," Lee Kyung Koh agreed, "but I am sure also many times he wished me a son and not a daughter, a man and not a woman, and I wish that too. Whatever I have done wrong with my life, it would seem certain there is no man for me, and I shall live, and I shall die, a woman – loved by no man, and barren."

Ai Fah was very upset. "But that is wrong, my Lady, we all love you."

Lee Kyung Koh smiled again. "I do know that, Ai Fah, I do know that you and all my people have very great affection for me, and I am highly pleased. But no man loves me, no man lies with me, and you well know, Ai Fah, of all women, that a woman without a man is not a woman."

She has known of my men all the time, Ai Fah thought, and she is envious of me because of them – poor woman, but how truly she speaks. Her sadness for her mistress was great and sincere, and she knew she must be even more daring.

"Then, my Lady, there can be only one answer – you must change your way of life."

"Change – change to what?" Lee Kyung Koh asked.

Ai Fah thought a while. She knew what she wanted to say, but dare she say it? Yes, she must. "You should give up your way of life in the Triad – you must travel, travel and find the man who is looking for you."

This was just like those Chinese films she watched so often, and it was the truth as far as she was concerned, whether her mistress liked it or not. She was relieved, however, to find that her mistress liked it.

"I have thought of that," Lee Kyung Koh admitted, "but would I be allowed to do it?"

Ai Fah was pleased with herself. The conversation was going well, and she saw herself as the number one adviser to the head of the Triad, who was so much in need of this talk at the same level. Who better, Ai Fah thought, than me to give her this advice. I love her, I know what she wants, I know all the activities of the Triad, I know the feelings of the high, as well as the low, know how this could affect them all, but I am also a woman, and I know what I am talking about.

"It would be a mighty change for us all," she told her mistress, "and for you, my Lady. But surely the Minister would see what advantages it has for you, if not for the Triad, and he is a very wise man."

"It could well be so," Lee Kyung Koh was very thoughtful, and though Ai Fah could not know it, her remarks were much what her mistress thought herself and wanted to hear. "Yes, it could be so. After all, Kings have abdicated, why not Queens? It could even be better for the Triad, but " – a pause – "would travel bring me what I seek?"

Ai Fah was ready with her reply, "That, no one could tell, but if the stars are right, and we know they are, then there is a man somewhere waiting for you."

"Would you come with me, Ai Fah?"

The question from her mistress did not take her by surprise. Those films had prepared her for it in a way, and it was just as she had often pictured, even though there was as yet no handsome prince to carry off Lee Kyung Koh, but she would find him on her travels. Of that, Ai Fah was sure.

"I would come of course, my Lady, if you wanted me," she replied at once. She knew she could not hesitate about that answer, though it was something she did not relish, all this travelling, "But I think it best the younger ones should go with you. I am ancient, set in my ways, but they are young and strong, and I have trained them well for you. They will serve you faithfully wherever it may be – better them than me."

She hoped her mistress would understand, would not think she was deserting her after all their years together. Oh no, it was not that, it was the truth as she saw it. She was sure travelling was not for her. To go with Lee Kyung Koh to one place – yes, but to travel to many places, many countries, was not for her.

Lee Kyung Koh must have thought it so. "Perhaps you are right, Ai Fah," she agreed, "but I would miss you greatly. It is something we cannot concern ourselves about at the moment. Perhaps it will all come to naught. There is much thought to be given to it, much discussion with the Minister and with all the Council before anything comes of it, even if I dare to suggest it."

"But you must dare, my Lady," Ai Fah insisted. "It is something you really want, I feel sure, and you must dare."

"Yes I must," Lee Kyung Koh told her, "and perhaps when I do, it will be better for the Triad." But then her thoughts came back to the present. "It will be discussed, Ai Fah, but not at the moment. Now there is much danger, and there will be much trouble in Hong Kong. The Minister is much worried, and I am the one they all worry about."

Ai Fah knew something of the trouble, and of the recent fighting in which some of the Triad had been involved, but she had not thought of any possible danger to her mistress.

"How can that be, my Lady?" she asked, "surely they know your guards will protect you."

"Oh yes, they do know that," Lee Kyung Koh said, "but our enemies are most dangerous and very strong, perhaps even stronger than my guards."

"Nonsense, my Lady," Ai Fah dared to be indignant again. This conversation had given her new confidence, and a new feeling of some power, so she could speak this way. She knew much of the bravery and the skill of the guards, all specially chosen from the best in Taiwan, whilst her present lover had no doubts about the result of any conflict and their ability to protect Lee Kyung Koh. "That is old women's talk, and it is wrong to even suggest it. The Minister knows full well you will be protected by the bravest of men, and knows no harm can come to you."

This was exactly what Lee Kyung Koh had really wanted to say to her Minister earlier in the day, and something she was now highly pleased to hear. Of course, her guards were competent, and there could not really be that danger at the Golden Lotus about which he had warned her. He was being wise but over cautious, as he would need to be with her, and she had not failed to notice, when she had been out on her visit, that her plain clothed guards had been increased, so she fully agreed with Ai Fah, she was safe enough.

It did not occur to her that Ai Fah could really know so little of the state of affairs in Hong Kong, whilst her Minister would know so much. Such are the remarks, the observations, which can be so wrong, as it has always been throughout history. The views of Ai Fah, delivered so strongly, and with such conviction, reassured Lee Kyung Koh completely.

She must respect her Minister's care for her, and she was pleased that he and all the Council were so concerned for her, but her supreme vanity made her sure she would be safe at the Golden Lotus, where she would have so many personal guards around her, and where emergencies had been planned for by the Minister, and her movements to and from the night club were such that she was well protected, so, of course, Ai Fah was right, as she was right – there really could be no danger to her.

Later, the two of them went shopping in Hong Kong, but now, Lee Kyung Koh was dressed in the same manner as Ai Fah, in a sombre black samfoo, a snugly cut jacket and trouser suit. Now she was not the glamorous lady who so often appeared so well groomed and dressed in the height of luxury at the big functions of the Colony, but just another Chinese woman of the lower orders, and she could look the part alongside the more dumpy Ai Fah, stooping to hide the height which people might know her by. Two more women in the crowded streets, but still well guarded by the many highly trained men who would give their lives in her service if need be.

They visited some of the shops of the Triad, and she was known at once to those in charge, but they could not, on these occasions, afford her the honour due to her as their head.

It was a policy she had carried out for many years, this way of visiting her people. Always it was well planned in advance, and she would be sure the ricksha boy would be a member of the Triad if she was travelling by ricksha, or the taxi driver if by taxi, whilst, if she was going on a bus or a tram, members of her bodyguard would have embarked at earlier stops, and others would get on around her when she did. It was the same when she ever crossed to Kowloon by the Star Ferry – that ferry boat would carry many of her guards, unobtrusive, but alert.

The official occasions, such events as the opening of a school or a hospital, when she would have to mix freely with the high officials of the Colony, both British and Chinese, were the real danger. Then she was Lee Kyung Koh, head of the Triad, and there could be no disguise, and though she would still have some protection from her own guards, as well as the normal police security, there was great risk. But she carried out all these duties bravely, and without fuss, never really thinking she could be in the great danger her Minister knew she faced.

So she enjoyed her shopping expeditions with Ai Fah, and she enjoyed the one today. She ordered a camphorwood chest, which, when completed, would be a present for the new baby, so that the mother could store all the baby clothes originally, and then other clothes as he grew older, until it would eventually pass into his possession altogether, and become a treasured family item as it had been a present from her.

She chose the style of the chest, and watched the master craftsman who owned the shop, and who made many items for her, start the pattern. This would be a fisherman fishing in a pool with the natural grains of the wood forming the ripples on the water. The old man used just a hammer and chisel to trace the outlines of the pattern, gently, but firmly, and without mistake. After he had finished, making it all seem so very easy, which she knew was not so, she stayed awhile to watch two of his young boys continue the work, commencing the filling in of the figures and the landscape, again using just hammer and chisel.

The chest would be entirely of camphorwood and not, as so many chests were nowadays, of rosewood or ivory, with a camphorwood lining. This was to her order and would be the very best. The shop was modern and roomy, and well lit, as was the workshop behind the shop, so that the owner and his employees worked in good conditions, and not like many other Hong Kong shops and workshops, when the shop itself was presentable, but the conditions of the workshops behind really awful, and where the youthful employees worked in bad conditions, in bad lighting, and very poorly paid. This modern shop was typical of all those of her Triad, and she herself insisted on the best possible throughout all the activities.

In the adjoining shop they examined some jade. Lee Kyung Koh was a good judge of jade, and was delighted with the perfection of the carvings of the figurines, and the jewellery. Jade was in good supply from Burma, and she knew it was a hard substance and very difficult to carve.

These visits to her own people were so much more enjoyable than the official duties which she had to perform almost daily on behalf of her Triad. These functions could be difficult for her because she was a woman in what was really a man's world. She knew she was resented by some of the older Chinese men she had to mix with on these occasions, but this was something she had to put up with and overcome.

It was not the same in her Council, although this was a man's world also except for her. The members respected her, as well as loved her, because they knew of the great interest she took in all the work of the Triad, and her desire to give her very best for her people, and to want the best for them.

Perhaps it was because she wore the simple samfoo as most Chinese women wore, and was not dressed in the elegant cheongsams she wore for official functions, when she would be in the company of the high Chinese of the Executive Council, and the Legislative Council of the Colony, that her people could talk to her freely, but always with great respect.

She would hear about their lives, their hopes and fears, their families and their work, and would study all the photographs with great interest. She knew many of them well, and all about the relations who were spread all over the world, but still connected with the Triad. She learned of the joys and the sorrows, of the births and the deaths, their plans for the future, and how the businesses were progressing.

From her fishing folk, she would be told where they were fishing, and what they were catching, and was happy to know that the newer boats were so much an improvement on the old ones, with modern engines making sails unnecessary, and the children of the fishing fleet now attending school and not living, as they always had done in the past, on the boats.

She would hear the latest news from those who still had relations in China, still waiting patiently to get out from the rigid rule imposed by the Red Guards to Hong Kong, where there was a chance to live freely and to work without being in constant fear. She would be told of the sombreness of dress and life in those cities of Red China, how the females were not allowed to wear the gay and colourful cheongsams they yearned for, and how very dismal and cruel life was still for them, and she would know, even if the relations did not, that it was necessary for some of the Triad to remain in China, whatever the conditions, so that information could be passed out to the Minister, and to the outer world.

They would tell her of the problems of other people, those Chinese in other Triads, with whom her own people were in constant contact, and of the vice of the Colony, especially that of drugs. She was amazed at the knowledge some of the women had of drugs, and was shocked with the stories of heroin. How it could be smoked in a cigarette, but generally it was wrapped in tinfoil, and heated over a flame, then the fumes were inhaled through a short length of bamboo, or rolled paper.

She knew a lot about opium, which had been a part of Chinese life back through centuries, and that an opium smoker could smoke the pipe for years, as her father had done, but heroin, she was told, was much stronger than opium, and would cause physical ruin and death in the space of just a few months.

Heroin is derived from morphine, which, in turn, is derived from opium, and was very expensive. A heroin addict needed a lot of money, and it was because of the craving for heroin that crime was so high in the Colony, as an addict had to turn to crime to get the money to pay for the heroin.

It was illegal to grow opium in Hong Kong, but it was smuggled in to the Colony in large quantities, in spite of the efforts of the Hong Kong police department to prevent it. Though large quantities were seized, some continued to get in – dumped overboard from ships in waterproof containers, and picked up by one of the many small boats using these busy waters, or brought in by passengers on aircraft or on ships, and sometimes by airdrop.

A lot of it came from the Shan states of Eastern Burma, and generally through Bangkok, the last stop prior to Hong Kong for many ships and aircraft. Some came from the Yannan province in south west China, and some from north west Laos and from Thailand. But it was still got in by all sorts of means, and it was really impossible for the Police to prevent all of it coming in, no matter how hard they tried and how vigilant they were.

It was from her people, on visits such as this today, as well as from her daily talks with the Minister and other members of the Council, that she built up her knowledge of Hong Kong and world affairs, and the affairs her Triad were engaged in, her factories, her shipping, her shops and stores, and the farms. She had a better all-round knowledge than any member of the Council, apart from the Minister, so that this knowledge often astounded individual members, which was why they respected and trusted her so much. She never, in any way, interfered with the work they had to do, always gave them ample time for their audience with her, listened carefully to them, often making a comment or a suggestion, which they knew to be real good sense as well as womanly intuition, whilst it was the same at a full Council meeting, where she would have her say, but never at the expense of a member, and made her final decisions after much thought and sound reasoning.

It was dark, with the typhoon much nearer, when she and Ai Fah had returned, and not long now before it would be time for her to go off to the Golden Lotus. She had thought earlier that she would respect the wish of the Minister and keep away, but had changed her mind after the conversation with Ai Fah, whilst the ease of her movements today, and the knowledge that there were even more of her guards around her, convinced her she was quite safe. In any case, had the Minister really thought there was the danger he had told her about, he would surely have insisted she stayed away – he was too wise not to have done this had it been really necessary.

She had dinner – her big meal of the day – in her saloon, in much the same style as she had taken her breakfast, brought in by the same two young amahs and served by Ai Fah. Lee Kyung Koh sat alone at the highly polished round dining table at the opposite end of the room to that occupied by the large desk at which she sat for business affairs.

The napery, the cutlery, the plates, dishes and glassware, were all of the very finest, the napery appliqued with the deep blue Hong Kong orchid. The room, only dimly lit except for a small, exquisitely carved jade lampholder on the table, which gave her light for her meal, peaceful and a perfect setting for a lovely lady, of noble birth, and elegantly gowned in golden cheongsam trimmed with white fur, sat erect as befitted such a beautiful woman.

She commenced with consommé and melba toast, taking her time, as she always did when eating. This finished, Ai Fah put on the table a large glass dish of King prawns. Lee Kyung Koh ate just four of these, separating the head from the rest of the body first, and then removing the shell from the body with her delicate fingers, and then, when she had eaten the body of the prawn, she took up the head to suck out the brains and the plankton, which to her, as to many, was more of a delicacy than the body itself.

This course completed, she drank a glass of ice cold water, previously boiled, as all her drinking water was, and waited for Ai Fah to continue the service.

This was roast chicken, prepared in a special way by her cook amah, and one of Lee Kyung Koh's favourite dishes. The chicken, beautifully plump, stuffed with chestnuts, previously boiled soft and skinned, herbs and shredded cabbage, had been wrapped in lotus leaves and baked in clay for many hours. Now it was so tender that the flesh came away from the bone, as Lee Kyung Koh carved what she required, and cut into small pieces before taking up her chopsticks. With it came boiled new potatoes, tiny carrots, which had been steamed and not boiled, a thin highly spiced sauce, and a side plate of salad – cos lettuce, tomatoes, sliced onions, radish and onions. Lee Kyung Koh ate well and with obvious enjoyment, thoroughly chewing every mouthful.

She drank another glass of the ice cold water, and then had a small portion of fruit salad – oranges, pineapples, pears and lychees, with a lot of very thick cream. Finally, a cup of black coffee.

This, and her breakfast, were the only two meals of her normal day, and she liked to eat a sustaining dinner, which was a meal to take time over and enjoy fully. She hated those days when there was an official luncheon for her to attend, and the fact that she must eat a little of the lunch, whatever it was, to avoid offending her hosts. Such luncheons put her in a bad mood and would mean an extra meal she did not want, which would, in any event, spoil her evening meal.

As she finished the fruit salad, Ai Fah placed a glorious golden finger bowl in front of her mistress. Lee Kyung Koh dipped her long graceful fingers in to the warm water of the bowl, and dried them on the snow white napkin her amah had placed on the table for her.

She finished her coffee. Ai Fah moved to her rear to take the chair away a little from the table, so that her mistress could rise.

A few minutes for her to take off the gorgeous cheongsam, to change again into another samfoo, to turn once more from a Chinese of high birth to just an ordinary Chinese woman, and then Ai Fah would accompany her the short distance to the Golden Lotus Night Club.

No word had passed between the two women during the whole meal, nor was there any praise for the cook amah when Lee Kyung Koh had finished eating. But Ai Fah could see how much the meal had been enjoyed, which she would pass on herself to the cook amah, and woe betide that woman if there was not another roast chicken prepared in the same way for Ai Fah's meal yet to come. A lonely meal tonight as her man was on duty guarding Lee Kyung Koh.

10

AND – A WOMAN FOR EVERY MAN

Carrie Jane, the senior receptionist, was on duty when Rankin came in through the swing doors. She looked up at once, and kept looking, pushing her glasses up on to her forehead, to make sure about what she was looking at.

Rankin grinned as he came up to the desk. He had stayed at the hotel twice before and knew Carrie Jane. She was nice.

She adjusted her glasses, still looking hard at him. "Hell soldier," she exclaimed, "you got your own private war somewhere?"

"Not exactly," he told her, "there was a bad accident on the road coming into Kowloon, and I've been helping the Police."

"Helping them?" she asked, "hell, if that's what you look like helping them, what'll it be like if you was fighting them?"

He looked down at her, grinning still. Carrie Jane was Eurasian, born of a liaison between a British sailor and a Chinese shop girl. A liaison which was short and happy, lasting all of three hectic days and nights, and finishing up with a night spent in a cheap hotel room somewhere along the waterfront of Hong Kong. The next day the main units of the British fleet had up-anchored and gone, and the sailor had never been seen or heard of again.

Carrie Jane had not been told a lot about her father, so wasn't worried about him at all, but she had been well brought up by a doting mother, and equally doting grandparents, none of whom seemed to bother that a young British sailor had left them a permanent souvenir of his shore leave in Hong Kong. She had been taught English at school, but, because of the many American films she watched, and was so passionately fond of, she had purposely developed a trace of an American southern drawl.

Carrie Jane's mother and her parents never knew that the young sailor had tried to keep contact. In the first place, he had overstayed shore leave because of the Chinese girl he had met, and British Naval discipline always frowned on those who could not distinguish between one day and three days authorised shore leave, whilst, because of the girl's poor English, the young man had not known her full name, nor her address. He did write to Naval headquarters to see if she could be found, but she could not be, so, as the Navy did not bring him back to Hong Kong again, time brought forgetfulness.

Carrie Jane was a happy person, and a very competent receptionist, who ran the accommodation of the hotel in a manner which would have made the manager bless all British sailors, had he known of her parentage. He was no fool, and could guess how it all had happened that she was there, and he treated all British sailors well. She had a fantastic memory, and was particularly pleasant to all serving men – British and American, which were the majority of the hotel patrons.

Many, like Rankin now, away from duty for a spell, glad of a reasonable and not expensive hotel room, clean and with the convenience of a shower, toilet and hot and cold running water, except when the water was cut off, due to the water rationing in the Colony, whilst, at an extra cost, the further convenience of a bed mate was readily available.

Carrie Jane was a natural red head and kept her hair nice – she was a girl who believed that money spent on a good hairdo was not wasted. Slim, but well proportioned, she wore dresses, not cheongsams, dresses cut low at the front to expose a fair amount of her firm breasts. She had a pleasant, rather than a lovely, face, with a wide generous mouth and lovely teeth, big brown eyes and a smooth complexion. The pearl rimmed glasses she wore for her poor short eye sight, as well as her clothes and her hair, were evidence of a reasonable affluence. She earned good money, and spent it on herself and on her mother and her grandparents.

"Can I have a room?" he asked her.

"You can," she replied at once, "a good one, with bath and toilet?"

"With bath and toilet," he agreed, knowing well that the bath was a shower and not a bath.

"Just for tonight?"

"No, Miss," he told her, "for two nights."

She looked up at him, the brown eyes soft behind the glasses. She liked the look of him, remembering him well from his previous visits. He was a mighty handsome hunk of man, in her opinion, and she was enjoying this conversation.

"The name's Carrie Jane, like it says here." She lifted a nicely carved ivory name plate from the desk, straightening up, and holding it right to the level of his eyes and right in front of him, then lowered it back to the desk again,." And I'm not a Miss – I'm married."

He was enjoying it all too, and knew she was in a very good mood. Her stance, bending a little low over the reception desk before she had straightened up, gave him a good view down the front of her dress – as he knew she knew.

"I'm sure you are," he said softly, "the lovely women always are."

She looked straight at him. "That's a nice thing to say, real nice, if you mean it."

"I'm a truthful lad," equally softly this time as before. "And as far as you're concerned, I mean it."

She kept looking at him, stood straight up. He could see her eyes were moist. Yes, she was really nice –

"I sure think you do mean it," she told him, her voice soft and warm, "and that is nice."

She pushed a large book across to him, turning it round as she did so.

"I have to have the details," she said, handing him a pen.

He didn't take his gaze from her as he took the pen, making sure, as he was certain she wanted to make sure, that their fingers touched.

"Fair enough, Carrie Jane, I've nothing to hide," he told her, then let his eyes drop to the book, filled in his rank and name, but not his unit or address, then turned the book round to her again.

"Rankin," she read out what he had written. "Sergeant David Rankin." She looked up at him again – "English?"

"Welsh," he replied, then added, "much the same in a way."

"It isn't," she said, "I know that."

"Have you been to England?" he asked.

"Sure have," but it was a big white lie, and then quickly, to avoid the obvious questions he could ask her, "but it was only passing through really."

But he didn't ask anymore about that, but took up his grip.

"You looking for company?" she asked him.

"No," he said, very abruptly, knowing the comforts which could be provided in the hotel.

She hadn't meant it like that, however, and knew at once she had said the wrong thing, and acted fast to rectify it, "I don't mean a sleeping partner," she paused – "I meant . . ." she stopped, not knowing quite how to finish it.

He was puzzled. Her question, which he had thought meant paying for a prostitute who could be brought in, had put a stop to the intimate conversation they had been enjoying.

"You mean what, Carrie Jane?" But his voice was soft again, and had lost the abruptness, and she knew she could bring the conversation back to the way it had been.

"Well, I thought you and me might go somewhere. I know the right places, they won't frighten you and won't cost you a fortune."

Rankin was genuinely pleased, he felt it was a sincere invitation, made shyly, which, in a way, was strange for someone he knew must be a worldly woman. It couldn't be tonight though. He was going to the Golden Lotus, and that really was the reason for this bit of leave in Hong Kong.

"Thanks, Carrie Jane, I'd like that, but it can't be tonight I have to go over to Hong Kong."

She didn't change her expression, and he couldn't tell if she was disappointed, but her business instincts were aroused at once, "To Hong Kong, hell Sergeant Rankin, you'd better be thinking of getting over there right away. Hold it a minute."

She picked up the telephone from her desk, and was soon speaking in rapid Chinese, with her right hand making all sorts of movements to emphasise some of her points. He waited for her, whatever it was it had to do with him, he was sure. Gosh, she was nice to look at – the pearl rimmed glasses didn't take anything away from her. A night out with her would be fun, she would be excellent company, and she would, as she had said, know the right places to go. He needn't really go to Hong Kong, or did he? There were many decent places in Kowloon she and he could go to. But then, his military training came up within him, he had come to go over to Hong Kong, and he would stick with that, but tomorrow night perhaps—

She put the telephone down.

"That was the ferry," she explained, "I sure thought with this typhoon coming up, they might be stopping, but they say not. They're all right and they do say the wind will drop, but there'll be a hell of a lot of rain. Take my advice though, sergeant, don't leave it too long, they've been wrong before."

"Thanks a lot," Rankin said, his eyes still taking her all in. She was a honey, nice figure, nice smile, nice teeth, nice everything he could bet. He wasn't a ladies man, but he ought to take her up on that outing together, after all, she had made the offer.

"Tell you what," he continued, "if you could make that a date for tomorrow night, it would be very nice."

He was sure she flushed a little, and that again was a surprise to him.

"You're sure about that?" she asked.

"I am if you are, but what about that husband of yours, what will he say?"

She smiled broadly, "I haven't seen him for a year, he's in America or somewhere, and I sure won't try to find him to ask him."

"Right then," he said, the decision made, "tomorrow night, what time?"

"It'll be late," she replied, "I have to be around tomorrow night, like every night – and every morning. In the morning it's a big time for business. I have to see the bills are paid, sometimes some of our guests don't want to pay" – Rankin could imagine it. "And at night I watch for who they try to bring in – we don't allow any girls in here unless we bring them in, and they have to be certified – so it'll be round about nine, nine thirty, OK?"

"That'll suit me, I'll look forward to it, and thanks, for everything." He pushed his face close to hers, "You're a smasher," and turned to move away.

She watched him go, not understanding the term, "smasher", but then suddenly shouted after him – "Hell, sergeant, I forgot about that uniform of yours, leave it on the bed in the morning. I'll have the amah wash it good."

He stopped and turned around.•, "Thanks again, Carrie Jane," he shouted back, "You *are* a smasher."

In his room he thought over what she had told him. Of course she was right about the girls – the prostitutes – and the hotel would make a good commission. He had got hot under the collar when she had asked him did he want company. He was glad he had been wrong in his thoughts of what she might have meant. Prostitutes were not for him – thank God.

How naive she had been in her manner, and how shy, throughout most of their conversation. It was a bit of a puzzle for him, but she seemed very sincere towards him, and he was looking forward to that night out with her. It was about time he enjoyed some female company.

It was not until he was over eighteen years of age, a strong healthy young man, that he came to realise what sex was, but he had known about it a long time before that.

His was a closely knit family, and his eldest brother, James, had always been his idol. Much of David's good behaviour and good manners came from the example set by James, as well as from the care and affection of his parents.

It was one evening at home, and James, who was the family chiropodist, was cutting David's toe nails on the younger brother's single bed in the room they shared. David was then nearly fourteen years of age, and very inquisitive.

"How do babies get born, James?" he asked.

James looked down at his young brother, lying flat on his back on the bed. If he was surprised at the question, he did not show it, his face did not alter one bit.

"Why do you want to know?"

The young lad pushed himself up with his hands behind his back on the bed, and waited a minute before replying, "Well, Cyril Davies says when a nipper's going to be born, its mother has her belly opened and out pops the baby."

"Does she now?" James mused, still very serious, examining the toes on the boy's left closely. "Does she now?"

"Well, that's what Cyril says," David said, "right from her belly button to her fanny, and out comes the baby."

This time James did laugh. "So that's what you young lads call it – fanny, eh," he said, "and that's how it happens."

"I don't know, James," David was truthful, "but Cyril says he knows, and his mom's had enough babies, hasn't she?"

"She has that," agreed James, and went on trimming the nails carefully.

"Well, is that what happens?" David asked again after a while.

"No, not quite," James told him, "but I think our Dad should tell you what does happen, he knows better than me at any rate – I'll have a word with him."

So that was it until a few days later when his father explained it all to him. He came up to the bedroom in the evening to sit at the side of David's bed, as he often did, especially when David had been playing football in the afternoon, and on those occasions, the two of them would have a quiet talk together, in the peace of the bedroom, and away from the women of the family.

But he didn't talk about football that evening.

He was quiet and sincere, as was always his manner, as he carefully explained all the mysteries of the human body of both males and females, then went on to the mating act, and finally, to how babies are born.

His youngest son listened with great interest. They were wonderful times for him, up here in the simple plainly furnished bedroom, with a picture over both beds – that of the younger brother tucked away in the corner, and of the elder brother right under the window.

"You remember that time Bella had her kittens?" his father asked, "can you remember I had to pull a couple of the kittens out of Bella?"

He did remember it. Bella was the family cat, and it was something forever stamped on his memory, to watch his father pulling those tiny kittens, seemingly out of the backside of the cat.

"Do they have to pull babies out like that then, Da?" And before his father had time to answer that question – "Did I have to be pulled out of Mom?"

His father continued the boy's further education in simple terms, answering the various questions put to him quite honestly.

Another evening he went on to the subject of venereal disease, in the same honest straightforward way. "Sometimes men and women do the mating act when they are not married, and that's a sin, although a lot of people don't seem to think so nowadays. Then sometimes, especially on the continent, men pay women to do it with them – those women are called prostitutes. There are some prostitutes in the big cities here – in Swansea and Cardiff, for instance, though they are not supposed to be encouraged, but there's a lot more of them in the cities like London, and everywhere on the continent. In France, and in Germany, and those other countries, a man can go to a special house – it's called a brothel – pay his money and choose a woman to sleep with. Though he doesn't go there to sleep with one, he goes to have sexual intercourse with her."

This was still all very interesting to David, although the continent was, to him, somewhere far distant, a place of mystery and intrigue, and he wasn't at all surprised to hear about these brothel houses they had there.

"Have you ever done that, Da?"

Even this did not flummox his father, "No, never son, and I never will, and I shouldn't advise you to do it when you grow up, in fact I trust you won't ever. Some of those sort of women have a bad disease. It's known as venereal disease, very contagious and very bad." He went on to explain it all.

David tried to discuss his new learned knowledge again with James, but his brother was no more talkative about it than before. "It doesn't interest me yet, David," he told his young brother, quite severely. "I can wait until I get married, and you just see that you wait too." David was certain that, as far as big brother James was concerned, there was nothing more to be discussed about the subject.

He continued to talk about it at times with his father. There never seemed anything wrong in doing so, and his father never discouraged an honest question, and always gave his son a truthful and correct reply.

He put Cyril Davies and the other boys at school right about the mysteries, and he was sorry for them that their fathers did not seem to be able to talk to them in the same way as his father did with him. He felt so proud of his father, and pleased that he was being told the truth about these things which, after all, were a part of life. To him, it didn't seem a subject to be hidden, but as he grew older, he found that it was much of a secret to most people, and not to be generally discussed when there were women about.

Certain newspapers and books were not allowed in the house, and he never heard his father, or James, use a wrong word to his mother and sisters, or in their presence. He sometimes wondered had his mother told his sisters all about everything, as his father had told him. He hoped she had, otherwise, as his father had put it, they were surely in grave danger from ignorance.

"It's much worse for a woman than for a man, David," his father had said. "There's many a nice girl been taken in by a man, told her he would marry her all right, she's let him do the sex act with her – just once – and taffy oh – she's pregnant. It's a terrible thing when that happens. It means they have to get married, but sometimes the man just clears off and leaves the poor girl on her own."

He learned that drink could be a big factor in sex. How drink excited a person, made some quarrelsome, made some moody, made others merry, and how it often happened that a young man would take his girl friend into a pub for a couple of drinks – "port and lemon," his father said – then for a walk up in the hills, as a preliminary to the sex act. This didn't mean much to David, he had never been into a public house, though he had seen a lot of drunkenness from time to time, and he knew his father and James enjoyed a drink, and the odd visit to the local pub.

During their conversations, his father spoke about the sex act, or a mating, and sometimes sexual intercourse, but the lads at school called it several other more lurid names. As the years passed, and he remained in the company of the lads he had been at school with, it came to be no secret which of them was having sex, which girl would perform, if a lad was prepared to take her out a time or two, and how you could get it fairly easy if you frequented some of the popular places in Swansea, but David was aloof from it all. His football, his job and his family, were the important things in his life, and he was aware a lot of the great stories the lads came out with were all bravado and not really true.

The lads in the football team continued to make the usual jokes about venereal disease and about sex, but David knew there was no truth in the talk that, if you got VD, the organ would drop off, though he knew that it was very serious, and he considered it stupid if you placed yourself in any danger of it.

In the winter, he kept fit for his football, and the summer was a time of much wandering around the local hills and valleys, when he had time, always on his own, keeping fit and getting to know many local farmers and shepherds. He was pleased he had his job with the Henshalls and that he wasn't of a family of farmers, it seemed to be a very hard life, even if it was healthy. He wasn't as keen on cricket as were his father and James, but sometimes he would spend a day at the county ground in Swansea watching Glamorgan play. A good outing it always was, taking their own lunch in a big bag his father carried, hard boiled egg sandwiches, and home made sausage rolls, and pies, made by his mother or his sisters, and very enjoyable, even though the cricket was a bit slow, he thought.

In the last year of his schooldays, he started a morning paper round for Albert and Alice Henshall who kept the local store and paper shop. It was a good job for a lad who was always an early riser like him, and they provided him with a brand new bicycle, whilst it also meant some money of his own. He talked over the finance with his father, and saved as much as he could, needing only a few shillings a week for his pocket money to spend at the Youth Club or the pictures, whilst he could borrow all the books he wanted from the shop free.

When he left school he went full time into the employment of the Henshalls, who badly needed a willing lad to cope with the increase in their business. He did the paper round every morning, then went home for a few hours, and had his midday meal with his mother and sisters. Every afternoon except Saturday, he was back at the shop until it closed at seven p.m., helping in everything, serving, running errands, and re-stocking the shelves. It was a friendly place, doing an excellent trade, and there was tea for the three of them – Albert, Alice and he at four o'clock, with lovely home made scones and cake baked by Alice.

Now he was receiving a weekly wage, quite a fair sum, and paid his mother for his keep, bought his own clothes, and still saved some money. It was a happy home life, though James was often away in Swansea for weeks at a time working in the electrical firm he had joined, which gave David a room to himself, almost, and the family prospered. His mother was a very good cook, and she was passing this knowledge on at any rate, to his two sisters, so they ate well, whilst, in the outside world, things still continued to improve after those grim war years about which David knew so little, as he had been so young.

He thought more and more about joining the Army, and anything military was of great interest to him. His father had served in the Royal Army Service Corps in the war, and it was the stories he told David about his service, some of which had been in Egypt, which brought on the thoughts of a more active life, and one in which he was told there would be ample opportunity for sporting activities, and for seeing a bit of the world.

He played football for the village team in the Swansea and District League, so his name was often in the local weekly newspaper. He received every encouragement from his father, who watched him in every game, helped run the village team, and knew that, even this early, Swansea were watching the boy.

Saturdays were grand days. David finished work at midday and would have a light meal at home, generally a couple of poached eggs on toast, before he and his father went off to the match. If it was an away match, the coach owned by Dai Lewis, would be waiting at the club for the team and the supporters, all paying one and sixpence each, even the players to help pay expenses.

After the match, it was a steak and kidney pudding tea at the Rankin home. With baked potatoes, peas and cabbage, home made bread, and strong tea, with his mother never failing to say, at least once – "We must feed our David after the match", but he would soon have to be back at the shop, calling at the bus stop at the other side of the road to meet the evening bus from Swansea bringing the football papers, eagerly awaited by the males of the village at the shop.

Later, it would be an hour or two at the club with the lads, when they would all talk about what they should have done to their opponents that afternoon, but hadn't done, and how it would all be different next Saturday.

He was early to bed on a Saturday night as well – Sunday brought a big paper round, and when that was done, and, after a late breakfast, they all went off to church to morning service – mostly now without James, who could seldom get home at weekends.

Life was good, the village was growing, more houses were being built, and more and more people were coming out from Swansea to live in the surrounding villages, such as this one.

One morning, Albert Henshall collapsed in the shop. Alice and David got him into the back room and laid him flat on the couch, and David ran his fastest to bring Doctor Stanley. It was a heart attack, and they remembered that his father had died of a weak heart. Not serious, the doctor said – Albert would have to take great care from now on, but he would last a long time yet.

So Alice took over complete control of the shop, with David, at sixteen years of age, her assistant. A new single bed was bought for Albert, and put up in the back room, as he was not allowed to climb stairs, whilst a new bathroom, with a toilet, had to be built in the back yard, with the door to it where the window had been.

Albert could do a bit in the shop, and sit doing the accounts in the back room, which was now his office, as well as a bedroom, but no lifting, no carrying – all this became David's work. David did not go home to dinner, and he would have this in the kitchen, whilst Alice carried Albert's meals in to him in the back room. He realised what a great difference Albert's illness had made, he was now very much a part of the Henshall's life and their plans, so, for a while, thoughts of the Army receded into the background.

Albert began to teach him the accounts, and suggested David should go off to night classes at Swansea, to take a course on simple accounting. His family greeted this with great enthusiasm, and David put up with it twice a week for their sakes, and because Albert thought it necessary. On other nights, after the shop closed, he spent a lot of time with Albert, playing draughts, learning to play chess, and they became very close.

As soon as David was eighteen, Alice began teaching him to drive the car, a Wolseley, kept in wonderful running order by Dai Lewis at the garage down the hill. They used the car a lot one way and the other for business, and it was essential for someone other than Alice to drive. She was a good teacher, and he an excellent pupil, so he passed the driving test in Swansea at the first attempt, which pleased them all.

But Albert's health was deteriorating. His slow walks in the open air on fine days to see his mother down in the crescent were fewer. He never went in the shop, and was often in bed for days at a spell. He passed the accounts over completely to David. People came less often to visit him, so David spent even more time with him, keeping him up to date with all the news of the village, whilst Albert, for his part, preferred David's company to anyone else, even to Alice.

The village knew of his condition, knew he was failing fast, and it was no surprise to anyone, least of all to Alice and David when it happened.

It was a hot, sultry morning in July when Alice came in to the shop in great anxiety. He knew what it was before she spoke –

"He's been in the bathroom a long time, David, the door's locked and he hasn't answered me – I've been calling and calling—"

David brushed past her into the back – "stay here a minute, Alice," he said, but he knew what he would find, and he had often told Albert not to lock that door.

He had to use all his strength to force the door open. Albert lay sprawled on the floor, face down alongside the bath, having obviously toppled head forward off the toilet seat. David had no doubt he was dead.

It was at the funeral, four days later, stood on the other side of the open grave to her, that he became vividly aware of Alice.

Alice Henshall – Alice James before she had married Albert – was his mother's youngest cousin, and had known David all her life. She had been his teacher at Sunday School, and, though he couldn't remember it, he had been present at church when she had married Albert, and, afterwards, at the reception his parents had put on at the Rankin home, made necessary because her own mother and father had died soon after each other a year before the wedding, and Alice had no other family.

It had been Auntie Alice in those days, and Auntie Alice until just two years ago, when she had told him to drop the Auntie and call her Alice.

She was a kind, pleasant person, with a very warm nature, and both she and Albert had always been very good to him, taken him into their business, treated him almost as their son, and it was in this manner he had thought of himself until now.

Now he wasn't thinking that way at all, his thoughts were far different. Good Lord, I fancy her – I do fancy her. Whatever would his mother and father say if they knew, and what would Alice say? What a thing for him to be thinking about when they were burying her husband – Albert, with whom he had been so friendly.

He looked across at Alice, only at her, the sunshine on her brightly, so that he could see her clearly, even though his eyes were wet with tears. She must be thirty-nine or forty, he judged, and he wasn't yet nineteen. She was in deep black, of course, and though she wasn't a beauty, she was nice. A bit plump, perhaps, especially her top half, but she had nice legs, and always looked clean and fresh and tidy.

Heavens, it was true – it wasn't just natural sympathy for her at her loss – his loss too – he was really gone on her.

11

IN WONDERLAND – WITH ALICE

Rankin had often wondered why it had all happened, and that it had been so wonderful for both of them.

He finished shaving and rubbed his smooth chin – he used an electric razor, and found this ideal in the humidity of Hong Kong, where it was necessary to shave twice a day, and not harmful or wearisome to do so with an electric razor.

He was thinking of Alice now. The pleasant encounter with Carrie Jane, and the promise of tomorrow with her, had brought his thoughts back to the only woman he had ever known.

Alice had been good for him, and he for her, and he knew that she had kept him on the 'straight and narrow', as his Father would have said. Because of her, he hadn't been interested in other girls, not even when he was away from her after he finally joined the Army. Not even during his time in Hong Kong, where there were temptations galore, and some very nice temptations at that, and he had hardly thought of another woman until Carrie Jane tonight.

The first realisation of his feelings for Alice as they were lowering Albert into his grave had shocked him and worried him for a long time.

He had no girl friends, never wanted one, though some of his pals had been courting since they were fifteen and sixteen. Happy and content in his home life within his family, and in his job with the Henshalls, he had never thought of a girl, but now it had come right at him – wallop – and it was something big to worry about.

So it did worry him, more than he could ever have thought, and much more than he cared to admit to himself, as the summer went and he settled down to his new life in the shop, with much more responsibility and almost as a partner to Alice, working alongside her, very close to her, every day of his life. It was so frightening to know what his feelings for her really were.

Football began again. Previously the passing of summer and the coming of the football season had been a time of great joy to him, but not so much this year. He soon realised he wasn't playing with anything like the zest he usually put into his game, and others realised it also, but they didn't know the reason. He managed to keep that to himself.

His father was as puzzled as anyone. "Do you think you're working too hard at the shop, David? Perhaps all those nights doing the accounts are making you stale."

"Could be, Da." he replied, "but I feel fit enough. Don't forget some of these teams are playing me hard now they know me. Don't worry, I'll get over it, I'll be all right."

This was true – he had acquired quite a reputation in the League, and he was a marked man on the field. Young as he was, he could hold his own physically, but some of the older players he was coming up against knew more than he did about the game. He took hard knocks, they were a part of football, but he came in for more than his share of late tackles, tackles over the ball, and being pulled down from behind. He finished most games battered and bruised, but took everything in good spirit – too good a spirit, some of the lads told him – and never resorted to foul means, or retaliation, he was not that type. He kept doing his best, but the results were not as good as the two previous seasons, and he wasn't playing as well as he had done.

It wasn't the work or the nights spent on the accounts, nights when he and she were alone in the house, that worried and upset him. It was the ever growing feeling he had for her, wanting her more and more. Hard as he tried to suppress his feelings, telling himself it was utterly impossible, and would ruin their lives, it was terrible with her always so close to him. He was sure his parents hadn't realised the truth, or his father would have spoken to him in his usual frank manner, and it was something he could not, and dare not, speak to his father about.

Alice was a much smarter person than she had been. She wore her skirts shorter, wore nicer stockings. She was slimmer, had a weekly visit to the hairdresser, where his younger sister, Mary worked. The perfume she used was devastating and different from that she had previously used. She had been sensible about the loss of Albert. It had happened, and she had to look forward, not back. She was very friendly with all the customers, as pleasant with him as she had ever been, and did not go out very much.

When she did go out in the evenings, it was generally to the Rankin house, to see his mother and sister Mary, and especially when his sister, Elsie, was home on the two days she was allowed every second week, from the hospital in Swansea. She would leave about ten o'clock, and most nights he walked her home and left her outside, or inside, the shop. On occasions, she would hold his arm or his hand for a moment or two, as she thanked him and said goodnight, sending the shocks flying through him, and heightening the desire for her.

They worked so closely together, and he still stayed at the shop for his midday meal, when they closed the shop for an hour and ate their meal together in the back room, which was now again a lounge. He purposely often stood closer to her than he need have done, and she never seemed to mind, whilst, now and then, she gave him a little hug, if she was especially pleased about something, and it sent the blood racing through him, so he thought he must burst.

She must know, he told himself, she really must. She was charming to him in every way, and they never failed to agree on anything. They were a perfect team in the shop, he was in complete control of the newspaper side, and had two boys to do the paper rounds. He was there very early each morning, sorting out the rounds, finding time to make a pot of tea for himself and the boys in the kitchen, then sending the boys off and shouting up the stairs to Alice there was a fresh brew made for her to come down to. He went home then for breakfast, and was back for half past ten, and, in the meantime, Alice opened the shop at nine o'clock, sometimes earlier.

If they were busy, the two of them would serve in the shop together, but she always had time to do all her housework, and cook a good midday meal for them both. Sundays, he was in early to sort out the rounds, and go home to breakfast, after which the family would go to church. Alice ran the shop on Sunday mornings, until midday, and then came to the Rankins for her Sunday dinner, and often spent the rest of the day with them.

By early winter, only David and Mary lived at home with their parents. Elsie was courting strongly with a young chemist in Swansea, and spent quite a lot of her off-duty time at his house with his family, and though James had his own car, his visits were infrequent, but the family spirit remained very strong, and they made Alice a part of it.

It made it so much harder for David that he was in such close contact with Alice every day. His longing for her grew, his football suffered, and, hard as he tried not to show it, his parents knew there was something wrong with him, and they worried and talked about it together, and couldn't understand what was wrong.

His mother brought it up one Sunday. "I'm sure you're working David too hard at the shop, Alice," she said, "he seems so listless these days, isn't that right, Dad?"

David blushed and protested; "Oh no, Mom, that's wrong. I don't work any harder than Alice does."

Alice was concerned. "Do you really think so?" she asked, and turned to David. "Perhaps it's true, David, you never stop do you, and me being with you every day, I don't notice it." Then back to his mother, "I'm glad you told me, I can do a bit more in the shop myself."

David kept up his protest, "Don't worry, Alice," he told her, "I'm all right, I really am, and I enjoy it – it's good to be so busy, besides you work very hard yourself."

But it had gone home, as his mother had meant it should, and Alice began to spend more time with David in the shop. This didn't help at all, as it brought them even more in close contact.

She watched him closely and seriously. There was no doubt he did enjoy the work. He was good with customers, and very popular. He was a very nice young man, and then she knew he wasn't a young man anymore. He was a man, and a very attractive man at that. Big, strong, good complexion, healthy, cheerful, happy, how lucky she was to have him with her.

Not only because he's such a good worker, she told herself, and such an asset to the business, but because he is a man, and it was so nice to have him around the house, and be with him. He meant an awful lot to her, and his presence had helped her a very great deal in all her troubles. She began to think much more about him, and knew she was very fond of him.

David was thinking again about the Army. It would take him away from her and, though it would be hard at first, he just had to get away. If he didn't, he would get hold of her one day, he knew that would come, and then what? Heavens, she would be furious, and it would ruin everything.

But, would she be furious? Perhaps, and perhaps not. He didn't know anything about women, but he remembered some of the things his father had told him about their clever ways, how they chased a man, without making it obvious that they were doing the chasing, and sometimes not realising they were doing the chasing. Look at Alice now, she was much more attractive than when Albert was alive. It was true she had gone through a lot of worry about him, but she was now very different. What had brought this about? According to his father, it would certainly be a man. If this was so, who was it?

He checked through all those he knew in the village, all the customers, and was sure it was none of them. She didn't go out anywhere on her own, and, if she did go to Swansea, it was in the car with his mother or Mary, so it wasn't someone outside the village. It wasn't one of the many travellers who called at the shop, though she was nice with all of them, but nothing more – he was sure of that. So, who was it, if it was anybody, could it be him? Was the change, the improvement because of him? Gosh, it couldn't be, it just couldn't be –

He spoke to his father about the Army, in the same way as he discussed everything with him, everything except his feelings for Alice.

"It is a good life, David, and it would suit you." His father wasn't against it at all. "You'll have to go soon to do your national service, so why not wait till then. Give it a go, and if it is what you want, then it's up to you and you can sign on as a regular. Think it over a while, after all, you've got a good job here, and we don't want to lose you. Besides, you might not like the Army, some don't, but if it is your choice, then you make the decision – Mom and me won't oppose you."

That was right, he knew, perhaps it was because he was under such a strain here that he wanted to join up, perhaps he might not like it, would regret it. His father was right, he would think it over, but he thought it only fair to tell Alice.

"I'm thinking of joining the Army, Alice," he told her one day when they were having their dinner together. "I'll have to go soon in any case, but I thought it might be a good thing if I joined on what they call a regular engagement."

It was a big surprise to her, and a shock, and she showed it, "Oh, David, I would miss you," she exclaimed, and he knew it was the truth.

"Whatever I'll do without you I can't think, and the village would miss you, and the club, and your mother and father. We'd all miss you."

He was pleased in a way, and could tell by her face that it was a big shock to her. He knew her very well, and it had been a big blow, though she too knew he would have to go and do his national service almost at any time now. But she could have only been thinking about the business and the shop.

It was more than the shop, and more than the business, and she knew it. She had begun to think so from that moment his mother had first mentioned her feelings that Sunday, when she had thought her first reaction had been concern for him, but it was more than concern, there was a lot more to it than that.

The last few years had been busy ones, the shop had grown, business boomed, her finances were good, but her own life had been hard work, and not brimming full of joy. It had been a happy and companionable marriage to Albert, but one without real passion, as he had never been a great lover. Life had been difficult for her through Albert's long illness, and even before that, and though she had the satisfaction of a job well done, something had been missing, and she had no doubt now what that something was.

She knew also what was troubling David, could tell now by his every action, by this action of wanting to join the Army, and it pleased her. It was silly, impossible really, but very pleasing to know he thought about her as a woman.

She hadn't thought anyone would do again, though she had thought there could come a time when she could love again, but – oh God; it can't be David – he's so young, young enough to be my son.

It *was* David, and she was well aware of it. She had no doubt at all what his thoughts were about her. It was all so plain now, in his eyes, in the way he stood so close to her, in the way he was so eager to help her and be with her. It was a ridiculous situation, she knew that, but inside her, just a little part of her, or a big part of her, knew that he was a splendid man, and he wanted her, and – oh, my God – she wanted him.

He realised she had changed, she was nearer to him, warmer with him in a way she had never been before. Walking her home the first night after he had told her of wanting to join the Army, he had put his hand in her coat pocket and found her hand, without gloves, warm and responsive, and from then on, he knew they were very close to each other. He was content to wait for her now – he didn't know how to start anything, and she knew so very much more than him, if he was right about her now, and he was sure he was, she would make the first move.

The Sunday night before Christmas, he walked her home in the rain, and she opened the door of the shop, letting him in with her to say goodnight. She stood very close to him, he could smell the perfume of her, knew the warmth of her, and she could tell by his tenseness what he was feeling about her.

"Thank you, David," she said, her face close to him, her breath against his mouth.

He did not speak, could not speak, did not know what to say.

She put her hands on his shoulders, reached up high on her toes to him, and kissed him, gently, tenderly . . .

She felt him gasp, knew the breath had all drawn up inside him, but his arms did not move. She turned him to the door which she had left open. "Goodnight now," softly, very softly, "see you tomorrow" – and, as he went, she pushed the door shut and stood against it – waiting – tense.

Oh, if he turns back now –

He didn't turn back, he was dazed with it all, and it was a minute or two before he realised where he was going, and before he recovered himself.

She had kissed him, the first time ever, the first time any girl, except his sisters. It had been lovely, it had made him feel like – well, he couldn't rightly think how it made him feel – but she had kissed him.

After a while, Alice locked the door quietly, went through the shop to the lounge, put on the light, and went into the kitchen, taking off her wet coat.

What had she done? What was the matter with her? You fool, she told herself, it's David – you must be quite mad – you fool – you utter fool.

She slept little that night, and was surprised to find David so calm the next day, and, as if nothing had happened.

It mustn't happen again, she told herself, it mustn't, it mustn't, it mustn't, and was very determined it wouldn't, and was glad it was a busy time for them both in the shop, and there was nothing unusual in David's behaviour.

She spent Christmas Day with the Rankins. James was home, but

Elsie away and on duty at the hospital. It was a good day, and good to think of an extra day off from the shop tomorrow – Boxing Day, but she was disappointed that James got up when it was time for her to go home, and said he would walk down the road with her and David.

She didn't show the disappointment, and was, in a way, pleased to have two men take her home, so it was a happy threesome, laughing and joking, with her arm in arm between the two brothers. Outside the shop she kissed them both – James first. Her kiss for David was quite different to the one for James, and she knew then, as she had known before, that she wanted him to put his arms around her and return the kiss, but, of course, he could not do that tonight.

Oh, my God; she told herself up in her room – I want him. Oh, good Lord, forgive me, please don't let me want him.

She nearly decided not to go back to the Rankins the next day, telling herself all through a sleepless night that it would be wrong to do so. But she put all that away from her the next day, and when it was time to go so she would be in time for the meal, she went gladly, gaily, and looking very attractive in a new blue coat and matching hat she had recently bought.

James left for Swansea early in the evening, so David walked her home alone that night. It was early, just after nine o'clock, when she said it was time for her to go.

"I haven't had any exercise all day," David told his mother and father and Mary, more than her, "so I'll walk Alice home, then I'll go along the road a bit as far as Harvey's farm. Must have a bit of a walk, blow the cobwebs away, an' I've eaten too much – our Mom's such a good cook."

They walked to the shop in silence, his hand in her pocket holding her hand, warm and responsive. There was magic in the air – a cold crisp night, the moon more than half full, and frost around in plenty. There was not another person about, the only sound that of their feet – it was as if they were in a world of their own.

David's heart was pounding. She had looked wonderful all day, whilst the little smiles and glances between the two of them were sure evidence of an ever growing intimacy. He felt tremendous, it was glorious to be warmly arm in arm with this wonderful person.

They went in through the front door of the shop, as they had done the previous Sunday night, but this time, David pushed the door to and the yale lock clicked home. He followed her through the shop ,with just the light of the street lamp outside to give some illumination, into the lounge, where again he pushed the door shut behind him.

She turned to him at once, in the dark, putting her hands on his shoulders, exactly as she had done that previous time, reached up, and kissed him, letting her lips remain on his.

His lips came open slightly, not a lot, he really didn't know how to kiss, but it was nice, soft lips and his chin smooth. She opened her mouth a little more, and his lips came open with hers. He drew his body a little away from her, and undid the big buttons of her coat, put his arms inside the coat, and behind her back to draw her close to him again. He was breathing hard, enchanted, amazed, in a world he had never known before.

His hands came slowly down her back to her buttocks, pressing her in against him low. They held the kiss for minutes, mouths more open now, and her tongue gently probing. She could feel his firmness against her, and gently began to ease her body against him, slowly, from side to side. Her left hand reached round from his right shoulder to stroke the back of his neck.

How strong he is, she thought, as he held her to him, how wonderfully strong. Their mouths were very wet, and she was moaning. "David – oh, David." She forced the lower part of her body right into him, enjoying the feel of his strength against her. He eased a little away from her to bring his right hand from her buttocks to her left breast, but still held her very firm with his left arm and hand.

Her mouth came right open, as his fingers gently massaged the underside of her breast, and she forced her tongue right back into his mouth –

Her desire, her eagerness, engulfed him and amazed him. He had not thought it would be like this. It was devastating, supreme, everything it ought to be, and more. He had thought she would be quite passive, and he would need to rouse her, but she was all his for him to take, and her wanting for him equal to his need for her.

"David," she moaned – "Oh, David – dooooooooon't – David."

They might as well have got in the car, driven to the Mumbles, and tried to hold back the incoming tide as try to stop the tide of passion which had risen within them both.

She eased her mouth away from him –

"Let's go upstairs," she said, her voice tense and commanding.

She had not put on any lights, but it was lighter in the bedroom than it had been downstairs, because of the street light shining in the window. She did not pull the curtains.

"We'd better get undressed," she told him, and took a dressing gown off a hook at the back of the door.

She undressed quickly, throwing her clothes on to a chair under the window. He could clearly see her back and bottom, very white, before she put on the dressing gown.

"I'll be back in a minute," she told him, moving past him to go out the door. When she came back, with a towel in her hand, he was standing in his shirt and trousers.

"Quickly David," she said, and got into the bed. He took his shoes off, and the remainder of his clothes, as fast as he could.

"This side," she told him, holding the bed clothes down for him to move in beside her.

His eyes were used to the light, and he could see her white body exposed to him. She had opened her dressing gown but was still lying in it. For the first time ever, he was looking at a nude woman, and his eyes took in her full breasts, and the large patch of pubic hair, jet black against her skin. He eased carefully down alongside her – surprisingly calm. This much he knew, he just had to stay calm, or he would spoil it all.

He lay on his left side against her, and she moved half right to him. He put his left arm under her head, knew he had not to get on top of her just yet, and moved his mouth down to find hers. Her mouth was wide open for him, her tongue darting in and out of his mouth – it was lovely.

He rubbed his right hand on the sheet beyond her body – "my hand is cold," he managed to say, then he brought it back to her body. She gasped with the cold of it.

"Do you know what to do?" she asked.

"I think so," he replied.

"Have you done it before?"

"Oh no, Alice," he almost protested – "you're the first woman I've ever seen like this."

"Oh, David," she said, and she was smiling and very happy. She pulled his head down to her again, smothering his face with kisses for a while, and moved her left leg over him to hold him into her with the back of it.

"We'll just have to make sure it's nice for you . . ."

It had been nice for him, very nice, and he knew it had been nice for her also. Delightful, thrilling and so satisfying, a wonderful experience, and complete ecstasy, a togetherness that neither of them could have dreamed of in their wildest dreams. A supreme passion for each other with the utmost opportunity to indulge themselves to the full.

Alice had told him she had never thought this was possible, that she would find so much strength in a man, and one so willing and happy to give it all to her as often as she would take it. It made him feel very proud that she thought him so wonderful a lover.

She brought out a book she had purchased many years before, not long after she had married Albert, and which she had hoped would help them, but it was not to be, as Albert was not interested and thought it vulgar. She and David had studied it together – the full descriptions and pictures of the various positions 'married couples were advised to try', and they tried out each position without shame of any kind, enjoying each other and delighting in the harmony of their intimate association.

She taught him so much, and learned so much from him, both so close and so very together in their love. They found so much satisfaction in the afterglow the book had taught them, when he would lie within her after their climax, playing and caressing, whispering sweet talk to each other, until his strength returned to him again and it was time for more love.

They had long talks about the association, and were surprised they each enjoyed their love making without any real sense of guilt, or wrong doing. For the first few days after the Boxing Day night, when they had first come together, Alice was very worried, and had told herself it could not go on. But it had gone on, better and better, more joyous in every way, so doubt receded as day followed day, and she bloomed in the full glory of their love.

As he was rampant and sure with her, strong and dominant, masterful yet tender, so this became his whole character. His powers on the football field returned with a rush, he was so tremendously happy, his life so full, and it was something to get out on that football field and show them all how he could play. No longer was there any worry for him. His father, his friends, the team, knew that David Rankin was right back to the top of his form, and he was the talk of local football. Swansea were watching him again, and his father was approached about a trial for him down at Vetch Field.

The real reason for it all, their happiness, was known only to them, though they were astonished that no one, not even his parents, had any idea of their association. Much time as David spent at the shop, it was nothing more than usual. Alice quickly learned to do the accounts, taking them over from him, and keeping them up to date in the afternoons, so that the evening time could be spent in their lovemaking, and though they would have wished to spend more time together, they did not do so. When she came to the Rankin house, it was the same as it had always been, and when he walked her home, they would say goodnight outside the shop with not a kiss in parting.

It had to be that way. Had she offered her lips to him, as she wanted to do, the desire would have flooded them both at once, so they knew, if the secret was to be kept, and it had to be kept, their time together was only the time David normally spent at the shop, so there was never the slightest thought within the village of what was really happening with the two of them.

He remembered, when he had been called up to do his national service, Alice had acted very sensibly. He had to go, and that was that, and as much as they missed each other, they could wait until he was on leave, and anyway, the two years would soon pass, and he would be home again. What they would do after that they didn't think about, all that was for the future.

When he first came on leave, it was as though they had never been apart, their love making resumed naturally, and as passionately as before, but when he was away from her, he thought about their situation a great deal, and knew it could not go on much longer in the same fashion.

He realised that when his national service ended, if he was to return to the village for good, it had to be put on a proper footing. They would have to get married, no matter the difference in their ages, and no matter what his parents and the village thought, or he would have to give her up.

His decision was made easier, because he was so happy in his new life in the Army. Whilst others were grumbling and discontented, he was happy and making good progress. He was the best recruit in his squad, though he had never handled a rifle before, quickly became a good shot, was very smart on the drill square, and enjoyed the outdoor training, the physical training, and most of all, the opportunity for sporting activities.

Within the first year, he knew it was to be the Army for him, and, on one of his weekend leave periods, he talked it over, first with his mother and father, then with Alice.

Alice knew he was right. They had been terribly fortunate no-one had discovered their romantic life together. It was as well, it could have spoiled their whole way of life in the village. Her love, and it was love, for him was no less, she was a sensible woman and knew his decision was the wisest course.

As his father had said, once he had made up his mind his parents would not object at all. They would miss him, of course, but they were so proud of him when he came home in uniform, and knew he would do well.

A lot of water had run down the valleys and into the sea since then, and he had matured and done well in the Army, never regretting the decision he had made.

He remembered Alice now, as he would always remember her – with the greatest of affection. She had been wonderful to him, for him, had taught him so much, given him so much, and she had been the only woman in his life.

He had remained true and faithful to her love over the years, until just that evening, when he had thrilled at the prospect of a night out with Carrie Jane.

There was just one other, one he had thought about for weeks now. The wonderful Chinese lady he had met at the Golden Lotus, and the real attraction that was taking him there tonight.

She was the most beautiful woman he had ever seen. He couldn't believe his luck that she had consented to dance with him that night after the football match, her touch had thrilled him beyond anything else he had ever known, and she had come alive in his arms.

The manager of the nightclub – the man he simply knew as Mr Lee – the same name as her – had told him she had never ever danced with any man there before, but she had certainly danced with him that night, and because of her, he was sure Mr Lee had been most hospitable to him when he had gone there again.

This Chinese lady was of high birth, and the thought of her was impossible really. But she did attract him strongly, and come to think of it, Alice had seemed well out of his reach at one time, but she hadn't been.

He was looking forward to the night – hoping hard he would see her, and then there was tomorrow night with Carrie Jane. That could be very good fun and romantic, he could bet.

Heavens – all of a sudden he was getting as bad as Bob Denton, with his eager thoughts of the Chinese lady and Carrie Jane. They would be getting ready for the ball back there in the mess – he just hoped Bob would never be found out in his affair with Natalie Hibbert. But who was he, David Rankin, to criticise or condemn, with his thoughts the way they were, and after his great love life with Alice?

12

TABLE FOR TWO

It was a thousand to one against Rankin getting into the Golden Lotus that night.

The orders were very clear – in this the Minister had been adamant. There was to be no admission at the door for clients who had not made previous reservations. Such reservations had been checked, as far as it had been possible to do so, and the strictest security measures were in force.

In every case every table had been booked, so it was just a case of a refusal for those who came without having made reservations.

Extra tables had been put in, making the restaurant more crowded than usual, but these were for extra security guards of the Triad, both men and women – women having long been employed on such duties by the Golden Lotus – and all, like most of the clients, in faultless evening clothes.

But the thousand to one chance came off, as such chances sometimes do.

Rankin was late really, and lucky that the ferry had still been operating, though the trip over from Kowloon had not been as bad as he had expected. It was obvious that the rain was near, so he took a taxi from the Ferry to the nightclub.

Mr Lee was at the door as the taxi arrived, having been called there a few minutes previously to speak to a small party of Chinese, well known customers of the establishment, who had not made reservations, and rightly been refused admission. He was making his explanations, and apologising, when the taxi drove up. Rankin saw him at once, paid the taxi driver, and waited for Mr Lee to finish what he was doing.

Mr Lee – tall, slim, yet powerful, sleek black hair well plastered down – was glad of the diversion Rankin's arrival afforded him –

"Hi, Mr Rankin – go in will you and wait at the bar," he greeted. It was as simple as that. Had he not been at the door, Rankin would have been turned away graciously, but firmly.

Mr Lee said something to three Chinese in white jackets who were outside with him, and one of them led Rankin through the outside swing door, then through a further set of doors, turning right inside the door, and along to the bar which ran from one side of the nightclub to the central doors.

"Order what you like," he told Rankin, "Mr Lee will be here as soon as he can, and look after you."

Rankin had no idea that he had been extremely fortunate to be admitted. To him, it was almost like the other times, though it was very crowded tonight.

The whole atmosphere was luxury – step through those doors and into the Golden Lotus, and you stepped into another world – a world of the best of everything, the most expensive of everything – furnishings, furniture, cutlery, glassware, napery, decor, service, catering, entertainment – everything. Only the very rich of Hong Kong, or very rich visitors to the Colony, could afford to be customers, unless you were taken there – as Rankin had originally been taken in the party after the football match, and unless you didn't have to pay, as had happened each time to Rankin.

He ordered a Dubonnet, long, with ice and soda, admiring the decor of the bar, and the vast stock of bottles, with so many of the Scotch whiskies, Booths or Gordon's Gin, and all the good brandies.

The service was slick, the barmen neat and tidy, wearing smart pale blue jackets, and a smile, as the drinks were served. He was the only person at the bar, though the waiter service at the far end was very busy, but unusually for such a place with a large cluster of wine waiters demanding attention, it was very quiet. Only the guests could be noisy at the Golden Lotus – the service, the music, the entertainment, were all quiet.

He turned to look at the tables. The place was crowded, every table occupied on this floor as far as he could see. In the centre of this mass of tables was a small space for dancing, and beyond, across the room from him was a large stage, with a large gold coloured backcloth plentifully sprinkled with blue stars. The electricity arrangements behind the backcloth were clever, and created a most beautiful and realistic twinkling effect in the stars. On the stage, an orchestra – Fillipinos – played sweet sentimental music, it was in keeping with the place.

Everything was excellent the curtains, the light fittings, the few pictures, the thickly padded carpets, and there were seemingly hundreds of captains and waiters to serve the guests.

A wide staircase – very wide at the bottom, but narrowing at the top – led to the Bar of Heaven, as they called it. What tables he could see up there were full.

Looking around, he could see a few Europeans, but it mostly looked as if the high and mighty of the Chinese population had gathered here tonight to celebrate the birthday of the Queen – or would they be doing that? Probably so, and he knew the high Chinese executives of the Colony were most loyal to Her Majesty. Only a few of the men were not in tuxedos or dinner jackets, but he was glad there were a few others like him, in a lounge suit.

The atmosphere, as yet, was quiet. He knew it would become more rowdy as the night wore on. It had been the pattern when he had been here previously, the noise increasing as the wine flowed, and there was always plenty of wine. He had learned that it was customary for the Chinese to take a full glass of neat brandy or whisky between each course, in addition to the wine. Oh well, they were welcome to that – it would kill him.

He looked up at the chandeliers, gorgeous and large, and in the same style throughout, though only the two over the bar were lit at this time. They must have cost a fortune. On each table there were electric imitation candles, one or two, depending on the size of the table, whilst an upward glow – now a deep rose hue – came from the glass panels set in the floor. These floor lights changed at regular intervals to bring a different coloured glow to the scene.

The thickly padded carpet was gold in colour, matching the gold of the backcloth of the stage, because of the name of the nightclub, he thought. The curtains all bore a small blue flower – an orchid – and that must be to do with someone or something he reckoned.

It was a lovely orchestra, the music just right, the amplification system perfect. The music was slow, smoochy, and he knew from that one dance he had enjoyed here, weeks before, that you held close and moved slowly, sometimes more with your body than with your feet.

What a night that had been. The other lads in the Army team had dared him to ask her to dance, and he could not refuse the dare. He had been surprised when she had accepted, and he hadn't been able to say much to her, but it had been a terrific experience.

She had come warm in his arms as they moved, and what a beautiful mover she was. Tall, graceful, terrific, she was super – marvellous long legs and very light. She had moved her legs apart a little as they danced, so he could move his right knee in between – not too far, just enough to make it thrilling, and he had dared to move in very close holding her firm against him, the fragrance and the charm of her enchanting him, her perfume intoxicating him, and the fullness of her breasts against him giving him all sorts of sensations to go with the others. Gosh, she was big up there.

Her voice, when they had finished the dance, and he escorted her back to her table, in a company which was otherwise all male, had been rich music in his ears. Her silvery-toned, "Thank you very much, I did enjoy that," had him walking back to join the lads, six inches off the floor and in a daze. What a woman, what a woman!

He had seen her on each of the other occasions he had come back to the nightclub after that – she always seemed to be here – and she had smiled graciously at him with her lips forming a "Good evening", even though he could not hear the actual words because of the noise of the place. Would she be here tonight, he wondered.

It was some time before Mr Lee joined him.

"Sorry, Mr Rankin," he apologised, "they were a little hard to pacify. Now, how are you? No football – what to do all day?"

"Oh, we work hard enough," Rankin told him, "they keep us busy."

"I can be sure of that," Mr Lee agreed. "Now, we have to find you somewhere to sit."

It was Rankin's turn to be apologetic, "I can see you are very busy." He looked around again. "The place is packed, don't worry. I can finish my drink and get back to Kowloon."

"We wouldn't think of you doing that," Mr Lee was firm. "You have taken the trouble to come here, we must take the trouble to look after you. In any case, the storm has commenced – you were only just in time getting here."

Rankin grinned – "well, as long as you think it's all right, I'm happy to stay."

"Sure it is all right," Mr Lee was confident about that. "We have the answer, I'm certain – just a few minutes more please."

He was off as he finished the sentence, up the stairs, moving fast, and on to the balcony – the Bar of Heaven.

Amazing fellow, Rankin thought, I'm sure he was telling that party they could not get in, yet here I am. Hope he finds something, I'm hungry.

He watched Mr Lee return down the stairs. In the dim light he seemed to be smiling. Watched him thread his way through the tables back to the bar, stopping at two of the tables to be told something, or say something to the captains. He was smiling – broadly – as he rejoined Rankin.

"We're lucky tonight, Mr Rankin – just one seat at a table for two, and with another English gentleman, do you mind?"

"Well, no," though Rankin was a bit doubtful, "as long as you think it's all right and he doesn't mind."

"He will be glad of your company, I think," the manager assured him, then, with the supreme courtesy of his calling, "Come with me please."

Hamilton had been in the Golden Lotus for nearly an hour, watching the place fill up and making good inroads into a bottle of wine. He had got himself in to a good mood, and had just been about to order his meal, when Mr Lee had approached him to fill the empty seat opposite.

He didn't mind, glad of a bit of company really. What an idiot he had been not to have that glorious BOAC stewardess sitting with him – what a night it could have been then.

Rankin followed Mr Lee up the wide staircase to the balcony, which ran right the way around in a huge circle, and so cleverly designed, that almost everyone sitting up there – with the tables right up alongside the balcony wall – could see most of the small dance floor, even if they all could not see the stage.

The decor was white puffy clouds and blue sky, with the same type and colours of carpets and curtains as down in the main restaurant. A small bar – the Bar of Heaven, with golden angels afloat in the clouds and the sky, filled one corner, and back from the tables in what little space remained, there were a few private cubicles for those who did not want to dance, did not want to watch the dancing, or the entertainment, but just wanted a meal and privacy. Mr Lee had told Rankin, on a previous visit, that the cubicles were very expensive and very popular, though it was the policy of the nightclub not to provide hostesses or girls – the only nightclub of this type which did not do so. "But, of course, Mr Rankin, if a good client brings a lady. That's his business," Mr Lee had said. Rankin didn't doubt the popularity of the cubicles, but had never seen inside one.

Rankin stood at the table for a moment, as Mr Lee said, "This is the other gentleman, sir," to the man already seated at the table.

"It's very nice of you to let me sit here, sir," he said, "are you sure you don't mind?"

Hamilton looked up at the large figure standing across the table from him. The light was better up in the Heaven because of the lighting from the stairs. What a strikingly handsome fellow – great strength, no doubt he was a rugby man. Bet he could hit a golf ball some distance with those mighty shoulders behind the swing. He was surprised at the use of the word "sir".

"Don't mind a bit, old chap," he replied – "glad of some company really. Not a night to be on one's own – birthday of Her Majesty, eh? My name's Hamilton – just call me Ham – most people do."

"My name's Rankin – David Rankin – I'm in the Army," Rankin told him, and reached over to grasp Hamilton's hand before sitting down.

Hamilton had got up to shake hands, and knew he had been right about the strength of this fellow, as their hands gripped.

"You just got in?" he asked. "Storm hasn't started then – will, no doubt before we leave here."

"No, I just got here in time," Rankin eased himself down into his chair, being careful not to disturb the Chinese people on the table close behind him, "but the manager says it has started now."

"Funny things these typhoons," Hamilton said. "Still we won't get wet in here, at least not outside, In the Army, eh? That's good – I used to be in the Army myself. Have a drink – I'm drinking Blue Nun – it's a good wine, I like it." He motioned to one of the attendant waiters. "Pour out the drinks, will you, and tell the captain to send up another bottle."

Within minutes they were getting on famously, and Rankin had warmed to the very decent fellow, who had made him so welcome and was obviously glad of his company.

"I was just going to select the meal," Hamilton said, "now what about you – can you eat anything, or are you choosey?"

Rankin was enjoying the wine – as Hamilton had said, it was good, "Don't worry about me, I can eat anything. You make the choice, you're the expert, I'm sure."

That pleased Hamilton. "Well I've lived out here on and off for many years – born out here in fact, grew up here, love the place – and the food. Live in Singapore now. You just leave all this to me, we'll have a real banquet, and what better time than tonight, eh?"

Rankin agreed, what an interesting fellow the other was – it was a lucky night for him to have got in the place, and now to be with Ham – so very much a gentleman.

Hamilton ordered baked Pomfret to commence with – a local fish, he told Rankin.

"Now," he went on, "we'll have Peking Duck as it's on the menu, not generally on the menu, as it takes days to prepare properly, but this is the Golden Lotus, and they would expect to have a lot of orders for this tonight. It really is, in my opinion, the number one Chinese dish, and you'll like it."

Hamilton was enjoying himself – "I used to prefer Mongolian hot-pot, but this is too good an opportunity to be missed – to have Peking Duck as it should be." He paused a while, looking through the menu – the patient captain waiting for him. "Then we'll have some pancakes, they'll be just right – with ginger syrup," he looked up at Rankin. "Hope you'll have room for them," he said as he passed the menu back to the captain.

"Sounds great," Rankin said, "and I'm very hungry, seems ages since I had anything to eat."

"We'll keep to the same wine," Hamilton said, rather than asked. "You like it?"

"I do – it's nice – but I won't drink too much – I'm not a drinker really."

"Nor me," Hamilton interrupted – "like wine though." Rankin thought this an understatement, in view of the amount the other was drinking, though it was probably because this was a special occasion. "Good for you too," Hamilton went on. "Can't really get bad on wine – mixing it's the trouble. Good wine this Blue Nun – you can drink a lot more white wine than red wine – like red wine too, that's a bit more potent."

Rankin let Hamilton ramble on, content to listen, and not knowing much about wine in any case. He had seen that every table on the balcony was completely taken, and the noise was increasing rapidly – oh yes, the wine was flowing at other tables as well as at this one.

They were sat at a small table, quite close to the head of the staircase. Rankin was facing backwards and away from the happenings below, so he had to half turn to see what was going on down below on the dance floor, even though he did have a good view of anyone coming up or going down the stairs, and of one or two of the cubicles.

It was great to be here on a night such as this. He kept wondering about the Chinese lady – would she appear as she had done on the other nights he had been here?

The mess Ball would be in full swing by now back at the camp. Pity in a way he had to miss it, though he was glad to be in the Golden Lotus, where it was different and exciting. Old Gerry Hibbert and others would be consuming vast quantities of beer and whisky by now – he was sure of that – when his mess celebrated, they did it properly – as a lot of those here in the nightclub would no doubt.

He and Hamilton were the best of friends by the time the first course arrived. Hamilton had been telling him about the Japanese soldiers who had conquered Hong Kong.

"Brutes, fiends, devils, everything you can call them," Hamilton remembered it so well, "and their atrocities still give me nightmares" – his voice cool now, after all these years, but the hatred of the remembrance was clear. "It was always their nature, to their enemies and to their own troops even. Did you know that in the Japanese Army a senior can beat a junior rank, kick him, whip him, anything, to punish him or to maintain discipline?"

Rankin had heard something about them, but not much.

"Saw it myself, old chap," Hamilton continued, "many times, vicious sadistic brutes, but then, what have they to look forward to, only death – the soldier is told that death is the highest honour and all they can expect from war, that, if they are killed in battle, they will leave this horrid earth, and go to their valhallah where they will be waited on hand and foot by the loveliest of geisha girls waiting for them up there, wherever there is" – he waved his arm around – "they were fanatics."

"And they believed it?" Rankin asked.

"Course they believed it, David, old chap – course they did. Why not? They had nothing else to believe in except their patriotism and the life to come – all of them – officers as well, even the most educated of them. That's how the Kamakaze pilots were picked. Die for the Emperor with honour, and claim your reward from those millions of geisha girls – with life thereafter one hell of an orgy of wine, women and song!"

The fish arrived just then, steaming hot, succulent, tender, falling away from the bones easily, as the waiter picked out choice pieces for them.

"This is great," Rankin said, after his first mouthful, watching Hamilton use chopsticks most capably.

"Thought you'd like it," Hamilton said. "Local fish, very fresh, probably only caught this morning – s'always good this fish."It was just as well the food had come, as Hamilton had drunk a lot of wine, but like Rankin, he ate well, and it was delicious.

"You know, old chap," Hamilton remarked, as they were taking the plates away, "We should have a glass of brandy between courses to do it properly – what do you say?"

"Oh, Heavens no – thank you, Ham," Rankin replied, "it would kill me!"

Hamilton laughed. "Don't think it would!" He was in excellent mood and talkative. It was good to have Rankin for company, better really in a way than that BOAC female. Really he was scared about girls, trouble was he hadn't ever had much to do with them.

"Used to come to a lot of big Chinese parties with my parents when I was growing up – terrific really – loads to eat, and to drink. How my poor Papa kept up with some of the Chinese, I never knew, but he did – God rest his soul – suffered for it a lot though!"

He had to talk loudly now to get above the babel of noise. "We used to leave all the dishes and plates piled up high on the table – and the bottles – show how much we'd eaten and drank – those were the days all right – 'fore the blasted Japs spoiled it all."

The Peking Duck and the trimmings took three waiters to serve, with a couple of captains to direct operations. A small table was brought alongside in the already limited space, but the service was managed most capably.

A whole duck, brown, crispy, on a vast bed of rice, with a liberal sprinkling of boiled cherries to add the colour, served on a great silver platter, and dish after dish of mushrooms, peas, almonds, small white turnips, bamboo shoots, cauliflower, white cabbage, bean curd, sliced oranges – both tables were full.

"I can't believe it," Rankin said, pushing back as far as he could against the chair to the rear of him, to allow the waiters more room – "I've never seen anything like this!"

"Must admit it's well done," Hamilton agreed, "though I expected it here, the place has a wonderful reputation for food." Hamilton saw Rankin needed some prompting to start. "Now, just take what you want when you want – that's what happens at a Chinese feast – you all eat out of the dishes – a bit here, a bit there – if you see what I mean."

Rankin did as he was told, and both men were soon giving their full attention to the meal.

"Try some of the skin," Hamilton said, motioning to the duck with his chopsticks, "you'll find that very good" –

Rankin liked vegetables, and had never eaten anything nicer than the duck, he really was enjoying it, ladling great forkfuls of the different dishes on to his plate. One thing puzzled him.

"Don't see any carrots," he remarked, "don't they grow them out here?"

"They do," Hamilton was sure of that, "but they're not considered a dish for the higher classes – only for the working people."

Rankin considered this very strange.

The meal did Hamilton a lot of good, sobering him fast. "You should try using chopsticks," he told Rankin.

"Not likely, but I must say you're an expert," Hamilton made the use of them seem so easy, "I really am lucky tonight, meeting you. I'd have settled for Chow Fan."

"A good choice, it would be excellent here," Hamilton knew that. "Now, we ought to have one glass of brandy to wash that lot down. Won't do any harm at all. Do you good in fact, we've had plenty of good food to soak it up."

He ordered the brandy without waiting for a reply, and they soon had a full glass in front of each of them.

"Now, try it in one, like the Chinese do. Say what you like – down the hatch, bottoms up, same thing really." He took one long swig and finished the whole glass.

Rankin could not manage it, the fire in the liquid too much for him, but he managed half the glass.

"Can't manage it all in one go, sorry," he apologised, "first time I've ever tasted brandy. I'll finish it later."

Hamilton nodded agreement. It had been an excellent meal so far, and he could see how much his companion had enjoyed it. In fact, they had both done full justice to it.

"The preparation of a Chinese meal is so thorough," he explained, "they do everything so well, take so much trouble over it. Those bamboo shoots were delicious, very young and very tender. Haven't enjoyed anything so much for years, and you'll like the pancakes."

Rankin did like the pancakes, and the ginger sauce, just tangy enough for him.

"This is the way I like ginger," Hamilton said, soaking a piece of pancake in the sauce. "The Chinese also eat ginger as a vegetable, but they prepare it very young, and before there's any real taste of ginger in the plant. This is the way to have it, it's very tasty."

He looked across the table at Rankin and grinned. "Some Chinese say that ginger is a good aphrodisiac – 'course they say that about a lot of things, powdered buffalo horn, and all that sort of stuff." He laughed. "Shouldn't think you need it."

Rankin sat back, wiping his mouth and fingers with his napkin, well content. "No, I don't think I do, Army life keeps you fit."

"I agree – I agree," Hamilton said. "I enjoyed it myself in the Army – kept very fit – still try to do."

The waiter brought coffee, and Hamilton ordered Rankin's glass to be topped up with brandy, and another glassful for himself. He chose a cigar from the box offered by the captain.

"I smoke these, not cigarettes." He was in a very expansive mood.

"Must say," he went on, "that dinner was first-class. Damn glad you happened along, I was feeling a bit sorry for myself. Done me a lot of good, your company – and it is the place to come – really first-class place."

"Oh, yes," Rankin agreed, feeling very well and happy himself. "I first came here with the Army football team one night; we played the Chinese in one of those annual matches, you know about them!" Hamilton nodded, but did not interrupt, quite sober again now, and interested in what his companion had to tell him. "Had a wonderful night, and I was lucky enough to have a dance with the owner."

It took a second or two for this to sink in, but then Hamilton sat up very sharply. "You did what?" he asked, taking his cigar out of his mouth and letting out a big puff of cigar smoke. "That does surprise me."

Rankin could see this was obvious. "Surprised me too," he admitted, "the lads dared me to ask her, you know how it is, she was sitting at a table down near the bar." He turned, "Down there, not as crowded as it is tonight. I went across and asked her, she said yes and we danced. She is a beautiful woman," he paused a moment, but Hamilton did not speak. "Since then I've been here two or three times, the manager always looks after me very well, and here I am tonight."

Hamilton put his elbows on the table, leaned forward and looked hard at Rankin. "You know who she is?" he asked very quietly.

"Sort of," Rankin replied, somewhat surprised at the other's intent interest. "Her name's Lee something, and she must be the most striking woman I've ever seen in my life."

"You and everybody else," Hamilton agreed. "Shall I tell you who she is?" Then, before Rankin could reply, "We'll have some more coffee."

He beckoned the attendant waiter. "Never do it yourself," he told Rankin, "that's what the waiter's here for, to serve, and if you serve yourself, at a place like this, a waiter could be in big trouble if the captain saw it – it's protocol, but very important."

The waiter served them more coffee and refilled Hamilton's glass with brandy. Rankin had left his filled glass untouched but he had a small sip now.

Hamilton still spoke quietly, leaning right across the table towards Rankin. "This Lee is Lee Kyung Koh, and she's the head of a very powerful Triad. You know what a Triad is? – A Tong." Rankin did know that. "It's a very law-abiding Triad, most helpful to the Hong Kong government, and" – he nearly said 'to the British government', but checked himself in time – "and the Police," he went on quickly. "And she is just about the richest person in Hong Kong where there are, believe me, some very rich people."

"She does own this place?" Rankin was impressed.

"They say so," Hamilton agreed, "but she has so much money, as the Triad has, it doesn't make any difference – the one is the other, if you see what I mean. She's a good woman, done a great deal for charity."

"Is she married?" Rankin interrupted.

Hamilton grinned his wry grin. "She is not, I know that for certain.

Who could marry her? Nobody in this Colony, nobody in China. Why? Do you fancy a try?"

"You're pulling my leg," Rankin said simply, not understanding why nobody in the Colony, or China, could marry her.

"I am," agreed Hamilton, grinning again, "but only because I knew you would take it in the correct way. I can't see who she could marry, or who could marry her, and she's a very big problem at the moment."

"How's that?" Rankin asked. He was very interested.

"Well," Hamilton was keeping his voice very low, and Rankin had to lean forward himself to hear him. "I have a friend in the Police, who tells me there is another Triad – there are lots of them, big and small, like secret societies in a way – who want to oust her Triad, and the battle could start any moment now."

"You're pulling my leg again," Rankin truly thought that.

"I'm not this time," Hamilton said, very serious. "This is no fairy tale, this is the truth. That's what I'm told, and I believe it, and when it does start, I think," very slowly and seriously now, "I think this other Triad will try to abduct Lee Kyung Koh!"

"Kidnap her?" Rankin was amazed. It was so hard to believe, even though Hamilton was so very serious.

"Exactly that," Hamilton agreed.

"Could they do it?"

"Hard to say – hard to say. The Triad of Lee Kyung Koh – the Golden Lotus, hence the name of the nightclub – are pretty good, well, very good, they should know their business, and the others would have to be that much better to get her."

Rankin sat back, thinking.

"But they'll try all right," Hamilton hadn't finished, "they'll try, because if they get her, it means such a hell of a lot – they could even try here tonight."

Rankin leaned forward again, his face showing all the amazement he felt.

"You really think so, Ham. Here with all these people around?"

"That's the danger. Who are these people? Mostly Chinese and all alike – look around, can you tell one from another? Can you tell friend from foe?"

Rankin could see his point. "No, of course not, they are all alike."

"Almost true," Hamilton nodded.

"But surely," Rankin was thinking hard as he spoke. "Her own people can tell who the enemy are. Hasn't she any guards?"

"The place is thick with them tonight," Hamilton was very sure about it. "I should say that at least one third of the Chinese here, men and women, are her guards."

"So, she's safe then?"

"No one's ever safe, not even in a place like this."

"They might try to shoot her," Rankin suggested.

"No, I hardly think that," Hamilton said, taking another large swig at his brandy. "They want her alive if possible, she's no use to them dead."

Rankin looked around him, then turned back to Hamilton. "So, any of these could be the other lot?"

"Most certainly there are some here somewhere," Hamilton agreed.

"Then, we won't see her tonight?" Rankin asked.

"I think not. That'll disappoint you?"

Rankin smiled. "Yes, I suppose so. She's so much worth looking at, but if it is a question of her safety, I'd rather she kept out of sight."

"Nobly spoken," Hamilton said, bringing his cigar out of his mouth, and inspecting it keenly. "But there is still a danger." He paused for a few seconds. "They say she is very headstrong, she is the head of the Triad, she makes that very clear, and she might just be foolish enough to look in tonight. After all," with the wry grin again, "she is a woman. What happens when she comes, is she downstairs all the time?"

Rankin knew something about this, "Well, when I've seen her here before, she comes in at the top there – behind you." Hamilton turned in his chair to look. "Then she goes downstairs, and previously, she has sat at a table down there, where I told you," he turned himself around, "near the bar, but there's no room there tonight."

Hamilton was very interested. "What happens, she isn't alone, of course, does she talk to anyone?"

Rankin thought awhile, gathering his memories together. "No, she doesn't, at least, I don't think so. She was with four men, they all sat down with her – that's why the lads dared me to ask her to dance, they wanted to see me thrown out on my neck."

"But you weren't?"

"No, I wasn't, I was lucky."

"What did the men do when you went to the table. Did any of them try to stop you?"

Rankin thought again. "I think one did, but I expect I took them by surprise, I don't think anyone had ever asked her before – that's what I gathered from the manager – but she said something to this one lad, who had stood up, and any case, I wasn't looking at him."

Hamilton thought awhile and looked around, weighing it all up in his mind. Her entry at the top of the stairs – he could imagine the scene as Rankin had approached the table – of course, no one had ever done that before. But he could not understand how Rankin had got away with it.

"You were lucky," he said.

Rankin knew that, it was even more evident to him now he knew something of who she was than it had been when it had happened. Then, she was just an attractive Chinese lady – Heavens, dare or not, if he'd known who she was, he would have sat tight – or would he?

It had struck Rankin that Hamilton was very interested in Lee Kyung Koh. He wondered why. Who was he, this quiet Englishman, who seemed to know so much about her, and about affairs in Hong Kong, even though he had said he lived in Singapore now.

Hamilton was thinking hard, looking at Rankin, and going over again in his mind all Rankin had told him.

"Interesting, damned interesting," he said at last – "I think you will be disappointed tonight, David – I don't think she will be in attendance."

As he spoke, the lighting on the stairs became brighter, and then, almost at once, the noise began to decrease – upstairs at first, then downstairs.

Hamilton was sitting with his back to the top of the stairs, and could not fail to notice the occupants of other tables turning to look in his direction, but it was not at him they were looking.

Rankin was looking in the right direction.

"You're wrong, Ham," his voice was loud, very loud. "You're wrong – she's coming now." He stood up, excited, face flushed, looking over, and beyond his table companion.

Hamilton saw everyone standing up and turning around, was aware how quiet it had gone.

He stood up himself, and turned around to see what it was all about.

13

THE NINETY-SEVEN ATTACK

Hamilton could hardly believe the evidence of his own eyes.

It was true, she was making her appearance, and what an appearance.

She was escorted by six of her special guards, two by two by two, with the leader of the Triad between the second pair of guards. The men were dressed in a type of bush jacket, deep blue in colour, black trousers and pumps.

They looked tough and, no doubt, were tough, six highly trained skilled men, ready to die for the woman they now escorted.

Up here it was very quiet, though there was still some noise from down below, as the little procession came slowly to the top of the stairs, and on down. Slowly, very slowly.

There was nothing different about these six guards than the Japanese he had been telling Rankin about earlier on. Just as the Japanese would have died so willingly for their Emperor, so these six, and many more he knew, would be prepared to die for Lee Kyung Koh. This was part of their creed, and if the training was good, as it had been with the Japanese, they would be prepared to do what they were trained for without hesitation.

Hamilton knew that all her guards came from Taiwan, where, undoubtedly, the training was as good as that of the Japanese. What absolute fanatics these Asiatics were.

Lee Kyung Koh looked regal, taller than the six guards, who were much of a size, she was dressed, as far as Hamilton could see, in a cheongsam of shimmering gold material, trimmed with blue, it would be the orchid, of course. Her hair had been brought back severely from the front of the head, and was piled up high at the back, giving her added height which she did not really need. She wore long jade earrings – he could not see her hands, which she held down at her sides, and did not know if she was wearing any other jewellery, but he knew the earrings would be of perfect jade. His knowledge of Chinese customs made him certain that jade was for the spring, and it was now summer, but, of course, Lee Kyung Koh was a law unto herself. In the older days, Chinese ladies had worn only the jewel of the season, and it would have been considered bad luck to have done otherwise.

"The idiot, the utter idiot," he told himself, "what in hell is all this for – what purpose?" The vanity of the woman – who did she think she was – a second Cleopatra? Whatever else he had thought might happen, he had not considered this sort of show.

Slowly, the procession moved down the stairs. There was no noise now from the restaurant where, he was sure, not everyone yet could see what was happening. They could not yet see the procession – there was no other word for it – but they knew something was happening, something exciting.

She had seen Rankin. Hamilton could see she was looking at the soldier stood alongside him, saw her give a slight bow of the head, and her lips frame the words "Good evening" – he was sure of that.

He felt, rather than saw, Rankin, bow in recognition. It pleased Hamilton above his other thoughts. Rankin had good breeding, instilled in him from somewhere back in time. Perhaps his ancestors had been amongst the valiant Knights of Wales. Well done – it had pleased him when Rankin had first come to the table they had shared, and used the word, "sir".

The procession went on down past them. How strange she should look for Rankin, must have known he was there. Then, of course, the manager would have told her, but why? How important was he? Just because once Rankin had danced with her. That must have been an event – something which would astound them all and impress her greatly. Good Lord, he was probably the only person who had ever held her in his arms – the only man, that is. Again – a modern knight – it all was so fantastic, but she had certainly looked for him, and only for him.

Along from their table, the guests had crowded to the low balcony wall, leaning over, watching the procession go past. It was packed up here at the balcony, with people behind them pushing and shoving to get another look, or a better view.

It was more noisy again up here – the excitement was over for a while until she came back up the stairs, whenever that might be. Then, the onlookers, who were now getting back to their tables – to their meals – to their wine – would come flocking back to the balcony. No doubt about that.

He sat down and picked up his glass, still highly perplexed by it all. Rankin remained standing, looking down over the balcony, still highly flushed, and Hamilton knew it wasn't because of the wine or brandy.

Rankin had probably been the first to see the procession appearing from the back of the landing there beyond Hamilton. As soon as he had seen the first two guards, his heart gave a jump, he knew what it meant – she was coming.

She had come down the stairs when he had been here before, but not in this manner. Then, she had been escorted by the manager, and flanked by a couple of other men. He hadn't thought of them as security guards, but he now knew they were, though they had not been dressed in the blue jackets her guards were wearing tonight.

It was now obvious that all Hamilton had told him about Lee Kyung Koh, about her Triad, and about the danger to her, was correct. Rankin was not reasoning why she had made an appearance, and in this manner, he had been very pleased to look at her again.

Heavens, what a beautiful woman she is, he told himself, looking straight at her and hardly noticing the guards, or the commotion of the other guests around him, not realising it had gone so quiet up here, and was quietening down in the same manner in the restaurant below.

She looked gorgeous, head held high, elegant hair style, long earrings, and the shimmering gold cheongsam. He could only see the top part of her – she was much taller than the guards. His heart bounded madly as she approached the top of the stairs.

She was looking straight at him, her eyes fixed on him. Her lips formed the "Good evening," as on previous occasions, slowly, clearly, and she made a very slight bow to him, a gracious acknowledgement of his presence, which was almost unbelievable.

He made his bow in return, very proud, but his lips did not move, and he watched as she slowly began the descent of the stairs, head turned to the front now, to where the procession was leading her, into the restaurant, where it was crowded and hushed, the crowds waiting to see her.

He was flushed, perspiring freely, thrilled, excited, all the emotions, because he had seen her. What a woman, what a truly magnificent woman! He knew those guards would die for her, and was sure he could do just that. Let anyone try to harm her – just let them try – and my heavens, he would kill for her and die for her.

She had looked straight at him, looked for him. She must have known he was here. Mr Lee must have told her – why? What did he matter to her, he had danced with her just the once, and that was all. His eyes probably told her how much he admired her, how much he could desire her, but that was all. It was so confusing.

He turned back to the table, where Hamilton was sat sipping his brandy, deep in thought. Rankin sat down and took up his glass. He needed something to steady him down a bit after all that. What a woman!

Lee Kyung Koh had seen him as she approached the top of the staircase, and was pleased. He was so handsome, so very handsome. She knew he had great strength to go with that handsome appearance, because of the easy way he had held her when they had danced. How that had excited her, thrilled her, pleased her.

It was all so clear in her mind and memory. It had surprised her at first, but she had been quick enough to realise why he had come to her table and had immediately restrained her guards from any intervention. He had asked so nicely, soberly, and she had accepted his invitation to dance without hesitation. It was as though he had commanded her to dance with him, rather than asked.

It had been wonderful to dance with him – he was so easy to dance with. She had danced with men in this western fashion before, in America, and when she was much younger, but it had never been as this dance had been. He held her firmly, snugly, comfortably – not afraid of her in any way, and she had moved happily, easily, with him, coming close in to him in obeyance to his arms, as tall as him, taller even, and he had looked into her eyes, smiled warmly, his eyes telling her all his thoughts, and he had obviously been very thrilled.

She had thought about it many times since. Why had it happened? Because it was in the stars for her, of course – perhaps he was the man who awaited for her, the one man Ai Fah had spoken must be waiting for her. She had seen him three times in the nightclub since then, and he had not again asked her to dance, there hadn't been the opportunity there was on that night, but she had seen, and read, the look on his face, in his eyes, each time, knew well what it meant, and was happy in her thoughts of him.

She had not thought anything wrong about dancing with him. The Minister must have been told about it, though she had never mentioned it, and he had not spoken of it with her. She had been correct, she thought, in not letting her guards stop him – if they had done so, there might well have been an incident, and that would have been wrong. She was glad they had danced, would dance with him every night if he asked her. He was so much a man – a man she could want, desire, thrill, respond to, please. He was what was missing in her life – a man.

She had told Mr Lee to look after him when he had returned for his second visit, and he was to be a guest of the house whenever he came. That instruction had not been questioned, and she knew Mr Lee thought highly of him. It was the manager, of course, who had told her he was in again tonight – Mr Rankin, he had said – he was a soldier she knew, but knew not much more than that.

He interested her greatly. He had held her in his arms in a way no other man had done. She knew the interest, the feelings, were mutual – all the stars were working for them both, she was sure, and if she was ever going to give herself to a man, she would like it to be someone such as him, no, she would like it to be him. But it was all impossible – impossible – impossible.

She walked slowly down the stairs, well aware of the excitement and the sensation she was causing. It had been her own idea, and backed by Mr Lee, this procession. She did not insist on her usual table by the bar, where she generally spent an hour or so, but tonight would simply look in on the festivities, this should please the Minister. Then, she would come back up to her own private suite at the back, and on the second floor of the building, change again into the clothing she always wore for her journeying to and from the nightclub, and return, early for once, to her own palatial apartment. She was pleased she had come tonight, she had at least seen the soldier – Mr Rankin.

The first two of her guards reached the bottom of the staircase, where Mr Lee waited them. They moved left to go around past the bar. It was so quiet down here in the restaurant, but upstairs the noise had re-commenced.

She followed the first two guards, who, in turn, were led by Mr Lee, secure between the men on either side of her, closer to her now in the more confined space – the whole procession was now more bunched up – this made her even more secure, there could not possibly be any danger. She was aware the service had stopped, aware that everyone in the place was watching her and the procession, and she was clearly in view, the chandelier lights having all been switched on long before the procession had reached the foot of the stairs.

She was half way along the clear space in front of the bar, still walking very slowly, the crowded tables very close, and all the guests – male and female – standing to watch her go past, when the attack came.

In seconds, a concerted rush of men from the tables nearest to her, nearest to the bar, engulfed her guards and herself. She realised immediately she was in very grave danger, realised the Minister had been quite right.

Upstairs Hamilton had lit another cigar, and had his brandy glass refilled. "Insane, idiotic, stupid – never known anything so ridiculous in my life," he had told Rankin. "She has no right to expose herself to danger in this way."

Rankin didn't agree – he had not the knowledge Hamilton had about Chinese affairs, "But surely she must be safe in here, with so many of her own people around?" he said.

"No, she's not," Hamilton argued. "She's doing exactly what the other side want her to do – playing into their hands."

Rankin didn't agree, he was sure she and her guards must know what they were doing, and what the risks were.

Hamilton was equally sure of the danger. "God knows what'll happen if they attempt to spring her down there," he waved his arm angrily towards the restaurant below. "It'll be murder – she has no right to give them this opportunity." Rankin could see how annoyed he was about it all. "She must be quite mad, who does she, who does she—"

Whatever else he was going to say was left unsaid as the uproar broke out down below. He jumped to his feet at once, looking over the wall. Rankin was up at once beside him, amazed at the scene below him, and again, most of those up in the Bar of Heaven were crowding to the balcony wall – some pushing in against the two of them as they looked down.

Along by the bar was a struggling mass of humanity – shrieks of the women caught up in the melée rising above any other noise. They could not see Lee Kyung Koh, but they knew she was in the middle of it somewhere. Hamilton knew what Rankin would be thinking, he grabbed his arm.

"Stay here," he ordered, "you'll gain nothing by getting into that."

Rankin knew that was true, and watched in horror as the fighting spread to the rest of the tables they could see, with women joining in. Some of the women up here in the Bar of Heaven were shrieking – Rankin couldn't think why.

The uproar grew, downstairs there was fighting everywhere, tables being overturned, waiters scrambling over tables to get into the fighting or to get out of it – more men in those blue bush jackets – more of her guards – dashing down the stairs to join in the fray.

"You were right, Ham, you were right," Rankin shouted in Hamilton's ear, meaning the danger to Lee Kyung Koh, and also that he was right about staying here on the balcony – it would be ridiculous for him to try and get down there, he wouldn't be able to get anywhere near her. It was all up to her guards, they had to save her – get her out of this.

Hamilton knew how desperate the situation was. To jump the Golden Lotus in the way they had here, the Ninety Seven – he was sure it was them – must be in great strength. He had wondered how they might do it, and now realised they were doing it in the only way the Asian mind knew, and always relied on – strength of numbers. But how had they achieved this strength in the nightclub, without it being obvious to the Golden Lotus Triad and the management?

There were no guns being used down there – knives certainly, bottles – and more men than there were guards.

Hamilton held tight to Rankin – he could understand his feelings –

"It's no use," he shouted at the soldier above the din. "No use at all. You can't get down there – and her own people wouldn't know what you were doing. You stay where you are."

Would anyone send for the Police, he wondered? If they had done so, could the Police stop this? If the Ninety Seven were in strength inside as they were, then they had prepared well and would be in strength outside. It would need a Police riot squad to get this under control.

The whole of the restaurant floor, as far as they could see, was a mass of fighting men and women – many women were on the floor, there were crumpled figures of men stretched out against the overturned tables – the noise was deafening. Hamilton was surprised nothing had started up here on the balcony.

Then Rankin caught a glimpse of Lee Kyung Koh. She was in a tight circle of the blue jacketed guards, forcing their way back to the staircase. Hamilton had seen her too, and held tight hold on him.

Her guards were winning – those protecting Lee Kyung Koh had gained the foot of the stairs with her. But there was fighting at the top where the blue jackets there were struggling with Chinese in evening dress. The Ninety Seven had planned well – they were up here as Hamilton knew they would be.

Rankin watched the blue jackets down below form a solid line across the foot of the stairs – how great their courage, how good their training, he thought. Then he saw Lee Kyung Koh. She was in great distress, her hair down, but still holding herself erect, with her arms across her front to keep her cheongsam together.

Mr Lee was with her, and now, with two of the guards, he was bringing her up the stairs.

Hamilton knew it was not all over yet. She was still not safe, far from it in fact.

Over the balcony leaped more Chinese in evening dress. It flashed through Hamilton's mind how thorough the Ninety Seven were. They had planned for this, for everything.

Some of the men leaping over had big drops to make, two did not land well and stayed down, but others did make it, and outnumbered the little group with Lee Kyung Koh.

"I'm going," Rankin shouted, and Hamilton released his hold on him. He could not stop him now, did not want to do so. Lee Kyung Koh needed Rankin's help, and nobody could have stopped him now.

Easily, as cool as if he had been in the camp gymnasium, he vaulted over the low wall, and on to the staircase, bracing himself for the uneven landing, and coming down asprawl one of the attacking Chinese. He was up in a flash, but the man beneath him did not get up. He pulled the nearest evening clothed man away from a guard, turned him around and hit him a mighty blow on the face – the man dropped flat.

He turned to face another, a little below him on the stairs. This one had a knife in his hand. Rankin thrust at him with his right leg, the sole of his right foot catching the man in the chest, and hurtled him full length down the stairs on to those fighting below.

Another attacker came at him low down, grabbing him round the knees in a rugby tackle, and almost pulling him to the ground. Rankin hit him a tremendous blow with the base of his fist right up in the small of the back, then, as the grip loosened, brought his right knee up hard into the man's chin. It hurt his knee, but he knew it would hurt the other a hell of a sight more, and he regained his balance quickly, as his attacker fell away, screaming in pain.

He scrambled up to Lee Kyung Koh – she screamed something at the two guards, still fighting the attackers off – he was sure it would be that he was on their side. From above, another man came at him, and Rankin met him with his left side and shoulder – a hard crunching shock – which shattered him away to bound into the wall of the staircase, and slowly slump to the ground.

He saw Mr Lee just below him, fighting valiantly, bleeding badly from the side of the head. The stairs, the bodies of the fallen, made it difficult to keep balance, and another opponent, leaping over the balcony, landed alongside him and lurched at him. Rankin hit him with a vicious short jab on the chin, and saw his eyes widen and go blank, while the man turned slowly around, and fell backwards down the stairs.

He got his left arm around Lee Kyung Koh. She was bleeding from the right shoulder, where there were long scratch marks from the top of her shoulder and down her right arm. In the fighting, her dress had been badly torn, and she was doing her best to hold it against her chest and around her middle.

"You'll be all right," he told her. "I've got you."

She smiled at him – still proud, still erect, doing her best to retain her composure, in spite of the difficulties she was having with the cheongsam, which they must have been trying to rip off her.

The fighting still raged below them, but they seemed to have beaten off the attackers on the stairs, whilst the blue jackets above had control at the top.

On the balcony, Hamilton had watched his chance and played his part. One of the attackers had jumped from the balcony opposite, landed in the centre of the staircase, staggered, and fell over just below him. Hamilton reached back to the table for the bottle of brandy, more than half full, leaned over the balcony, and, as the man picked himself up, crashed the bottle down on his head. It was a fearful blow, and the man had collapsed immediately, brandy and blood running down his face, leaving Hamilton holding on to the jagged part of the bottle – a good weapon, he thought, as he turned to face inwards again, just in case any other of the attackers had seen what had happened – but there were none.

Mr Lee went past Rankin up the stairs. "Bring her up, Mr Rankin," he said.

Rankin followed him, supporting Lee Kyung Koh. They passed through the line of blue jackets at the top, stepping over crumpled figures on the floor, and along the passage to the rear of the building.

Mr Lee opened a door of a room. "In here please," he said, almost as if he was showing them to a table in the restaurant. He closed and locked the door after them, then opened a cupboard at the side of the room, moved clothing on hangers on a rail to one side, fiddled at something on the rear wall, and a partition slid away.

He moved through the opening and switched on a light at the other side.

"Quickly, Mr Rankin," he called back, and Rankin helped Lee Kyung Koh through to where he was standing waiting for them.

"Careful," Mr Lee warned, "not too far." In the dim light, Rankin could see an iron staircase just along from him.

Mr Lee moved back into the cupboard, closed the door, re-arranged the clothing, and then, coming back to them, closed the partition on their side.

Rankin had taken off his jacket while they waited – there was a lot of blood on it, but, surprisingly, it wasn't torn.

"Put this on," he told Lee Kyung Koh, and she released one arm at a time from the cheongsam she was holding to do so, half turning away from him as she did. Rankin saw she had nothing on from the waist up, had she been wearing a brassiere, it had been torn off her when the cheongsam had been half ripped off her. Still turned away from him, he heard her rip the cheongsam and fiddle with it at the side. When she turned back she was holding it at the waist with one hand, as a skirt.

Mr Lee moved past them again, up the iron staircase, and into a long brick passage – smelling very musty. They hurried along, first Mr Lee, then Lee Kyung Koh, and then Rankin close behind her. The passage turned right and then left, inclining downwards to another flight of iron steps, this time downwards, to a large door, heavily bolted on the inside.

Mr Lee had difficulty in getting this door open. Rankin, holding on to Lee Kyung Koh, was just about to help when the last bolt clanged back, and the door opened. The wind and the rain of the storm swept in at them.

They followed Mr Lee out into the night and into the storm, the rain sheeting down, the cold shock of it making him gasp, and he felt Lee Kyung Koh cringe back into him. They were soaked in seconds.

Mr Lee shouted something to Lee Kyung Koh in Chinese, and bowed to her as he spoke – even here, Rankin thought – then turned to Rankin, still shouting.

"Stay with her, Mr Rankin," just that, an order, not a request, and went back through the door, slamming it hard behind him. Rankin heard the bolts being shut on the inside, and they were left, the two of them, in the street, and already wet through to the skin.

"Are you all right?" He had to shout at her to get above the noise of the storm. "Can you walk?"

She nodded her head, the water pouring down her off her long black hair, what was left of her make-up coming down in black streaks on either side of her nose, and red streaks down her chin. Like him, she was saturated and cold, but she was elated – she had escaped from the grave danger she knew she had been in, for a while, at any rate, and she was with this man who had been so brave, and, like her guards, had fought so hard to help her.

She had watched him jump down to her aid, seen how he had dealt with some of the attackers. Had it not been for him just at those crucial moments, they might have succeeded in their aims. It had been very close, and his intervention had probably saved her life, and the Triad.

She held his arm tightly, and led him down the poorly lit street. Away in front of them, some distance yet, was a better lit street, a main street perhaps, but Rankin had no idea where he was. He didn't care, he was too happy, thrilled to be with her – how glad he had been to get down to her on the staircase and get to her. Heavens, he had never hit anybody as hard as he had hit those devils, or fought like that.

About twenty yards from the end of the street, she stopped at a door, looked for a moment, went on to the next one, paused a moment, and then grabbed the door handle. It was locked. She shook it, and Rankin banged hard on the door with his clenched fist.

She shook the door again – impatient now, and Rankin banged even harder. They heard a noise from the inside, a screeching of bolts being moved, just saw a glimmer of light, and the door was flung open.

She said something sharply, and Rankin followed her inside, to a bare room, with a rickety old bed in one corner, on which the occupant had been sleeping, when their banging had awakened him.

He was old, thin, unkempt, and still half asleep, but he shouted something through an opening in the far wall, and soon two younger men appeared. These were sleepy looking also, but tough, thick-set – more of her guards, Rankin judged at once, though they were not wearing blue jackets. They kowtowed at once to Lee Kyung Koh when they saw her.

It was a bizarre scene, she in his coat and the remnants of her cheongsam, still having to hold on to it to keep the skirt part around her. Wet and dishevelled, like himself – and the three Chinese, and this dank old brick room – was Rankin dreaming all this?

The two young men were let out of the front door. Rankin knew the rain would soon wash all the sleep away, and in five minutes one of them was back. He spoke to Lee Kyung Koh, who turned and took Rankin's arm – she did not speak. They went out again into the pouring rain, leaving the old man behind to close the door after them, turned right into the main street, to where the second of the young men waited with a ricksha – the shafts down on the ground.

Still without a word, she clambered in – Rankin helping her, before getting in beside her. The rain beat down, driving under the hood of the ricksha. One of the men tried to put a plastic cover over their legs, but Rankin took it from him and wrapped it around her thighs and legs, tucking it in firmly – not that it was any good as she was wet through.

The man at the front took up the shafts and they started moving. Rankin could hear the other man running behind and feel him pushing. He put his left arm around her, pulling her in very close to him, bracing his feet hard down, and cowering back with her as much as he could under the hood, but it was very little protection.

The storm raged overhead, the rain hissed down. Fork lightning, sheet lightning, lit the sky for seconds at a time. The thunder rumbled and crackled, seemingly just over the top of them. The man pulling the ricksha jogged steadily on, aided by the efforts of the man pushing behind.

Rankin did not know where they were going, nor how far from the nightclub they were. They had gone quite a long distance down those passages with Mr Lee. He was content enough, wet as he was. She would know where they were making for, it was enough to be with her. Taxis passed them at intervals, lights blazing, wheels splashing up great waves of water as they passed, but the streets were otherwise deserted. Rankin didn't wonder about that, only criminals, thugs, imbeciles, Police – though he hadn't seen any Police – refugees, as they were, would be out on a night such as this.

Trams passed them, they were still running, like the taxis spurting up big waves of water as they passed. There were minor torrents of water everywhere, rushing down the side streets from the higher ground to their right, and about fifty yards in front of them, he could see another ricksha – it had been the same distance in front of them since they started off.

He did not know that, less than fifty yards behind, was yet another ricksha, or, that both the ricksha in front and the one behind were manned by Lee Kyung Koh's guards.

They were heading for the typhoon anchorage just beyond Kellett island, one of the escape routes for an occasion of danger as there had been tonight. The Minister and his security chief had always been prepared for this happening. There had been others of her guards in the house they had entered, who had been sent on immediately, down the route they were taking now, to ensure that more guards were strategically placed, and prepared to meet any further attack.

She nestled close to him. He had his left arm under her left side, his left hand just below her left breast, his right hand holding firm to the small rail of the ricksha, his feet braced hard down, keeping as steady and balanced as he could with her.

His thoughts raced. What a night it had been – so much had happened so quickly, and now here he was with this wonderful woman – wet through but happy, not caring where they were going and he would stay with her, wherever it was, as Mr Lee had asked him to do.

Bob Denton wouldn't believe any of it when he went back after his 48-hour pass was up – he could imagine what he would say when Rankin told him. Bob would be happy enough himself now, back at the mess, where events would be in full swing, but not as happy as Rankin was. What about Hamilton? Hope he's all right. Rankin had seen him lean over the balcony, and nearly brain one of the attackers with that bottle.

She moved her position a little, and his left hand came higher up to hold her, to her breast. Gosh, she's big breasted. She didn't try to move his hand away, but she turned her face up to him.

"You are a very brave man," the first words she had spoken to him in all this time, the first words he had heard her utter in English, apart from her thanks that time he had danced with her. It was lovely, silver toned music, in his ears.

He did not know what to say in return, but he moved his face down close to hers, down the wet black hair, brushing her cheeks with his nose, excitement sparkling within him, happy, proud, thrilled, and held her even closer to him.

They were moving along the waterfront. Lightning revealing the open space to their left, lighting up the buildings to their right, and the sky above in an awesome electrical display. The thunder roared, cracked and banged, as they went steadily on whilst the rain lashed at them, pouring and splashing off the hood on to them, running down the plastic he had wrapped around her, and to the floor of the ricksha where their feet were deep in water.

His left hand grew warm against her breast, her breast warming to his hand. Soaked as they were, the age old wonders of nature were stirring within them both and warming them.

They turned left, it was very dark here, unlit, then right again, and the ricksha men eased down to a walk. In the lightning flashes, Rankin could see boats to his left – they were almost at the side of whatever it was – a place where vessels had crowded in for shelter from "Judy", and from the elements that fickle typhoon lady was hurling down at them.

The ricksha came to a halt, the man in front holding on to the shafts. He shouted to the man at the back. They waited some minutes, huddled together, until the man returned from out of the darkness to say something to Lee Kyung Koh, and at once the man in front put down the shafts to the ground.

"Please come with me," she said, as he released his hold on her. She got down from the ricksha and he followed her, a few yards along the side of the road. A sampan moved into a clear space, and he heard her speak to the man on the boat, stood upright, easing alongside the quay wall.

She jumped aboard, and he followed her at once, the sampan rocking as he landed, then rocked again, as the man who had been pushing behind the ricksha, jumped on as well.

He braced himself against a canvas shelter built up on the deck of the sampan, and she reached for his hand, and directed him through one side held open by the boatman. He bent double, as she had done to get inside, moving down into the well of the boat with her. It was pitch black inside, he knelt down close to her.

He heard the men talking above their heads – it was dry inside this shelter, but the noise of the rain beating on the canvas was very loud – and he felt the sampan moving. He couldn't care where they were going to now, he was still with her.

She rummaged around and passed him a blanket. His eyes were becoming accustomed to the darkness.

"There are only blankets," she told him. "You must dry yourself." –

Unbelievable, absolutely unbelievable. I must be dreaming it, he told himself, but knew she was right. He took off his shirt and rubbed his hair and chest vigorously, then slipped off his trousers and underpants, sitting down to do so, and continued drying himself.

He was used to blankets, and they weren't as rough as some he had known, but they must have been rough for her to use.

The sampan bumped against another boat, and she was thrown against him. She had taken off the jacket he had given her, and the skirt, and was drying herself as best she could, kneeling with her back towards him.

He helped her kneel up again, feeling her back wet against him –

"Let me dry your back," he said, and without waiting for her to answer, turned and knelt behind her, and began rubbing her with his blanket. First the top of her back and her shoulders, gently but firmly, then her waist, then lower to her bottom and the sides of her thighs. She continued drying her front and her long black hair.

"Not too rough, am I?" he asked.

"It is good," she replied, "I was very cold. Now you must let me dry your back also." He turned round on his knees in the confined space, and she rubbed hard at him, as he had done to her, at the top, then the waist, then the lower part.

"It is good," he agreed, "I'm getting warm now."

He sat down again with his back towards her – her legs and feet, still wet, along his left side. He dried her feet, then her legs, rubbing the blanket up as far as her knees, whilst she continued rubbing at her hair.

He took off his shoes and socks, squelching wet, and put them as far away from him as he could, where he had put his clothes.

The sampan bumped again, rocking violently, and the bump brought them close together. She put her left hand on his bare shoulder – sending electric shocks buzzing through him. He took her hand in his left hand, and put it to his lips, kissing the back of it. She turned her hand over in his grasp, and moved her fingers gently along his top lip and lower lip, and then stroked his cheek.

She was very close to his back, her breasts against him. "You are very brave," she whispered, "so wonderfully brave."

The heat rose within him, he moved back a little more, as much as he could on his bottom, half turning to his left as he did so. She put her right hand on his right shoulder, and slowly round and down to his chest. He moved back to her, half turning to the left as he did so, back against her breasts and upper body – his face to her. His lips moved along her cheek, and she tightened her hold on him. His lips found hers.

After a while, he moved his mouth from hers. "Are there any more blankets?" he asked.

"There are more," she whispered, leaning back away from him and rummaging again. "Yes, there are three."

He took one from her and spread it down on the bottom of the deck, then another in the same way. It wasn't easy in what little space there was, and his hands moved against her legs, her thighs and her bottom, as he manoeuvred the blankets into place.

"Now, let's get these wet blankets out of the way," he said, throwing them to where he had put his wet clothes, and turned to her again, his mouth coming to hers at once. She clasped him tightly, fiercely, her mouth wide open to him. She was trembling violently, but from the rising heat of her body, he knew it was not because of the cold.

His right hand moved down to her left breast, holding the fullness of it for a few seconds, and gently playing with the nipple with his first finger.

He moved his mouth away from her again, and whispered, "Can I have the other blanket?"

She passed it to him, and he spread it out along his feet – changing his position to come alongside her. It was a tight squeeze, and he moved his hand down to bring her feet forward, stroking her all the way down her body and her thighs as he did so, but holding her firmly with his left arm.

His lips found hers again, their mouths opening wide, their tongues darting into each others' mouths. He slowly pushed her back to lie on the blankets he had placed on the deck, easing carefully alongside her, full stretch to her, and reached down to pull the blanket over them.

There was just room for them lying facing each other. He made himself comfortable with her, making sure he was not yet lying on her, just against her – his left arm under her neck, his right hand free to caress her.

His body was on fire now, and so was hers. The cold, the wet, the outside world and all its happenings, forgotten. His right hand moved her left leg over and around his legs – higher and higher around him.

14

ESCAPE TO HAPPINESS

Rankin had long been convinced that his romance with Alice had been the best thing that could have happened to him, as well as being a wonderful experience, and tonight was the certain proof of it.

It had given him a mature outlook on life in the most satisfying way, given him an understanding and appreciation of women he could not otherwise have gained, and made him certain that sex was an enjoyment which could only come with great respect, warmth and affection, which grew into love.

For Rankin, it had been perfection in the greatest of comfort, and with the most accomplished and receptive woman to instruct him, enjoy him, and love and respect him for the pleasure and happiness he brought to her. Rankin had always treated Alice with the utmost courtesy, had considered her a lovely woman, thrilled to her, loved her, enjoyed her, and respected her body for what it was a– paradise for him to enter and enjoy to the full.

This was the way he always thought of women because of Alice, what he had thought about Lee Kyung Koh when he had first seen and danced with her.

Rankin was at his very best with all the expertise Alice had taught him. He needed to be, had to be, only that was good enough for this gorgeous woman – all arms, all legs, all body, and mouth and deep passion. Carefully, tenderly, Rankin wooed her with hands and mouth and tongue, whilst she made queer moaning sounds, held him fiercely, her long nails digging deep into his shoulders and back.

She spoke only once, bringing her lips to his right ear, biting his ear and sucking it – then whispered, "Please be careful" – a pause whilst she bit again, then kissed the ear. "No man has entered me, no man has ever touched me."

He was surprised in a way, though he hadn't time to think about it, but it was obvious she was inexperienced in the art of love. She tried to hold him too close to her – he didn't want that just yet, and was all movement – too much movement.

"Careful – careful – careful," he whispered to her – "ease your mouth a little – open it – careful, beautiful."

The sampan rocked – he wondered what the men up above would be thinking. They would know what was happening, he could be sure of that, but it wasn't any of their business, though perhaps it would remind them of some of their own amorous adventures.

Funny what you think about at a time like this – Rankin was sure the Chinese would have their feelings and their memories. How funny life is, fate is, for him to be here with this beautiful Chinese woman in a sampan, lying on blankets. He had heard tales from some of the men that the sampans the water prostitutes used were very comfortable, the rain beating down on the canvas shelter which protected them, the thunder rumbling above, lightning keeping the skies almost permanently ablaze.

Carefully – slowly – he eased himself over on to her, forcing her legs wide with his knees, wincing as his right knee, the one he had half-killed one of the Ninety Seven with in the nightclub, banged the deck. He felt her shudder – moved away slightly, then back, gently but firmly. She shuddered again, cried aloud – and he was there.

He came to his climax quickly, this first time, but she was with him, he knew that, moaning, her mouth wide open, holding on to him with all her strength, her nails scratching him right down the back, her legs wrapped around him – and now the sampan rocked more violently – their storm as magnificent as the one raging overhead, and he gave – and gave – and gave.

When it was over, he came naturally to the "afterglow" position he had always known with Alice, moving his legs outside hers, still lying on her, forcing her legs close together to hold him within her – taking most of his own weight on his elbows, kissing her gently, letting his mouth play all around her face, and into her long black hair which had sleeked down her left side, over her shoulder and arm in her violent movements, biting her ear tenderly, kissing her neck – her hands the while running up and down his back from the nape of his neck slowly, lovingly, down, to his bottom.

This was the wonderful part of loving the book and Alice had taught him, the glorious intimate respite in between the give, the take, the action. This was the delicacy of love.

He lowered himself as much as he could into her body, enjoying the splendid feel of their togetherness all the way down, pushing his chest into her great breasts, though still not heavy on her.

"You are wonderful, truly, truly wonderful," he whispered in her ear.

"I'm so happy," she whispered back. "So very happy it is you who have made me a woman."

Happiness engulfed Lee Kyung Koh. How wonderful this man was, how gentle, how strong, how accomplished, how vital. All her hopes, her dreams, her desires, had suddenly come true. She was at last a woman.

How strange she had discussed her feelings with Ai Fah that very morning. The first time she had ever spoken in such intimate fashion with her number one amah. Now she knew what love was all about – what men and women found in each other – why men wanted women, and why women wanted men. Many times in her life she had known how empty it was, in spite of all her activities, and this morning she had been sure there could never be anything for her as a woman, only to be sadly jealous of that mother and her new born child, and to be a woman who was a leader of a Triad, but had no man to call her own, to love, to adore, to be with always.

Travel, Ai Fah had said – find the one man who is waiting for you. But could she have done that, could she have left the Triad and the only life she knew, and if she could, would she have done?

But now all that was not necessary, it had all happened for her. Ai Fah was right, there *is* a man for every woman, there *is* a man for me. And he is lying on top of me now, lying within me, we are two people, and we are just one – how blessed am I – and how well worth waiting for this wonderful man.

There were no thoughts of the ordeal she had passed through at the nightclub. What the enemy would have done to her had they captured her, she did not know, nor was she thinking about it. Forgotten already the escape from the Golden Lotus, the ricksha ride to safety through the typhoon, still raging above them. She was safe now, she was certain of that.

No thoughts of the past, no time yet to think of the future, though that would have to be faced. The Minister would have to know about this, he would know something of it already. All the future plans would have to include this man. She wanted him in her life – would fight everyone for him.

It was obvious to her now that right from the very first time she had seen him, when he had asked her to dance, when she had danced with him, that he was the man for her, though she hadn't dared to think so then. But it had come true, just as Ai Fah had said, as it was written in the stars. There were some problems for her to overcome, but those problems could wait a while until she could give them her full attention. She never gave it a thought that there might be problems for him also.

The escape route – one of the many planned by the Minister – was simple. The more simple the plan, the easier to carry out. By ricksha or taxi to the anchorage, then to one of the Triad's junks, or to a motor boat, and straight across the water to Kowloon where she would be taken – again by ricksha or taxi to another of her apartments.

But it had not been that simple tonight, and she was glad, glad beyond all belief – so happy it had not worked as fast and as smoothly as it should have done. So happy she was here on the sampan – poor as it was – with this man. With him it wasn't a sampan it was a love boat, the blankets were pure silk, the atmosphere all romance – oh how fortunate a woman I am!

The nearness of "Judy" was the cause of it all, why they must stay in the anchorage. The junk was somewhere else in shelter, it was not just outside as it should have been, as it had been night after night for many months – that had been impossible with "Judy" throwing so much at Hong Kong.

Word had been sent to the Minister who would decide what the next action would be. In the meantime she was safe, surrounded by many other sampans, with a great number of men and women of the Triad all around her and alert. If, and when, the storm eased, the junk might come outside to pick her up – to pick them up – this man would be with her, but all that she did not care about. What she did care about was here on the sampan with her – lying here on top of her with just the canvas shelter above them, and they were warm and cosy though there were damp parts, and the rain had leaked in near their feet. But that they did not notice. The stars are right – he is here, my man . . .

His strength began to return to him and ecstacy ran through her as the tender kisses became more demanding. The fire came to her quickly as he moved firmly and strongly within her. The sampan rocked again. Her hands traced patterns on his broad back and down, down to his bottom, pushing him further into her. Her mouth, her body, her whole being, wide open to him and his great strength.

They loved and talked through the night – a wonderful night. A fantastic night, so close to each other in the limited space of the sampan with the musty fishy smell of the lived-in interior, the rough comforts of the blankets, the dampness, the noise of the rain and the storm outside, lessening, as "Judy" moved on, having never really centred near to Hong Kong. The lightning was infrequent now, the thunder rumblings fainter, whilst the two of them came close and deep into sweet intimate companionship – something Lee Kyung Koh had never known before, and more close even than he had been with Alice. A strange pair – how was it possible fate had brought them together like this?

Rankin was her equal, nay, more, he was her master, her hero, her heavenly delight. All other men except her father had been so careful, so correct, in their dealings with her, and she had not dreamed there could be this sort of relationship with a man. This perfection, this giving of everything, this taking of everything, and this great joyful possession of each other.

To Rankin, she was paradise, a deep treasure of tremendous fire and passion, a great length of loveliness, longer than he as they lay together, wondrous long arms and legs that wrapped around him possessingly, suppleness of body he had not known in Alice, delightful as she had been, with internal control which held him tight within her, and amazed him with the power of it, something he had read about in the book, but which Alice had not been able to master. Lee Kyung Koh's physical exercises daily had unknowingly given her this inward strength – strength that thrilled Rankin beyond anything he had ever known, and made her the most perfect of women.

Rankin's power and vitality filled her with great joy – she had never imagined that loving could give these great thrills. She ran her hands all over him, playing with him under the legs when he was not within her – holding his head down to her breasts whilst he filled his mouth with her nipples, enjoying him savagely, viciously – giving out loud cries of satisfaction, and glorifying that, with each succeeding encounter, he could be stronger and stronger with her.

Rankin knew the rocking of the sampan was full evidence of their coupling for the men above, let alone her shouts, her moans and her cries, but he was proud that he could achieve so much for this gorgeous woman. Inevitably he compared her to Alice – how glorious each was in her own way, but how different this one to the tender passiveness of Alice. "You're a lucky man, Rankin," he told himself. "How can any one man be so lucky?"

He encouraged her to talk between their loving – and after a while, she found it easy to do so. Surprisingly easy that she should want to say so much to him, to tell him so much about herself and about her life, to answer questions, to ask them, to talk and talk and talk, and then again to love.

She told him of her childhood, her father, the Triad, how she lived, of the old China she had known, and of Hong Kong and the dangers to her, such as had been tonight, and of her praise of his bravery, and how he had rescued her from a fate even she could not bear to think of.

He found her so intensely interesting, and so very loving in between all the many things she told him about.

She had never been one to accept that women could not share in the many liberties men enjoyed, never had she been a woman to be put in the background – not even her father could do that to her.

"It was always the way of men to maintain their privileges, even in the lowest household. The men, the master and the sons, had all the good things, the women, especially the daughters, were as servants, but I would not allow that, and have tried to encourage the younger women of the Triad to follow my example. Fortunately, the younger men, the educated men, especially those who have been to England and America, as many have, see it my way. They are not happy with the old customs, we are breaking away from them gradually."

She told him of the old custom of the number one wife, the "Tsai", as she was called, encouraging a husband to take other wives. This gave them a standing as head of the household, power over the other wives.

"Sometimes," said almost fiercely, "the number one wife chose the other wives for her husband – so ridiculous – of course they would only choose those they could be certain would treat the number one wife in the way she wished – as the head, in charge of all the women of the house. –

“Is it so” – this said so wistfully – “that a man is more powerful than a woman – does a man need more than one woman to exploit his sex?”

Rankin thought that one over carefully –

“Perhaps so,” he said, “you know how many wives the old Eastern rulers were supposed to have, or concubines at least. Some of them had hundreds.”

“And could they use them all?” she queried.

“I don’t know,” he confessed, “I don’t think so, but there is an old saying that variety is the spice of life, but I could not fancy that sort of life.” Then, with real feeling and great truth, he added – “I’d be more than content with you only.”

This pleased her so much, fitted in with all her thoughts and plans. This man was hers, and there was nothing she would not do to keep him. She had no idea what his situation was, whether he could stay with her in Hong Kong, or whether they would need to leave and go elsewhere?

Perhaps she would need to abdicate the leadership of the Triad, as Ai Fah had suggested when they had talked that morning. But need she? Could she not remain as the figurehead, leaving all the decisions to her Minister and the Council? That she had read, and been told, was how the Queen of England lived, and she still remained the Queen, led her own family life as far as possible, fitted in with the affairs of state. Surely she and he could do that with the Triad?

He was so marvellous with her – with his strength coming back to him at intervals, when he would start his love making again, using all his artistry, all his knowledge, with his mouth, lips, fingers, playing their full part before coming in to her again, and now, as his strength had been slower to return, so his control was greater, and he could use long magnificent thrusts which thrilled her fully, gasping, moaning, crying Chinese love expressions to him, holding on to him with all her strength, until at last would come his explosion of love within her, and she would cry aloud with happiness and thrilling passion.

At times, she would lie alongside him, fondling him all over with her left hand, holding on to him low down for a while. She told him of the time she had been sent to America as a young girl, and of the young men she had known there. There had been one who courted her strongly, but wanted more than she would give.

"He wanted me to allow him to put his spear into me," she said, "but I did not let him, did not let him touch me where he wanted to. He was nice, but not to be my man – I knew I was not for him."

Rankin chuckled – "I love the word, spear – it's beautiful."

"Do you not call it that?" she asked.

"Well, I've never heard it called that before"

"What do you call it then?"

He was highly amused. "There are several terms – some rude – but I think 'spear' is probably the best – it certainly sounds nice when you say it."

She was puzzled. "How can it be rude? It is a natural thing – it is part of the body."

"It is, it is indeed," he agreed, "but we don't often refer to it at all and I think it is a wonderful name for it – bless you."

"It is funny," she said, "we cover up all the sexual parts of ourselves as though everything is a dreadful secret, but you have taught me it is all so truly wonderful."

"It is wonderful – you are wonderful," he assured her, "and how we came to meet, how you danced with me, it is fate that we should meet, and all this was destined to be."

She agreed with him so wholeheartedly. "You are right, it is written in the stars for all of us, that I know. I was surprised when you asked me to dance, no man had ever asked me before, though I did dance with some young men in America. I was so happy when you asked, and I know now I have always wanted you, and wanted you immediately. I was always happy when you came to the Golden Lotus, just to see you," she rubbed her hand over his chest and trunk, "but I did not dare to think the stars would give me all this happiness."

She nestled her face close to his, kissing him, licking his lips with her tongue.

"You are happy?"

He held her very tight. "Wonderfully happy."

"This is paradise," she said.

"It is paradise," he agreed. "And without the bother and expense of dying."

He asked her why she had no pubic hair on her body, and she told him of the Parsee women, and how beautiful they are. He had not heard about them, nor the custom she practised, but he told her over and over again that no woman was as lovely as she, no woman ever could be.

Once he had to leave her to go on deck – he had left it as long as he could, and was pleased the rain had eased. His movements alarmed her –

"I must go," he told her, kneeling above her. "I have to make water."

She was relieved when she understood him. "To piss?" she asked, surprising him that she used the word, but then he realised she could use no other and this was the word in the dictionary.

On deck the rain had stopped, but the wind still blew strongly. His knee was sore and puffing badly. Away over the high hills of Kowloon he could see the lightning – marvellous to watch – a great and awesome wonder of nature, jagged fork lightning, splitting the sky with venomous coloured darts, and sheet lightning, exposing the darkness of the peaks and hills for seconds. Far away there was the rumbling of thunder, and it was chilly up here, out of the warmth of her arms.

They were in a sea of sampans – entirely surrounded by other small craft. He knew why – there was safety in such numbers. There were two figures sitting on the deck, patiently awaiting the orders, the whims, of their leader, or the person from whom the next instructions would come, he knew the Chinese were renowned for their patience.

Around him, as he grew accustomed to the semi-darkness, he could make out other figures on the deck of nearby sampans. She was safe enough here. He knelt down just behind the two figures on the deck, where there was a patch of water, and the nearest sampan on that side a couple of yards away. No need to worry – he had to do this, or burst, and he didn't want to burst. Anyway it was a natural act and wouldn't worry any of those who might be watching him – there were certainly no toilets on these little boats. He wondered what they would do, however, if Lee Kyung Koh felt the same way, and had to come up there on the deck.

She hadn't that urge, but she had the other as soon as he was back to the warmth of her embrace – the boat rocking again – her cries and moans half muffled by his mouth, her nails digging deep into his already scarred back, as they swept together up the magnificent waves of love – he very dominant, and with tremendous power, her arms, her legs, her everything, gripping him to her, to the final bursting surge of his strength into her.

Afterwards he held her against him – lying on his back with her lying half atop him on his left side, her long body against him, her left leg high up over his middle as far as the confines of the boat would allow.

Her thoughts were rampant – she was thinking of everything, and now much of his feelings. She knew of the pride of men – knew how proud he would be. Whatever was to be done to keep them together needed very careful thought. But this was love, real love – for her and for him. He had told her he could not do this with a woman unless he was in love with her, unless there was a spark for each other, as there was. She had so much money, enough, and more than enough, for them both, but this would be a problem. She would gladly give it all to him, and then it would be his money, not hers, but would he take it?

His thoughts were busy also, but not about problems. With all his experiences with Alice, he was still amazed at the loveliness and vitality of this woman. She was everything a man could desire.

"I have seen a lot of women in different countries," he told her, "but never one like you, never such a beautiful woman as you."

She would have liked to ask if he had been with many women. He must have been – he could not otherwise have had all this expertise – but she did not ask.

She ran her hands around his mouth – he liked this as he kissed her hands and her fingers. "I am so happy you tell me that, very happy, it is so nice you think that of a Chinese woman."

"The Chinese are very beautiful," he said at once, "and very smart, but you are the most lovely of them all by far. You are so wonderfully elegant, so luscious here" – he gave her breast a gentle squeeze, and brought his mouth down to give the nipple a tender bite. "These gorgeous legs, so long, so lovely" – he moved his hand down the inside of her leg – slowly – excitingly. "You have so much charm, you are so vital, all Chinese women cannot be like you."

This time she dared to ask, "You have been with other Chinese girls."

"No – never – nor with any other sort of girls except one."

He told her about Alice, lying there with her, paying great tribute to the woman who had given him his first love, and taught him so much about loving.

She appreciated the telling – he was a truthful man.

"And since then – nothing – until now?" she asked.

"Nothing, and never wanted it until you," which was almost true, he had always wanted her, and had forgotten all about Carrie Jane.

"I play football, so I train a lot," he explained, "so no time to worry about girls."

She could understand to a certain extent.

"Is it bad then for a man to do this?"

"Oh heavens, no, it's very good for you, really," He was most definite about that, "but as I've told you," – a pause while he kissed her – "it has to be like this as far as I'm concerned. I could not do it cold, can you understand that? – with a prostitute. For me, sex is love, and love is sex, I know no other way."

She understood him. "My Triad does not allow prostitutes, but we know other Triads do," she told him. "We know many young girls are still sold as slaves, and end up as prostitutes – here in Hong Kong, in Singapore, in Australia, in many countries. It is terrible, there are many bad houses here."

Rankin had heard a lot about the cat-houses, as they were known, from the high-class, very expensive, establishments, down to the lowest and dirtiest of places. Knew also of the prostitutes, who were possibly not part of an organised ring, who operated in the open air at night, wherever they could encourage a client, or in a taxi, or a hotel, if the client paid for the room. The "ten dollar jennies".

"It is hard to put the blame on the girls," he said, "it's a natural function, soldiers must have female company or they'd go mad, and there isn't any in Hong Kong at their level unless they find a Chinese girl, which many of them do."

She knew this, knew that many girls of her Triad had married British soldiers. "The Chinese girls are very western minded now, some of our girls are married to your soldiers, we have a lot who live in your country. It is bound to happen, and this Chinese person is so wonderfully happy that you like her."

"Liking is not the proper word," he retorted at once. "I'm sure it is love," another pause whilst he kissed her again. "Yes, I'm sure it's love."

Lee Kyung Koh was enraptured, it was exactly what she wished to hear – he was her man. She thought of the many things they could do together. She would make him the head of her personal bodyguard –

no, that wasn't enough for him, he was her prince – they would travel, she would go anywhere with him.

He too was enraptured, deeply engrossed already in this romance. She was a sheer delight, there could not be another woman like her. Conversation was so easy with her – he enjoyed listening to her – still chuckling at her use of the word 'spear', and wondered why, if she had known the proper dictionary word for making water, she had not known the real word, but perhaps it was a Chinese term translated to English.

"Perhaps I am not really Chinese," her thoughts simply had to come out, to be explained to him. "My father and my mother were true Chinese, but, perhaps far back, there was another strain. Many western people, western men, came to China long years ago, to my part of the country. I perhaps I have other than Chinese blood in me."

There really is no problem, she told herself, no obstacle at all why we should not always be together. There were many mixed marriages in Hong Kong nowadays, she mixed a lot with British officials. No, they could get over any problem.

"Perhaps you are right," he agreed – "these" – a gentle squeeze of her breast – "are so wonderful – I have not seen another Chinese woman, but it is said they do not have big breasts."

She hastened to the defence of her countrywomen – "Oh, that is wrong! Of course many of our women have big breasts, good figures, but I have always exercised each day, and that must have helped my development. It is good?"

"It is marvellous," he assured her, and there was silence as their lips became busy again, his free hand more active.

The boatman called something from above, and she started up at once, speaking very rapidly back to him in a commanding voice. The man said something else again, she replied quickly, but this time less forceful. Then she sank back to him, coming over to him to find his lips with hers for a moment.

"It will be time to go soon, the main part of the storm has passed. We will go to Kowloon," she could not keep the sadness out of her voice.

He knew the same sadness. "What a great pity we cannot stop time passing, that we cannot say now, 'stop', and it will always be like this, and we would always be together, just we two."

He amazed himself that he should think this way. It had never been thus with Alice, much as he had enjoyed their love making, but now he was lost – the Army – his career – football – all forgotten, only this woman mattered.

"You say wondrous things, you are a wonderful lover, a wonderful man. You fill my heart with gladness, and I would wish you to always stay with me."

"I will stay with you, as long as I can," he assured her.

"It will be for always," she said, and he knew she meant it. He was glad, and proud, but the full realisation had not possessed all his thoughts at that moment.

The fire was back with her, not that it had ever left her since he first roused her, but now she demanded him. He could feel the sudden heat of her right down his body. Her lips roamed his mouth, his cheeks, his neck, shoulders, chest. Her desire brought back his strength – she could feel him down against her, and her mouth and body grew even more possessive.

He lifted her gently over on top of him, and then carefully settled her on to him. She understood immediately what she had to do, firmly, fully, they locked together.

"Now," he told her, "this time you can do it all."

She needed no instruction as he took his hands away from her sides and brought them to her breasts. Leaning forward, she eased up and down above him, slowly at first, then quicker – her head coming down to him, her mouth seeking and finding his. He moved his hands down her back, slowly, right down from the top, right down to her bottom – slowly – everything he did easily, slowly, never hurry, Alice had once told him, never hurry until the great finale – slowly for the greatest effect. But her movement was much faster now – the rocking of the sampan was more violent than at any other time – and he thrust upwards – ever upwards – for the glory of his climax – and for hers.

He was still lying full beneath her when the canvas above his head opened, and one of the men said something to her. She raised herself from him to reply. Soon the sampan began to move, bumping hard against the others. The canvas opened again and something was put through on top of them – a bundle of clothing.

"We must go now," she said, and kissed him long and passionately, their mouths wide open to each other, her long hair falling all over his face and shoulders, as he held her to him with all his strength.

It was even more difficult to put on the clothing than it had been to take off his wet things earlier. Rankin found he had a pair of trousers of rough material, far too small for him, but he managed to button them around him, and a jacket, also very tight.

He searched back in his wet clothing for his wallet, as Lee Kyung Koh shouted something to the men above, and the canvas was thrust back to give them more light. She had managed to put on trousers and a blouse, or was it a jacket – he couldn't quite make out. His shoes were soaking wet still, and he did not bother to put them on – his knee was sore and had swollen up a lot.

He could not think what time it was. They had been in the sampan for hours, he knew that, but it seemed only minutes, and yet it seemed weeks – alas, time would not stand still for them. He hadn't any thoughts about the future – didn't even care that his knee was so sore, his brain too full of her. What a glorious woman – the most glorious in all the world – and he did not want all this to end.

They sat together, his arm around her. What contentment there was for them both in each other's company, and in each other's arms, even in this sampan.

"We will go on one of my junks to Kowloon," she told him, brushing his cheeks with her lips as she spoke, "there will be a taxi waiting for us at the dock, and we will go straight to my apartment. You will stay with me?"

"I will stay with you for ever," he said. It sounded so good to them both.

15

HAMILTON ABDUCTED

Hamilton held on to the jagged remains of the brandy bottle. It would be a handy weapon for him if he was attacked, and someone must have seen him crown that man on the staircase.

He moved back from the balcony towards the cubicles, near to a little group of Chinese – elderly men and women, very frightened, and obviously not Ninety Seven agents.

He saw Rankin and Lee Kyung Koh reach the top of the stairs, following the manager it looked like, then they vanished from his sight along the passage from where she had first appeared. He was sure there would be a good getaway plan, and they would be safe.

Downstairs was still bedlam, but it was quiet up here – there was no more balcony jumping. It looked as if the Ninety Seven men had all committed themselves to the fighting on the stairs. Some of the blue jacketed guards moved down – reinforcements for below, leaving just two of their number at the top.

After a while, Hamilton moved forward – the two guards at the top of the stairs took no notice of him. Close to the balcony, one table was still standing. On it – upright and unharmed – a bottle of brandy almost full, glasses, dishes and a jug of water. He transferred the jagged remains of the bottle to his left hand, and with his right hand, poured some water into a glass, rinsed it round, and threw the water into a dish. He repeated the movement, had a good look at the glass to see it was reasonably clean, then poured himself a good measure of brandy. He took a good sip – that's the stuff, he thought – Courvoisier – he liked good brandy. All the time he was alert, watchful, but didn't bother to look over the balcony to see what was still going on.

The manager came back along the passage. He looked battered, and had long streaks of blood down his face. He spoke to the guards at the top of the stairs, looked towards Hamilton, and turned to come around the balcony to him.

Suddenly shooting started below, Hamilton threw himself down at once, jerking the glass out of his right hand as he did so. Down on the floor against the balcony, he found he still held the jagged bottle remains in his left hand. He had been lucky not to injure himself.

The shooting lasted a minute only. Several single shots, then a burst from an automatic, then more single shots – a deeper bang this time. One bullet ricochéd, zinging up the staircase to plop into the roof somewhere above his head. He stayed down – surely the Police must be in by now.

Mr Lee saw Hamilton dive for the floor, and followed his example – the two guards remained standing.

A Police sergeant and two constables came slowly up the stairs, pistols in their hands. They looked around carefully, then the sergeant shouted something down to those below. Soon they were joined by another sergeant and more constables – all armed.

Hamilton got up off the floor, brushed his suit down and then, at last, put down the jagged part of the bottle he had held on to. He looked at the Police – their uniforms soaking wet, he had forgotten about the storm outside. Phew – damn glad they're in, he thought – time for another brandy.

He watched one of the sergeants and three constables move out the back way, and the other sergeant go down the stairs with the manager, leaving three constables at the top of the stairs with the two guards. He picked up a chair and set it at the table, rinsed himself another glass in the same way as he had done the first, poured himself another brandy.

A British inspector came up with a sergeant. Hamilton remained seated watching them. The inspector, like the others, was soaked. Apart from a few shouts downstairs, it was fairly quiet – Hamilton judged the danger was over.

The inspector, big, broad shouldered, sandy moustache well trimmed, took command.

"We do not wish anybody to leave for the present," he shouted, "we'll have the tables set up for you. Please sit down, make yourselves comfortable. There is no danger now, but we will want to take all your names and addresses. Now, is anyone hurt? Does anyone need medical treatment?"

Jolly well done, Hamilton thought. Couldn't have done it better myself.

The sergeant repeated what the inspector had said, in Chinese, but he wasn't as polite as the inspector had been, and he made it clear that nobody could leave until the Police gave them permission to do so.

Some captains and waiters reappeared, and commenced to pick up tables and chairs, set them in some sort of position, clear up the debris, and bring on fresh glasses. Mr Lee came bounding up the stairs then around the bar –

"Order what you wish," he called out, "with our compliments – there will be no bills for anyone tonight."

The guests began to settle back to tables, there had been no demand for medical attention, and soon the waiters were busy. Like Hamilton, most of the guests needed a drink after that experience.

The manager stopped at Hamilton's table. "All right, sir?" he asked.

Hamilton was quite composed. "Perfectly thanks. Did they get away all right?"

Mr Lee hesitated for a moment or two, then, "Yes, they did, I'm sure they will be safe."

"Good," Hamilton nodded his head in approval. "Well done, it must be bad down below"

"It's awful, a lot of people hurt, some very badly, some dead, it's like a battlefield."

Hamilton could imagine the scene. He would have liked to ask more, but didn't. "Thank you," he said simply, "spoilt a good night, eh?"

Eventually the Police took names and addresses. Hamilton vividly remembered the last time he had given his name to anyone in uniform in this manner. Eighteen years before when Hong Kong had fallen,' Then it had been to a Japanese soldier, who had spoken excellent English, and then they had filed past him, whilst sullen bitter looking Japanese guards jabbed them with rifles, spat at them, kicked them, as they moved slowly on in a long queue.

In this case, the Police came to each table, were most correct, and by this time, most of the debris had been cleared up, the Bar of Heaven nearly back to normal.

The inspector found time to have a word with Hamilton. He looked hard at the brandy bottle, but Hamilton knew better than to offer him a glass on duty.

"Oh, I'm perfectly all right," Hamilton assured him, "but it was nasty whilst it lasted. Gang fight, was it?" testing out what the Police might or might not know.

"No doubt about that," the inspector agreed. "Bloody nasty, two rival gangs, one lot owns the place, the other lot either wanted it, or wanted to wreck it."

Hamilton knew this was the stock answer. It was more than likely the inspector would know something about the real object – the attempted capture of Lee Kyung Koh, but, of course, he couldn't disclose any of that.

"I'm only up here for a few days from Singapore," Hamilton said, "you often get this sort of affair up here, don't you?"

The inspector could be truthful now. "Not lately, it's been quiet," but looking around for a second, and lowering his voice, "we think this lot has been brewing up for quite some time, could well be a big showdown, and this is the start of it."

"Oh lor, I hope not, I've a few days before I go back to Singapore yet, don't want to get mixed up in anything like this again." A pause, then "What was the shooting?"

The typical way to ask a question, switch quickly from one subject to another, tends to throw the other person off his guard for a moment.

"The attackers getting out," the inspector kept his voice low, "could well have been the signal to call it off, to get out as best they could. A lot of them didn't get out, we're sorting it all out down below."

Hamilton was nearer to the balcony than any of the others. The tables, apart from the one he was using, had been kept well back on the orders of the Police. He didn't bother to look over to see what was going on – he'd seen enough scenes of carnage in his time.

Gradually the place emptied, most people leaving as soon as the Police had finished questioning them, escorted out the back way, but Hamilton stayed on.

Mr Lee – up and down the stairs at frequent intervals, encouraged him to do so – "There's a terrible storm outside, the rain is coming down in buckets, that's how you term it, I think. I should stay here for a while."

"I will," Hamilton agreed, "as long as I'm not a nuisance to you. In any case, I've got to get back to Kowloon. I wonder if the ferry is still running?"

He wasn't at all bored, wasn't keen on going out whilst the storm was raging, content to wait, sip coffee and brandy. He'd been pleased when they brought him the coffee, listening to the odd snatches of conversation and the shouting between the waiters as they went about their work amongst the tables and the litter.

Mr Lee came back again. Hamilton was sure the manager wanted to ask him about the coffee.

"It's excellent, much prefer coffee to tea myself ," he replied, "only drink tea during the day. Coffee goes far better with brandy. Sure there's no bill for me to square up?"

"No sir, nothing, it's all with our compliments." Then, "Are you all right here? You can use my office if you wish, it's much more comfortable than this, with all this clearing up going on. I'll have the brandy and coffee sent in for you."

Oh ho, Hamilton thought, he wants me in there to ask the questions. What can he think I'll know about Rankin, or anything else? It would have been most interesting, and he knew he could hold his own with any questioner, providing all things were equal. He might learn a lot himself about Lee Kyung Koh, but no, he would stay where he was.

"No thanks – quite all right here – thanks all the same."

He was surprised, and pleased, when Sam Reynolds came up the stairs. Glad now he had refused the invitation into the office. He might well have missed Reynolds.

A grin broke over Reynold's serious face when he saw Hamilton, and he came over to the table immediately, his wet appearance proof of the bad weather outside. Hamilton stood up, smiling, happy to see Reynolds.

"Hello, Ham," Reynolds greeted him, "you been here all the time?"

"Yes indeed, came in before nine. It's been quite a night."

"Looks to have been," Reynolds agreed. "I've only just got here, I was at Repulse Bay when we got the first message, but there were others here so I didn't have to come."

"Trouble over at Repulse Bay?" Hamilton asked.

"No, not a thing, but we got a tip-off there would be – probably a false alarm to throw some strength from here. Then on the way back, I was pushed to Causeway Bay – it's bad up in the shacks behind there again – you know the sort of thing – hundreds of shacks washed away down the rocks. You know how they perch them up the sides of the hills there – it always happens when we have this sort of rain."

Hamilton knew what he meant. This was a typical part of Hong Kong life, he could well imagine the chaos going on in many such areas in Hong Kong and Kowloon.

"It's bad down there too," he waved his hand to the stairs.

"It was, they tell me," Reynolds agreed, "but they've got it pretty well cleaned up – three dead, including a woman – a lot of people badly beaten up, a lot of women hurt. Some walking wounded, and a lot of them taken for questioning it's been threatening a long time."

"Any trouble anywhere else?"

"Surprisingly not, this seems to have been the only effort – can't think why."

Hamilton knew well that Reynolds could think why, but he wasn't going to say so. "It's good brandy," he nodded his head at the bottle. "Like just a wee taste?"

"I could do with a wee taste," Reynolds said, "but of the good stuff, whisky. Not on duty though."

"Thought not," Hamilton said, "but we could go in the manager's office, he's just asked me in – nice chap."

Reynolds thought awhile, "No thanks, Ham, not here," he looked around, looked over the balcony for a minute. "I've a better idea. I'm going home for an hour or so, must change this wet uniform. Come up with me, and we'll have a drink at my place. You can't get home yet, weather's bad, but not as bad as we thought it might be. That's it – we'll go to my place – I'll find out about the ferry and run you down later. Might have to go over myself later, so we could get you home on one of our boats – what do you say?"

Hamilton thought it excellent, especially when he was assured Mrs Reynolds would not be in bed, and would be waiting up for her husband, as she often did.

Reynolds insisted on Hamilton using his macintosh. "I'm wet through now," he said, "can't get any wetter," and the waiting Police car soon had them away from the nightclub. The restaurant was cleared except for the captains, the waiters and cleaning women, still hard at work, a Police guard left inside and outside. Up the hill, half way up the Peak, through the storm. "It's easing a lot now," Reynolds shouted, as they hurried into the house from the car.

Mrs Reynolds, buxom, Scottish, a jolly woman and a good conversationist, was not at all taken aback to see Hamilton. This was part of the life she had accepted, the hours, the company, the unexpected. The life she had lived for many years, improving in status as her husband had progressed, content in Hong Kong, where the advantages far outweighed the disadvantages, their ties with Scotland decreasing as the years went by.

She and Hamilton got on well – it was good to have him to talk to – something different, and though they had only met briefly once before, they were good friends by the time Reynolds had showered, dried himself briskly, and changed to another suit of uniform.

"No, not yet finished," he told them, as he rejoined them. "Might have to go over to Kowloon, in which case I'll take Ham over with me."

She didn't complain, he was in the top bracket now, and she knew he did what he had to do gladly, happy in his life, and that meant much to her. The life demanded thoroughness and long hours, which he gave unstintingly, and she put up with it with good grace.

Mrs Reynolds was proud of her hospitality, and Hamilton thought the fresh salmon sandwiches with thin slices of cucumber really excellent. He hadn't wanted one, having had a good meal in the nightclub, but couldn't refuse and enjoyed what he ate. Reynolds tucked in well, then had two big slices of home made fruit cake with his coffee.

"This coffee's really delicious," Hamilton said, pleasing his hostess, "never tasted as good." He looked at her, "I'm a good judge of coffee, you know, love the stuff – goes jolly well with this brandy, thanks," with a nod to Reynolds who had poured it. "Drink China tea in the day, if I have to. Don't like it though, goes right through me since my days with the Japs, if you see what I mean."

They both knew what he meant, they had many personal contacts with people who had been held prisoners in Hong Kong, Singapore and the rest of that part of the world.

"Aye, Ham," Reynolds had comfortably settled into a big armchair, with a glass half full of whisky and a little water. "You can say I'm well looked after. She's a good lass is my Doris, and I've never wanted to swop her for anyone else. Wouldn't swop my whisky either for your brandy."

Time passed quickly, pleasantly, with Reynolds on the telephone now and then, and Doris Reynolds and Hamilton talking, of everything, the old days, of Singapore, up to the present day and the shacks of Hong Kong, where many thousands of people would be homeless again tonight.

"It's terrible, it really is," she said. "Their hovels – you can't call them anything else – are washed away every time there's rain like there is tonight. I do wish Government could stop all this shack dwelling, but there's so many of the poor devils always getting in, nobody could deal with them all."

Hamilton agreed. He knew what a great job the authorities had done, and were doing, with the tremendous problem of entrants to the Colony from China.

It was nearly five a.m. when they left the 'castle', as Reynolds called his home, with a promise of dinner somewhere – the three of them – when Sam was free, and before Hamilton went back to Singapore.

"Come back whenever you wish, Ham," Doris Reynolds told him. "You're always most welcome." Hamilton was pleased, he knew it was the truth.

He was pleased also that Reynolds had to go over to Kowloon, so could offer him a lift in a Police launch, and that the rain had stopped, though it was still blowing hard.

"Got to have a quick look around the Causeway Bay area," Reynolds indicated as they went aboard, "see what's happening at the anchorage there, then we can go over to Kowloon."

The launch bumped its way along the Hong Kong side of the water as far as the anchorage, dipping and rising steeply in the strong sea, waves and spray beating hard at them. Hamilton was sorry it was too rough for them to stay on deck. On their right, on shore, neon signs still blazed, the street lighting going upwards in a crazy zig-zag pattern to the black of the high ground behind, with many of the big houses still well lit up, cars moving up and down, their headlights cutting strong white beams through the night.

Near the anchorage, they met a formation of three large junks, pitching and tossing badly. The black and white Police launch nosed near to them inquisitively – its searchlight stabbing the darkness at each junk in turn. The leading junk was very big, the painted image of the human eye on the bow pointing downwards, which Hamilton knew denoted a fishing junk – the magic eye searching for fish. On the other two junks, the painted eye was central – these were trading junks, plying around the waters of the mainland and the island of Hong Kong.

Even in the light of the searchlight, the junks were still picturesque, the high sterns, the large anchors, most familiar to Hamilton, but these three, like most of the junks nowadays, were powered by diesel engines, and did not rely on the wind as they had done in the past.

Hamilton could just see a little group of Chinese huddled together on the lower deck of the leading junk, sheltering against the ladder which led to the high stern behind them. There were a lot of other Chinese – a lot of figures anyway on the high stern, and lots on the other two junks as well. This is funny, he thought, who the devil are these people? It seems certain the Police knew of the junks.

The searchlight was switched off, and the launch headed for Kowloon. As they left the comparative shelter of the Hong Kong side, and into more open water, they bumped and pitched even more deeply. It was impossible to talk because of the noise of the sea and the engines, so Hamilton let his thoughts roam. He admired the way the coxswain handled the vessel, not a bit worried, and even enjoying it all. He was at home on the sea, never had any fears, knew the launch would be all right, otherwise they would not have attempted the crossing.

Whoops! It was going into those troughs of the waves really hard – pat yourself on the back, Hamilton, that you're a good sailor – this is really something – not like those damn aircraft which he hated. Not looking forward to that return flight at all. Think I'll try to get a passage down on a ship, cable the office at Singapore, explain when I get there. Now that was a fine idea.

The lights of Kowloon looked close. The distance between Hong Kong and Kowloon always seemed less at night. Must be because of the way the lights shone out in the darkness, and how they reflected back from the water. Going towards Kowloon, as they were, wasn't as good as coming the other way – from Kowloon to Hong Kong – when, by night, surely Hong Kong was one of the grandest sights in the world – an island of light.

The riding lights of the many anchored ships, and the smaller lights of the moving small craft – like fireflies flitting over the black of the water were a familiar sight to him. Always within his memory, this had been a busy stretch of water, as busy as anywhere in the world. Now everything was getting back into action. These men of the sea and the big ships, and the men who served those ships in the smaller vessels, didn't waste time. The worst of the storm had passed over – lighters were moving out again to nestle against, and cosset, the bigger ships – starting the loading or the unloading again – time is money.

Away to the left front, he caught flashes of the brilliance and colour against the very bright static lights of the shipyards. He wondered if they had stopped work during the storm. Fantastic world that, building ships.

The runway of Kai Tak airport, far out into the water on their right front. That had been a marvellous project that he had seen something of. Levelling a small mountain on the approach to the airport, using vast hordes of Chinese men and women for labour, and with the materials from the mountain building the runway into the sea. Manpower no object – that must have been the way they built the pyramids, and that was the Chinese nation. Untold numbers and thousands upon thousands were born every day. "They'll never stop the Chinese," he had often heard his father say, "too many of them. Take a deep breath, and there's a thousand more. They'll rule the world one day, just by sheer force of numbers." He well thought his father could be proved correct.

They neared the Kowloon side, still in very rough water. The harbour buildings became more prominent, more recognisable. Neon signs still burned – did they never switch them off? What a fabulous place this Hong Kong is. Wrong really to call it just Hong Kong, misled so many people. It's more than Hong Kong, lots more, must put it all straight some day. There's the Peninsula, soon be back in the hotel – been a long night – what a night – wonder what happened to Rankin and Lee Kyung Koh?

Pity we couldn't have got up on deck, much better up there, would have blown some of the cobwebs away, far too rough though. You've had a lot to drink tonight, Hamilton, one way and the other – feel all right though – nice chap Sam – what a peach Doris is – take them out and give them a damn good night somewhere. Pity about that BOAC charmer – stupid man I am – must do something about all this – fed up being a batchelor. Look at old Sam – how happy and comfortable he is – that's the life – must find myself a wife.

There was a Police car to pick up Reynolds when they disembarked.

"We'll run you to the hotel, Ham," he said, "no trouble, feel it's my duty to get you to the hotel safe after what's happened tonight."

Hamilton could have walked the short distance, would rather have done so, but didn't argue. Grand lad, old Sam – had a damn fine night – celebrated Her Majesty's birthday good and proper – so I should – very fond of Elizabeth – wonderful girl – there's another lucky man – Philip.

The Police car dropped him at the main door of the hotel. Hamilton was most profuse in his thanks. It had been a splendid night, plenty of excitement, and finished up well, thanks to Reynolds – good old Sam.

"You'll be all right now, Ham," Reynolds told him. "I'll telephone you this afternoon, try to arrange that night out for tonight. Doris and I will just love it. You get to bed and have some sleep – wish I could."

Hamilton watched the Police car drive away. He suddenly felt very weary and worried.

There were a couple of cleaners working in the lounge as he went through. Several people were clustered at the far end, on the big settees and chairs, probably waiting for an aircraft. There were two or three men at the reception desk. The Peninsula was always busy.

He went up in the lift to his floor, and along the corridor to his room. He was jolly tired now. He fumbled about with the key for a few seconds, managed to find the lock, turned the key and threw the door open. He went in and found the light switch – turned on the lights. The door was closed behind him.

It was a few seconds before he realised someone must have closed the door, a few seconds in which his eyes were focusing to the lights. There was a man sitting on his bed, pillows back against the headboard. Chinese, smart, dapper, big thick glasses – a luger pistol in his hand.

Alongside him now stood another man, this must have been the one who had closed the door. From the bathroom came another, smartly dressed in western style. They were all well dressed. This chap who came out of the bathroom was a tough looking specimen.

"Good morning, Mr Hamilton," the man on the bed said, "You're very late."

16

LEE FINDS TRUE LOVE

The sampan rocked violently as they approached the entrance to the anchorage. Rankin and Lee Kyung Koh stood, holding on to the side frame of the canvas shelter, he with one arm around her. It was blowing hard, the sea outside was very rough.

Right in front of them, square across the entrance, was the junk. Rankin could hear the throbbing of the engine over the noise of the storm, as the crew fought to keep it steady against the force of the wind and the sea. As they approached, he could make out the shapes of two other junks to the rear and further out.

The sampan bumped hard into the junk, and eased alongside, until the man at the front could grab a rope ladder hanging down from the lower deck. He shouted something to Lee Kyung Koh. Rankin was trying to make out the painting on the bow of the junk. It looked like a big eye – some queer significance.

She moved across him, up and along the sampan to the rope ladder. A light was flashed down from the junk, right in her face. She screamed something as she grabbed the rope and the light was switched off at once. Quickly, she climbed the ladder, her movements graceful and certain.

He moved to the rope ladder, his knee sore, and climbed it more slowly and uncertainly than she had done. The sampan banged madly against the junk, the man at the rope ladder holding it as steady as he could as Rankin climbed. He was sure the two men on the sampan would be pleased to get all this over, and get back into the shelter of the anchorage.

He came on to the lower deck of the junk, where she stood beside a bulky figure. He heard a shout from the rear, and the junk began to move, the engine picking up rapidly, heading out into the open fairway, tossing and heaving in the strong sea. He hoped the sampan men had managed to push away safely.

Lee Kyung Koh had put on a huge black cloak, and she passed another to him. It was like a monk's cowl, and he was glad to wear it, needing the warmth. The jacket and trousers hadn't given him much protection, and the trousers were far too tight for him. Still, better than just wrapping a blanket round him, as he had done when he went on deck on the sampan to make water.

The other person said something to Lee Kyung Koh – it was a woman's voice. Lee Kyung Koh turned to him, clutching his arm possessively.

"Shall we go into the cabin?" she asked. "It will be warmer."

"If you wish," he replied, shouting to make sure she would hear, "but it is all right here now I have this cloak." He fingered the cloak appreciatively, he was getting warmer. "We are sheltered here from the wind."

"I would rather stay here also," she shouted in his ear, "as long as you are warm." She came even closer to him, the other woman about a yard from her, and two other figures nearby. She shouted something to the other woman.

They stood back, in the shelter of the ladder which led up to the high deck behind.

"We are going to Kowloon," she shouted, "that's Causeway Bay behind us, where we were. I shall never forget it."

He held her as close to him as he could, balancing himself against the ladder. "I will never forget it either," he shouted back.

Suddenly they were lit up, and almost blinded by the fierceness of a searchlight from a little craft which had come close in to them. The searchlight probed the full length of the junk, then moved off, presumably to the other two junks, if they were still with the leading junk. He couldn't think what all that was about – must be the Police – wonder why – looking for drug runners probably, trying to bring their stuff in under the cover of this storm –

It was grey, bleak, streaks of white light appearing in the sky. The clouds racing along overhead, the wind strong, fairly screeching through the ropes of the junk, the vessel bowing deep into and through the waves, rolling hard. The rain had gone, but there would not be much of a dawn this morning.

Lee Kyung Koh was happy, completely unafraid – she loved the sea. But it was this man she was happy about – he had told her he would stay with her for ever, and she had no doubt he meant it. She had made her plan, and would confront the Minister with her decision immediately. Whatever happened, she would make her life with the man she knew was for her – the first man she had ever known as a man – the first and only man she had ever given herself too. This is the man. The stars are correct – I have my man.

The Triad would manage without her. She would remain the figurehead if the Council wished, but they would now make all the decisions, not her. The vast fortune her father and she had built up, would be available to the Council, she would be advised by the Minister on all money matters, about the property she owned, and about her future duties.

That was not the problem, she was sure of that. The problem was how to get this man to accept all this. Would he feel he was living on her money – that was how the novels described it – it was the theme of a lot of the novels she had read. It would have to be handled very carefully, but it could be done. She would give her money to him, then *he* would have the money, not her.

They would travel, go where they wished, live where they wanted to live – she would like to see more of the world. They would go to America, to England, anywhere, everywhere. They would be married, she would have his children, lots of children. That she was Chinese and he was not meant nothing, this is a world where everything is accepted – there are many liaisons between Chinese and foreigners at every level – there is no problem about a mixed marriage now.

What pleasures she and he would find together. She would need to tell Ai Fah what had happened, how she had been right about there being a man for every woman, as is written in the stars. Her number one amah must be amazed at all this, wondering what it is all about. Oh, I will tell you, Ai Fah – I will – all in good time.

Ai Fah was neither amazed nor wondering what had happened. She had been cross they had not gone into the cabin where they would have been much more comfortable – she hadn't her man with her to put his arms around her as this man – a white man – was doing with her mistress.

Ai Fah's womanly experience told her that, when a woman held on to a man in the way Lee Kyung Koh was doing here, and he to her, there was a lot to it, and they were very close indeed. She knew they had been in the sampan for some hours, knew that clothing had been passed to them to replace the wet clothes they had worn, and there were no separate changing rooms on a sampan. She was annoyed about those clothes – rough old clothing – she had sent good clothing for her mistress, but the carefully folded pack could not have reached her. Where was that?

Oh no, there were no separate changing rooms in the sampan, but there was room for other things to happen – they would be very close to each other, huddled up in that shelter. It had happened to Lee Kyung Koh for certain – it shone all over her – she was radiant, even in these conditions, in those wretched old clothes, the happiness seeped out of her, Ai Fah knew well what had occurred on the sampan, her mistress was a woman – but the Chinese films had never shown the gallant prince in this fashion – wearing a dirty old jacket and trousers, and limping badly at that.

Now what? Ai Fah knew where they were going, the apartment in Kowloon was all arranged – the household staff from Hong Kong were on this junk with her. She knew her job, and her mistress would have all the comforts she was entitled to and would be expecting, and it seemed this Englishman would be along with them. She had heard the shouts, and understood a little English. No doubt Lee Kyung Koh would tell her all about it when they got to Kowloon – she was sure of that – it was evident as they had met on the deck of the junk. It will be interesting all right, and the man, in spite of his limp, was a big fellow.

They neared Kowloon. Not far now, Lee Kyung Koh thought, confident all the arrangements on the Kowloon side would be made for her. Soon she would have this man – she only knew him as Mr Rankin – he had not said much about himself, but she had called him the most wonderful Chinese names and terms in her passion. In her apartment – she would have to leave him there – but there was tonight to look forward to – and a thousand nights of the future – a thousand and more, many more.

They pulled into the quay wall at Kowloon between two large lighters. Rankin did not know much about the sea, but he appreciated the clever way the junk was eased into the space which could well have been left for it – most probably was. The other two junks held off a short distance away – bobbing up and down alarmingly in the rough sea and against the wind.

The two lighters were being unloaded, and the hard lights of the dockside shone down on swarms of men moving on to the lighters on one gangplank and off another, fully loaded, all dressed in black jacket and trouser, as Rankin himself was dressed. They reminded him of ants following each other along a set line, going on to the lighters empty handed, coming off bent double almost with their huge loads – sacks, tea chests, small crates, whilst large crates were being swung off one of the lighters at the stern. On the quayside, vehicles – large and small – moving, stopping, starting, reversing, horns blaring, weaving in and out. There were a lot of children round about, and a lot of men who were not working. It was not difficult for him to guess the non-working men were more of her guards.

Rankin limped slowly down the gangplank from the junk behind Lee Kyung Koh, moving through the lines of workers, to where three cars were parked about thirty yards from the gangplank . He caught glimpses of familiar names on some of the boxes and crates being unloaded – Heinz – Kelloggs – Teachers – and some of the larger crates were marked, "Made in Birmingham, England", which stirred him a bit.

The rear door of the second car was held open for them. He winced as he got into the back seat alongside her. A Chinese man, dressed in western style, closed the door after him, then got in the front seat next to the driver.

"Your leg is bad," she said, quite concerned for him – "I will have someone to attend to it very soon now."

"It is a bit painful," he agreed, "some fluid on the knee." It was more than a bit painful, it was a bad knock, he knew that. It was some satisfaction that he was sure the man he had kneed in the face would be sore that morning – would have been in great pain all night.

The car began to move, following very closely to the one in front. He did not look back, but was sure the third car would be equally close behind them.

She moved closer to him, holding tight to his arm. He took her hands in his, turned her left hand over, and brought it to his mouth to kiss. She moved her fingers gently along his lips as she had done in the sampan, and the thrills all began again. He looked at her a moment, saw the wonder of her love in her eyes, shining for a fleeting second in the bright light of a street lamp, as they slowed to turn a corner. He nestled his face against hers, kissed her brow, then her nose, then her lips – she opened her mouth wide with his. The guard in front kept his eyes straight ahead and the driver did not look in his mirror.

"You're wonderful – beautiful – delicious – all that's heavenly," he whispered, "really gorgeous." She had him very much in the mood again.

They sped up Nathan Road for a short distance, then turned left, and as the car turned more corners, right and left, he held her close to him. He was not the slightest bit interested in where they were going, content to be with her. He drew away from her only when the car slowed, then stopped.

"We will be safe here," she said, "please come with me."

Full daylight had not yet come, the street lights here were poor, the wind blew gustily up the street, the pavements were very wet with large pools of water here and there on the road.

There were at least six men on the pavement, alert, watchful, as they got out of the car, bumper to bumper, against the cars in front and behind. He followed her into a shop full of flowers – he looked twice and thought they must be artificial, through into a rear room, then out down alleyways that twisted and turned, poorly lit, and into a large hall with many games machines around the walls – through a door on the left, and to a passage where a lift door was being held open for them.

The fattish little Chinaman waiting at the lift was all smiles, as he bowed to Lee Kyung Koh – he certainly looked very pleased to see her. They rode up three floors, the lift stopped and the door opened – the Chinaman bowed again, still smiling broadly. Rankin followed Lee Kyung Koh down the passage, through a large door – it looked very strong, probably steel – down the continuation of the passage to a door at the far end.

She opened the door and went on in front of him, to the centre of a very large room.

"This is my apartment," she told him – nearly said, "one of my apartments", and was glad she had not done so. "It is yours now as well as mine."

The words did not sink in – he was simply amazed at what he saw. The room was carpeted completely, a large tiger skin rug near their feet, contrasting sharply with the white of the carpet. On the left, at this end of the room, a double bed draped in white net curtain – wide carved bed posts. A door towards the middle of the room on that side, and beyond that, a vast settee and three matching armchairs, covered with a blue and white striped material, and heaped with deep blue cushions – beautiful, and he could bet, very expensive.

Wall lights on each wall. Twin old-fashioned lights, with blue the dominant colour of the shades. On the walls, pictures of a Chinese dancer – a series of pictures of different poses – of a young girl with a blazing red flower in her hair.

On the right side, down at the far end, another door, and along the complete right side of the room from that door to end – large windows, curtained in the same material as used for the bed.

The utter luxury of it all was staggering. He had never seen anything like it, nor imagined anything such as the beauty and comfort of the room.

She saw the look on his face – it worried her.

"The bathroom is there," she indicated the first door. "And that," pointing to the door at the far end, "is my dressing room. It is all yours now, use it as you wish."

He turned to her. "It is beautiful," he told her. "It really is – the most super room I have ever seen, and it suits you because you're the most beautiful woman I have ever seen. You really are."

She knew he was speaking the truth – could see it in his eyes, and the simple words were supreme music in her ears – took all her doubts and worries away. He would adapt to this life with her – he deserved to. They would be happy together – just let her set in motion her plans this morning.

She stood very close to him. It thrilled him she was so tall, and stood on the same level as him – perhaps even a little taller than him. How gorgeous she is, even in this plain garb – how perfect her complexion, how smooth her skin, not one blemish. How lovely the smell, the perfume of her.

A lovely high forehead, big eyes – what colour are they? Grey – blue – both – shining with love for him. The eyebrows long and beautifully tended, narrowing evenly. Her mouth, with all the beauty of the rest of her, the mouth was the supreme feature – wide, generous lips, kissing lips, perfect teeth – a superb woman, with that terrific pliable body, beautiful breasts and long clinging legs. A fabulous woman – made for a man – how is it no man has touched her until me, why should I be so fortunate? Why?

He put his hands on her shoulders. He had to reach up a tiny bit to kiss her – tenderly at first, then more passionately, the desire great within him again.

She knew, and knew the same desire as she nestled into his arms. Much as she wanted to stay, she could not, just then. She moved her lips from his, kissing the side of his face and then his left ear, whispering as she had done in the sampan.

"You must be tired," though she was aware his body was anything but tired. "The bed is there, try to get some sleep for a time. I have some things I must do immediately, but I will come to you as soon as I can. Perhaps you wish to take a bath, the water will be very hot, there will be a boy to look after you. I will send someone to see your leg. Use all this apartment as you will, I wish you to do so, wish so much for you to be – how do you say – at home here.

"I must go," her voice hoarse and deep. "I do not wish to go – you can tell, but I will come back soon, that I promise. I cannot bear to be parted from you, but I must, there are things I must do."

He held her less closely, knew well of the fire within her, but he knew also not to force himself upon her – he would not do that, passionate as she was for him. She would come back to him when she could, he was certain of that.

"There will be clothes for you," she told him, "my medical amah will come to see your leg. Rest well, I will come to you as soon as I can. I love you so – want you so."

She kissed him – this time so softly – for a few seconds. "I love you – I am completely yours – I have waited so long for you. Be patient a little while, as I must be."

When she had gone, he moved into the bathroom – large, elegant – in pink. A great bath, shower, shower curtains – huge bath rail piled with towels. A bath and a shower was the first thing, and she was right, he was tired, but he would never be too tired for her.

Back in the room the fat little Chinaman from the lift was waiting for him. A jolly little man, dressed in a smart white jacket now, high collar, a blue flower – what was it – an orchid? The same flower was on all the towels – on the left breast above the breast pocket, well creased black trousers and black shining pumps. He was still smiling all over his face.

"Me, Johnnie," he greeted Rankin. "Me, your boy – Lady tell me look after you good. Me very good boy – work long time Mirimar Hotel. Me happy to be your boy. You tell me what you want – I do – I get – you like some bleakfast?"

Now he had mentioned it – "bleakfast" – just what the boys in the mess always said – never "breakfast" – Rankin felt hungry.

"Yes, Johnnie," he agreed. "I'd like some breakfast," careful to say breakfast, not bleakfast, careful not to make fun, Rankin never did that, though some of the others in the mess often did.

"You say what you like, I get," Johnnie told him. "You like eggs, bacon, tea, coffee, toast, we have everything here. This plenty fine place me tell you, best cook amah in all Hong Kong. You say what you like" –

Rankin thought a while. "Well, I'll have some eggs and bacon, some toast and a nice big pot of tea."

"That's good," Johnnie said, well pleased. "Me already tell Cookie that, me say, 'Big man English, he eat eggs, bacon, tea, toast, for breakfast, all English mens eat same in Mirimar Hotel' – me tell cookie get plenty ready, he big man – he eat big bleakfast."

Rankin laughed – he was going to like Johnnie, liked him already. "Well done, Johnnie, but first I'm going to have a bath and shower. Is there something I can put on afterwards?"

"Oh yes, sure thing," Johnnie replied. "Lady tell me bling robe, I put on bed for you."

"That's fine." Rankin limped over to the bed, pulled the curtains aside, and picked up the multi-coloured dressing gown. He turned back to Johnnie. "Give me about twenty minutes to bath, then I'll be ready for that breakfast."

"Twenty minutes OK – but better you take thirty minutes – more time for you – no need much hurry." Johnnie had it all planned. "Lady say doctor amah come after bleakfast, then you sleep. Me take your suit to tailor maker, he clean pless that suit plenty quick, make new suit same time. He come later bling shirts, what you say, vests, drawer things, new shoes. You look very smart."

Rankin felt much better after the bath and a cold shower, but was dismayed at the state of his knee. It was badly swollen and painful. He limped out of the bathroom to find Johnnie and breakfast waiting for him, the delicious odour of fried bacon greeting his nostrils. A small table in the centre of the room, white tablecloth and napkin, a deep blue little flower showing up on the white of the cloth, gleaming cutlery – one chair. Johnnie stood alongside with a large trolley, on which he could see silver dishes, plates, a large tea pots. Heavens! There's enough here to feed the Battalion, he thought.

He ate well, he was hungry, and it was excellent food. Eggs, bacon, mushrooms, tomatoes, toast, all perfect, and strong, hot tea. Johnnie knew his job and did it well, quickly, efficiently, and kept up a stream of chatter.

"Barber man wait outside, perhaps you want shavee now or after you sleep some time. You say when – barber man wait – I get."

Rankin fingered his chin, it was a bit bristly and it was natural for him to shave every morning. Besides, she had told him she would be back soon.

"I'll have a shave after I've finished this lot," he said.

"You please eat all," Johnnie requested. "Cookie say she cook lot, I tell her I know English mens – English mens all time eat plenty bleakfast – eggs, bacon, at hotel. Then I get barber man – I tell him you want shavee soon – Johnnie know English mens shavee in morning time."

Rankin ate more than he intended to, but he had to please Johnnie. It would not do to let him down with the cook – he had to be right.

The shave was first-class. A good barber, wizened, old, slow and careful, using a large old-fashioned razor in masterly style, and a very stringent lotion afterwards.

Whilst he was working on Rankin, Johnnie took the table and trolley out, and when he saw the barber had finished, he hurried him out. Rankin thought Johnnie very terse in whatever it was he said to the old man.

"Doctor amah outside now," Johnnie told Rankin, "you please lie on bed I think best." He pulled the net curtains on one side, hooked them up, as Rankin lay down.

It was only when he saw the medical amah that he realised it was a woman. He hadn't been listening much when Lee Kyung Koh had told him that she would send someone to see his knee, and it hadn't registered when Johnnie had spoken about the doctor amah. Now he knew why Johnnie had hurried the old barber out – the medical amah would be an important person.

Johnnie wheeled in another trolley – set up with white enamel basins and gleaming instruments. The medical amah had come well prepared.

She was thorough, careful and firm. Prodding the knee, around the swollen area, and underneath the knee. Bringing his leg up, bending it – noting how he winced and reacted to the movements. Then she moved her hands searchingly up the inside of his right leg, prodding, pinching, right up until her long fingers reached the groin. Rankin pulled the robe up, tucking it around himself as best he could, as she moved his right leg upwards, then bent the knee, first slowly, then quickly – the pain brought him out into a sweat.

She said something to Johnnie, who was watching all she was doing with great interest. He struck a match and lit a small stove on the top deck of the trolley,

Rankin watched her closely – it was the first time he had been in the hands of a woman doctor. Thank God, he hadn't needed doctors much in his life as far as he could remember.

She was thirtyish, he reckoned, tall, nearly as tall as Lee Kyung Koh. A thin, delicate face, pronounced cheek bones, good skin, large intense eyes, and he was fascinated by the pigtail which swung behind her as she moved. She was dressed in the uniform style of Chinese women, a severely cut jacket and long trousers, but the quality of the material was good, and the drab black was relieved by blue trimmings to the sleeve cuffs, and the ends of the trouser legs.

She rolled back the sleeves of the jacket, almost to the elbow – she was indeed thin – and put on long rubber gloves. He judged her to be a very able woman, and felt safe in her hands.

Rankin knew a bit about knees, footballers were often plagued with knee troubles, especially fluid because of knocks, and he expected something antiphlogistic to be used, to reduce the swelling.

The woman took some long thin needles from the middle tray of the trolley, and Rankin thought again about the treatment. This looked like acupuncture, the Chinese medical science they often talked about in the mess. Nobody understood what it was, and he had heard many suggestions and stories about it – well, he would soon know.

She said something to Johnnie, quite a long speech. Johnnie laughed and nodded. Rankin was curious.

"What was that all about, Johnnie?" he asked.

Johnnie laughed again and looked at the woman, and Rankin was surprised when she replied.

"I told him I thought you are a tough man – very strong – so needles won't hurt you."

"Oh," was all Rankin could say for a few seconds, though he thought there was more to what she had said than that. "This is acupuncture, isn't it?"

"It is," she replied, "do you object?"

"Oh no," he assured her quickly, "you carry on, do what you want as long as it will get the swelling down."

"It must have been a very hard knock," she said, "it is bad, but this will soon bring improvement, much faster than any other way. Now, will you please turn over."

She spoke beautiful English, almost as good as Lee Kyung Koh. Yet, like her, she couldn't use it much, unless she used it with Lee Kyung Koh, which he doubted, or mixed with English medical people at hospitals, which was possible. But he had long since stopped being surprised at anything the Chinese accomplished. He was very pro-Chinese, thought them an amazing race, with the same good and evil as every other race, yet with a wonderful background and history of medical science and beliefs. He liked the Chinese, he knew, and the Chinese servants in the mess were very fond of him.

Rankin turned over slowly on to his front, grunting with pain, as he felt the pressure of the bed under the thick towels against his knee.

"Keep your leg as flat as you can," she instructed, and he felt the hands in the rubber gloves exploring the back of his leg, right up to the backside, then down to the ankle and to the toes.

She spoke to Johnnie who carefully re-arranged the towels under his leg.

"Doctor amah, she very good," Johnnie said, very happily, "needles not hurt – plenty soon your leg get better fast – you OK with that?"

"I'm quite happy, Johnnie," he said, turning his head to one side, and wishing he could see what was going on, "your doctor amah is doing a great job. Don't worry about me, I'll be all right."

"It is good you have faith in me, and the treatment," the woman told him, "many people in the western world call those of us who practise acupuncture silly names."

"Is that so?" he asked, but he had heard the science often referred to as a joke, and those who practised it as quack doctors.

"But we are not quacks," she went on, as if reading his thoughts, "at least, we do not think so" – he could feel her rubbing the back of his leg with a liquid, a spirit no doubt. "My people have made many wonderful cures in this manner, we have learned, and are still learning, much about the human body, and have known about acupuncture for a long time."

He heard the needles clicking together – this was it –

"I have heard about acupuncture," he said, "but very little, some of our doctors seem to think it is dangerous."

"Of course, all surgery is dangerous," she agreed, then there was quite a break, as she busied herself at what she was doing, but there were no needle pricks. "We know there are many points in the body which respond to activating," she went on, "good needle points, many that are bad, and many more that are neutral, so we take great care to use only the good points."

Johnnie said something to her but there was no laughing now,

"I have inserted three needles into your leg," he was surprised, he had not thought she had started with the needles, and was holding himself for the pain of insertion. "You must be patient a while now."

"Don't worry – I'm all right," still amazed at not feeling any pain.

"You are a good patient, very good, so I can tell you something of what I am doing – shall I?"

"Oh, please do," he replied, "I'm very interested"

"Good," she said, "I have inserted one needle into the top of your leg here" – he felt a little pressure high up under his backside – "another here" again a little pressure slightly above the knee – "and the third, here" – lower down, below the knee – "this will stimulate energy in one part of the leg, and reduce it in another."

Rankin listened carefully, still wondering why he had not felt the needles being put in.

"The human body is a wonderful machine, and truly complicated, there are many things yet we do not fully understand." A pause. "The blood is carried by different channels to where it has to go, and studies have enabled us to make the best use of these channels, they are very important, it is a case of sending the right thing to the right place, and stopping the wrong thing – in a little while I shall remove the needles and you should feel much easier."

He hoped so, it would be great, he remembered that antiphlogistic treatment took quite a long time to reduce swelling.

"There is another treatment we know of for which we use a plant which is named Moxa. That is a heat treatment, again the western world think it is a nonsense, but acupuncture will improve your knee much faster." He felt her hands on his leg again. "I am removing the needles now – one" – he felt nothing, felt her hands move upwards to the top of his leg – "two" – again he felt nothing, then her hands moved down below his knee – "three" – again no pain.

"You may move your leg now," she said.

He moved it – it seemed much easier – or was he just imagining it?

"Turn over," she continued, and he moved over on to his back. It was not as difficult as it had been when he had turned on to his front.

She moved his leg, as she had done in her first examination of him – up and bent the knee – slowly, steadily, then moved his leg up even higher, and again bent the knee – it was painful, but not as bad as it had been, he was sure of that.

Johnnie had no doubts about it. He gave the knee a careful inspection – "Leg plenty better – she first class doctor amah."

The doctor amah prodded her fingers into the knee – it pained him, but not badly. She was pleased with what she saw. "The swelling is down," she said, "how does that feel?"

"Much better, much better – nothing like as painful as it was."

"Good" – for the first time there was something of a smile on her face as she looked at him. "I'm pleased you have faith in acupuncture, now we will apply a little more treatment."

She put his leg down on the bed, moving over to the trolley to pick up a bottle. "This is iodine – please turn over again."

He turned over much quicker, easier, than the previous time he had turned on his front. Oh yes, there was no doubt, it felt much better. He felt her applying the liquid to the back of his leg, to the three places where she had made the insertion with the needles.

"Turn back again now," she said after a while, and he did as he was told. He had not been able to keep the robe tucked around him in all his movements, but tucked it back between his legs as he came round to lie on his back this time. Johnnie was watching him – still grinning – he had enjoyed it all.

She applied the iodine liberally to his knee with a brush. "The swelling is moving quickly," she told him. " I am very pleased. Now you will know what acupuncture can do."

"I don't know how to thank you," he said, looking up at her as she finished with the iodine, corked the bottle, and put it back on the trolley. "I expected you to use something antiphlogistic to take down the swelling, and thought it might be weeks before it was better."

"There is no need to thank me," she replied, "and your knee will be better very soon. It was something interesting for me – we like to do different things in medicine – dull routine can be very depressing." He could appreciate all that, "but rest the leg all you can – rest is a good aid for many ailments – don't move from the bed until you have to" – a little smile, Rankin wondered why – "the knee will be completely good again in one week, and I will come in and see you again tomorrow."

"Thank you," he said, and was thinking hard. She had a sense of humour, this woman. The reference to the movement from the bed, did it somehow imply his relationship with Lee Kyung Koh, something had amused her when she had told him not to move from the bed. She had done a good job on his knee, they would not believe him in the mess when he told them about it. He hoped it would be back to normal in a week, bit optimistic perhaps, he would have to report sick with it when he got back to Camp – that was a long time off – over twenty-four hours, he still had a lot of his pass time left – make the most of it, Rankin lad, you'll be with Lee Kyung Koh again tonight – lucky lad – get a bit of sleep now – he was tired – he didn't wonder at it really – weigh it all up a bit later – he could do with some sleep.

Johnnie came back into the room – he had wheeled out the trolley for the doctor amah. Rankin was still wondering what had amused Johnnie so much earlier on – what was it the woman had said to him?

"What did doctor amah say to you, Johnnie?" he asked, "did she really say I was tough? No need to be tough – those needles didn't hurt. Come on, old lad, what did she say?"

Johnnie thought a few moments, and his grin even more broad, "Oh yes, I remember, doctor amah say you very strong, tough – needles not hurt – then she say you like an oxe, not need any powder to eat," he laughed out loud as he finished the statement.

Rankin hadn't got it. "Won't need any powder. What would I need powder for?"

It was a great joke to Johnnie. "Doctor amah know plenty much, she know you not need rhinoceros horn, like old Chinese mens need it to pokey girls."

Rankin understood – it was common talk in Hong Kong – the aphrodisiac qualities of rhino horn ground to a powder, and snake blood and other things, and that venerable old Chinese gentlemen were said to consume these various ingredients in large quantities, and at high price to retain their sexual powers. Whether it was true or not, Rankin did not know, but he had heard a lot about it. One thing was certain, he didn't need any.

He laughed also. "You're right Johnnie, I don't need any powder, but what I do need is some sleep."

"You quite right," Johnnie agreed. "You sleep now – me come back three clock perhaps with lunch – how you like it – salad – cold ham – ice kleam – you say – I get."

"That'll be great, Johnnie," wouldn't do to disappoint him even after the large breakfast he had eaten. "A salad will be just right, and some cold ham. I'll leave it to you, you're a good boy – best ever – you wake me at three then."

17

TIME FOR DECISIONS

He was fast asleep, dreaming of Lee Kyung Koh.

She was with him – what a wonderful dream – on his right side, as he lay there, her long body cool against him, her hands fondling him – the left hand with fingures running along his lips, her right hand caressingly moving across his chest and down his middle, then lower to where he was firmly alive.

Her lips against his face, then to his mouth – her breath warm and sweet, her body heat increasing rapidly –

Then he awoke. It isn't a dream – it is all real – she has come back to me as she said she would.

She lifted herself up to bring her mouth fully on to his, his hands explored her – how quickly the heat came to her – she was all liquid, the fierce possessiveness of her engulfed him.

She climbed on to him, as she had done that last time on the sampan, extending her legs across him, using her right hand to bring him into position – "Oh quickly, quickly, angel, I am nearly there," easily she clamped on to him – right down on him – and his volcano erupted within her mightily. She screamed loud in ecstasy – a tremendous bundle of fire herself, her hands in his hair, her mouth slobbering all over him – their movements strong, passionate, fierce, then slowing, slowing, slowing, slowing, until she collapsed on him, and he held her tight to him.

"You gorgeous, gorgeous angel," he told her fiercely, you are devastating – terrific – tremendous – marvellous – everything that is wonderful – I wish I was all liquid and could shoot all of myself into you."

"Oh no," she gasped, "you must stay as you are, so strong, so wonderful yourself – I love you so, I love you so.

"How is your leg?" she asked him later.

"Much, much better."

"I am so glad – she is good – the medical amah?"

"Excellent," he replied, "and it is so good – acupuncture – I have heard about it, of course."

But she did not want to talk about acupuncture – only about him and her.

"I am a very poor person," she told him, "I have a wonderful man, a mighty lover, but I do not know his name. I do not know how to call you – how should I?"

"My name is David Rankin," he said simply, "just call me David."

"It is nice – David – that is – how you say – a forename?"

"Yes, my Christian name, one of them. Say it again, you say it so nicely."

"David – David – David," she repeated, "yes, it is a nice name."

"I also do not know your name," he had been puzzled what to call her. "I know it – is the first part just Lee – like a Christian name – is that how I should call you?"

"It is my name," she agreed, "in some fashion much as your way of names, but then we have other names. We call ourselves heavenly flower, or little blossom, but you called me a wonderful name, just – just then – it is what my mother always called me – so nice – Angel."

"It suits you," Rankin said, giving her a big squeeze, his right hand and arm under and around her, his hand clasping her right breast – "you really are an Angel – a super Angel – full of love and so terrifically passionate. I shall call you Angel."

"I am pleased, my mother was the only one to call me that, it is lovely you should want to say it also. It is so difficult for me to have a name, sometimes I think I do not have one. My own people all call me Lady; when I am out I am only called Madam. I do not know what it is to have a name – even my father only called me daughter, never a name."

"That's settled then, Angel," he said. "I shall call you Angel."

"You are happy?" she asked.

"Happy – there isn't a word for how I feel. I have the most magnificent woman in my arms," he found her lips to kiss her for a few seconds, "she is an Angel," he lowered his voice – "a very sensuous Angel, bless her, I am more than happy, I am enchanted – that's the word – enchanted – you enchantress."

"Then you make me the most happy woman in the world," she was so pleased, the conversation was going so well – "You are in the Army, I know," she continued, "are you high in the Army?"

He was silent a while – puzzled what to say, "Not really," he replied, "I am a sergeant," wondering whether she would understand the rank.

"Oh, that is good," she was enthusiastic. "It is very hard to be a sergeant – it is very responsible – yes?"

"It is very responsible," he could say that with certainty. He realised much of this conversation was difficult for her, appreciating she must come on to their status, their future, what was to happen to them. He must give her all the help he could.

He held her close to him on his right side, and even in their passiveness, the little love-acts were multiple. She is so wonderful, this woman – this Angel has given me everything – everything I could desire in the short while we have been together – such passion as I never thought possible – we must continue – it must not end.

She was supremely happy. How marvellous it is to lay with this man – my man – the only man I have ever lain with – he is so wonderful to hold – I cannot keep my hands off him – but there are so many problems – please he will not leave me – he must not.

"Are you always in the Army?" she asked, and he guessed what she meant.

"It is semi-permanent," he told her, "I have a few more years to serve yet, but" – as an afterthought – "I can always buy myself out."

She thought a few seconds. "You mean you can leave when you decide?"

"In a way," he agreed. "I pay so much money and they will probably allow me to leave."

"Will you pay a lot of money?" she was thinking very high, he was such a wonderful man, a strong man, he must be such a fine soldier.

"Oh, yes, well sounds a lot," he was a little confused, her ideas of a lot of money were probably not in line with his. "No, not a great amount really, say, two hundred pounds, something like that."

He was surprised at the easy way he could say – that he could talk about the Army – talk about buying himself out like that. He – Sergeant Rankin, whose life was the Army – this time yesterday, he would not have thought it possible in the wildest of dreams. Today – because of this woman, because of what they had shared, what she had given him – their ecstatic joy together – well, it was possible all right.

"Would you do that – for me – and stay in Hong Kong – with me?"

Now she had said it, what she so much wanted to say – had wanted to say for many hours, had thought so hard how to say it – had thought could she say it to him. It was said. Had she said it well enough?

He could answer – he hadn't thought she would ask it in this way, but had long considered it in his thoughts – knew the question must come, would come. He had been most sincere last night, when he had told her that he would stay with her for ever. He felt even more that way now. There were big problems for them both, things to be sorted out, but, by heavens, he wanted to be with her, knew he loved her, it wasn't just her body, glorious as that was, she was so wonderful – so much for him – she needed him, and he needed her. Whatever the obstacles were, they could be overcome.

He brought his head down to her face, nosing aside the thick tresses of her lovely hair – found her lips. Fire was stirring again in him – already. Their lips met – for seconds – his tongue probing gently into her mouth.

"Yes – I would – I would stay in Hong Kong with you," another long kiss. "There are difficulties, you are a very rich woman, I know that. You are head of your Triad – and I – I am nothing."

"Do not say that," she told him, most concerned, her voice fierce, angry. "Please do not say that. You are everything – you are mine" – her voice softened – "you will be the father of my children – I want there to be many children – our children. I love you so much – only you. I will give up everything for you if you will be with me" –

She is very strong-willed – he ought to have known that. His choice of words had not been the best, but he must get the difference between them over to her in some way.

"I want to be with you, Angel," he reassured her, "but you cannot deny you have a high position, and you cannot deny you are rich – a man—"

"That part is easy," she interrupted – "we can settle that now – I will give you all my money – then you will be the rich one, and I will be the poor person."

He laughed – he couldn't help it – but knew he must not upset her.

"You're super gorgeous Angel, really you are," he kissed her again, a longer kiss this time. "But we can't do that—"

"We can," she began, and he held his mouth to hers. "We can," she tried to say again – "of course" a much longer kiss – "David" –

Her hands were in his hair, she turned to him, her mouth wide open. The desire great in her, as in him. She started to climb on top of him again, but he held her back –

"Easy, Angel," he told her. "My turn this time."

He slowly pushed her on to her back, gently, lovingly, but surely, turning on his right side to her.

"Your knee," she managed to say – "take care."

"I'm being careful," he said, moving on to her, as she moved under him – waiting to receive him, and there was no pain he could feel from the bad knee – not that you ever noticed pain at a time such as this.

This time was the best yet, tremendous as the other times had been. Then they had been eager, fierce, demanding, hungry for each other. This time it was pure love, reaching the utmost peak of splendour, the utter joy of giving all and taking all.

He entered her beautifully – perfectly – and they began long, easy, rhythmic movements, mouths together, clasped tightly, comfortable in her arms, with his arms under her back and shoulders, taking some of his weight from her. They went slowly on and on and on, thrilling to the most magnificent of sensations – on and on until his movements became stronger, more rapid – her long nails dug deep into him – her cries ringing in his ears – on and on, faster and faster – to their climax – a triumph of ecstatic joy – satisfaction beyond all belief – a complete and absolute surrender to each other – he thought he would never stop giving.

"Oh, David" – she was almost breathless – "oh, my wonderful David."

He could not speak – he was so full with emotion and love of her, filled with awe at the perfection of their coupling. Could not speak, but could think, and knew he could never give this woman up. She is mine, as I am hers – nothing matters but that – we will – we must – find a way to be together. She will have my child – twins – triplets – the way we are going on – what a fabulous woman.

Nothing will make me give him up, she told herself – I will never give him up – never, never, never. There cannot be another love such as this in all the world – the stars can hold nothing but beauty for us both – there is no other joy to equal the joy of having this man with me – he is supreme – magnificent – there is one other joy which will be nearly as perfect – the joy of having his children – our children – nothing else matters except that we are together.

How can we arrange it, he asked himself. We must, but how? Where will we live – what work can I do here in Hong Kong – she has so much – can I be a part of her life, can I fit into her life – should I not leave when she has gone – no – no – not that – I cannot do that – I will not – whatever the consequences – as long as she wants me – and thank God she does – I stay with her – she is everything a man could ask for, everything and more.

They lay quiet for some time – a long time – happy to be together in the loveliness of their afterglow. She held him tight within her – he looked down at her lovely face, kissed her brows, her eyes, her nose, cheeks, lips, as she held him in her embrace, a tremendous love-light in her eyes, her face full proof of her joy and satisfaction. How lucky you are, Rankin, how lucky , he told himself.

"We will talk much tonight," she said at last.

"If we have time," he agreed, smiling down at her.

She was puzzled, it showed in her face, "Will there not be time then, tonight?"

"Of course, Angel," he replied and kissed her nose again, "but we have so little time between our love-making."

She knew what he meant now – the concern left her face, she smiled with him. "That is true David – you are so strong."

His smile broadened – he kissed her again. "I like that," he said, "I am strong, and what about you? You are terrific, so demanding, so quick to want more—"

He eased his head down to find the nipple of her left breast with his mouth, and she ran her fingers through his hair, around his ears, and down his back –

"It's so wonderful, our love, David. This poor person is poor no longer. I waited so long for you – but you are worth all the waiting – I had to wait for you , the stars knew this, I did not know until this that such a love Heaven exists, but it does. Now I know much more about the stories I have read about lovers – now I know it is all true what men and women will do for love – and I am yours, David – for now and for ever."

He felt so humble, and yet so proud. "You Angel," he said, "you make me so very proud – so proud – that a woman such as you loves me

– and I am yours, all yours and only yours—"

She did not speak for a while, and he pushed himself up from her to look at her. Her face showed concern again.

"What is it, Angel – do you not believe me?" he asked.

"I do, oh I do," she stopped – began again. "We can" – stopped again.

He knew she wanted to ask him something very important, knew even what it was, knew he had to help her –

"Tell me, Angel," he leaned down to her again and gently kissed her lips – "or is it something that I should ask you?"

How wonderful to hear these words from him – he knew what she meant, what she was wanting to say. Stupid fool she was, here together in the most intimate position there could be – and yet she had been frightened to say what was in her heart – frightened of how it would affect him, but it was easy now because of what he had said –

"In your country, yes," she replied, "but in my country, as you must know, these things, marriages" – she had said it – "are still arranged by parents, but I have no parents" –

"Then we must arrange it," he told her, kissing her again. "My parents will not object – so we will be married, if you will have me."

How happy it made her, forcing the problems into the background – how good it all seemed, how fortunate a person she was.

"Oh, I will have you David – I am sure, but are you sure you want to marry a Chinese woman?"

"I'm sure, Angel," he countered, "are you sure you want to marry a Welshman?"

It puzzled her again, he knew that. "I am Welsh," he said, "Wales is a separate country from England, though we are all part of Great Britain. You sure you want to marry me?"

"I do, I do," she repeated, with great conviction.

"And there will be no objections from your people?"

There could well be – she must tell him the truth. This was the problem she had to overcome.

"Not from the people, or at least, I think not, but there might well be from my Council – the Council have much to say in all things connected with the Triad – they could well have much to say about my marriage" – even as she spoke she knew it may well be the other way – may well be the people who would object, the Council all worldly-wise and knowing her so well, would – she felt sure now – agree to her proposals to them – that she would abdicate, leave them to run the Triad, "but that will all be settled today. That is why I have to leave you now, I must see the Council, obtain their agreement."

"I'm sure you must," he said, encouragingly. "I don't want our children to be born illegitimate" – he kissed her again – "nor do I want to live in sin."

"What is that?" she asked, and he explained.

She agreed with him wholeheartedly. "You are such a good man," she told him, "such a fine soldier also of that I am certain – will there be no objection from your Army?"

"None that I can think of," he assured her.

"Then how soon" – she hesitated. "How soon could we be married?"

"Whenever you say, Angel," and he meant it. "I'm completely yours. We know there are difficulties, but I'm so much in love with you – and you with me, bless you" – with another kiss – "that it must be. We must be married, and soon."

"We will, David – we will – for us it is written in the stars."

He was kissing her and his mouth roaming all over her face, his hands busy also.

"I must go, David," she said – a few minutes more and she would not – she knew. "But I must, my love, I have many appointments – I do not wish to go – never wish to leave you – you must know that – but I must, I must" –

He eased carefully from her and to one side, pleased that his knee gave no pain, had not done so during all the time he had been on top of her.

She raised herself and knelt above him, looking down at him. The beauty of her smothered him in emotion, the loveliness of her face, no make-up but absolute perfection, the intense eyes filled with longing for him. If ever he had seen love, it was in her big eyes, a love flowed out to him from every part of her, from those eyes, her mouth, hands, arms, and her body. She was love incarnate.

Her glorious long black hair fell down her front in rippling sheens, but her breasts pushed out, as if determined not to be hidden from his gaze. Her very white skin had not a blemish or a mark, as his gaze took in the sweep of her middle down to where her legs joined her body. She is a lovely woman, he told himself, a thoroughbred in every way. The most wonderful woman he had ever seen, the most glorious sight in the world. How very lucky he was.

"Don't worry, Angel," he told her, as she moved across him to get out of the bed, "there will be other times."

She stood for a moment, then bent down to kiss him. How thrilling her movements, every action sheer delight. There could not be another woman so lovely as her.

"Oh yes, David," she agreed, her lips so close to his. "So many times. I cannot bear to wait until tonight even. I will arrange a special dinner here for us two, I am sure I will have much to tell you. Then afterwards we can be together again, I want that so much."

It was a long kiss, tender, her tongue just gently moving across his lips, but no probing, and much as he wanted to, he did not reach up for her. She must leave him, he knew that, or she would still be on the bed with him.

She said something in Chinese, kissed him more firmly for a few seconds, then she was gone. The curtain fell down behind her, and he knew that she went into the bathroom, knew also there was soon someone else in the room, heard them talking quietly, then tiredness overtook him and he slept.

He did not know that she came back to the bed, lifted the curtain, and stood again looking down at him as he slept.

She was in a black samfoo, her head of hair severely combed and tied behind her in a pigtail. She must now go out for there were no conference rooms in this apartment, and elsewhere in Kowloon, her Council would be waiting for her as she had wished.

She stood for several minutes looking down at her lover, whilst Ai Fah waited patiently behind her. He lay almost flat on his back, naked, except for a large towel which barely covered his loins, and she was thrilled with the immense chest, the slim middle and the great strength of his legs – he is a man indeed – the stars have brought me a great lover, I must be worthy of him.

She stooped and kissed him just below the left nipple – just on the heart – once only, and told his heart in a whisper how much she adored him, and how much she belonged to him. She was not to know then, could not foresee, that she would regret all the rest of her life that she left him on this day when they could well have been together.

Johnnie woke him at three o'clock. His knee was sore, but he sat up and had a good look at it, was able to raise it easily, and saw how much of the swelling had gone. When he got out of bed, he walked quite well, only a slight limp, convinced he was cured, and forgetting the doctor amah had told him that rest was a great aid to complete recovery.

"Just a minute or two," he told Johnnie, and went into the bathroom, where he showered and dried quickly, noting the great red scratches that ran down his back, and the love bites on his neck and shoulders – what a passionate woman she was. He put on the robe and came back into the apartment.

The trolley Johnnie had brought in was full again, and the same table set with the same fineries – a new snow white tablecloth with the little blue flower, a napkin, everything so perfect.

He ate well, large slices of cold ham, thin slivers of cold chicken, crisp lettuce, tomatoes, onions, all delicious. A thick, creamy dressing which was highly spiced, and which he thought terrific, rolls and butter, followed by ice cream, and then coffee. A beautiful meal, he could not have done better anywhere. He was surprised at his appetite after that large breakfast he had eaten earlier, then grinned a little, as he told himself the old story of not being able to make love off nothing.

Johnnie saw the grin. "You like lunchee?" he asked.

"Great, Johnnie, just great," he replied, "didn't think I could eat so much"

Johnnie grinned with him. "You eat plenty – velly good thing, keep you velly stlong – not need rhinocleous powder."

So Johnnie knows what's going on, Rankin thought, and knew better than to continue the conversation.

He looked around the apartment, whilst Johnnie busied himself clearing the table and stacking the trolley. A wonderful place – the furniture sumptious – it must have cost an awful lot of money.

He looked at the pictures on the wall which had attracted him earlier. They were paintings, not photographs. All of the same young Chinese girl in various dancing poses. A very beautiful girl, hair piled high on her head, a long black fringe, long whisp of sidehair, and wearing a blazing red flower in her hair. She was gorgeously gowned, with long pantaloons, or long boots, beneath a voluminous skirt – in some of the paintings she carried an umbrella.

He looked at the paintings. Of course, it must be Kyung Koh. He asked Johnnie. "Who is this, Johnnie?"

"That Lady," came Johnnie's quick answer. "Lady when she velly little, me not know her, but she velly wonderful dance lady. That special style Chinese dance – that velly special, velly good – many Chinese ladies dance same way, but not good like Lady."

Rankin thought the paintings beautiful. She would be about twelve years old, hard to say, but the beauty of her was already there for all to see, and the poetry of her movements. The frames were beautiful also, some sort of gold material all fashioned in the same way. They were a lovely set, and would be a great treasure, he was sure.

Johnnie interrupted his studies of the paintings, "Tailor maker he ready outside see you now. You OK him come see you?"

The tailor was accompanied by two boys, and they were all loaded with clothing and boxes. Rankin found his own suit cleaned and ready to wear, but also had to try on another suit, in a light grey thin material, and very nice. It fitted perfectly, though the cotton stitching showed it was not yet finished. The tailor spoke to Johnnie.

"Tailor man say this suitee plenty same you suitee – stitches same for same," Johnnie told him. "You like?"

Rankin liked it very much.

"OK. Tailor man say tonight bling back for you. You OK with that?"

"That's great, Johnnie," Rankin replied, "I'm OK with that." He chose underwear and a cream shirt, went into the bathroom and returned with these, and his trousers on, still limping a little.

He chose socks and shoes from the many offered for his choice.

"These are very good," he told Johnnie. "You tell the tailor he has good things. Now what about paying for them?"

Johnnie was shocked. "Oh, no paying, Lady velly closs. Tailor man not need money." He rattled away ninety to the dozen to the tailor, who nodded his head often, but said little in reply, while the boys looked on with wonder and awe showing clear on their faces.

Lee Kyung Koh will pay the tailor certainly, Rankin thought, and there's very little I can do about that, and it again struck him what problems could arise, as she would want to give him everything. Something I must talk to her about, he thought.

Johnnie bustled the tailor and the two boys out, then busied himself tidying up. Rankin put on the socks and shoes he had chosen, and a tie. He noted that the tailor had taken very little away, most of the boxes had been left with Johnnie – that tailor must have judged his size well from his suit.

Well, what should he do now?

Johnnie read his thoughts. "You like papers – magazines?"

Rankin was restless, he felt well, his knee felt better, he had eaten well. He ought to go down to the hotel, collect his things, pay his bill, and tell Carrie Jane he could not be with her that night. He owed that to her, and he had to collect his things he had left at the hotel.

"I think I'll just go down to the hotel," he told Johnnie. "Collect my shaving things, pyjamas, pay my bill."

Johnnie was not sure about it, but, in the many instructions Lee Kyung Koh had given him personally, there had been nothing about going out. There had been nothing about staying in either. There was doubt in his mind, but he had been told to look after this Englishman and please him.

"That plenty good idea," he agreed. "You go me come too, I get ricksha, we go – I show you way – velly difficult – me take you hotel – OK."

He had no idea yet what hotel it was, but his conscience was clear, he was pleasing this big man and, as long as he was with him, he would be OK.

Rankin had no objection, judging by all the precautions there had been coming in, he knew he could not possibly get out without Johnnie. In a way, he was very surprised nobody tried to stop them.

Carrie Jane was not on duty at the hotel. He had guessed from what she had told him last night – was it only last night? – she would be off at this time. The girl on the desk was intelligent. Chinese, small, fat faced, big glasses, alert and capable. He asked her to tell Carrie Jane that he could not be there that evening, made it clear he was booking out from his room, taking his things, paying his bill, and he would come back and explain it all to Carrie Jane another time.

Fortunately, Johnnie was not very interested in the conversation, but Rankin thought it safer to take him up to the room with him, rather than let him stay talking to the girl in reception.

The room did not impress Johnnie. He sniffed his disapproval.

"Not nice like Mirimar. Why you not go Mirimar."

"It's not as costly as the Mirimar, nothing like," Rankin replied. He had seen the Mirimar from the outside and could guess what it was like inside. He could also have a good guess at the price. This hotel suited him, as it suited many – inexpensive, good, central, convenient.

Johnnie didn't like the lift, reception, or the Chinese girl. Rankin felt he had rather gone down in Johnnie's estimation. It was silly, but typical of the class stature in any language. He was glad to pack his bag, which Johnnie insisted on carrying, and get back in the ricksha.

His knee was sore again, his limp more pronounced. He knew now he should have rested it, as the doctor amah had instructed, and told Johnnie to send someone to the hotel to collect what he wanted. Still, soon be back in the apartment again.

The early evening was cool, clouds hanging dismally overhead. The streets wet, the pavements crowded as they always were, littered with paper and rubble, waste, rotten fruit. They had turned off Nathan Road, but were still in a busy area with stalls stocked with produce, vegetables, fruit, ducks, chickens, fancy goods, clothing – men lounging at street corners, others hurrying as fast as their legs would carry them, weighed down with huge loads of merchandise across their shoulders. Hordes of children, all ages, all sizes, in coloured shirts or sweat shirts and shorts of every known colour, many in bare feet, some in sandals. The ricksha man just missed a fat little girl, only a child herself, carrying her baby brother or sister in a sling on her back. Above the calligraphic signs of the shops gave a little colour. What a place – Hong Kong. Rankin loved it, the turmoil, the crowds, the atmosphere – even here in these streets, in this poorer area of the city.

Johnnie shouted something at the ricksha man, and he stopped with a jerk. Johnnie motioned him over to the other side of the street to a café, with the white and blue sign contrasting badly with a huge coca-cola advertisement. The man put the shafts down carefully.

"This belong my blother," Johnnie informed Rankin, "you OK, we go see, dlink cokey cokey?"

Rankin had no objection. In any case he was thirsty, that creamy dressing had been excellent, but given him quite a thirst. It didn't look too bad a place, no dirtier, if no cleaner, than other cafés.

Johnnie sat him on a chair at the only table on the pavement in front of the café – moving two men and another chair away. A thin man came out to see what was happening, and was greeted by Johnnie, as if they had not seen each other for many years. After they had finished hugging each other, Johnnie introduced him.

"This my blother" – no name – "he velly pleased you come see him at this poor place."

That's not very loyal, Johnnie, Rankin thought, as he shook hands very correctly with the thin man. He would never have guessed they were brothers – the other man obviously much older, much more serious, with none of Johnnie's happy qualities.

They soon retired to the interior of the shop – it was much more a shop than a café – leaving Rankin to sip a very cold coca-cola, and to think.

Yes, he loved Hong Kong, and would find no hardship in living in the Colony, but was he doing the right thing? Was he being fair to Lee Kyung Koh? It was terribly difficult. Could he fit into her world, and could she fit into the world they would need to create together?

Marrying a Chinese woman did not worry him, though his parents would be astonished. But she wasn't just Chinese, she was international in every way, the most elegant beauty he had ever seen, and she really had more problems than he. He was aware she had only left him today to put her proposals to – as she had called them – her Council. What would they think, would they allow her to go ahead with her plans? Maybe not.

Then there was the money problem. He grinned again, as he recalled how she had said she would settle that – by giving him all her money, so he would have it, and she would have nothing, but it was not as easy as that. Then he would have to ask his commanding officer for permission to get married. It would be granted, of course, but would cause a bit of commotion. Wonder what old Bob will think?

But he had made up his mind. If she would have him, they would be married, the sooner the better. He could fit in here in Hong Kong, if he had to. Had he stayed with Alice, he had visions of building up a chain of shops. There was great scope for him, perhaps he could be of great use to her Triad.

In any case, he was hers. He was the luckiest man in the world to have such a woman in love with him, and he was really in love with her. He would give her all his love, his devotion, his loyalty, his strength. Sure there were difficulties ahead, but together they could get over them.

Soon he would be back with her again – they would have many hours together tonight – to talk, to make love. She is so marvellous, a glorious woman, and she is mine.

It was about time they were moving. He was just about to get up to call Johnnie when he and his brother appeared. There was a third man with them – little, mean looking, a rogue, if ever there is one, Rankin thought.

Johnnie had lost his smile. "You lucky English mans out here with me," he blurted out at Rankin. "You happy, this man says nother English mans not velly happy like you, that English mans plisoner, in that stinking place" – he threw out an arm to motion to a large godown along the street and on the other side.

Rankin was surprised at the outburst, and puzzled. "What's all this about, Johnnie?"

"This man says nother English mans plenty much tlouble." Johnnie was very serious. "He plisoner, down there, he English mans – chained in wall – he velly sick no doubt."

It was still difficult for Rankin to understand. "How does he know this?" he asked Johnnie.

"He go look see," Johnnie answered at once, "English mans velly sick. He chained in wall – he little mans – like this man – wear glasses – velly sick no doubt."

"Well then, let's go and tell the Police," Rankin said. To him it was simple – a matter for the Police.

However much of the conversation the little man understood, he certainly knew the word, "Police" – he started shouting at Johnnie at once.

"This man says 'No bling Police'," Johnnie explained at last. "Police not think this man tell tluth – then bad mans no doubt kill English mans plenty quick."

Rankin could not understand it. "What about if I go tell the Police?" he asked.

There was more shouting from the little man, and again it was some time before Johnnie explained.

"This man say no bling Police. Police come bad mans kill this man plenty quick – kill English mans plenty quick same time."

"Are there other bad men over there, in that place?" Rankin queried.

Johnnie consulted the other man, "Yes, no bad mans there this time – bad mans come this morning bling English mans chain him in wall – bad mans not there now but come back soon. English mans plenty sick ask this man bling help – say him get much money but this man says he no bling Police – OK you go see that English mans – you velly blave, velly stlong – we go quick no bad mans there – we get English mans quick – this man get plenty money."

No doubt, Rankin thought, and you get a share, Johnnie. What was it all about – was there really an English man there, a prisoner? Surely it couldn't be a trick – not from Johnnie.

"How does he know this man is English – did he see him chained to a wall?"

Johnnie knew the answer to this already, this was what had kept him a long time inside. "Oh yes, no doubt – he see all this – he know English mans talk – he understand much English talk – this man say help quick or bad mans kill sick man – one – two." He swept his hand across his throat to indicate how it would be done.

"How can we get in to that place?" Rankin asked.

Johnnie knew that one also. "Walk in quickly – bad mans not there now – come back soon no doubt – but no mans there now – we go quick – we get English mans – this man get plenty money."

You rogue, Johnnie, Rankin thought. The English man doesn't matter, it's the money you're thinking about, and your share. He had made his mind up – foolish, dangerous, but he had to see now what it was all about.

"Come on then," he said, "what are we waiting for?"

There was more shouting, then Johnnie said: "This man says some money first – then he show you English mans chained in wall."

Rankin was annoyed. "How much then, Johnnie – quickly?"

They spoke a minute. "How much you got?" Johnnie asked.

Rankin nearly exploded. "Two hundred dollars – no more."

Johnnie and the little man conferred for another minute. "OK," Johnnie said. "Two hundled now – then this man get more when you get English mans in that place."

18

PRISONER OF THE NINETY-SEVEN

By the early evening Hamilton was in a very bad way. Physically, he was utterly weary – it had been a long, weary day after a night which he had enjoyed, but had been exhausting, too much to drink and no sleep, whilst all the day, because of the way he had been chained, he had to remain upright.

His mental state grew worse as the hours went by, and he was now at a low ebb. Surprised at the way he had been treated – in a way, he had almost been neglected.

The three men had brought him out of the hotel – one man on each side of him, with the third man just behind. It was this man who had been sat on the bed in his room, and he had made the position quite clear.

"I shall shoot immediately if you try to escape," he told Hamilton – "but believe me, I have no wish to do so. Please, therefore, do not give me the opportunity – we just want to have a little talk to you."

Hamilton was aware he was in grave danger, and had no doubt the man meant what he said. He was also perfectly sure that, after the little talk, he would be disposed of – could not think they would let him go free. But he thought, as always, whilst there is life there is hope, so he gave no trouble. In any case, he was too tired, perhaps a little too fuddled, to have got away.

He was bundled into a taxi outside the Peninsula, into the back seat, between the two men who had flanked him. The third man got in front with the driver. He was sure the taxi had waited all the night as the men had done.

He retained one very great advantage – no-one knew he could speak Chinese. He was certain of that, and listened carefully to what the men were saying. The men were quite free in their conversation, not knowing he could understand most of it.

They were from the Ninety Seven, and there was big trouble in the Triad. He gathered that Mong Lin San, the overall leader, had been killed in a car accident in Kowloon the evening before – that was a surprise to Hamilton – and the number two – he couldn't catch the name – was in conflict with Lin Poh, the Hong Kong leader, who was now bidding to take over the Triad, but there were too many of the big boys now in from China, all of whom supported Mong's number two, so now it was a battle of personalities. These three were Lin Poh's men, of course, with the man who spoke such good English very close to Lin.

It was only a short journey, and he had no idea where he was going. They had stopped, and waited a long time in a poorly lit street, whilst one of the men went off. The other two continued to talk, but there was nothing about what had taken place in the Golden Lotus – these men would not know about it, as they had waited for him in the room in the hotel throughout the night.

Eventually the third man returned, gave some directions to the driver, and the taxi drove on again – a short distance only, then stopped. He was taken into a large building – a godown – down a long passage, up a flight of stone steps and into a large room, bare of any furniture, with a doorway to another room at the far end. He was taken to a central stone column, where handcuffs on chains hung down from a long iron rod in the wall about six feet up the column. The handcuffs had been locked on to his wrists – like the chain they were new, but the iron rod looked as if it had been in position a long time, and obviously used in this manner on previous occasions.

"We shall leave you now," the English speaking man said – "you will be looked after, and we shall come back for you later." He gave the chains a shake almost pulling Hamilton off his feet. "Don't waste your time trying to get out of these, and shout if you wish, nobody will hear you."

Polite bastard, Hamilton thought. He could not understand it. He had expected to be taken to a house somewhere, questioned at once. Not to a place such as this, and left. He tried the chains – they were right, he would not get out of the handcuffs or the chains, but what about the iron rod?

He reached up to grab it, protruding some twelve inches out from the column. Luckily, the chains did not restrict him in this, and there was a slight movement in the rod. He pulled and pushed at it with all his strength. It was his only chance of escape, and it was going to be damn hard work.

After a while, he had to give up, and knew he had made no impression on the rod. He had chafed his wrists badly, and his hands were sore. He must have a rest before trying again. It was uncomfortable, because he could not sit down, had to remain standing, and the electric lights above him were very bright.

Now what? They'll come back for me, he told himself, take me to see whoever it is I am to see – then – the sea perhaps. Not a nice thought. Wonder how they got on to me, what has been started up. What will it be – torture, or just a truth drug?

He tried again at the iron rod, but soon had to give up. He wasn't strong enough, and he was tired. Drank too much last night – too old for this sort of lark.

After about an hour – so he judged – two Chinamen came in. Young, hefty, tough. One of them unlocked the handcuffs, and they took him into the other room, where there was a toilet and a wash basin. He needed the toilet badly. It was dirty, stinking, but it was a toilet, and it pleased him. Fastidious as he was, he would have hated to answer any calls of nature standing up, and chained.

There was a table in the room, two chairs, a big old-fashioned chest of drawers, and some pictures on the wall – pictures of nude women. He was allowed to wash his hands though there was no towel. He drank some of the water from the tap, felt a bit better.

When they locked the handcuffs back on his wrists, the bigger of the men thumped him hard on the chest, staggering him. The chains prevented him from falling, but gave him an awful jerk through his arms and wrists. When they had gone, he started again on the rod, he had to do it, there was no other way of escape. He soon tired again, this was too hard for him. He would have felt better if he could have moved the rod a bit, given him some hope, but it wasn't moving at all – bloody hell fire.

What a ridiculous situation – is this how I am going to finish up?

After the talk with whatever bastard wants to talk to you, it will be the sea – taken out in a junk, and thrown overboard, to drown, if you're not finished off before then. Ghastly prospect, how the hell have they got on to me?

Sam Reynolds had told him he would ring that afternoon – would that help? No, they would just say there is no answer from his room, so Sam would think he was out somewhere, and by the time he started worrying, it would be too late. You've just got to try that bloody rod again.

He tried hard, his hands bleeding, his wrists also. Was it easing just a little? Not anything like enough – what a stupid bloody performance.

Some time in the afternoon, he thought, the two men came back to repeat the process of the toilet. They looked at his hands and laughed. The bigger of the two spat at him, and told him how much of a fool he was, he would never move that rod, not knowing that Hamilton understood everything he said.

Should he appeal to them – in Chinese – to let him go. Offer them money, a large sum. His knowledge of Chinese was still his trump card, should he play it now? He decided against it – was sure it wouldn't do any good – not with these two thugs, both members of the Ninety Seven, no doubt, they dare not help him.

The big man spat at him again, when they brought him back from the toilet, and called him the foulest of names. Hamilton could not evade the spit – ugh the dirty bastard. Then, as he was about to leave, the big man thumped him again like the first time – full in the chest, but harder this time. Hamilton fell back, brought up sharp by the chains, crying out loud in agony of the pain to his wrists, and the strain on his arms and shoulders. The big man laughed, cleared his throat, and spat again – he was enjoying it.

When they had gone, the depression set in. The dirty swine. Come on, come on and get me – what's keeping you – get it over – he could not understand it – why had he been left so long –

The day wore on, with Hamilton very weary, his spirits low. He thought his eyes were playing tricks, when he saw the door slowly opening, watched in amazement, as a face carefully appeared around the door, and a man, a little Chinaman, dirty, ragged, came in to the room. He advanced slowly towards Hamilton, but kept out of his reach, looking at the chains and up at the rod to which the chains were fixed.

Hamilton watched him. Who is he? He is not a different jailor, surely? Who the devil is this, something to do with the godown, perhaps, a watchman.

The man kept well clear, but his eyes had taken it all in. Hamilton thought hard – take it carefully, very carefully – this is definitely not one of the Ninety Seven, it might be just the help you need. He held himself still, a move and the man might run. Keep calm, Hamilton, take it easy – should he speak in Chinese, was this the time to risk everything, or should he try first in English? Try the English, he decided.

"You speak English?" he asked quietly.

The man's eyes lit up – he nodded his head. "No speakee lot – me know lot."

Hamilton's heart bounded. How much will he know, might be a lot, as he said, but might be just a little. Some of them know a lot more than they admit, some of them understand a lot of English – pray he is one who does.

He spoke slowly, spacing each word. "You – go – quick – bring – help – take – off – these," he shook the handcuffs and chain. "I – pay – you – much – money – lot – of – money – ten – thousand – dollars – you – bring – help – you understand."

The man nodded his head again. "Me know," he said simply, looking straight at Hamilton, thinking, searching for the words he wanted, remembering the little English he knew, "me go."

He turned and went out, closing the door quietly behind him. Thank God, Hamilton told himself. Now there is a chance, he could only wait, and hope, and pray. What would the man do? Would he go to the Police – Doubt it – purposely did not mention the word, "Police," fully aware of the feeling of many Chinese about officials and Police, especially a man such as this – contact with the Police would be the last thing he would want to do – he looks a sneak thief. Keep your pecker up, Hamilton – he'll do something for ten thousand dollars – he'll do something – he must – he's got to do something.

Time went by and his hopes sank, the black depression returned. It must be getting on for evening now. The Ninety Seven must come back for him soon – what the hell is happening out there – what's going on – my God, you're in a spot now, Hamilton, but keep cool, keep hoping, keep praying – remember what you've always said – whilst there's life, there's hope.

He was dead tired, and it was hard work to keep upright, but he could not sink down because of the handcuffs and the chain. He kept his eyes glued to the door. Could that little beggar bring help? If not, it was all up with him.

He had given up – convinced he was finished, when the door slowly opened. His heart jumped, he held his breath, it must be the man, knew it must be, because of the slow way the door was pushed open, so cruelly slowly – oh, my God, it must be. It was, and the same face appeared round the door, looked at Hamilton for a second or two, then the little man came in slowly followed by Rankin and another Chinaman.

Oh, my God. I'm dreaming, or I've gone mad, Hamilton thought. It can't be true – Rankin – the man I met in the Golden Lotus last night.

If Hamilton's astonishment was great, so too was Rankin's. He also could not believe it. He paused in amazement at the sight which greeted him. Hamilton of all people, and what the man had said was true – in chains, and looking in a bad way. Rankin had been kicking himself for getting into this affair – had been sure it was a hoax, and there was something behind it he could not fathom, but the last thing he had expected to see – the last person – was Hamilton.

They had got into the godown without trouble, out of the rapidly increasing dark of the evening – the mean looking little man leading the way up a narrow passage, with a peculiar bulging bend in it, just before they arrived at the door he had so carefully opened, and here was Hamilton – an Englishman in chains, just as the man had said – it was hard to believe. What was it all about?

He moved past the little man to Hamilton, saw how bad a state he was in, took up the handcuffs, chains, and Hamilton's wrists in his hands. He saw the chaffed wrists, the bleeding hands – looked up at the iron rod – cripes, that looked something difficult.

"Fancy meeting you," he said simply, then, with a grin. "We meet in the nicest places."

Hamilton only just managed a grin in return, he was far nearer to tears, though his spirits had risen quickly, he knew there was hope now, but what could he say?

"David," the voice thick with emotion. "Thank God, thank God."

Rankin realised the depths Hamilton must have sunk into, would have liked to know what it all meant, but it wasn't the time to ask. He reached up, took hold of the rod, pushed and pulled at it, took a good look at the chains, pulled at them, then went back to the rod.

"Don't worry, Ham," he said, "I'll soon have you out of this," hoping he sounded convincing. He pushed again at the rod. "Just have to get this out to free you," but knew it wouldn't be easy.

He took off his jacket, which he gave to Johnnie to hold. How typical of a trained British soldier Hamilton thought, and moved back as far as the chains would allow him, to give Rankin room. He watched, as Rankin rolled up the sleeves of his cream shirt – nice shirt that, Hamilton thought.

Rankin reached up again for the rod, began to pull, then push, pull and push, putting all the power of his great shoulders and the strength of his arms and wrists into the task.

There was no conversation – both men knew the urgency. There would be time to talk later, perhaps. Johnnie came up as close as he could, holding on to Rankin's jacket carefully, but the little man remained near the door. An amazing scene, one that Hamilton would never forget; the hard electric light blazing down on the mighty efforts of Rankin, pushing up, pulling down, rhythmic, easy, a splendid display of great strength.

It wasn't easy, and he had to pause a while, "It's coming," he knew he must keep Hamilton assured he could be rescued. "Won't be long now." Rankin's hands and wrists were bleeding, the sweat poured off him. His knee, sore again, was a handicap, couldn't put all the power into his movements he could have done, had his knee been sound.

"Here we go again," he said, and his efforts re-commenced. A push up, a downward pull – the rod was definitely moving – push – pull – push – pull – yes – yes – it was moving all right – the knowledge increased his strength

"Got it," he roared loud in triumph, and with a jerk, pulled out the rod – full twenty four inches long, and with a vicious spike where it had been in the wall – dust and dry mortar coming out with it and falling to the floor. "Got it," he repeated, holding the rod aloft – "How about that, Ham?"

He was jubilant – not many men could have done it, as he well knew, it was a triumph of coordination of movement and tremendous strength. He was suddenly very happy – pleased he was here to help this unfortunate man. Cripes, has he been here like this all day? And pleased it had not been a cock-and-bull mission after all.

It was hard for Hamilton to speak. It was a miracle, and just when he had thought himself finished. He had been right, whilst there is life, there is hope, and thank God for a man such as Rankin, and how amazing it should be him.

"I can't tell you how I feel," he gasped. "But I'm in your debt for ever. How in heaven's name did you get here?"

"We'll save that for later," Rankin replied, very cheerful now. "Let's get out of here. You'll have to carry the damn thing, and we'll get the handcuffs off when we get outside somewhere." He looked around, "Johnnie, where are you, Johnnie?"

Johnnie had gone into the other room, but he came back as soon as he was called, still carefully carrying Rankin's jacket, but there was no sign of the little man.

"Where's he gone?" Rankin asked, but there was no need for an answer as the man came rushing in through the half open door, babbling something rapidly to Johnnie. Hamilton realised what it was – they were not out of danger yet.

"Mans coming," Johnnie told Rankin. "Bad mans" – there was fear in his voice.

"Shut the door," Hamilton said. "Keep inside, it's our only chance" –

Rankin closed the door quietly, then pushed Johnnie and the little man to one side so they would be behind the door when it was opened – "not a sound from you two," he ordered fiercely.

"There'll be two of them," Hamilton continued. "I hope only two, they've been in twice before. Let them come in. Stay behind the door, get them when they're inside. I'll go back to the wall."

He went back to the position he had been in such a long time that day, forcing the spike end of the rod back into the wall. Rankin kept the two Chinese men behind him. "Not a sound," he ordered, and motioned to both of them with clenched fist, fear was written all over their faces.

The door opened and the same two men as before came in, the bigger of the two leading, the other close up behind him. Only the two of them, thank God, Hamilton thought – they stood a chance with two.

Rankin let them get right in the room, then slammed the door behind them. The element of surprise was much in their favour as they turned, startled. Rankin advanced to the second man and struck him a smashing right hand blow – straight to the chin. The man toppled, knocked clean out, crashing in to the other man and both fell to the ground.

Hamilton pulled out the iron rod as the big man got up again, managing to grip the spike end in both hands as a club. This was the man who had spat at him, called him foul names, struck him, and as he rose, Hamilton summoned all his strength to bring the rod round as hard as he could, hitting the man across the right side of the face with a sickening thud, throwing him back against the wall where he slowly collapsed, blood pouring from his shattered face.

Johnnie and the little man squealed in fright. "Shut up," Rankin shouted at them, shaking his fist at them both. They stopped the squealing – they had seen what that fist had done to one of the men, unconscious on the floor.

"Well done, Ham," Rankin said, in a way amazed at the viciousness of Hamilton's attack. He went over to the man he had hit, turned him over and looked at him. "He'll be round in a few minutes, have to watch this one." Then he went over to the other man, against the wall, bent down on one knee alongside him, then stood up again and turned to Hamilton. "This lad's in a bad way, needs medical attention – we'll send someone in to him when we get out."

Hamilton felt no remorse. He knew it had been a fearful blow, he had put all his remaining strength in to it, knowing it was a case of them or him, and well aware what they would have done to him, had they been given the chance. He held the iron rod in his two hands – because of the way he was handcuffed.

They heard Johnnie in the other room, and now he came to the doorway to call Rankin.

"Some things you come see here OK? Some things like gun." He had got over his fright quickly.

"Watch the door, Ham," Rankin said, and went in to the other room, to where Johnnie was standing by the big chest of drawers, one of the drawers open. Rankin picked up a revolver and broke it. It was a 38 revolver, dusty, but in good condition, and loaded with six bullets – stolen from some military unit for sure.

Johnnie watched Rankin break the revolver. "You take that gun – you take shoot other mans."

"What other men?" Rankin was puzzled.

"More mans come back soon," Johnnie replied. "You shoot bang."

Wonder what the devil he means went through Rankin's mind. He could be right, we should get out of here, but he pulled open the next drawer, empty except for a coil of rope, then the bottom drawer. An object rolled forward as he pulled the drawer open. Rankin stopped it rolling with his left hand, put the revolver in his trouser pocket, then had a good look at the object. He knew what it was, that was why he had stopped it rolling. A grenade – another trophy from a raid on some unit. He inspected it carefully, like the revolver, it was dusty, but it was primed. Good job Johnnie had not got hold of it.

"David," he heard Hamilton shout from the other room – "David" –

He moved back quickly, Johnnie close behind him, still carrying Rankin's jacket very correctly. Hamilton was standing by the door, the little man cowering behind him.

"This beggar was just about to do a bunk, but he heard something and came rushing back – he's scared to death."

Rankin opened the door a little – they could hear a great deal of noise down the passage. Johnnie said something to the little man who jabbered away fast in reply – there was no doubt he was scared. "This man say many mans come for other place inside – big place velly much store things – many mans there last night this time same place."

Hamilton knew what it meant – "Some sort of meeting, and they held one last night. Must be the Ninety Seven, remember I told you about them last night. "He spoke slowly to Johnnie: "Ask the man where other place inside."

Johnnie spoke quickly to the other Chinese man who jabbered again, motioning with his hand and arm. Rankin held the door partly open, listening, alert for what was happening outside.

"This man say other mans talk long time same place last night," Johnnie told Hamilton. "Many mans – many shouting – other place inside along here plenty near – big place much store things."

"What sort of store things?" Hamilton asked.

Johnnie and the other man spoke again. "Many things here this store place," Johnnie said eventually. "Things like palafin, klackers, big klackers go bang, bang, bang, how you call plastic things – many things."

"So that's it," Hamilton told Rankin. "This godown stores a hell of a lot of stuff, from the length of the passage it's a big store, certain to open up on to the dockside. Johnnie's friend says paraffin, fire crackers, plastic items, a lot of them, are stored here, and it looks as though the Ninety Seven are holding their meeting in the big store – must be a hell of a lot of them."

"Must be," Rankin agreed, "judging by the noise they made, but it's all quiet out there now." He opened the door wider. "They must have all gone in the big store, and it doesn't look as if we will get any more visitors."

"Don't count on that," Hamilton told him. "They won't have forgotten me, they'll be along soon. I wonder if these two," he motioned at the two men on the floor, "were sent for me? Doubt it. Soon see though – wonder if there's any chance of seeing what's going on." For the first time, he noticed the grenade in Rankin's left hand. "Where did you find that little beauty?"

"Inside, in a drawer. This as well," Rankin pulled the revolver out of his pocket. "Loaded too."

"Good, we might need them, especially that grenade, if it's primed," Hamilton was quite sure about that.

"It's primed all right," Rankin said. He saw one of the two men on the floor moving, the one he had hit. He closed the door. "Bring me that rope from inside, Johnnie," he ordered, and moved over to the man, who was coming round quickly now. Rankin put the grenade down very carefully in a corner, and put the revolver back in his pocket. Johnnie brought him the rope. There was just enough to tie the man up securely, first the hands behind the back, then the hands to the feet, bending the legs up backward at the knees. Rankin made a good job of it.

"Give me my jacket, Johnnie," he said, and taking it from the puzzled Johnnie, he tore it upwards from the centre vent, and across to give himself a big piece of material, which he stuffed in the man's mouth and tied it tight behind his head, "This lad'll give us no trouble now," he said, and moved over to the other man. He turned back to Hamilton, "In a bad way, he won't last long." He picked up the grenade again. "Let's see if we can get out of here."

19

ANXIETY

It was well after six o'clock with the evening closing in fast, when Lee Kyung Koh, accompanied as always by Ai Fah, came back to the apartment.

There was great joy in her heart, happy anticipation of a life ahead with the man who had found her and loved her, as she loved him.

The man – strong – courteous, dominant, who had said he would stay with her for ever, and asked her to marry him. A wonderful man, who had delighted her with his love making, made her a woman, given her ecstatic, passionate thrilling hours she had not ever thought possible, until she had been in his arms, and together they had achieved a love union that was pure heaven in every way.

He was hers, in her stars, and there was so much to look forward to – to tonight with all the thrills he would bring to her again, to the soon when they would be married, to the bearing of his children. How fortunate a person she was.

Her meeting with her Council had been all she had wished, all she wanted to do would be hers to do. Led by the Minister, they had been very understanding. It was not something that amazed them. They were men and had knowledge of the feelings she spoke about.

In any case, in their wisdom, they knew there could be no man, no husband, for her, in her own race, and in truth they were glad. If there were such a man, he would have to be given a high place in the Triad, and would weaken the power of the Council. It was she and them who had done so much to build the Triad, they saw no reason why another man of their own race should rise in power over them, and no reason why their leader – a woman – should not find happiness with a white man without detriment to the well being of them all.

The world today had a new understanding between peoples – mixed marriages were commonplace. A man was a man, and a woman a woman, and their coming together was as natural as if they both belonged to the same race. They understood and appreciated a natural mating, it was the unnatural things of the world they could not understand – men were made for women and not for other men.

There would be children, of course, but plans could be made for the future. The wise Chinese are too mature to worry over such things as children – they were only content that such children would be born in wedlock.

Nor was the money a problem. She had so much to offer to the Triad, and then enough to spare for herself. They wished her always to live in the manner and style to which she was long accustomed. She and her man must discuss all this properly, and he would see that money would not be allowed to affect their romance.

Her people would be told about it in the proper manner. The handling of this was their affair, she was not to worry about it. They were the chosen leaders of the Triad, chosen to act with her, and they would, and could, convince her people that what was to happen would be best for the Triad, and for her.

So it was a radiant Lee Kyung Koh who came back to her man. A radiance that could not be dimmed by the severe samfoo she wore and the long discussion she had endured. First, of course, she must change into her proper attire to be received by him. He must not ever see her in this plain garb she used for such occasions as today, when it was necessary for her to move around without becoming a target for her enemies. She must bathe, have Ai Fah prepare her hair, choose and wear her finest gown, before he would come to her, and her whole being throbbed with the eagerness of the want of him, his love and his body.

She had so much to tell him – from herself, from the Council. She must convey to him their gratitude for saving her from her enemies the night before. The Council knew of his actions and his bravery – knew well that, without his intervention, she might well have been taken by the Ninety Seven. The Council and the Triad would be forever in his debt.

It was all so very wonderful, so exciting, and she must not see him, or be seen by him, until she was properly attired, and there were several things she must check about the evening she had planned for them both.

Ai Fah was startled when she was told that the man was not in the apartment. That he had gone out much earlier with the servant, Johnnie, and had not yet returned.

Ai Fah was perplexed. Should she inform her Lady? Surely not, they would be back any minute. Surely yes, or she would be in great trouble for concealing something from her mistress. It was a sore problem for the number one amah, but she had to do her duty. She broke the news to Lee Kyung Koh.

The information shocked her mistress – a sudden foreboding of dread seized her. She was angry, but held her anger in check. She must not yet blame the servant she had chosen to look after her man – in all fairness, she had not given any orders about leaving the apartment, had no thought that he would want to go out. In any event, he would be back very soon, and then she could be angry with the servant. She continued her preparations to receive her Lord, as he must now be called.

Six o'clock became seven o'clock, and then seven o'clock became eight o'clock. She kept as calm as she could, with acute anxiety rising within her.

The household waited, their thoughts with their mistress. Fear grew in her heart something must have happened to him, he would not surely leave her. Oh no, he had just gone out with his servant and would return soon. She must, she must be patient – he would return soon.

But he did not return, and the fear, the anguish, the agony, increased with each terrible passing minute.

20

THE NINETY-SEVEN ARE ANNIHILATED

Rankin questioned the little man through Johnnie, to make sure of his bearings.

"This mans say we go stlaight that way," Johnnie motioned with his right arm "down steps long passage stlaight out door that ways." Another arm motion, "near down steps big door store place, that velly big door. This way," a motion in the opposite direction, "funny place this mans say, can see big store place – other steps go roof."

Rankin thought for a few moments, trying hard to picture it as they had come in, down the long passage and up the steps to this room.

"This is the way I see it then," he told Hamilton. "We go straight for the door, and hope there's nobody to stop us." He pointed to himself. "I go first," pointed to Johnnie, "then Johnnie," pointed to the little man, "then him," and finally pointed to Hamilton, "then you, Ham. You tell the man that quick Johnnie."

Johnnie spoke quickly to the little man, pointing to each one of them in turn as Rankin had done.

"Tell him," Rankin went on. "If I stop, you stop, and he must stop. The noise – understand?" Then more fiercely, "No noise."

Johnnie continued to translate to the little man, the last few words very fierce.

Rankin had not quite finished. "You tell him if he make noise this man here," – he pointed to Hamilton, "will hit him with this," he indicated the iron rod in Hamilton's hands, "like he hit other man there." He pointed to the man on the floor, lying very still, the head covered in blood.

Johnnie spoke again, and the little man looked in horror at the man on the floor. Rankin was sure the message had gone home. He turned to Johnnie. "And no noise from you, understand? If any men down there at the door I will stop, when I stop you must stop, stay still. No noise, understand?" Johnnie nodded his head. He understood.

"If we are stopped, Ham," Rankin said to Hamilton. "What do we do? Fight our way out, use this" – he transferred the grenade to his left hand, and brought out the revolver with his right hand "and this?"

"Sure thing," Hamilton agreed. He had recovered well and, though very tired, and his eyes, without his customary sun-glasses all the day in the bright electric light, were sore, he was alert. "We've got to get out. I'd like to know what's going on at that meeting," that thought intrigued him greatly, some vital decisions would be made for certain. "Don't worry about this little fellow, he'll be all right, I owe him ten thousand dollars."

"You what?" Rankin asked, amazed.

Hamilton managed a smile. "When he came in first, I promised him ten thousand dollars if he would get help. It worked, he did his part, brought you. It's worth it."

"Wonder why he wanted to scoot off just now then?" Rankin was puzzled, but knew now why Johnnie had been so keen on getting him here. The money would be shared, of course – Rankin grinned – couldn't blame Johnnie, it was big money and, as Hamilton said, well worth it.

"Right then," he said, "let's go."

He opened the door very carefully, revolver in the right hand, grenade gripped safely in the left hand – paused a moment as he looked out – the passage was empty. He moved out, followed by the other three, and went slowly down the stone steps, his eyes becoming accustomed to the dim light of the passage. He had got to the bottom of the steps when a big door, a few yards ahead on the right side of the passage was opened – a man came out and went down the passage away from them, shouting loudly. Rankin froze against the wall, how fortunate the door opened to conceal them, how lucky they had not started a few seconds earlier – they must have been seen. He heard Johnnie gasp behind him, the little man kept quiet – he knew all about that iron rod.

Rankin heard a lot of noise along the passage and sounds of men coming towards the caller. "Back," he shouted urgently, as loud as he dared. "Quickly!" They moved back up the stone steps, turning a corner in the passage, almost opposite to the door of the room they had emerged from, in to a large open space. Rankin knew they could not be seen.

He risked a look back around the corner of the wall, was in time to see men going back through that big door – that must be the door to the big store – he heard the door shut hard.

They were in a much wider passage, with some light coming from in front of them. To the right a few yards further along was an open arch, that must be the way to the roof.

"Wait here," he ordered in a fierce whisper. "I'll have a look down that passage again. See how many there are at the door – agree, Ham. Keep them quiet."

He moved out again, down the steps. His knee was very sore, but it was a damn good job for Hamilton he had not stayed in the apartment to rest it. Wonder what the time is – wonder if she's back yet – got to get out of here. He moved past the big door, keeping close to the right hand wall.

Suddenly he stopped. There was much brighter light ahead, figures, talking, loud talk, the guard on the door. Funny no one else came to look for those two men we clobbered.

He backed down the passage – he knew the score now – they would have to fight their way through – hope the surprise would help them. He backed past the big door – heard a shout from the inside – it was a strong door, with a big wooden bar hanging down at the wall on one side – if I fix that bar across and clamp it down in the socket across there – that's what it's for, of course – keep those beggars in there – but he didn't do it, kept on backing, up the stone steps, back around the corner to Johnnie and the little man. He could not see Hamilton – "Ham," he called – "where are you?"

Hamilton appeared out of the darkness, the iron rod held in front of him. "There's a crowd of them at the door," Rankin said. "Impossible to see how many, we'll have to rush them. Keep together – I'll fire a few shots and we'll get through – agree?"

"Not just yet, David," Hamilton replied. Rankin could sense the difference in his voice now – he was strangely excited, tense. "There's an iron grating up here, I've got a first class view of the meeting – can hear something of what's going on. Come and look." He turned back into the gloom, not heeding Rankin's "Come on Ham, we've got to get out fast!"

Blast him, he thought, but followed. "Down on your hands and knees,"

Hamilton said, in a loud whisper. "Careful – quiet."

Rankin got down on his knees – that knee was painful again, and crawled up as best he could to Hamilton, to where light shone out between iron bars. He heard loud voices, and, as he reached Hamilton, a great shout came from inside, startling him for a moment.

"Rub some dirt from the floor on your face," Hamilton said, "blacken your forehead, then take a look – careful."

Rankin did as he was told – intelligent lad old Ham, he thought, even with my training, I hadn't thought of that. He raised himself a little and peered in through the bars. There were some men on a platform right across from where he was looking – facing him, but the majority of them were sat on their haunches, facing the platform, but with their backs to him. He watched for a few seconds, so this was a Triad meeting. It was like a scene from a film – hard to think he wasn't dreaming all this.

Hamilton pulled him down. "Sit down a minute, David, and listen very carefully, please."

Rankin turned around, made himself comfortable on his backside, his back against the wall. Hamilton moved himself up so that their faces were very close together.

"We've only a minute or two, so listen – don't ask questions," his voice was fierce. "Down there are all the big boys of the Ninety Seven, some bloody picnic that." He paused, then "And some bloody target."

"Target?" Rankin asked, he hadn't quite got the hang of it.

"If that mob carry out what they plan to do, intend to do, the bastards, they'll rip Hong Kong apart – they'll rip the whole of the East apart – they'll take over from the Triad of that woman you rescued last night, and there'll be all hell let loose in this Colony. We've got to stop them."

Rankin sensed the bitterness and the urgency in Hamilton, but he still could not understand it. "How, how can we stop them?"

"Easy," Hamilton said, he had it all planned, "at least, we can stop them. Listen carefully. Down on the far side there – you saw it – there's a huge dump of paraffin cans – great big cans – all sorts of other stuff too – we go down to that door down there – I open it – and you throw that grenade at the paraffin dump – got it?"

Rankin had got it – it amazed him – horrified him for a moment. "We can't do that, Ham," he said, "not like that, in cold blood."

Hamilton's anger blazed. "We bloody can, and we bloody will," he pushed Rankin with the iron rod. "Think what it's all about, think of how they chained me! Think. Think carefully – of what they would have done to that woman last night"

"To Lee Kyung Koh?" Rankin asked. It was all coming clear now.

"To Lee Kyung Koh," Hamilton agreed, "they'd have taken her, and let some of the strong young men get at her, one at a time, one after another, then delivered their terms to her Triad. And they would have razed Hong Kong, killed, looted. I know it all, David, believe me," he paused, thinking. "What happened to you last night, when you left the Golden Lotus?"

The memories, golden memories of the night came flooding back to Rankin. "I stayed with her all night," he said simply and truthfully, "She's a wonderful woman – we're going to be married – it's all arranged."

It was Hamilton's turn to be amazed, but it was possible, sure it was possible. Good, it added strength to what he was telling Rankin. "David," he said, "we've got to be quick, but I must tell you this – very few people know it, and I've never ever told a living soul before, and you must never tell anybody – understand? I'm the head of British secret service for Hong Kong, and I do know what I am talking about. I can't throw that grenade, you *can*, you can lob it just where it should go. Will you do it?"

Again the thought flashed through Rankin's mind. It's a dream, it isn't really happening. If it isn't a dream, then what have I got myself into? It must be true what Ham says, otherwise why had he been chained, and what about the Golden Lotus last night, that had all happened, and those swine would have done what Ham said to Lee Kyung Koh – Ham was not exaggerating – those bastards been let loose on Lee Kyung Koh – never – not while he was alive to stop it. He didn't understand all of it, but he understood what Ham had meant about Lee Kyung Koh.

Hamilton waited, whilst the shouting and talking went on back there almost underneath them. How amazing it all was, the two of them sitting there with the whole of the Ninety Seven theirs for the taking – and the seconds ticking away.

"Right, Ham," Rankin said at last. "I'll do it, for you and for her. Let's have another look." He turned, raised himself again, peering through the iron bars, and the relief flooded through Hamilton. If all went well for them, they could stop the Ninety Seven for a long, long time,

Rankin took his time. Cripes, what a noise they are making. He looked hard at the large dump of big cans – what a bloody explosion that'll be if I can land the grenade there.

He lowered himself to Hamilton, ready to do what he had been asked. "What about us, and what about these two lads?" he pointed to Johnnie and the little man.

"We take our chance," Hamilton replied quickly. "We might be lucky, the cans are all down at the far end away from us, the blast will be at that end. That big door at the end will be closed and locked – it might hold, I hope it does – it looks bloody strong. Get those bastards down there, David, I hate all they stand for."

"Don't worry, Ham," Rankin told him. "I'll get 'em, I can do it on my own – don't need you to open the door. You get in that archway over there," he indicated the other side of the passage to where the little man had said there was a way up to the roof. "That might get you some protection, I'll get back to you if I can. Hope the grenade is all right!"

"Good luck, David," Hamilton said quietly, "and thanks."

Rankin moved off quickly down the passage, past the two Chinese who had waited quietly, but in great fear and wonder. He put the revolver in his trouser pocket again.

Hamilton and the two Chinamen moved back into the archway, as Rankin had suggested.

Rankin came up to the big door, remembered which way it opened and paused a second. Then he pulled the door wide open – looked at the scene inside – a haze reaching up to the electric lights, there must be a hundred men here.

He stepped inside a few paces, cooly, calmly, just as he would have done on the training range – pulled the grenade from the pin, and carefully lobbed it at the dump of cans. Turned back at once through the door, which he slammed hard behind him, and slumped down to the ground, back to the near wall.

His aim was true, the grenade landed exactly right – there was a bang and a huge flash, a roar, another huge flash, then more explosions, more and more and more, the great door thudding to each explosion, but holding firm, then the fire crackers started to explode.

Rankin knew luck had been on his side, he hadn't been seen at all. He wondered what it was like inside – a lot of noise – hope there's a lot of damage, hope that main door has held as this one has. He stood up, and pulled over the great bar to ram it down in the socket – that would stop any of the bastards from getting out. The fire crackers banged and swooshed, and now there was a continuous roar from the inside – fire – it must be an inferno inside there, unless the big doors at the dockside end had been blown open in the blast.

It was an inferno inside – a raging tide of flame, as the paraffin cans had burst and the liquid caught fire, and spread quickly across the big store – fire crackers banging and shrieking. The fire had rapidly engulfed a great stock of plastic goods so that thick smoke now added to the horror, and the main door had held firm. The men inside had been shocked by the initial explosions, dumbfounded as they continued, and then panicked as they rushed and fought for the doors for a few minutes. Some of them, those who had been near the paraffin cans had been viciously burned in the first movements, and others had clawed at each other to get away from the vast sheet of flame which enveloped them so very speedily. Not one of those inside was to escape.

The main doors were burning and buckling in the great heat, and the incoming draught of air swooshed the flames even higher. Thick greeny grey smoke poured out from where those vast doors had stood, with flames licking into the open air after the smoke.

The flames and smoke roared out of the grating through which Hamilton and Rankin had looked down at the meeting taking place inside. My God, what a holocaust, Hamilton thought – hope those bloody doors have held – hope every bloody one of those men of the Ninety Seven were still inside – every bloody one – we've been lucky so far – got to get out fast – marvellous bloody man that Rankin – and the grenade had done just what he had hoped for – more than he had hoped for.

He moved out once more into the passage – shepherding Johnnie and the other man in front of him. "David," he shouted. "David, are you there? We're coming down."

Rankin waited for them at the bottom of the stone steps. The heat from the nearside wall was building up fast – the smoke from inside billowing out of that grating back there, as first, Johnnie and the little man, both terrified, then Hamilton emerged, Rankin grinned a little, heard Hamilton shout: "Bloody well done." Then turned to lead down towards the door, limping, the revolver again in his right hand – alert – they were not out of it yet.

"Get down," he shouted as he saw figures ahead, and dived for the stone floor. Hamilton dived at once, landing hard on the iron rod, but not noticing the pain.

A long burst of fire from some sort of automatic screamed over him. Cripes, what have they got down there. He heard Johnnie cry out, Johnnie and the little man were not trained – had not understood – had stayed upright – most of the burst hit Johnnie – he cried out once only – then was gone – life oozing out of him mercifully fast, much quicker than the blood, which seeped over his body, as he lay where he had been smashed to the ground by the force of the burst.

One shot – one shot only – had hit the little man – straight in the centre of his forehead – the perfect shot for any marksman. The little man made no sound – toppled back, his feet striking Hamilton on the ground, as he fell backwards, beyond where Hamilton lay.

Rankin raised himself a little – pushed the revolver forward, took steady aim at the nearest of the figures less than ten yards away from him. The revolver cracked once. His shot went home, straight and central in the chest. He saw the man stagger and fall forward, heard a crash as the automatic hit the ground.

There were more men down there – he could hear them shouting, even above the noise of the fire behind them. Visibility was bad, with smoke coming down the passage way, clouding the entire length, as it thickened and spread towards the door ahead, but Rankin saw another man come forward and bend down to pick up the automatic, whatever it was. His strong wrists held the revolver firm, as he pulled the trigger again and it cracked the bullet away. He saw the man jerk upright, then fall again – two out of two – not bad – but he knew there were more yet.

He scrambled back to Hamilton as fast as he could, crawling past the body of Johnnie – poor Johnnie – now with his ancestors wherever they were.

"Let's get back," Hamilton shouted. "Try for the roof – it's our only chance."

"Don't think so," Rankin argued. "The way that fire's going, the whole place will come crashing down soon."

"True enough," Hamilton agreed, "but we may be able to get off the roof on to another building if we can get up there. Some of these godowns are built very close together. In any case, we'll not get past that lot down there, As the fire increases, they'll stand away from the door and pot at any one who comes out."

There was no time to argue further, and he may be right about the roof. Why didn't we think about it at first, flashed through Rankin's mind? We might have got Johnnie and the other lad out. Ham's right about the door though, that automatic'll just murder us.

"Right," he said. "You go first – I'll keep a watch behind in case they come for us."

"They won't do that," Hamilton snapped – "they'll just wait."

They went back up the stone steps again, treading across the body of the little man. No ten thousand dollars for him, Rankin thought, won't need it where he is. How many times have I been up and down these steps, and with this gammy leg. They turned in to the archway – only just in time as another burst from the automatic splattered viciously along the passage they had just left. Ham had been wrong, they hadn't just waited at the door, those lads, one of them must have come up the passage a bit.

They climbed up the narrow steps to the first floor. It was very dark. "Better keep on going," Hamilton grunted, "doesn't look to be any way out here."

They could hear the fire crackling and roaring, it must be one hell of a blaze now. Another big explosion rocked the building, and the steps shook violently. Up again – quite a climb – steep steps. It would be a long way down to the ground if they had to jump.

At the top was a trap door. Hamilton could not open it. Rankin came alongside him, felt with his hands, pulled aside a wooden bar, and pushed upwards. The trap door separated into two parts and fell downward on the hinges – one side just missing Rankin's head. The coolness of fresh air greeted them, the sight of the stars twinkling high, high above them, particularly welcome.

Rankin reached up again, took hold of one of the sides, and sprung upwards, mostly from his left leg. Trained athlete that he was, it was easy for him. He came up into the Hong Kong night, saw tremendous flames to his left, thick smoke billowing upwards. That side of the building was a raging furnace.

He lay flat on his stomach and reached down for Hamilton. "Lift up the rod as far as you can, Ham," he instructed, "keep your hands at the ends of the rod, let me put my hands in between yours," he searched with his hands, as Hamilton held the rod up as high as he could. Rankin heaved, slowly lifted Hamilton upwards – good job he wasn't a big man, but it was hard work just the same, awkward, and a great strain on Rankin's strong arms and terrific shoulders. The rod, and then Hamilton's head, came up through the opening as Rankin inched back, now Hamilton got his elbows on the roof – then it was easy, but thank God, thank God, for a man as strong as Rankin.

There was a low parapet all around the roof, and to their left, a stone building – was it a lift shaft? Couldn't be. They heard the familiar sounds of sirens loud below them – the Hong Kong Fire Service and the Police would be there – there were a hell of a lot of sirens going – it would be a general alarm.

The flames and smoke to their left half-screened the majestic sight of Hong Kong across the water from them, reaching up into the night sky with all its blazing lights. Over there on the island, thousands upon thousands of people were staring across to Kowloon, watching the fierce blaze – they had no time for the familiar sights of the famous stretch of water between Kowloon and Hong Kong, with the moving lights, red, green and white, of ships of all sizes, and the stationary lights of the big ships at anchor, loading and unloading, but Rankin clearly heard the roar of a big aircraft overhead, making for Kai Tak Airport.

"This way," he shouted to Hamilton, "keep away from that side, the building might go at any time."

They moved to the land side, away from the blaze and the smoke, looked around as best as they could – there was no chance of getting on to another roof – this building was higher than those on either side – no chance of jumping either. But all was not lost yet, the Fire Service were in action, ladders up, hoses spurting water at this side of the building, and on the buildings on either side.

The low parapet was three feet wide – Rankin stood up and shouted. There was a roar from below – they had been seen. Rankin was amazed at what he saw below – a dozen fire engines, cars, Police cars – every street, as far as he could see, crowded with people – a severe handicap to the Fire Service and the Police, no doubt, and thousands more making their way nearer, attracted by the fire, as people always are. The upturned faces were an amazing sight.

Searchlights stabbed the sky and held on him. Hamilton got up beside him and there was another great roar from the people.

"What a fantastic sight," Hamilton said. "Look at them, millions of them" –

They watched a rescue truck ease as near as the driver could get it to the building below, then the ladder reached up, a small figure climbing as the ladder extended.

"Good lad," Rankin exclaimed, "wonderful lads these firemen."

They were both so cool, so calm – fascinated by the scene down under them, thrilled by the ladder which probed now right up to them – the helmeted Chinese fireman grinning at them.

"You first, Ham," Rankin said, "and make it snappy – don't want to be up here too long – that other side's not going to last much longer."

He helped Hamilton climb on to the ladder as the fireman moved down the rungs of the ladder to make room for him – Hamilton hung on tight as best he could as the ladder swung away. Rankin stepped down from the parapet and leant against it – looking over, watching the progress of Hamilton to the ground. Soon be back for him – hold on Rankin – soon be out of this – she'll be waiting for you – hope she's not too mad at you – you've been out a long time old lad – bet she's worried what's happened to you – you'll have to be at your best tonight for her – how can you be otherwise with a gorgeous woman such as she is – you're a lucky old lad really, Rankin – you sure are.

Now, with Hamilton safely down on the ground, she was all he could think about. He looked down, not seeing what was happening below, hardly noticed the ladder and the fireman coming up to him – stood motionless, sprawling against the parapet, revolver still in his right hand.

Up through the trap door opening, pushed up from below, climbed a man in black in the uniform jacket and trousers of the Chinese. He looked carefully at Rankin leaning against the parapet, then reached down for the automatic weapon handed up to him. He moved quickly to the cover of the low building – loaded the automatic – moved out from the side of the building towards Rankin – paused about six yards from him – knelt down on one knee and took aim.

Rankin heard a faint sound, and because of his training, sensed danger – hurtled himself to the right. He was a fraction of a second too late. As he moved, however, the man slightly changed his aim downwards and the burst, meant for the middle of the back, tore into Rankin's left side – at the waist, the hip and the buttock. The shock pulled him over to his left side immediately. He fell – the pain intense, and he could feel the blood pumping out of him, soaking him all the way down his left side. He lay still in the dark of the parapet.

The man in black was sure Rankin was dead – advanced to look, intending to drag the body out from the parapet into comparative light.

Rankin pushed up a little on his right side, still holding the revolver – a great roar shook the building, some of it at the far side away from him crashed down on to the dockside. The man in black paused above him, startled by the explosion. He knew that he himself was in great danger now.

Rankin pulled the trigger for the third time – for the last time, and again his aim was true, though this time he had not taken aim. The bullet, travelling upwards, hit the man in the lower part of the abdomen, and spun him backwards and down.

Below, the people roared as the ladder held a little away from the parapet – more and more of the building was crashing. The fireman was puzzled, there was no sign of Rankin. He said so into the microphone strapped to his chest, asking for orders.

Rankin raised himself on his knees, the revolver slipped out of his hands. His left hand held close to his waist, the left arm close down the side – the blood continued to pump . . . He crawled on to the parapet and got to his knees again, for just a few seconds.

The fireman looked at him horrified – saw the blood soaking all down his left side. The searchlights picked up the hunched figure of Rankin – the crowd roared again – he swayed forward, seeing nothing, wanting only to go to her, and the crowds broke into a great wail, as his body pitched forward, and over and down into the street below.

21

HAMILTON'S REPORT

Hamilton was pleased Sam Reynolds was able to help him dress, wrists and hands plastered and bandaged, it would otherwise have been a hard task, but the hotel barber had given him a jolly good shave.

He had refused to stay in the hospital he had been taken to – was adamant he wasn't bad enough for a hospital bed – but he was bloody distressed, and had got back to the Peninsula at about the same time Reynolds had got there, having heard some of the news. Wisely, Reynolds did not worry him – he had a few hours sleep – didn't think he would have done, but he was utterly weary and slept well, not knowing that a Police constable stood guard all night on his room, and now – thanks to Sam – he looked fairly presentable, even if his heart was terribly sad.

Reynolds accompanied him to Police Headquarters, where Hamilton gave the Commissioner a very accurate report of what had happened to him, and what a tremendous part Rankin had taken in it all. This was all faithfully recorded by a Police stenographer. Then he went with the Commissioner to Government House, where he repeated exactly the same story to the Governor, and the Commander of the British Land Forces – with again great and rightful praise to Rankin.

"I'm absolutely certain," he summed up, "that not one of them could have got out of the godown. No-one got out of the door where we were whilst the fire spread so rapidly that, unless the big doors on the dockside were blown out by the blast, and I am told they were not, no-one could have got out that way."

"I feel sure Mr Hamilton is right, your Excellency," the Commissioner agreed – "My forensic department are continuing their investigations, of course – they're still searching through what is left of the place, and they are sure the doors held until the heat buckled them, and they caught fire – that would be some time. My latest report is that they think – and they are generally very accurate in this ghastly business – that they have at least ninety bodies."

"I'm certain also," Hamilton stated – "that Lin Poh was in there. The main quarrel was between him – it must have been him – and three others on the platform as I watched – Mong's number two must have been one of those three and there is no question what the argument was about."

"Yes," again the Commissioner was in agreement – "our information is that all the big boys were here, must have been in at the meeting. Mong Lin San died in that crash at Kowloon, of course, but he had brought all his strength with him, knew they had to be here to deal with Lin Poh, who was a most ambitious man. So I should think it safe to assume they were all in that godown."

"Good," Hamilton said, leaning back gingerly in his chair – he had no remorse for any of them. "That will finish the Ninety Seven."

"For a long time, no doubt," the Governor said, "but we cannot say for all time, though we can be sure there will be no immediate trouble here – nor in Taiwan for that matter. And, unless I am sadly mistaken, there will be no trouble for a long time to come."

The Commissioner nodded his agreement. "The Golden Lotus will retain their hold, which is an excellent thing. We have never had trouble from them, on the contrary, they always give us the greatest help."

"And all due to Rankin," Hamilton put in, "a very great man."

"A very good soldier," the Commander, British Land Forces, could say that with great conviction. "I knew him well, saw him up at their mess only two days ago, the Birthday Parade. Yes, a very good soldier: very sad blow to the Battalion."

"He'll get a medal?" Hamilton asked. "He deserves the VC."

The General looked at the Governor a moment before replying. "Well, he won't get that, and I don't think he'll get a medal. What can we say, Mr Hamilton, that he deserves a medal for rescuing you?"

"Rescuing me, General, only that?" Hamilton lost his usual calm, his temper flared. "Yes, he did that, thank God, but he also saved Hong Kong."

"True, Mr Hamilton," the Governor said, quietly and firmly. "We must put the matter in the proper perspective. We know that, as least we know what he did, and we know what it can mean, but in all fairness, and you must allow me to say this" – his voice had become more firm – "he threw the grenade on your instructions remember, you have told us of his initial reluctance."

"I only said that to point out what a wonderful fellow he is – was – his sense of fairness, but he did throw the grenade."

"Allow me to finish what I was saying, please," the Governor is in his most executive voice, Hamilton thought, and displeased at my interruption. "We know that grenade started the fire, which we think has decimated the Ninety Seven, but there are other implications which you well know about, and which will prevent us recommending adequate reward for a very brave action by a very brave man."

Hamilton cooled down. The Governor had spoken the truth. "Thank you, sir," he replied, "but it was Rankin who did it all. I would have never got out of there without him, wouldn't be here now." He turned to the General. "I still think something should be done – he does deserve recognition – he was tremendous, as his Excellency has fairly stated. He was a very brave man."

"We know you are right, Mr Hamilton," the General to some extent was on his side, "and neither his Excellency, nor I, not anyone, have any wish to deny him one iota of praise. You well know, however, that our hands are tied, as his Excellency has said." He looked straight at Hamilton – he knew Hamilton's military history. "You, personally, also know that's what the training of soldiers is all about, so that they will be very brave when the occasion arises." That's perfectly true, and fair, Hamilton thought. "Sergeant Rankin was a very good example, there are many brave soldiers, always have been, please God, there always will be. We understand your feelings and appreciate them, and you are right – his Battalion, the Service, and all of us can be very proud of him, but you must leave it to us to do what we have to do, you understand that, I'm sure."

Hamilton knew they were right, but he was sad about it, and would be sad for a very long time.

Sam Reynolds was waiting for him back at Police Headquarters

"Doris would like you to come and stay with us for the rest of your time here, Ham," he said. "I'd like it too. I've a couple of free days I can claim, now that the heat's off a bit, we can rest up, or we can be more active – just as you wish – but we'd like to have you."

It pleased Hamilton immensely. That hotel room wasn't attractive any more, and he didn't want to mope around on his own.

"Thanks, Sam, I'd like it very much. It's kind of you and Doris, very kind."

"That's fixed then," Reynolds was happy, knew his wife would be equally happy. "I'll get you back over to the hotel, we can pick up your things, and be back in time for lunch – all right?"

"That's good of you, Sam," Hamilton said, "but I have one thing I must do first. I'll get back to the hotel, but, if I'm not asking too much, could I be picked up about three o'clock? That'll be in good time to get over to your place before the funeral."

"Of course, Ham – no trouble – I'll pick you up myself at three."

Reynolds dropped Hamilton at the ferry, where he joined the jostling crowds thoughtfully. There was one thing he was resolved to do, to see Taipan Chin as soon as possible. He had seen the look on Rankin's face, even in the gloom of that passage, when he had talked about Lee Kyung Koh, noted the difference in the voice, how warm it became. Something big had happened between these two after Rankin had taken her out of the Golden Lotus, as Rankin had disclosed, when he had said he was going to marry the woman.

Hamilton badly wanted to see Lee Kyung Koh – he wanted her to know all that had happened. There was no other way she would know the details, and of his great bravery, other than from him. He owed it to Rankin, and he owed it to Lee Kyung Koh. He thought about it all the time, thought of that, and only that, as he got off the ferry on the Kowloon side. He hoped Taipan Chin would be able to arrange for him to meet the woman, and the sooner he saw the old man so that he could make the arrangements, the better.

He went in to the tobacco shop. The owner saw him at once and came to him. Did he never stop smiling?

"You want more good cigars, no doubt?"

"Yes," Hamilton replied. "I do, just one." He held one finger up. "Just one."

22

IN THE STARS

The Battalion buried Sergeant David Rankin, as was their right and their duty, at the Hong Kong British Military Cemetery, at five thirty p.m. that afternoon.

It was at that exact time Rankin would have been reporting to the pick-up point for the return journey back to Camp – his 48-hour pass over.

It had been a hectic day, saddened for them all by the news. Many of them still could not believe it had happened, it was in many ways so unreal.

A staff officer from Headquarters British Land Forces arrived at the Battalion at ten o'clock, and fifteen minutes later, orders were issued for the Battalion to parade at midday.

What was the reason for the parade, they could not think. It could not be anything to do with the military situation, if so, the Royal Air Force next to them would have been involved, and there was nothing to indicate that was happening, no more aircraft than normal taking to the air.

Had something of a political situation occurred? Perhaps they were in for a quick move to – to where – elsewhere or home. No, it could not be home, that was too much. There were some wild guesses, and they waited eagerly for midday.

After an hour's discussion with his second-in-command, Rankin's company commander, Major Achingdon, the adjutant, and the Battalion sergeant-major, and a long telephone conversation with the General in Hong Kong, the commanding officer was ready to give the Battalion the news.

It was a simple statement completely true, but hiding the full story, of course. Sergeant Rankin had been killed in a big fire which had burned a large storehouse to the ground, in Kowloon, the night before. Rankin had gone in to help rescue the people trapped inside, had been forced on to the roof with one man he had rescued, got that man on to a fireman's ladder, and brought down away from the burning building, but, before that ladder, or another ladder, could be got to him, badly burned, he had fallen to his death as the burning building collapsed.

The Battalion were dismissed to dinner, then to get ready for the funeral, transport to leave at three p.m. No time to waste.

There were many sad hearts, and many had no thought – nor wish – for food.

It was typical of Tanko – just typical – to rescue someone without thought of his own danger. They could see him doing it – knew it was just what he would do. Great fellow, Tanko, only he could have done it.

Great fellow, Tanko – great lad – that was what he generally called them – lads. Tanko had his own encouraging style. Steady lad; think carefully lad; hold the rifle steady lad; what would they do without him? What would the football team do without him next season? And the boxing team? Cripes, old Tanko would be sorely missed.

Bob Denton went into the billet they had shared – he did not want any food. He stood and stared at the bed Rankin had used, would never sleep in again.

"What the hell fire did you have to go and do that for, Tanko?" he asked the empty bed.

Just after three p.m., the trucks moved on their journey down to Kowloon, and then across to Hong Kong. The movement well organised, as was typical of a first class British Army unit, the men quiet as they boarded the trucks. No 'comedians' today, and all still sad and in some wonder about it all.

Escorted by the Military Police down to Kowloon, and then taken over by the Hong Kong Police Force.

All ranks in their number one dress, the uniforms they had worn for the parade two days earlier, and rushed back from the laundry that morning, only now their left arms wore black crepe arm bands – neatly, tidily, all the same measurement above the elbow, whatever the length of the upper arm.

Lance Corporal Anderson drove one of the trucks, expertly as always, keeping the correct convoy distance from the truck in front. He was thinking hard, but did not let his thoughts affect his concentration, or his driving. I'd have been bringing him back to Camp tonight if this hadn't happened – hard to believe it all – he was a damn fine man.

At the Military Cemetery, they disembarked from the trucks and formed up quickly.

Rankin's entire company was on parade, with a platoon from each of the other companies, and all the Battalion represented. Some of the wives had travelled down in a special coach.

The band, with drums black creped and muffled, led the solemn procession. The parade slow marched well – evenly – left – right – left foot stabbed through the air – toe pointed forward and down – and glide on.

The proud, mournful music – not overloud – sounded out clearly over the green sward, over the rows of white memorial stones, and seemed to hang overhead for a while, before rolling, slowly rolling, down the slopes of the cemetery, and out to the sea beyond, out into the shimmering haze, and to the islands which could just be seen.

The six sergeants, Denton one of them, eased the coffin – carefully – tenderly – off the gun carriage and on to their shoulders. The next two smallest sergeants, one at each side at the front – then the next two sized – then the two tallest – Denton and "nifty" Smith – performing their last service for their brother sergeant.

The coffin, draped with the Union Jack, bore one solitary wreath – from the commanding officer and all ranks of the Battalion. There were many other wreaths – from his own sergeants' mess – from the Hong Kong Football Association. From the commander, British Land Forces, from the Wives Club, one from Hamilton, and many others.

The Battalion chief clerk carefully noted all the wreaths. The commanding officer and Major Achingdon would have letters to write to Rankin's father – his next of kin, and a full list of the wreaths would be enclosed.

By this time, his parents would already know about his death, their home in South Wales shattered by the sad news, and Alice particularly so. But the Army buries its dead quickly in tropical climes, and there was no time for his father and mother to be brought out to Hong Kong – they would be sent a full report and some photographs.

There was one tremendous bunch of flowers – glorious blooms of many colours, which puzzled the chief clerk. A gold rimmed white card bore some Chinese characters and the beautifully written words: "Wait for me in the stars my love." The chief clerk could not know that the Chinese characters meant exactly the same as the English words so clearly written, and he was puzzled by the small deep blue orchid printed at the bottom right hand corner of the card.

Hamilton, with Sam Reynolds, on their left arms a black crepe band, took his place a little away from the grave. The Battalion owned Rankin for just this little while longer, and others – apart from the General's representative – must be well back.

Hamilton was very sad, it would be a long time before he got over all this. Behind him and Reynolds, he had seen without really noticing two Chinese women in severe black samfoo and black conical hats. Had Hamilton been more alert – less sad – he might well have guessed who one of them might be.

The service was brief but so very impressive. The British Army Padre had known Rankin well.

Reverently, gently, lovingly, the coffin was lowered into the open grave. There were many wet eyed men, and women, as the volley was fired, many sobbing bitterly as the Last Post was played by the Battalion buglers – the sharp notes trilling out crisply in the still air.

The officers and senior ranks filed past the grave, one by one, and saluted. Their tribute to a good soldier. Then the Battalion reformed – reformed and marched away, leaving behind them one of the Battalion's sons to rest for ever in the Colony of Hong Kong. As they marched, they passed the two Chinese women.

Bob Denton could not help but see them. What the bloody hell are they doing here? he wondered. Communist bloody spies, I'll bet. "Did you see them?" He asked his company sergeant major, Gerry Hibbert, as they boarded the trucks. "Typical of this bloody place – you can't bury a decent bloody British sergeant without the Reds having their spies out to report to Mao."

Hamilton waited patiently until all the Military personnel departed. "Give me a few more minutes, Sam," he said softly to Sam Reynolds, then moved forward to the graveside.

One of the two Chinese women came up behind him, moving very carefully, and slowly edged around the grave, to stand opposite to him.

Deep in thought, Hamilton bent down and picked up a handful of earth, held it for quite some time, then threw it into the open grave.

The woman opposite bent down also to pick up some earth – as much as she could take in her hand. Then, as he had done, threw it into the grave.

They looked at each other across the open grave. She was crying, and she muttered something Hamilton could barely understand, but some of it came back to him from his boyhood – something about the stars.

She was sobbing now, but she stood proudly – quite tall for a Chinese woman, he thought.

He knew now who she was.